SEVEN
YEARS
OF
GRACE

Achsa Sprague, c. 1860, in a fashionable silk brocade dress with wide pagoda sleeves trimmed with fringe. Courtesy of the author.

SEVEN YEARS OF GRACE

The Inspired Mission of Achsa W. Sprague

Sara Rath

PUBLISHED BY THE
VERMONT HISTORICAL SOCIETY
BARRE AND MONTPELIER

Library of Congress Cataloging-in-Publication Data

Names: Rath, Sara, author.
Title: Seven years of grace : the inspired mission of Achsa W. Sprague / Sara
  Rath.
Description: Barre, Vermont : Vermont Historical Society, [2016]
Identifiers: LCCN 2015044763 | ISBN 9780934720663 (softcover : acid-free
  paper)
Subjects: LCSH: Sprague, Achsa W. (Achsa White), 1827-1862--Fiction. |
  Spiritualists--Vermont--History--19th century--Fiction. | GSAFD:
  Biographical fiction. | Historical fiction.
Classification: LCC PS3568.A718 S49 2016 | DDC 813/.54--dc23
LC record available at http://lccn.loc.gov/2015044763

Printed in Canada

18 17 16   1 2 3

Designed by James F. Brisson

ISBN: 978-0-934720-66-3

First Printing, March 2016

For
Celia

❧ CONTENTS ❧

INTRODUCTION 1

PART ONE (1827–1856)

Weary Wanderer 5
To Suffer and Be Strong 27
Thoughts of a Long-Tried Heart 43
Passing Strange 54
Slave or Butterfly 71
The Day of Small Things 93

PART TWO (1856–1859)

Floating on the Billows 125
A Convention of Moral Lunatics 148
All the World Should Run Nightly Mad 178
At Darling's Gap 200
Songs Without Words 217
The Heart's Dream 239
Home Again 256
Darkeyed Lass 277

PART THREE (1860–1862)

Misanthrope 311
Birds of Passage 333
No Unholy Kiss 351
Angry and Sorry By Turns 369
My Burning Thought Leaps Up 380
Like Some Bright Evening Star 406

AFTERWORD 419

GRACE NOTES 433

ACKNOWLEDGMENTS 449

The Vermont Historical Society
expresses thanks to the following people
for their generous support of
this publication:

In honor of our spiritual ancestors
Patricia Passmore Alley

Virginia L. Coolidge

There is a <u>Great Within</u> to every human history,
And strangely changed would human judgment be
could it but read it right.

ACHSA SPRAGUE
"Notes by the Wayside"
The World's Paper
February 1858

Achsa Sprague lived in the little house across the road
from the schoolhouse. They were a very intellectual
family, but nervously imbalanced. I presume my stepmother
may have had some [of her works] as I think she was a
relative…
This great family was gone before my recollection.

PRESIDENT CALVIN COOLIDGE
May 15, 1930

⊰ INTRODUCTION ⊱

I OFTEN MARVEL THAT SOME PERSONS are born with minds inspired. They can think, speak or write with but very little effort on their part—or if effort is required they have that within which causes them to struggle on. For my sister, Achsa White Sprague, it was always an easy task to think, speak or write with but very little effort but with me it has always been the reverse, and if I undertake to write upon a topic it requires more time and rewriting than it does good after it is written. I worry that I am throwing away time whenever I sit down and attempt to compose a sentence. I do believe it would take an eternity to make me an easy writer.

My sister dwelt in her mortal body thirty-four years, seven months and nineteen days. Not long before her passing, she had been instructed by her Guardians to "Have mediums for thyself, those who shall speak for thee, those who shall give to earth the lessons thou has taught in word and deed."

When I came to Wisconsin in 1853 I was seeking a mission in my life. I had never yet engaged in anything in which I could excel.

I am not a medium. Having admitted my lack of purpose and my limitations as an author, I beg your forbearance as I sit at my kitchen table here on our Wisconsin farm and endeavor to acquaint you with my beloved sister and her extraordinary life.

Celia

CELIA SPRAGUE STEEN
Oakfield, Fond du Lac County,
Wisconsin—September 1862
(1830–1867)

❧PART ONE❧

(1827–1856)

Woman must be either slave or butterfly,
Or at least she is so at the present time…

ACHSA SPRAGUE'S *DIARY*
Monday, December 10, 1855

The little hamlet of Plymouth Notch lies in the folds of Vermont's Green Mountains. The Sprague farmhouse may be seen at the far left.

⊰ 1 ⊱

Weary Wanderer

M Y SISTER AND I WERE BORN two and a half years apart: she
in 1827 and I in 1830, in a modest New England clapboard
farmhouse in the small hamlet of Plymouth Notch, Vermont, in the
foothills of Saltash Mountain. Eight children were brought forth
there by Charles Sprague and Betsey Moore. Father was an inveterate
drinker and Mother suffered the pity of townspeople for her
regrettable marriage. When we children were sent to the General
Store we sometimes overheard gossips claim that our entire family
was unstable and nervously unbalanced. Those cruel neighbors claimed
that our oldest brother Nathan and sister Malvina were morons and
simpletons. The women were astounded when Axy once spun around
to repudiate their tittle and tattle in high dudgeon. (I was, by that
time, in the doorway securely clutching our modest parcels.)

After a while we became inured to such rude comments. Our
family *was* somewhat unusual. Our eldest sister, poor dull-witted
Malvina, was given to sudden seizures that frightened us all when
she broke into uncontrollable laughter or fits of bitter weeping that
ceased with fainting and froth issuing from her mouth. Nathan,
slow but gentle, remained at home for most of his life where he
helped Father with the horses or in the fields.

Only two years younger than Malvina, we all imagined Orvilla's
destiny would be that of a spinster until at age twenty-eight she
readily accepted a proposal of marriage from a forty-four-year-old
widower, Jarius Josselyn, and moved to Tyson Furnace to become
stepmother to his five-year-old son. Axy was outspoken about the

lopsided match and Orvilla never forgave her. I can vouch that Orvilla only became more disagreeable and tedious after her marriage. Mr. Josselyn had many disagreeable words for Axy, too.

Ephraim and Charles William, our adored brothers, were normal in every way. Sarah, the youngest of our siblings, followed after me by two years and except for her propensity for hypochondria, seemed ordinary enough. Fortunately Sarah and I were still at home to help when Axy fell ill at age seventeen with what was diagnosed as a scrofulous disease of the joints. We helped with her baths, combed out her hair and attended to her needs. Our sister was not demanding in her requests; everyone realized her affliction was a sobering encumbrance.

Axy. Our family and her closest friends used that pet name for Achsa, a name from the Bible where it was spelled "Achsah," the daughter of Caleb, a mighty man of God. A long-ago ancestor must have had that name and brought it across the sea, although some Puritans merely opened their Bible and chose the first name they came upon and that may have been the case. Axy felt it had a harsh sound and could be misconstrued as "Axe Her."

Before her illness my sister had been a robust child, a natural leader. She was my dearest friend. Less than five feet tall, Axy possessed dark hair, hazel eyes, full lips and a determined jaw. I was more faint-hearted in temperament but of similar build and color and gladly inherited her well-worn hand-me-downs already faded from hard use by Malvina and Orvilla. I followed the quick tread of this strong-willed, exuberant girl on trails up East Mountain, down to Pinney Hollow and over to the Blueberry Ledges, but I was more apt to obey Mother's warnings of forbidden activities and watch from the sidelines. Axy would wait until Mother was not watching, then merrily join the boys in their more daring escapades with her black hair loose, swinging in the wind. She enjoyed skating on the pond with Charles and Ephraim and could not resist the wild thrill of sledding down Schoolhouse Hill all the way to the General Store—while I shied back from the edge of the pond or the top of the hill, in awe.

Father never expressed the least regret over producing five daughters, though he may have wished for even more sons to help

Tintype of Achsa as young
school teacher, date unknown.

Gift to author by Plymouth historian
Eliza Ward. (Note: a tintype produces
a mirror image.)

with his chores. We had a small farm and only a few head of livestock; he mostly worked for our neighbor, Calvin Galusha Coolidge, who was developing a special breed of black-and-white milk cows called Jarvis that had been introduced from Holland. Mr. Coolidge also took great pride in raising his spotted Arabians.

Before he began farming, Father had enjoyed an education and encouraged those of us who could, to learn to read from his library of classics. On winter evenings (when he was sober) the entire family gathered around the lamp on the center table in the parlor while he wove thrilling tales and recited much-loved poems that remain with me still—like these words of William Wordsworth,

> *My heart leaps up when I behold*
> *A rainbow in the sky;*
> *So was it when my life began;*
> *So is it now I am a man.*

Plenty of beaux wished to court her, but Axy rebuffed their advances. Orvilla had made her own unfortunate match and Sarah eventually did the same when she married Nathaniel Randall. I will say more of them and of my own future in due time.

My siblings and I were constant witness to our parent's lamentable marriage. Perhaps that is why Axy and I were excited by the Seneca Falls Convention for Woman's Rights in 1848 and welcomed newspaper accounts of the speeches and bold opinions proclaimed. We carefully scrutinized the women's "Declaration of Sentiments" (deemed scandalous by many) and found our hopes raised that more promising times for women were close at hand.

Axy declared she never intended to become the property of *any man*, since women possessed precious enough freedoms. She encouraged me to join her in envisioning a much different path as well, a grander and more significant destiny. To fulfill our shared thirst after knowledge, we wished to attend college, a luxury currently forbidden to women almost everywhere.

On my eighteenth birthday Axy composed the following:

> *Sister, our life is but a dream*
> *And we are hastening down the stream*
> *That glides so fast;*
> *Just eighteen years have passed away*
> *Since thou beheld the light of day, —*
> *How soon it past…*
>
> *I well remember how we dressed*
> *Our dolls up in their very best,*
> *To make them show;*
> *And William then would plague and tease,*
> *And never give us any ease,*
> *Or peace, you know.*
>
> *And when we must to school away,*
> *We almost wished at home to stay,*
> *To tend them well;*
> *But when once there, we soon forgot*

Their wants, in learning in that spot,
To read and spell.

And when the winter came with snow
And ice, — when all the boys could go,
And slide so smart;
While you stood back with timid fear,
I always thought the "coast was clear,"
And took a part...

But childhood's hours have passed away,
And with them all our merry play,
And dreams of bliss;
For after years bring pain and care,
And we must learn such things to bear
In a world like this...

Twenty foreboding stanzas warned of disillusionment and myriad sorrows that may lie ahead.

'Tis thus that life appears to me,
Yet brighter it may seem to thee
Than to my eyes...

Our mutual love of further learning was a very strong bond and my heart ached for my sister who was slowly becoming inundated with a crippling disease.

I have never attributed my leaving home to her portent words, but not long thereafter I exited Plymouth Notch to teach school in nearby Tyson Furnace, where I reluctantly consented to board with sister Orvilla and her middle-aged husband in exchange for my assistance in caring for their growing family. I thence accompanied them the following year when they moved to Troy, New York. But in Troy I chose to board with strangers near my schoolhouse in

Rensselaer County (where I met the Catholic, Mr. Rausch, but more about that to come). After I left home, Axy's nursing care was left to our overworked mother and our younger sister Sarah.

Only recently have I learned of Axy's diary and journal in which she began writing a year after I departed for The Furnace in June 1849. Of her illness she wrote, *I have been trying to amuse myself in some way, but can only think of what I had hoped and planned for the future.*

At the age of twelve she had begun teaching the primary grades in the little schoolhouse across the road, but this was becoming a dispiriting chore. *Once more I am unable to walk or do anything else; have not been a step without crutches since Sunday and see no prospect of being any better; see nothing before me but a life of miserable helplessness.*

All of us had attended the little stone schoolhouse, its exterior consisting of blocks of square hewn slate native to our area. Inside the one room, benches and desks sat two students apiece. The winter term began in November and lasted three months; the summer term began in June. When she penned the above, Axy had eleven scholars and little time to think about herself for six hours per day. Fortunately, the school was nearby as those few steps had become progressively more difficult, even with crutches. By candlelight at night she reread *Jane Eyre*. She also found that *Lallah Rookh* beguiled many an otherwise tedious hour—especially "the Fire Worshipers," a tragic tale of romance between a poet and a princess. I had encouraged her to read *The Life of Milton* but she said she found her mind wandering from that book very often.

Had I realized her eventual despair it would not have affected my departure. Axy strongly insisted that since her progress toward our mutual goal was deterred, I must seek whatever independence I might achieve. We were not aware that her suffering would become seven years of darkness during which she would beg and implore that she might no longer cumber the earth, a burden to our family and to herself.

By 1852 I was boarding in the German community of Brunswick, New York, which bordered the city of Troy, with the family of Timothy Adams and teaching school at the very school where the author Herman Melville had taught in 1840 since his mother lived nearby (I had not yet read his novel, *Moby Dick*, only recently published).

The bleakness of my family's home was behind me but my presence in Brunswick was not initially courted since I was neither Catholic nor Lutheran, those German congregations numbering the majority of inhabitants. As soon as my school day ended I chose to be alone unless there was some argument or subject for discussion among my hosts.

The Adams children and their parents formed the happiest family I had ever known, albeit Catholic. I admired the mutual respect among them and their contagious joyfulness of life. Mr. Adams played the violin and on warm evenings I was invited to sit on the porch and listen to the strains of pleasant German melodies wend through the woods and along the shores of the nearby Posten kill which flowed northerly toward the Hudson. The children sometimes joined their mother in song and encouraged me to sing. Foreign the words may have been, but so was the family's kindheartedness. And despite my pledge to Axy that I would remain independent and unmarried, I found myself contemplating an amiable family of my own.

The intoxicating lure of the West began to tempt Mr. Adams and his wife, who spoke of moving the farthest distance one could then travel in that direction by train. Rather than return to Vermont or remain with Orvilla and Mr. Josselyn, I eventually determined that my destiny must also lay in the West, although I later blamed my fickle heart for sending me all the way to Wisconsin after the completion of the school term the following winter.

I humbly confess that a man (Axy would have given me a stern lecture to reiterate the paucity of women's freedoms) expressed what I believed was an especial familiarity. Mr. Rausch—his given name was Carl—a friend of Mr. Adams, worked at the Burden Iron Works in Troy, which manufactured horseshoes. During late summer evenings, Mr. Rausch often called upon the Adamses after supper and we all sat outdoors and shared a pitcher of lemonade. Mr. Rausch usually gestured to a vacant seat by his side. And when the Adams's children were sent off to bed thus abandoning the porch swing, Mr. Rausch would invite me to share that squeaky apparatus.

Granted, the conversation among the group mostly concentrated on heartening stories of success from the edge of the western frontier, the "land flowing with milk and honey" that was cheap in Wisconsin, "the best farmland in the country" according to Mr. Adams's cousin who had migrated there two years before, "certain to double and triple in value." Speculators had snatched thousands of acres when the land had originally come onto the market but now that land was coming up for sale, most of it never even having been plowed. The cousin wrote of the health of his livestock, the height of his corn.

"It wouldn't take much of a nest egg to purchase a few acres," Mr. Adams coaxed Carl with a wink. "You're an able young man, you can swing an axe, hew logs, and build a cozy little house. Matter of fact, we could be neighbors!"

Carl was not only able, he was handsome as well, with blonde hair that fell across his blue eyes. I had to restrain myself from brushing it aside. I knew, working at the Iron Works, he must also be strong. And I knew he was fond of me, a consequence I found unnerving. I was *not* the Sprague sister who fended off beaux—that was my vivacious sister, Axy! I was the shy one, the girl who hung back and dared to show her face.

It was arranged, then, that Mr. Rausch would accompany the Adamses and help them trek to Wisconsin. The event would take place in a matter of weeks. If I came out in spring, I was to seek Mr. Rausch, who was waiting for me. He would write with explicit directions. Although no formal promises were made between us, Mrs. Adams assured me in confidence that a proposal of marriage would unquestionably be waiting, too.

I said nothing of this to Axy, who frequently wrote with concern for my welfare. Before the November term, after Mr. Rausch and the Adamses left for the West, I was obliged to seek a new place to board and was taken in by a benevolent family in Troy, Mr. and Mrs. Benjamin Starbuck. If not for the Starbuck's hospitality, I believe my guilt-ridden conscience would have caused me to be stricken with self-reproach for holding close the secret of my future hopes from everyone. The added burden of Mr. Rausch being a *Catholic*, with the prevailing anti-Catholic prejudice held not only by my family (and above all Axy), was of foremost concern.

Anti-Catholic literature disseminated by the Know-Nothing movement had warned of a Papal plot to invade the western part of our country. It was generally feared that the substantial stream of Irish and German Catholic immigrants had been called by the Pope to unite and invade the West, as far as the Mississippi River. I had never heard Mr. Rausch nor Mr. Adams mention a word about such a plot by the Pope, which should have helped to quell my unease on the matter of conspiracies. In my heart I suspected Mr. Rausch's wish to move West was instilled more by a desire for adventure than a farm of his own. I was more concerned about Mr. Adams's teasing remarks that in the German language, *einen Rausch haben*, meant "to be drunk."

I will say more at length about the Starbucks and my temporary sojourn in Troy, but to complete my removal to Wisconsin, let this brief account suffice:

I had inquired about Fond du Lac County while in Troy and had been reassured that many genial Vermonters were settled there. I was also told there was much need of schoolteachers in that area, so I should have felt confident, setting my course.

I desperately wanted to feel I had a *mission* in my life. Axy had (impatiently, I thought) asked me repeatedly to write to her when I had learned my wants, so I tried to decide upon something but my search yielded naught. I did not believe I was destined to do or be anything of importance in the world; I had never yet engaged in anything in which I could excel. I enjoyed teaching very well but was not sufficiently qualified to do as I wished. Nor was there enough originality about me. If I was younger I would work to graduate from some college, yet I knew I was not naturally a scholar. "I must be effectual," I complained to Axy from Troy, "I have fought with the world from infancy till now and very little has come to pass as I wished."

I left that city with reluctance, as the Starbucks had been so affectionate. However, there was still the matter of Mr. Rausch. A letter from Mrs. Adams had reached me, saying they had settled as planned in Fond du Lac County and I should be able to find Mr. Rausch in the vicinity when I arrived.

It took a great deal of courage to step onto the railroad cars by myself for the very first time. They were dusty and crowded, the wooden seats were far from comfortable. Privacy was unknown. I was unable to sleep, half-suffocated with sulphurous smoke, foul air and tremendous noise. If I did nod off, the scream of the steam whistle frightened me awake with heart pounding.

Ten hours after boarding at Troy, I reached Buffalo. The train stopped and passengers dismounted to rush to the refreshment saloon, where we had only minutes to bolt a dismal breakfast and stretch after having sat for so long in an upright position.

The next day Chicago provided quite a sight, as it had been raining very hard and the city had no pavement, only ruts and deep puddles. Mud collected on the hem of my skirt as I changed to a separate train. With the cholera epidemic raging in that city and its streets like open sewers, I wished to spend as little time in that city as possible.

My journey seemed never-ending and I was becoming disillusioned. My thoughts were caught up in second-guessing—going off on my own, my brief acquaintance with Mr. Rausch, and whether I was mistaken in going anywhere on the basis of my restless nature and a promising amity that might never advance into anything more.

Perhaps the freshness of Wisconsin would ameliorate what must be a fickle mind that caused me to be so impatient. And I did pin a few hopes on Mr. Rausch but was loath to admit that to my sister, especially!

During the final day of my journey, I spied rude log structures along the tracks that I took to be homes. Some had only patchwork quilts or blankets covering the doorways, and no windows. A few sad dwellings resembled dugouts. The villages had clapboard or brick structures, but in all they were so much less prepossessing or civilized than those I had left behind in New England. I had heard Mr. Adams speak repeatedly of "getting rich in the West," but the population I saw did not look at all rich, and many looked and sounded foreign.

There was much building going on, however, and with the train now running regularly surely progress would be swift. Land was Wisconsin's most precious resource, Mr. Adams informed me, but he'd also spoken of remaining vigilant for claim jumpers who might take advantage of the government's delay in recording ownership to illegally occupy another person's farm. "Some claim jumpers move from one new section of the West to another, endeavoring to seize the land of some timid or simple man and collect a pretty fee as an inducement to leave," he'd said. If a claim jumper was caught, he could be killed and his corpse allowed to swing in the breeze (that's exactly how he put it). Or if a claim jumper seized a farm during the winter, when its owner might be temporarily working in a city to carn hard cash, the neighbors might chop a hole in the ice of a nearby lake or river and submerge the interloper until he was all too happy to flee.

I did not inquire then as to Mr. Adams's motives or future plans, but I presumed he was not going to jump a claim! At any rate, I was not following him or his family in their quest, but going on my own. My intended destination was a reliable hotel on the plank road between Sheboygan and Fond du Lac built by Sylvanus Wade, a hotel of good standing and out of harm's way. I found it so, but filled to capacity almost every night by people coming to settle in that section and by emigrants on the road to points farther west. I asked if anyone knew a Mr. Carl Rausch, but received no encouraging response.

As I had been assured in Troy, I was soon able to find a school in nearby Greenbush and began boarding with one of many families who had moved to the frontier from Vermont.

I finally confessed the reason for my presence in that state to my beloved sister. In her swift and sharp reproof she asked if I had lost my presence of mind, following a *Catholic*! I immediately replied that she was very much mistaken, as I had never intended to become the property of a man or to accept Mr. Rausch's proposal. I dared not admit to Axy there had been *no proposal.* I could not convey my devastation when, after I found him, Mr. Rausch informed me he was traveling to California to seek his fortunes in the newly discovered gold fields. And that was that. And there I was.

Greenbush was a small community in an area of mostly unbroken wilderness with the added alarming prevalence of Red Indian tribes who lived in wigwams made of wild animal skins stretched over a conical frame of reeds or branches. Nervous townswomen enjoyed warning me of the Indians' propensity for scalping and plunder, although others assured me that the Redskins were peacefully occupied with farming and maple sugaring and most favorably disposed toward white settlers. They often brought fresh game and maple sugar to town to trade. Yet we often heard rumors of Indians that still roamed the state and committed various depredations including the burning of houses, taking off with furniture and provisions. Indeed, Indian trails were the only thoroughfares.

I purchased books and primers for twenty children, at $1.35, and felt well prepared for teaching. I had less than a dozen scholars in my first Greenbush school, referred to locally as "a shanty affair." For my own part, I would rather *attend* school than teach, but I always felt somewhat repaid for all my trouble and trials when I saw my students make such efforts to please me, for I had succeeded in getting up their interest. I wrote to Axy that I hoped to see even greater efforts when they became interested for their *own* improvement. It was quite an undertaking to have done as much as I had, for these country students seemed to me so stolid and dull.

Finding myself so far away from Vermont in a vast backwoods that to my eyes often appeared vulgar and foreign, Axy's letters were longed for and despite my deception regarding my initial lack of scruples and resulting relocation in that wild settlement, her correspondence remained constant and concerned.

It was not only the rough country location that caused my dejection, so I searched for words to express my melancholy and hoped she could understand my dissatisfaction with my lot, that my path seemed to be rugged and uneven with scarce a flower by the wayside. I begged my sister, "turn to your own feelings and think them as mine. Not knowing what I want or need, I submit myself to be tossed about by the tempestuous billows of life until I pass from this earth to another, knowing that my ruling motive has only been to do good."

To help time pass while not in school, I tried to learn to play the piano, but most evenings were spent sewing with friends. By then I was convinced that happiness was merely a web of delusion that charmed only to deceive. Whenever I felt inclined to be happy I checked it, because I knew the opposite reaction would inevitably follow. Obviously, the change in my surroundings had not brought contentment.

I despaired that I would never see my own family again. Axy encouraged me to "try to be happy" but poems she enclosed with her letters were grim with her own self-pity. I had been amused by her tendency toward drama when we were children—she loved to embellish and embroider her stories. Now I saw a severe lack of restraint in her indulgence. She insisted she was undergoing severe mental struggles but finding that life was almost too real, too hard in its requirements, too severe in its exactions.

Upon occasion my own letters of misery were a cause for self-reproach, as when Axy answered back that she was unable to sew or write but very little, although she still possessed the amusements of reading and riding horseback. *My horse is rather contrary though perfectly gentle every other way and with help I am still able to ride two or three times a week. I am thankful I can even have those activities and doubly thankful for the ability to enjoy myself in the world of books when the works of action seem shut from me.*

Her love of horses and the freedom riding provided soon became a dangerous pursuit, as she related:

One morning the autumn air was so pure and delightful while riding that I seemed to feel new life springing up within me as I inhaled its freshness. The many colored leaves whirled past in the breeze telling a tale of decay and death, but it seemed not so to me, for I felt in an uncommon mood to see beauty in all things. As fate would have it (which by the way is always playing us pranks) and I enjoying all this beauty and paying more attention to it than to my horse, he suddenly whirled, the rein slipped, and before I could recover myself, I was thrown to the ground. Luckily, I was unhurt but being unable to walk I had nothing to do but to wait until assistance offered itself. My horse, as if half ashamed of serving me so rude a caper, and willing to do all in his power to repair the mischief, stood patiently and humbly beside me, tossing his head as if he hardly knew what to make of it. Looking around I espied a man at work in a field at some distance and contrived to make myself heard, upon which he speedily came to my relief. I was soon safely on my horse's back again where I took care to remain until I was at home once more. Ashamed of my awkwardness and fearing I should not be trusted hereafter if it became known, I heartily hoped the man who helped me would keep his own counsel.

As originally pledged, my purpose with this story—I could call it my intended pursuit—is to describe my sister Achsa's inspired life. I fear I have wandered far from my objective and omitted critical details. It is now 1862. Through the years I have kept a scrapbook where I pasted newspaper notices of Axy's appearances, correspondence from Mother (including Axy's letters to her) and those essays and stories written by my sister that I have been able to collect. Of course Axy's letters, such as the above, are tucked in there as well.

A great many changes have occurred since the anecdote of Axy and her horse, which transpired before her skills as a lecturer were developed. I have lived here in Wisconsin for nearly a decade, I have married to a good and kind man born in Ireland, John Morrison Steen, and we live on his farm near Oakfield, where he has built me a house and fashioned many pieces of fine furniture. He is a Free Thinker (not a Catholic), a farmer and carpenter and well read.

Our blessed country is currently at war and circumstances nearly everywhere are wretched. Only a few short months ago, I paid my final visit to my beloved sister at our childhood home at the Notch.

Our weather was overly warm for June as I boarded the cars for Vermont, not knowing what I would find. Railroad travel has improved some, but not considerably. With each stop as I traveled east I witnessed groups of young, enthusiastic boys who are eager to fill up the ranks and "make food for powder," as my husband would say.

Wisconsin has currently mustered 24,000 troops. Morris joined up with the Oakfield Guards last year as a high private. It was hoped the County of Fond du Lac would raise one complete regiment. I was appointed by the Ladies of Oakfield to deliver a flag and address the company (Morris said that I did remarkably well). But before they were called into camp, the Oakfield Guards disbanded, having quarreled over the selection of officers. I rather selfishly hope, even now, that my husband will remain at home as long as there are already sufficient men to serve.

All in all, my recent departure from our farm this summer involved a sad journey, and for many reasons, an even more desolate voyage back home to our farm. Unlike Axy, I have never relished traveling by myself and find the train cars deafening, crowded and reeking with unpleasant odors. My dove grey journeying dress is filthy with ash and reeks of smoke. It should be destroyed.

Recompense for my train fare east involved sacrifice for Morris, as economic times have been difficult—over forty banks in Wisconsin have already failed and more are expected to fail every day—but my husband insisted that I must be go where I was needed. I kept Mother's telegram tucked in my bodice.

COME AT ONCE. AXY NEAR DEATH

After two days of miserable railroad travel, I caught the stagecoach at Ludlow and at last and none too soon we reached the heart of Plymouth Union. There was the familiar Balm of Gilead tree in front of Daniel Wilder's hotel. The horses made a sharp right turn and were reined to a stop while the driver handed the mail to the storekeeper and the pause allowed the horses to catch their breath before the steep climb up to the Notch.

Mossy scents from the hillside recalled favorite hidden nooks in the woods, and in the breeze I could distinguish the subtle sweetness of sugar maples in blossom. The buds on the Balm of Gilead tree would soon be ready for harvest. Pickled in alcohol, the resinous buds were only one of many disgusting nostrums we'd applied to Axy when the scrofulous joints in her wrists and ankles began to cause severe pain.

The coach arrived in front of Mr. Dana's store, but my little hamlet seemed unusually desolate. Of course the boys from the Notch, lovers of true freedom, would have been among the first brave and loyal hearts to volunteer their lives at the shrine of liberty. When Fort Sumter was fired upon, Vermont offered troops to President Lincoln even before Congress passed a Declaration of War! I'd been told that every Vermont soldier wore a distinctive green patch upon his cap to proudly denote his Green Mountain origin.

Within minutes of climbing the hill, I arrived at our farmhouse only to find my "near death" sister very much alive and, albeit weak, in a frenzied and animated state. The day before, she and Mother had returned home from a twenty-mile passage over the mountains to Rutland thanks to Axy's insistent marshalling of Uncle Thomas and his carriage.

After a brief hug and a fluttering motion of her hands—a frenetic nervousness most unlike her—my sister paced the floor of our mother's parlor in an agitated manner. I found her appearance as bewildering as her actions. Axy's face was partially covered with a dishtowel tied around her head, seemingly a sort of bandage for her left eye; the other eye was sunken deep into her skull but possessed a restive gaze. She was emaciated beyond even her sickest days as a child and her visage (that I was able to observe) bore an unhealthy pallor. Words spilled from her almost more swiftly than I could comprehend. Moreover, her garments were extremely ill-fitting. In the heat of the afternoon she clasped a deep green velvet cloak. It was so large it dragged on the floor, yet she shivered with chills.

"You must join me in a stroll," she whispered almost immediately. "I have an urgent need to confide in my beloved sister."

I exchanged a quick glance with Mother, who waved a weary hand behind Achsa's back to signal that I comply.

I longed for a bath and a restorative nap after my journey, but Axy's welfare *was* my objective.

"My own Green Mountains!" Axy sang with a tremulous voice as we departed our familiar dooryard. One fragile arm was locked in mine, but the other flailed hysterically, like an anxious bird. "I am so grateful to at last be secure within the folds of their embrace. And in *yours* as well, my dearest sweetest most beloved Celia!"

She leaned over to kiss my cheek with chapped lips so hot I unconsciously brought my free hand there fearing her kiss had left a mark.

Our pace was exceedingly slow. There were no neighbors about, yet Axy pulled the hood of the velvet cape over her head to conceal her tortured features.

I heard a feverish ecstasy in the words she uttered the moment we were beyond our mother's hearing. "Celia, I believe I am with child!"

The statement seemed so unlikely, I gasped and covered my mouth.

The grip on my arm tightened; her face bore a rictus grin.

"I was forced to flee in haste from Oswego. I will tell you all about it in detail, tomorrow. Oh, Celia—it became such an ungodly mess with Mr. Crawford's wife Elvira, who I sincerely believe is my friend, or *was*, until I fled. I became trapped in that city. I had no choice but to endure my recovery, such as it was, under their roof! For nearly a year! And then yesterday—I knew of Mr. Crawford's long-planned meeting with the railroad in Rutland, hence I begged Uncle Thomas to hasten me there so I could reveal our glorious news. As it happened, Mr. Crawford, *John*, was not at the hotel after all. Perhaps he had never even come. But his associate, Mr. Philo Chamberlin, had left an envelope for me that contained a very special poem. And oh! Such a poem, Dear Sister! I may have sometimes doubted my darling John's love, but I am now assured of it with all my heart."

I could barely apprehend her scurried jumble of words. My sister seemed *possessed*. She pulled a creased blue envelope from her sleeve, and clutched it to her heart. "I will carry this with me until death!"

We had reached the church that stood down the hill below our house. After only a moment, Axy pulled me inside its wide doors before we might be seen.

"Mother warned me it was foolhardy to journey to Oswego last year. As you know, I had been ill. And due to my illness, I cancelled a full slate of summer lectures in the West."

Her comments continued with ecstatic rapidity.

"When I reached Oswego with the sole intention of attending the National Convention of Spiritualists and greeting all my colleagues who were equally anxious for my presence, I found I was too unwell to appear and became obliged to depend on friends for my convalescence.

"And, of course as my health failed, Mr. Crawford *would* have me stay at his home on the shores of Lake Ontario. He was most insistent, Celia. There was no refusing him. He carried me there! In his arms! Even if he had known my recuperation would last through winter, he would not have reconsidered *for one moment*. You have no idea how charming he is. And how commanding! And what would happen *did* happen, of course."

I fumbled for a seat in a box pew, fearing I was close to collapse. Axy still clutched my hand in a fierce knot.

"It was a Spiritual relationship, Celia. You must believe me. After speaking out against it as stridently as I did across this country, North, South, East, West, I could never hold with acknowledging to anyone but you Dear Celia, that your sister, *Achsa Sprague, engaged in Free Love!*

"You must realize my Guardians and his were profoundly invested in our devotion; we were sincerely convinced of that. In Pope's *Essay on Man* he says *Whatever is, is right*, and John and I relied earnestly upon that phrase. And, oh! Celia! The bliss and the agonies we suffered!"

My sister tore her hand away and, leaning on the edges of pews for support, made her unsteady way to the front of the church where she threw back the hood of her velvet cape and paced back and forth before the altar. I could now see that her hair had been shorn. She ran her pitifully thin fingers through the matted curls, tugging angrily at her scalp.

"The night before I escaped from Lakeside View—yes, I had to escape from John's home, in due course it came to that! I played with various phrases until my fingers bled. Finally, my quill captured the

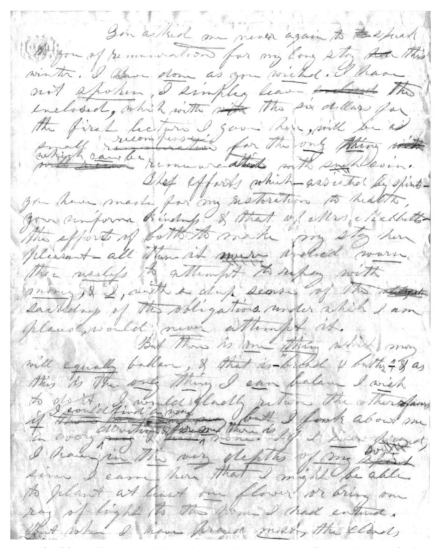

Draft of farewell composed by Achsa, April 1862, prior to fleeing the Crawford home in Oswego: "You asked me never again to speak to you of remuneration for my long stay this winter. I have done as you wished. I have not spoken…"

precise mix of my bitterness and sorrow. I dressed before my maid awoke and tiptoed downstairs at dawn, where I placed the letter and a poem for Mrs. Crawford on the silver tray with her silver coffee service along with six dollars from my purse. Six dollars, the total sum of my income for nine months. If you care to read the letter, Celia, I have an early draft."

Her voice now conveyed a shrill and peculiar air of peril.

"At that early hour," she gestured dramatically with both arms, "a perfect glissade of fog fanned out from Lake Ontario. Like a phantom pursued, I crossed the lawn from the house to the barn, the lively waves mocking me as they shattered invisibly upon nearby rocks. The dew was so heavy that morning that it soaked through my new kid boots.

"I had entrusted the little Irish boy who looks after the Crawfords' stable to be prepared with the black team harnessed and my trunks already in the carriage. I knew Mr. Crawford would return from Ogdensburgh on the steamer *Prairie State* before noon. I desperately wished to avoid saying farewell. As for Elvira, when she discovered the note and grasped the meaning of my poem I was certain she would remain in her bedchamber for most of the day."

"What did you say in the letter?" I asked at last. "Why would Mrs. Crawford be so singularly upset?"

"Because the poem referred to 'hearts tempted unto sin,' and 'deep despair' and even 'the sufferer's aching eye.' *My* eye. My recuperation at Lakeside View had evolved into the inevitable chaos one *would* expect."

There my sister paused and untied the linen from her head to wipe a flood of tears from her good eye. With her ragged hair and the formerly bandaged eye protruding from her face in an extremely hideous and gruesome manner, I could not but turn away and cover my own eyes even as I heard my gasp of horror.

> "When to thy heart and to thy home,
> Thy words have bid the wanderer come,
> And watched with earnest, heart-felt prayer,
> And with a mother's tender care...

There is no doubt that Elvira would have recognized herself.

When hearts are tempted unto sin—
If thou doest speak, their souls to win
From that dark midnight gulf of pain,
Making them strong and true again;
When wildly by the storms they're driven."

She stood at the pulpit and quoted the entire poem, which seemed to request forgiveness at the same time she admitted her own forbidden love.

Free Love, a Spiritualist practice my sister had preached against from New England to beyond the Mississippi River.

Free Love that was scorned by skeptics who cruelly christened it *Free Lust*.

My dearest beloved Axy looked and sounded like the madwoman I feared she had become.

Achsa White Sprague, c. 1843–1845.

To Suffer and Be Strong

(1849–1850)

I feel like one from whose path the Shadow of Death
has passed, leaving the sunlight of hope and the rainbow
of promise gleaming in my present Heaven.

ACHSA W. SPRAGUE
May 11, 1854

THE VILLAGE OF TYSON FURNACE was given that name due to iron ore having been discovered there in 1761. Mr. Tyson set up an iron works and began producing stoves and other products. Most of the settlers in Tyson Furnace were involved with the iron works—the mines and the blast furnaces. There were only a few families as the majority of workers were single, and thus the school did not have a great many students .

It seems so long ago now. When I left Plymouth Notch in June of 1849 to teach the summer term at the Furnace, our brother, Charles William (referred to by the family as "William"), moved to Boston with brother Ephraim in an effort to escape Father's tirades and the lack of opportunities available for ambitious young men in the Notch. Not long afterward William brought Ephraim back home, severely weakened by consumption. We worried that Mother would soon be sick herself, for she had so many invalids to wait upon—three, including Axy; Nathan had also fallen ill and Father was of no help. I wondered at my absence and was tempted to return, but confess I refrained, fearful I may perhaps become a helpless burden as well.

Ephraim was only twenty-five. He asked to have Dr. Spencer come up from Clarendon and at least make him comfortable. While the doctor was at our home he examined Axy and gave her a tonic to settle her nerves. Dr. Spencer conceded that Ephraim may not live through the summer. Nathan was holding his own.

Apparently impressed with her intelligence, Dr. Spencer suggested that Axy join his family in Clarendon, where she could tutor his children and consume the curative waters at the Clarendon Springs Hotel, Vermont's oldest and most famous spa. The sulfurous springs were claimed to be highly efficacious. Wealthy Southerners who sojourned there often brought their slave servants along.

The Spencers had two studious sons and Axy liked being at their home better than she had expected. She exercised a great deal, consumed gallons of mineral water by pinching her nose to cover the stench like rotten eggs, and struggled with guilt over leaving Ephraim's bedside.

Nathan recovered his health. Ephraim lingered for months. Axy returned from Clarendon and wrote to me that autumn's damp weather only increased her infirmity, but she enjoyed rainy days better than days of sunshine, which made her feel like a caged bird pining for its wildwood home.

Family incidents had been conveyed to me while I was teaching in the Furnace, but they were necessarily brief. During my visit this summer, Axy invited me to read the diary she had begun after I'd left home:

> *Yesterday afternoon I sat by Ephraim's bed while Nathan was occupied in the woodshed splitting firewood for the stove. Everyone else was absent. The house was blissfully hushed except for the grandfather clock whose unvarying cadence echoed from the parlor throughout deserted rooms. At times that old clock only serves to remind me of the heartache of*

passing hours, but now it seemed to comfort me with its tranquil measure. I caressed Ephraim's feverish forehead with a damp cloth and hummed a soothing tune.

Then as fate would have it, I heard Father's familiar footsteps and felt immediate unease. He burst through the front door and tripped over the rug with an angry, drunken bellow.

"Mother and Sarah have gone calling," I explained as I made my clumsy way from Ephraim's bedchamber with my crutches. Nathan rushed in from the woodshed to protect me and began to wail upon hearing Father's unleashed invectives. At the same time, I felt I must care for Ephraim who was startled by the sudden outburst and began to cough most wretchedly.

Father's rage was further fueled by shame and confusion.

"Idiot boy," he shouted at Nathan, "Stop your putrid mewling. And you, worthless old maid," he barked roughly at me, "Are you so pitiful you cannot even lend your poor suffering father a helping hand?"

Today Dr. Spencer again visited the Notch, this time at Father's insistence. Ephraim was cupped and bled, but for me the doctor had little to offer. I huddled beneath the faded quilt in the bed I now share with Sarah.

"I believe the girl is lovesick!" Dr. Spencer pronounced at last.

My cheeks blazed with embarrassment as if I had been slapped by the doctor. I had lived with his family, been entrusted to care for his children under his own roof! How could he be so heartless?

"Get out of bed, Daughter," Father admonished.

I cowered as the men whipped the quilt away to expose my thin cotton nightdress and my swollen, misshapen ankles. Mortified to be so rudely revealed, I pulled the quilt back to shield myself.

Despite my cries, Dr. Spencer grabbed my arms while Father slid my useless legs around to the side. Together they pulled me bodily to the floor, and then dropped their hold. Of course I collapsed.

"Walk!" Dr. Spencer ordered.

"Walk!" Father shouted.

I crouched on the rug in fear and covered my bare legs with the hem of my gown. Tears flowed freely; hot tears of pain and disgrace.

After reading about that episode, I directly expressed my regret to my sister. She said Sarah repeated claims that neighbors clucked and called her spoiled and ill-tempered. Father declared that all and sundry agreed with the doctor's "love-sick" diagnosis, and some folks in the village had advised him that all Axy needed was a good spanking.

Of course she dared not speak harshly to our Father, so Axy expressed her frustration in writing. She was then composing several poems a week, which in itself indicates her frame of mind. I would never have mentioned it, but those early poems she mailed to me were morbidly wretched, self-pitying, and maudlin with titles such as "The Invalid's Dream," and "'Tis a Hard Life to Live." For example, "They Bid Me Nerve My Drooping Soul" wearily addressed those who suggested that she look on the brighter side of life. Axy wrote that she could have coped with poverty, borne Father's fall from honor and truth and the disgrace of hearing him called a drunkard, but having her most cherished dreams destroyed by a relentless disease forbade her from finding a brighter side with such a dreary lot.

At last she unleashed her anger toward Father in "To One who Called Me Ungrateful."

> *I'm not ungrateful, though I seem*
> *To thee so base and weak;*
> *I'm not ungrateful – ne'er again*
> To me such dark words speak.

In late October she paid Dr. Spencer fifteen dollars to settle her account. Then she rode in the cars to Keene, where she saw Dr. Gwitchell, who prescribed for her and declared she should be well in the course of a year. This was the first time Axy had ridden in the railroad cars and she enjoyed the new experience, despite the roaring flames of the engine, the noise and the choking smoke. Unfortunately, she was obliged to walk some distance with her crutches in Keene, so she required a long time afterward to get rested.

Her daily diary continued with occasional entries, but soon even the surcease that writing provided was unavailable. Illness caused her thumb to swell so painfully that holding a pen was impossible. Before she put it down, she made a brief and bitter mention of our family's miserable Thanksgiving:

> *November 29, 1849: Thanksgiving Day. A joyful sound to some no doubt, but not to me, it only makes me feel more desolate. If Thanksgiving consists (as I have heard some people talk as though they thought it did) in rich food, then I truly had little reason for feeling thankful, for my food for the last five weeks has been only such as contained no butter, grease or sugar, which usually form so large a part in a Thanksgiving Supper, and therefore my share was small.*

Ephraim defied Dr. Spencer's ominous predictions and lived into winter, but our beloved brother finally succumbed on January 2, 1850. Mother wrote to me with the sad news, describing the kindness of Galusha's wife, Aunt Mede, and other neighbor women who laid out our brother's body and wrapped the casket and the mirrors and pictures in our parlor with white sheets. Our handsome young Ephraim, of so much promise to our family, rested in a plain wood coffin that Father had sorrowfully built for his youngest son that autumn and kept covered with a quilt in the woodshed because the sight of it so unnerved Mother. The Sprague house was dark with grief. Axy recorded our family's sorrow:

> *April 1, 1850, I take up my diary to write of the sharp loss we all suffered:*

Months have gone since I wrote the last line here, months that have passed like the shadows of storm clouds over some desolate spot that seemingly leave as many behind that frown yet as darkly. They have passed and death has been within our circle and taken one we have long known we must yield.

When her aching hands allowed, Axy wrote prodigiously, mostly poems that expressed her dejection and countenanced her despair. But after her recovery (for yes, my beloved sister recovered!) her life turned a corner that the most cunning soothsayers could not have imagined.

Axy's return to health at age twenty-six was widely regarded as a miracle bestowed by angels.

One afternoon during my visit to her sickbed this summer when she was unusually alert, Axy called my attention to a tapestry valise that had been shoved into the dust beneath her mattress along with some yellowed newspapers. Inside I encountered a thick sheaf of foolscap in her recognizable hand (due to her infirmities, her penmanship was often chaotic but I was accustomed to the idiosyncrasy). It seemed that during her recent illness in Oswego she had begun an autobiography of sorts.

"I had very little to occupy myself while I recovered," she explained, "so I spent many hours in my room summoning up events in the past and how they brought me to that moment in time."

Her chosen title was *My Own Sad History.* I could not (and still cannot!) imagine anyone but the most lugubrious picking up a book with such a gloomy title, but I will excerpt a small portion here that concerns her diverse attempts at recuperation.

My Own Sad History (excerpt)
– *Achsa W. Sprague* –

The appearance of spring, always tentative in Vermont, was cautious as ever in 1850. Snow continued to fall into late April and the spring peepers did not begin to sing until May. It seemed to me that the sun had gone backward and we were to have a second winter. I was restless and my attention again turned to finding a cure for my ailing health. Neither applications of leeches nor the ingestion of herbal compounds offered relief to my throbbing, swollen joints. My plight caused me to seek even more unconventional forms of treatment. Especially tantalizing were recently popularized electric and magnetic curatives suggested by brother William who provided magazines and newspapers crammed with testimonials and advertisements for electric belts, rings and batteries that purported to achieve astonishing effects upon all manner of ailments including harried nerves, congested lungs, bad feet, constipation, baldness and dandruff. William knew of a man in Boston who wore a pair of electric spectacles that featured a small zinc and copper plate that delivered a tiny current to the wearer at the bridge or nosepieces where it was thought to reach the optic nerves and thereby strengthen the eyesight. If his friend happened to be suffering from a cold, nasal congestion would also be relieved!

I thought it all complete Humbug, but after Ephraim's funeral, a set of Galvanic Bands arrived in the mail from William. The bands utilized a similar "theory of magneto-therapeutics." The devices incorporated magnetized metals and, when worn on the affected parts, were claimed to cure rheumatism. I humored William and diligently wore the galvanic bands on wrists and ankles for six weeks, but by April I had not noticed any positive benefits from them and was almost certain I would not.

Now that school was dismissed, I enrolled in a "penny post" correspondence course to develop the skill of <u>phonography</u>, a new system of phonetic shorthand that had recently been invented by

English educator Sir Isaac Pitman. It was thoroughly explained in his 1848 <u>Manual of Phonography, Or Writing by Sound</u>, available through mail order. Once my handbook arrived, I ceaselessly practiced Pitman's lessons. My quest exacted the price. I hardly knew what to do with myself for I had injured my eyes, so soon, studying, for they never tolerated much. I could see but very little and my thumb would not let me write much and only that by holding my pen loosely and letting it almost guide itself.

When my eyes healed, the only activity left for me was reading. Catherine Beecher, former principal of the Hartford Female Seminary and sister of the New York abolitionist and clergyman Henry Ward Beecher, had recently published her <u>Treatise on Domestic Economy</u> in which I found pearls of wisdom with regard to one's deportment among the aristocracy. Such mannered behavior was not practiced in the Notch, a location the prim Miss Beecher would have found unbearably rustic, but I was endeavoring to be positive: when I got well, I should be capable of proper etiquette. <u>When</u> I got well.

Also fascinating were articles in newspapers and periodicals written by or about independent women who, in their determination to achieve equality with men, aspired to roles beyond their customary status as wives and mothers. I greatly admired Elizabeth Cady Stanton and Susan B. Anthony for their work toward liberating women.

The much-debated question of slavery was also frequently discussed in such publications, as Stanton had been quoted as saying that women were treated no better than slaves. The women who signed the "Declaration of Rights and Sentiments" drawn up at the Woman's Rights Convention swore to use every instrumentality within their power to achieve their object. One of my most ambitious dreams, was to add my support and my voice to those of Lucretia Mott, Stanton, Anthony, Wendell Phillips, Frederick Douglass and William Lloyd Garrison, progressive thinkers all!

There was an enlightened woman in nearby Woodstock, Marenda Briggs Randall. She was nearly thirty years older than I, and a homeopathic physician with a modest practice. In 1834 she had married Nathaniel Randall, an apprentice watch-maker and jeweler ten years her junior who also practiced homeopathy. Both Randalls were earnest advocates of all manner of reforms—political, medical, scientific, social and religious. I was familiar with their home in Woodstock—a striking Greek Revival cottage with colonnaded front porch and dark shutters, built by Nathaniel's father, a shipwright. It was located on River Street at the base of Mt. Tom.

Marenda was the more controversial of the two because she strictly followed the theories of Sylvester Graham who advocated the consumption of coarsely ground whole-wheat flour and preached that excessive sexual desire and disease were caused by an unhealthy diet.

Eager for a woman physician's point of view, I rode the stage to Woodstock to consult her about my swollen joints. She was a large woman of pale complexion, with inquisitive eyes, brown hair and a ready smile. Her Grahamite philosophy decreed that I would be wise to shun tight corsets, heavy clothing, coffee, tea, alcohol, white bread, feather beds, pork, tobacco, salt, condiments, and hot mince pie. She also recommended that I undergo treatment by a "psychologist," Dr. John Gordon, of Windsor, Vermont, who often saw patients in a Woodstock hotel and had a reputation for the successful treatment of patients with ailments similar to mine. Dr. Gordon utilized magnetism in his treatments. This was not the magnetism utilized by galvanic bands, this was "animal magnetism," and the healing power came from the magnetic forces of the spirit.

I was skeptical.

As Marenda briefly explained it, magnetic healing involves the concept that Man is a magnet. Our magnetism contains the vital principles of physical life and is used to produce any and every manifestation of man, whether physical, mental, spiritual or psychical. "Live magnetism is permeated with the spirit influence of mortals," she said, "It is a material substance, perhaps a fluid."

All phenomena are produced by certain rates of vibration, and when a patient is suffering pain, that vibration must be re-attuned harmoniously by the laying on of hands.

I arranged to stay at Mrs. Willard's rooming house in Woodstock. Dr. Gordon's treatments would involve a transfer of his own magnetism, generated or gathered from unseen spiritual forces, and thus eliciting a harmonious vibration, temporarily or permanently, by placing his hands or mind or both upon me and my infirmity. A successful treatment would hypnotize me so that I would fall into a trance, thus "mesmerized."

On the day of my appointed meeting with the psychologist my fascination with the subject wavered, not only because he saw his patients in a hotel room, but I did not know how I could place my unconscious self in the hands of a stranger, much less an unfamiliar man.

Mary Willard, Mrs. Willard's daughter, offered to accompany me to the Inn, for which I was most grateful. She would remain seated outside the door while I received my first treatment and if I called out she vowed she would promptly come to my aid.

Mary's offer was even more appreciated when I first beheld Doctor Gordon, who, when I entered his sanctum, closed the door solidly behind me. The man was short and stocky. His bald head gleamed like a large pink egg above an unruly nest of black hair. His beard was equally wild and strung with gray throughout. Most unsettling was his piercing gaze. Through thick narrow spectacles his black eyes were magnified, unnaturally large and dark.

I was relieved of my crutches as I sat in the chair that he offered (not the bed, as I had feared!). Foremost in my mind was a comment by Miss Beecher in which the author warned women to be wary of doctors who might take sexual advantages while they were literally under his "spell." What was mesmerism, if not a spell?

Dr. Gordon explained in his Scottish brogue that in order to magnetize me he would place his right hand upon my forehead and *his left hand upon the back of my neck and head. The right hand, possessing a positive charge, would throw out the magnetism. The left hand (negative) would receive the magnetism after it circulated through me, passing from his right hand and through my brain, magnetizing my brain and charging my entire nervous system with his own electromagnetic vitality.*

His hand was warm but the moment he touched my neck, a chill immediately chased up and down my spine. The impact was so violent that acute shudders nearly caused me to slide from my chair.

"This is only natural," Dr. Gordon said, catching me and feeling me tremble beneath his fingers, "Electro-magnetism is generated by nerve cells in different parts of the body, but especially so by the spinal ganglion on either side of the spinal cord. This sensation occurs because my spirit forces are being applied to the nervous system at the base of your brain."

It may have been my imagination, but at the close of that session and each session thereafter, to my unfailing embarrassment and mortification, Dr. Gordon seemed to enjoy taking liberties by physically manipulating my body from head to foot, although I always remained fully clothed. He explained these actions were necessary to throw off all the infective magnetism from my system. He snapped it off at the tips of my fingers, careful not to draw it toward the vital organs but to throw it aside.

After that first treatment, Mary Willard helped me back to her mother's home, where I fell into a deep sleep.

By the first of May I had stepped four steps with very little help and had returned home as the doctor was going back to Windsor, where he belonged. Or so I felt. I could scarcely analyze my feelings. I wrote to Celia and confessed that I had a strange mixture of hope and fear, and it was puzzling to tell which predominated. I dared not think it possible that I could get well. I recalled the number of times that I had been disappointed and was wary of being too presumptuous.

Heavy rains pounded the mountains around Plymouth Notch that spring, causing the Black River to rise and flood the nearby town of Ludlow where it caused devastating damage for the brand new railroad. In Woodstock, where I again boarded so as to receive further treatments from Dr. Gordon, Mary Willard was ill with consumption. I worried that Mary's cough sounded very much like Ephraim's when he was near death.

I had not been present at Ephraim's moment of passing, but witnessing Mary's departure marked me for life. In her last moments when the breath went slowly but surely out of her body and I saw the look of peace that settled on her features, I thought in my heart, it is well. The next day I wrote "Lines on the death of Mary S. Willard," pleased that I was again able to grip a pen.

My second series of treatments with Dr. Gordon extended into early July, at which time I returned to Plymouth Notch where I found the sweetness of summer was already fleeting.

I kept a careful distance from Father, who had grown even more morose since Ephraim's death and ridiculed my magnetism treatments. He rose before sunrise and retired before sunset, working all day at his own chores with Nathan, in addition to assisting at the neighboring farm of Mr. Coolidge—Father called him Galoosh—whose spotted stallion was put out to stud, a purebred Arabian sired by a stallion once owned by the Sultan of Muscat in the Arabian country of Oman. Father had a way with livestock but possessed little patience for the peacocks and other exotic fowl that paraded around the Coolidge's fenced-in lot. Their farm was close enough that Father could come home for noon dinner when he wasn't working out in the fields or the maple orchard. At least he was careful not to drink until the evening, as he would surely have lost his job with Galoosh if he had.

Long after Father had gone to bed, when Mother's work was done for the day, I would often ask to be helped to a rocking chair in the dooryard where she and I could enjoy watching the shadow of night rise upon the side of East Mountain. I have always liked to inhale the clean, damp taste of our darkening hillside. Crickets sang in the dewy grass. Fireflies floated past like wayward sparks. Ribbons of cool air wafted up from Hollow Brook through the maple trees.

In the deepening twilight, the fragrance of newly-mown hay mingled with the climbing roses in Mother's garden. As she rocked and sighed, Mother tucked a pinch of tobacco into a little white clay pipe she puffed, as did most of the women in the Notch. The sweetness of the pipe smoke wound upward into the gloaming amid the lightning bugs and the last warbles of birds settling in.

I envisaged myself becoming as such, my greatest joy derived from frolicing fireflies and sunsets fading. Poor Mother. We pitied her, perhaps all the more so because she came from a prestigious family. Ephraim Moore, my grandfather, had been a representative from Plymouth to the Vermont General Assembly from 1809 to 1822. But Betsey Moore married into poverty — the son of a tavern owner who, in turn, was corrupted by drink.

One evening when she dozed off while smoking, I retrieved Mother's little clay pipe, cradling the warmth of its smooth bowl in my own hand. The residual heat eased the deep ache in my thumb. Soon I will take up a pipe, I thought, I will take up a pipe or chew snuff and toil my way through weary years with a long-suffering attitude like Mother's, and nothing to show but regret for my dreary lot. I pulled a tiny mouthful of smoke from the stem and stared into the growing dark before I exhaled.

If I sometimes chose to remain in the garden after Mother retired, Nathan would carry me back indoors. Slow and deliberate in his actions, Nathan was a kind soul. For years he had patiently struggled to learn the rudiments of reading and writing, although Father complained I was wasting my efforts with him.

Sitting in the garden with Nathan, I read Celia's letters aloud and my heart ached for her sympathetic companionship and for this brother who would always be limited in his abilities. In the dusk, I quoted a poem by Longfellow that had been in my thoughts for a very long time:

The night is come, but not too soon;
And sinking silently,
All silently, the little moon
Drops down behind the sky.

Longfellow had written "The Light of Stars" on a pleasant night such as this, I explained, and I offered Nathan advice taken from this poem that I carried in my heart:

As one by one thy hopes depart,
Be resolute and calm.

Oh, fear not in a world like this,
And thou shalt know erelong—
Know how sublime a thing it is
To suffer and be strong.

The "Glorious Fourth," the annual Independence Day Celebration, was a traditional time for social gathering and much festivity in Plymouth Notch. Families from miles around assembled for a pot-luck pic-nic. July 4, 1850, was no exception.

Twenty years before, Plymouth residents had purchased subscriptions for the casting of a five-hundred pound cannon at the Tyson Foundry that was fired in 1840 to announce the election of President William Henry Harrison. Every year after that the two communities, Plymouth Notch and Plymouth Union, connived, tussled and fought over who would have the honor of firing the gun on the Glorious Fourth.

From the open window of my darkened room, I could not escape the cannon's boom, the crack of Chinese fireworks, and patriotic songs like "Yankee Doodle" and "Hail Columbia" played with imperfect yet martial gusto by a local amateur brass band. I *felt no desire to pull the curtains aside and witness the merriment in detail as it reminded me of my own <u>dependence</u>, my own misery. Not until midnight would I make my way to the window and the cool light of the moon to seek a sign that my plight would improve.*

Fireflies were like sparkling fairies performing a mid-summer's night dance. When I was little, Father had told me that on nights such as this, Little Men in Green danced in the forest with great merriment. But the "Little Folks in Green" had all disappeared long ago or else they thought me not worthy of their care—for I never got a glimpse of them in their moonlight revels, nor caught one note of the song they were said to sing in the midnight hour.

According to Axy's diary, only a matter of a few weeks after the above, a new idea began to prosper that would change the course of her life. She paid a sympathetic visit to friends Delia and Abby Pollard down in Plymouth. Their mother, Ruth, had recently died. Among subjects the girls discussed was the enlightened notion that spirits could communicate with the living, as she recorded thus:

July 29, 1850: Today wrote a poem for Abby, "To My Mother's Spirit," suggested by a discussion among us as to whether spirits could communicate with mortals. 'Tis a beautiful idea, that our departed friends are around us and with us, that they can come back to guard us from temptation, to soothe us in affliction and win us from sin. 'Tis a beautiful idea, but if true, <u>could</u> the world be so sunk in wickedness? Yet if not true it might be still working and I am inclined to think it may be so. Is it not the influence of spirits when better thoughts come back to the heart which had almost yielded to sin?

July 24, 1850: Let me remember to cultivate a grateful disposition. Have written today 'Life is an Echo,' and every word I write—instead of thinking of my helplessness, let me be thankful that I can use my thumb in even so slight a degree and be happy in the thought.

⊰ 3 ⊱

Thoughts of a Long-Tried Heart

(1850–1854)

PLEASE PARDON THE INTERRUPTION, but at this point I must briefly deviate from my sister's story to include a revelation of my own that may have had an effect on her as events in our lives coincided.

When the iron works closed in Tyson Furnace, I then moved to Troy, New York, where I first boarded, as mentioned, in the cheerful home of Mr. and Mrs. Timothy Adams. After they packed up their belongings and headed west, I was invited to board with Mr. and Mrs. Benjamin Starbuck, a very kind couple who took me under their wings and bade me feel at home. The congeniality of the entire family was refreshing.

The Starbuck's household was a lively place, with two Irish servants and five children. Mr. Starbuck, of Starbuck and Gurley Troy Air Furnace, also owned and operated Benjamin Starbuck Bros. Iron Founders & Machinists. He had two business locations, one in the city and another on Centre Island in the Hudson River off the Troy shore.

Mr. Starbuck was jovial and good-natured, referring to his wife Evaline and their many children as "the Tribe of Benjamin." At that time we had no idea that he would be influential in Axy's future; I was only aware that I was provided with comfortable quarters and warm and companionable hosts.

One evening the Starbucks invited me to attend a spirit lecture at the Universalist Meeting House. This topic was entirely new to me, but the Starbucks were much interested. As Mr. Starbuck explained, it was very much discussed albeit little understood. During the lecture, the speaker would deliver messages from the spirit world that he ascertained while entranced.

"It is not premeditated, Celia," Mrs. Starbuck kindly assured me, "and you need not be afraid."

Mr. Starbuck explained that the invisible power of the spirit world had been revealed a few years before when two young sisters from Hydesville, New York—Catherine and Margaretta Fox—chanced upon their gift of spirit-communication. By establishing a simple code that involved a specific number of raps in response to verbal questions, the Fox sisters eventually determined that disturbances in their house were caused by the spirit of a murdered peddler. Catherine and Margaretta soon moved into the Rochester, New York, home of their older sister. Even more spirits began to communicate there, through a "spiritual telegraph" that rapped at appropriate intervals as the girls called out letters of the alphabet.

By the spring of 1850 the Fox sisters were celebrities. They arrived in New York City, where they held "circles" or séances three times a day at Barnum's Hotel and were invited to give private sittings for small parties as a form of fashionable amusement. Horace Greeley, editor of *The New York Tribune,* entertained the Fox sisters at his home with such guests as novelist James Fenimore Cooper and poet William Cullen Bryant.

Mr. Starbuck guided us to seats near the front of the Meeting House. I could overhear tidbits of conversations around us conveying skepticism and disbelief; yet others in attendance seemed to display indifference, perhaps even mischievousness in their countenance.

"I've heard he teaches pernicious doctrines," a woman behind us whispered to a neighbor, who replied, "What a fool he is, to throw himself away on this ridiculous humbug!" This assertion caused Mr. Starbuck to turn in his seat and sternly proclaim, "Let us wait until we hear and then decide," which so startled the women that they remained silent for the rest of the evening.

In all, it was a remarkable lecture. I cannot say whether I was offered, as promised, "divine revelations," but the speaker, Andrew Jackson

Davis, professed that he was able to reach and realize the presence and existence of spirits who were in fact the very persons who once walked and talked with us but whose bodies had been cast off forever, and whose conscious existence we may have erroneously believed to have ended with death. I found it a startling theory and Mr. Davis' revelations (divine or not), which he called his "Harmonial Philosophy," appeared to have been delivered while in a clairvoyant state.

During a discussion afterward in their parlor, Mr. Starbuck said most of the churches and their preachers were not pleased with this new belief—they blamed it on the Devil. But the Universalists, in response to the vast crisis of faith that our country was then undergoing, countered with tolerance and often invited traveling lecturers to demonstrate their philosophy.

I found a reassuring religious implication in this New Era, as the advent of Modern Spiritualism became to be known, for one no longer needed to depend upon a church for proof of the soul's immortality.

I had told the Starbucks about Axy, and they suggested that I write to her about these mysterious powers that might help alleviate her pain.

Axy, who had been studying this concept, agreed that the notion was heartening. In response to my letter, she wrote:

> *Could we but know the future is, as has been represented, a Higher Sphere and yet Higher Sphere, leaving all pain and sorrow with our frail earthly bodies here, we should grow wiser, happier, better through all Eternity when the soul frees from its earthly bonds like an uncaged bird should stretch forth its Heaven-born pinions through all Immensity.*

But she said nothing about inviting the Spirits to aid in her healing, nor did she reveal that she had discussed this New Era with Marenda Randall as early as May 1850, while she was receiving magnetizing treatments from the spine-chilling Dr. Gordon.

Axy began writing in her diary again. In February of 1853, she noted that she wanted *once more to trace upon the pages the thoughts of a long-tried heart... lain bowed down by disease, shut up from the world in darkness and solitude like a prisoner chained in his dungeon.*

Marenda Randall was once more influential in my sister's quest for renewed well-being. The phenomenon of healing occurred in an oddly intertwined yet spontaneous manner.

A Woodstock man, Gaius Cobb, was a shoemaker, beekeeper, and violin maker. He had been requested to construct a *rapping machine* that had 36 keys like a piano, 26 letters and 10 figures, so that Spirits could communicate by spelling out the answer.

Marenda and Nathaniel Randall were most eager to employ Mr. Cobb's invention. In 1852, Marenda received a spirit letter from General George Washington, who had been dead for fifty-three years! The message took six sessions to receive and transcribe as it was tapped out in an elaborate code. Washington expressed his feelings about slavery (he would not permit the spread of slavery to new states); railroads (he called for a nationally funded railroad all the way to Oregon); and urged that America assist fallen and oppressed people everywhere. The communiqué was subsequently published as a twelve-page pamphlet by the Randalls.

Of course this activity eventually came to the notice of the residents of Plymouth Notch, although Axy had not mentioned anything of the like to me.

As girls, our heroines were always valiant. We enjoyed sharing books that involved suffering and survival. While boarding with the Starbucks, I was advised that social reformers—advocates for prison reform, abolition and woman's rights—all who were attuned to a "harmonious progression," embraced the possibility of spirit communication.

Galvanic bands had failed my sister, Mesmerism had failed, physicians and their nostrums had failed. With Marenda Randall's encouragement, Axy conceded that Spiritualism might be her only hope.

The charismatic and increasingly eccentric Universalist minister John Murray Spear visited Woodstock in late March of that year. Spear, 49, wore an amiable smile, and had long black hair and a flowing black beard. The Randalls invited Axy to meet the eminent Spiritualist and hear him speak. She told me later that Spear appeared quite tall—in fact, he was several inches over six feet. Axy was immediately drawn to him, as Spear championed many of the issues that she carried in her own heart: He was a prominent abolitionist, active in the Underground Railroad in Boston, and devoted to helping prisoners—he vigorously campaigned against the death penalty. By 1852, encouraged by his daughter, Sophronia, Spear had begun to heed the direction of spirits who directed his presence toward people and places where his freelance ministry and his magnetic healing were needed. In late March 1853, his spirits guided him to Woodstock and to Axy.

Sophronia accompanied her father. She was a medium as well. Plump and gracious, Axy found Sophronia to be softness wrapped around a sturdy spine.

Despite muddy roads from recent snows and rain, Spear delivered a trance lecture on the subject of "Philanthropy" to a packed crowd at the Woodstock Town Hall on Sunday, March 27, from noon to three p.m. As he was wont to do, Spear delivered his lecture from the rear of the lecture hall, with his back to the audience. He declared he had been called to Woodstock at the behest of the spirit of Dr. Benjamin Rush, as his ministry and magnetic healing were required there.

Axy used her shorthand phonography to take notes during Spear's lecture:

"Reformers are not all philanthropists, because all have not yet approached that plane & felt their minds drawn particularly to each outward manifestation, yet all feel at times the want of humanity, & no heart was ever so hardened but that some voice of suffering has at times awakened it to sympathy."

Later that afternoon, Axy was granted a private audience with Mr. Spear and Sophronia at the Randall home, where the Mt. Tom Spiritual

Circle was holding a modest reception. Axy asked Spear if she might be healed. And, if healed, could she become a medium as well.

Mr. Spear took her crutches and asked that she be seated in a kitchen chair. He placed his hands firmly on her head while Sophronia gently held both of her hands in one of hers; Sophronia's other hand rested comfortably on Axy's right shoulder. Marenda Randall acted as amanuensis.

The room was absolutely silent; even the Mt. Tom Spiritual Circle was hushed, awaiting this singular blessing.

"Spirit-of-all-Spirits," Mr. Spear poured forth in his sonorous voice, his eyes tightly shut, "controller of all events, ruler of all worlds, up to thee the mind ascends in gratitude that one so faithful, so truthful, has been made willing to consecrate herself, all that she expects to have, to labors so useful, so important to man. While the New Era is but yet in its bud she has said, 'Do with me O God as thou in thy wisdom may direct.' Though the tear from time to time has moistened the eye, yet she has not faltered. Very few persons now living on this planet have exhibited a more constant fidelity than this noble woman."

Mr. Spear paused, as if intercepting a spectral influence. Axy said her senses were so heightened at that moment that she could smell the sour dishrag hanging over the edge of the Randall's sink. She could hear the purring of their tabby cat, curled in the corner near the cookstove as it stretched and yawned and went back to sleep.

Sophronia began to verbalize, also inspired but in a much softer tone.

"When this woman has determined on a course of action all the fires of Smithfield cannot deter it. When she sees that the path of wrong is open before her she will not walk therein, though worldly honor, riches and prosperity are presented to her view. This woman was born under the influence of the planet Pluto. She has a strength of character, a balance of intellect, a substantiality, compactness and rotundity of form which together form a beautiful and most valuable combination. Whatever she does, whatever she says, whatever she writes is in harmony with the light, wisdom and knowledge which have been influenced to her mind."

Mr. Spear took over, with his deep and masterful timbre.

"From a large class of persons this woman has purposely been selected as an able, untiring and faithful Teacheress. Every where she journeys she will command and without effort secure the confidence, respect, cooperation of persons with whom she from time to time may sojourn. This travel, this observation, this public teaching will in a few short years all tend to render her one of the noblest women of the nineteenth century.

"And now thou shalt receive thy true and thy appropriate name and thou shalt be called *The Teacheress*. Go then, Teacheress, teach man of himself. Teach him of the laws of his being. Teach him of his relation to his fellows. Teach him to commune with nature, teach him to see the divine in stars, to hear his voice in the rushing winds. Teach him that he is immortal, that woman is his equal, that no true sociality can be until woman and man have their individual rights.

"Tell him that unending futures are opening to his vision.

"And Teacheress, when clouds may gather around there shall be presented to thy vision one star. That star shall shine upon thee when all others are obscured. When thou shalt feel that thou art alone, that star shall comfort thee and shall guide thee."

As Sophronia had accurately noted, Axy was born a Scorpio, under Pluto. They had only met that day, so, according to my sister there was no way Sophronia could have known that without spiritual revelation.

Axy left Woodstock feeling for the first time that her physical system was under the control of an invisible, yet intelligent power. Knowing not whether this power was among the elements of the physical world or the spiritual, she had some reservations with regard to giving herself up to its mastery. She was still in need of crutches. But she was certain that Mr. Spear's words could scarcely injure her more, and she thought, perhaps, they might help. As she recorded with confidence in her diary, *The chains of disease are falling off my limbs.*

Mr. Starbuck had given me copies of many small newspapers to read, all being printed to spread the word of Modern Spiritualism. I learned that Axy subscribed to *The New Era*, and she later contributed inspirational articles and stories to *The World's Paper*, published in Sandusky, Vermont. She would eventually write personal columns for *The Banner of Light*, published in Boston, and *The Herald of Progress*, published by Andrew Jackson Davis in New York.

Release from the bonds of her affliction may have been gradual, but Axy would explain her cure in a lengthy melodramatic poem, "The Angel's Visit," which enjoyed wide publication in the above periodicals.

Her poem dated the beginning of her recovery to November 1852, *when winds were loud and high,* and *storm-clouds drifted through the sky.* Born in November, she closely identified with tempestuous autumn gales that swept through the Green Mountains. In her poem there was a sound *like some poor sufferer's dying moan* while an autumn dirge murmured *Gone, all gone.* Alone in a darkened room a young girl was *chained by disease,—a living tomb* (a favorite image that appears in many of her written works). The poem-girl wanted only to die, for she had been ill for many years, *such years as make the heart grow old.*

While lying, helpless, the storm increased and, as if a mighty spell touched her heart, the girl burst forth with *wild, impassioned, burning prayer…a prayer in which the blight of years, the bitter, burning, scalding tears, the blasted hopes, the burning thirst,* mingled and reached a peak of intense despair that was able to reach all the way up to God. In her anguish, the girl dared to accuse God of not listening to her plea!

Then abruptly, as if in response, her appeal was interrupted by the blinding, exquisite rush of angels' wings.

> *A glorious light filled all the place,*
> *Its radiance shone o'er all her face,*
> *Gone, gone, was all her pall-like gloom,*
> *As if bright angels filled the room…*
> *And strength through all her form was given—*

"Was she transported unto heaven?
Or had bright angels come to earth,
To raise her to a higher birth?"
As if in answer to this thought,
In melody these words she caught,—
Like angel voices through the room,—
<u>*"God heard thy prayer, we come, we come!"*</u>

In her poem, Achsa explained that her Guardians exacted a promise for their cure: She must agree to take up a holy mission; she must work to turn souls from sin to nobler truths and save others from pain and despair. Most importantly of all, it was her calling to *teach the soul it cannot die.*

This notion caused a dramatic shift in her attitude. To her amazement, my sister's physical health also began to improve.

The sensational story of her transformation from helpless invalid to spirit medium would become a long-standing lecture topic for Axy; it was a frequent request. Her most devoted followers, including her family, were not only intrigued by the miracle she attributed to the intervention of angels—we were also astonished by her progression from the home-bound world of women to the platform of the lecture circuit, a world deemed appropriate only to men.

Years later, in response to the entreaty of Boston editor and publisher, Alonzo Eliot Newton, she composed a detailed explanation of her miraculous conversion which appeared in *The New England Spiritualist* in 1855:

> *I was taken by invisible physicians, through a course of*
> *treatment (if I might so speak,) unlike anything which could*
> *have been devised by my own brain. First, my own hands were*
> *used involuntarily to magnetize myself; then I was caused to*

inhale the atmosphere by expanding the lungs for half or three quarters of an hour at a time, without being conscious of making any effort of myself. Then followed, as my strength increased, various bodily exercises, many of them to me totally unfamiliar, but, as I have since learned, such as are in some degree practiced at Water Cures.

In time I was raised upon my feet by this invisible yet powerful and <u>persevering</u> influence, and was made to walk about the room. This was done for many days before my strength was sufficient to <u>take one step at any other time,</u> let me make what effort I would.

About this time, my hand began to be used to write involuntarily. And now came communications purporting to be from friends who had gone before, and those whom I had never known. What could it be but spirits? Still I was fearful lest my desire to believe might influence my reason, and cause me to give credence without sufficient evidence. Was it indeed at the hands of my spirit-friends that I was receiving that strength which was returning me once more to the world?

Among my exercises for the lungs was that of singing. I was caused to sing, when under the influence, words and music wholly unfamiliar to me, apparently communications from spirits; although at that time I had never heard or thought of the like being done, through any medium.

Next came the development of speaking. I am always conscious while writing, speaking or singing, although wholly unable to control the power by which it is done. But I feel so unlike myself at such times, that to believe the powers of my own mind thus act, would be impossible.

While passing into the superior state before speaking or singing, I feel a mysterious influence stealing through my system, as if some subtle power were loosing the band that binds soul and body as one. My mind seems elevating and almost detached from earth. I am surrounded by an atmosphere of harmony, poetry, intelligence and spirituality, and a superior mind seems flowing into mine, filling it with power and energy, and imparting ideas which form themselves into words and sentences as I speak or sing. I seem to occupy a plane both of thought and vision midway between earth and the spirit-spheres. Earth is forgotten, save as I look down and behold her children in their darkened state, and wish to give them light. The light of the spirit-spheres is beaming through the depths of my soul. The spirits of the free seem around me and with me, (although I see nothing save with the spiritual perceptions) and I seem one of their number. Thus I felt at the time when developing as a speaker. I had tested, I had reasoned, I had thought; now came the internal evidence, and I believed.

And when spring came with its freshness and beauty, I was strengthened and prepared to meet it. I went forth once more, and looked upon the loveliness of earth. I mingled again with the outer world. I walked once more in the fields, upon the mountain, and in the forest; and in the Temple of Nature, listening to her thousand voices and her silent teachers, I learned to worship the Living God. And I was not alone. "Angels came and ministered unto me."

Many wonder at, what in olden times would have been called a miracle, and many believed. Yet as in olden times, many say "it is of evil." But it matters not to me. It is enough that "the shadow of death has been turned into morning," that the shroud has been cast aside and my spirit, touched by the quickening power of higher intelligences, once more is free. From that time forth my health has continued to improve. And though not yet fully established, I am able to do much, and my labor seems proportioned to my strength.

Passing Strange

(1854)

As I held my sister's dry hand this summer of 1862 and listened to her feverish ramblings, I well knew that reassurances of yet another miraculous recovery were implausible. Let her Spiritualist friends summon choirs of guardian angels. My beloved sister could not be healed again.

Axy was suffering from brain fever, or inflammation of the brain. While she slumbered I did nothing but trace her feeble pulse and watch the quilt move on her flat chest to be certain she still lived. Through those quiet hours I often thought of Morris back on our Wisconsin farm, handling the livestock and the housekeeping with only the help of the young Irish lads we'd recently taken on as hired hands.

Morris wrote to me often. I found his letters less than soothing. "The Wis. 1st regiment has returned one of the men who died yesterday. Mr. Spencer has just been up here giving notice of the funeral which takes place tomorrow at the Free Church."

He said our weather had been very dry and the crops looked fair though in much need of rain. "Business is very dull and a great cry of hard times although I do not see that it makes much difference to us so long as we have an abundance to live on." I felt confident he had added the latter to diminish my concerns for his well-being. Two years ago he suffered a severe head injury during the harvest and after that a bilious fever that confined him to his bed for many weeks. He had been making a washstand from a pattern he took from one of Mother's during our visit to the Notch, and I told Axy, "I expect my house as well as all my furniture will be made by the hand of my husband," as he was an excellent craftsman and carpenter.

THE BENNETT GAZETTE

APRIL 9, 1885   KILBOURN CITY, WISCONSIN   VOLUME XXIV NO 3

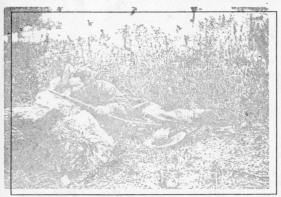

KIDS FOLLOW NEWPORT BAND DOWN STREET

When the sonorous strains of Vanderpool's Newport band was heard at Kilbourn City, every kid in school jumped from his seat and followed the band down the street.

REMEMBERING OUR HONORED DEAD

It has been twenty years since the end of the Civil War and today we recognize an important figure for the Union, Private Truman Head, commonly known as California Joe, who passed away almost ten years ago.

Immortalized here in an illustration by Larkin Mead, California Joe is pictured positioned as he often was to fulfill his sharpshooting duties. This illustration was first a photograph taken by George H. Houghton.

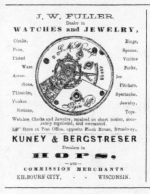

THOMPSON DISPOSES THE MIRROR (OF KILBOURN) TO DAVIS, WRIGHT & DAVIS

Mr. T. O. Thompson, finding it rather difficult to carry on a paper at Berlin and Kilbourn City at the same time, has disposed of the Mirror (of Kilbourn) to the firm Davis, Wright & Davis, the latter a lady, who are highly commended as fully capable of making a good paper. In their salutatory they say the paper will labor for the interests of its locality, making hop reports abroad and home a speciality.

Axy's curtains remained closed due to the distress of her bad eye, so it was too dim in her room for me to sew or to mend or do any clever thing. When she was awake I sang to calm her, framed muted light from a lantern to read aloud from her favorite books, and during moments of her lucidity asked if she wished me to pen more recollections of the lives she'd touched and the landscapes she had witnessed—in addition to those she had already recorded in *My Own Sad History*. She directed me to casual notes and random jottings she had chronicled at the Crawfords' Oswego home, beginning with those that noted her early, gradual development as a medium.

As I came to understand it, my sister's restoration to health empowered her with a mystical sense of control. With all medical remedies exhausted, her illness and her situation seemed curiously altered by divine intervention.

An old New England phrase describes such an anomaly: *passing strange*.

Axy's development, then, involved a kind of self-hypnosis, not far removed from Dr. Gordon's magnetism. Automatic writing, or spirit-writing, was encouraged as a means of practicing the dialogue between spirit and medium. Seeking absolute solitude, she climbed a trail into the mountains to our favorite grassy clearing in the woods. Writing pad on her lap and pencil in readiness, she waited. This was the closest thing to silence she could achieve, albeit she could not subdue the birdsongs or the rustling leaves. Cows lowed in a nearby meadow and she could hear their cowbells chime. She wondered if her time would be more productive if she helped manage Malvina or worked the spinning wheel for Mother. Even the bees on the clusters of nodding pink phlox distracted her. She began by scrawling lazy circles.

Marenda Randall had advised Axy to announce to the spirits that she was ready, each time she sat for a message. "I am ready," she declared softly, several times. Then, impatient, she turned her face to the sky, closed her eyes and shouted "I am ready!"

Gradually, penciled scribbles on the page gave way to more legible writing. Early experiments grew to be encouraging.

Then *an entire letter* came through in a hurried scrawl: the letter defined my sister's mission. She interpreted this as her contract with her Guardians in response for her restoration to health.

> *Keys silver and golden are given to thee that thou mayest unlock the treasure chambers of heart and brain and lead forth embodied and garmented in rich and varied speech the love and truths and joys of the inner life to the glad embrace of earth's children. From the valley of the Shadow of Death where gloom and anguish assume tangible and threatening aspects and the waters of affliction roll their dark ensanguined billows o'er swept by the whirlwinds of desolation and despair thou hast been led by angel hands upward to the lofty table lands and sunny mountain slopes of God's glorious Upper World of light and beauty. A teacher and a priestess divinely ordained and consecrated thou standest in the realm of the intermediate interfusing soul of love with the portent, grandeur and dignity of an uplifted intellect..And when weariness and exhaustion supersede thou shalt be folded in the arms of sweet repose and the ebbing tide of life shall return refluent and joyous kissing with golden waves of celestial Harmony all the circling shores of thy being and bearing to thy outstretched hands gifts immortal and divine from the boundless Wealth of the Infinite.*

Further spirit writings were received after that. Axy rehearsed becoming entranced. She preferred seclusion for these experiments, eventually trusting friends Abby and Delia Pollard to accompany her, or sometimes our sister Sarah, now twenty-one. The girls sat quietly until the spirits inspired Axy and she was motivated to speak. After these episodes, Sarah declared that the voice Axy used was very unlike her natural voice. It was low and emphatic; persuasive.

Convincing. Sometimes Axy found herself singing a hymn that was given to her, a hymn none of them had ever heard.

Marenda Randall had warned, "You may experience a sensation as falling or dizziness, as if you were going to faint; this may continue until you become entirely unconscious on the external plane, and you will know no more until you regain your normal condition, although, while under the influence of the operator, you may have been speaking more or less coherently."

To release control of her conscious state was a most daunting prospect, even though Axy trusted and was comforted by those friends who watched over her. In this way she could concentrate on breathing to let her body relax and she kept foremost in her mind the advice of the noted Spiritualist leader, Andrew Jackson Davis:

Behold! Here is thy magic staff. Under all circumstances keep an even mind. Take it, Try it, Walk with it, Talk with it. Lean on it. Believe on it. Forever!

As she set aside her crutches, Axy relied upon this invisible magic staff. Along with renewed health, she regained her strong self-will and her adventuresome disposition.

But the fear of public speaking appeared insurmountable. Women who spoke in public were forbidden or sternly discouraged from exercising their power of speech in settings where such an activity was seen as indecent and unladylike. Often mentioned was a contemptuous quote from Dr. Samuel Johnson: "A woman's preaching is like a dog's walking on its hind legs. It is not done well, but you are surprised to find it done at all."

Nevertheless, Axy's Guardians offered detailed instructions and exercises that were explicit in their counsel. The spirit of one of her Guardians, "Father Hopper" (a Quaker who had been active in the underground railroad, endorsed prison reform, gave aid to the infirm, free blacks, the sick and the insane), conferred a message in automatic writing but written in reverse as if using a mirror and it may only be deciphered in that fashion only, suggesting the following in response to her doubts:

My Dear Friend. Thee is like a bird in the morning brezes. Does a bird ask for a test of its power of flight? Thee is like a star high in the azure heaven needs no confirmation of its position thee must lean on thy own staf for God hast given thee a staf whereupon to lean. Thee is like a winged insect from flower to flower flying giving lessons to the very flower and …obtaining honey from the flowers…Thee must go forward For already Father Hopper has put credit marks & the number of thousands to thy name and each mark shall brightly shine in thy crown in the land of life love and light Thou cans't not always tell when Father Hopper is near and thou canst not always disern the star of hope that thy Angel Friends proffer to thee here must my good child if stars descend from heaven they shall fall on thy little rise of soil and thy spiritual life shall glisten in the rays of the spirit and as the drop glistens in the light of the morning orb I visit each one a little…I shall be with thee again today and feed thee a little or as much as thou dost relieve the hunger so shall thy hunger be appeased.

Thy Spirit Friend, I. T. Hopper

For Axy's twenty-sixth birthday, November 17, 1853, Delia Pollard composed a poem that invited the anniversary to bring new hope, strong faith and purpose:

Was it writing on the wall,—or didst
Thou read the words within my inmost soul—"thou shalt yet live?"

With the arrival of spring in 1854, my sister was strengthened and prepared to meet its freshness and beauty with her new life. She had

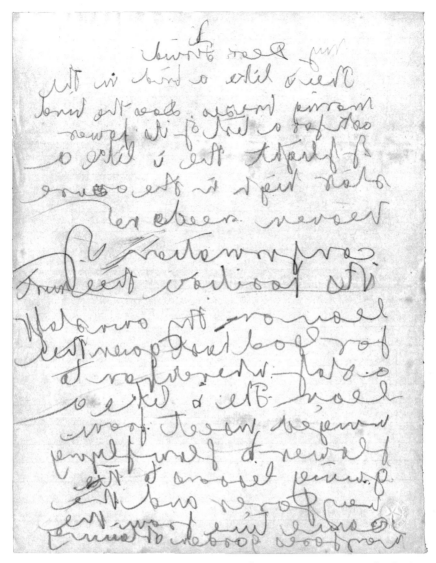

Automatic writing, mirror writing, message from I. T. Hopper, one of Achsa's spirit guardians: "My Dear Friend. Thee is like a bird in the morning brezes."

written to me of walking *in the Temple of Nature, listening to her thousand voices and her silent teachers. I learned to worship the Living God. And I was not alone. Angels came and ministered unto me.*

From that time forth her health continued to improve. Mother's letters were rife with accounts of Axy's achievements and the astonishment of friends, but in response I confessed that for me the spirit world remained a sealed book.

Later I will describe the concurrent progress of Spiritualism in Fond du Lac County and how it helped to draw Axy to visit our farm, but for now I shall continue with the progress made by her in the early days of being "inspired," as she called it.

Early in 1854 she again visited the Mt. Tom Spiritual Circle in Woodstock, where she sat in on séances conducted by Marenda Randall. Axy firmly stressed that becoming a spirit lecturer was not a gift she sought. Marenda reminded her that Lucretia Mott asked, "Why should not woman seek to be a reformer? If she is to be satisfied with the narrow sphere assigned her by man, nor aspire to a hither lest she should transcend the bounds of female delicacy; truly it is a mournful prospect for woman." And Elizabeth Cady Stanton declared that, "The best protection any woman can have…is courage."

Privately giving up consciousness among close friends was difficult enough. Unaccompanied on a stage where formidable women who proposed woman's rights had been spat upon or had mud thrown at them or been subjected to cruel taunts—well, Axy expressed regret. She felt she was wholly inadequate for that task.

And the notion of conducting her own private circle or séance was nearly as paralyzing as the concept of lecturing in public while entranced. She refused all such invitations until Marenda reminded her that the most influential Spiritualists advised "circle work" to be the very best way of developing one's mediumistic powers. "The home circle is the prayer meeting of Spiritualism," Marenda assured her. "If there is one place in all the world where the spirit is pleased to come, it is the sacred hearth, and the table around which they have gathered."

At least it was not necessary to hold a circle in complete darkness before an audience of strangers. The only true necessity was to surround oneself with persons of a certain type of psychical power, namely those who might be reservoirs upon which the spirits could draw. "You cannot expect growth unless you give the requisite conditions," Marenda promised. "You might as well anticipate a harvest without sowing the seed, just because you bought a sack of wheat!"

Axy grudgingly agreed to lead her first circle at the Pollard's home in Plymouth, where eight participants gathered in the parlor: Abby, Delia, and their father Moses Pollard; Mother and our sister Sarah; Uncle Thomas Moore, our mother's brother; and Mr. Daniel Wilder, a known Spiritualist who had a hotel in Plymouth Union. It was required that roughly half of the group should be of "passive temperament," or female, and they should be seated alternately around an uncovered table of convenient size.

Flames in the oil lamps were lowered and palms were placed flat upon the table.

Patience was essential, Axy forewarned. She knew Mother was uncomfortable, anticipating Father's scornful reproach when they returned. She knew, too, that Mother desperately wished for a message from our departed brother Ephraim. Perhaps the Pollards hoped to hear from Ruth. The convivial conversation of Uncle Thomas and Mr. Wilder helped everyone relax.

The group was to sit in silence for at least an hour. If nothing happened they agreed to try another time.

"If the table should move," Axy advised, "let your pressure be so gentle on its surface that you are sure you are not aiding its motions. When we think the time has come, I will take command of the Circle and act as spokesman. I will relate to the unseen Intelligence that an agreed code of signals is desirable."

One possible code would have her repeating the alphabet so the table might tilt at the letters forming the word the Spirit wished to spell. Another code involved tapping the alphabet with the Woodstock "rapping machine" that stood at the ready, on loan from the Randalls.

The evening was not a success, she reported to me.

> *You may think me selfish, Celia but…I sometimes feel as though my mediumship is of no worth because I have never relayed any communications to send to strangers save in three or four instances and I do not like to sit for that purpose, nor will I ever stand on a stage entranced and allow myself to be mentally undressed by any audience.*

I goaded her by teasing that perhaps she was reluctant to abandon "woman's lofty sphere" by appearing in public before a crowd of unfamiliar persons.

I was not aware that Daniel Wilder had already invited her to make her first public speaking appearance in nearby South Reading. My sister had refused.

Axy's initial séance may have been a failure, but the little post office in the Plymouth Notch General Store began to receive letters addressed for Miss A. W. Sprague from supporters in neighboring towns who had heard of her awe-inspiring cure and saw it as a "test" for their own beliefs. Thrilled with notice of her triumph, she was not disheartened if the correspondent challenged Spiritualism itself, or questioned her appearance or personal convictions.

> *I have nothing to say about myself, except that I am <u>as ugly looking</u> as nature could make me, and as for my <u>real self</u>, the "Internal," I shall let you draw your own conclusions from my style of writing, as I of course shall take the same <u>liberty</u> with regard to you. It is also a pleasure to me to correspond with people of intelligent minds even though they may differ from me in opinion.*

Mr. Wilder persisted with his invitation to speak at South Reading. Marenda Randall would not able to attend but her husband Nathaniel Randall and Axy's friend Delia Pollard promised to be there. Sarah and Mother gave assurances of their presence, as well. Fearing stage fright, a terrible silence or worse, Axy put off the invitation for as long as practicable.

She wrote to Mr. Spear for instruction, and he replied, "Thou has the individual work to do, Teacheress. Taught thyself, thou art to teach others."

Eventually, she accepted Mr. Wilder's invitation to speak with tangled emotions of ambiguity and despair. She wrote to me:

> *I can no longer shut my ears to the voice that is calling me to an even larger public field of labor. It requires much sacrifice of feeling, but gratitude demands it, and it is just. (Sacrifice for truth is no sacrifice). It seems that my devoted followers are not only intrigued by the miracle attributed to the intervention of angels, they are also eager to witness my grand progression from the home-bound world of women to the forbidden public platform of the lecture circuit, a world deemed appropriate only to men.*

I knew Axy did not seek homage. She was well aware of the blame and reproach that would be unkindly cast upon her for appearing in a public hall. She also knew she chanced being branded a blasphemous infidel.

> *When I stand before an audience, although experiencing the angelic mantle of delight falling upon me, yet my manner may appear peculiar. While in the trance state my breathing becomes rapid and irregular. If my eyes close, I am sometimes unable to open them. My hands and body may twitch and jerk as if I am being subjected to a series of galvanic shocks. If the trance is successful—if my powers leap up at will to burn and quicken—I am often conscious of an impulse to blurt out certain words.*

Every spasm, twitch and flutter would be analyzed and criticized, each wrinkle in her dress would be remarked upon; the style of her hair, her plain features, her scuffed, worn shoes.

It was terrifying to grasp how men's probing eyes would be free to devour her while she stood alone upon the stage. And men would surely jump at the opportunity to do so: Spiritualism may allow women to speak in public, but there was also a further significance and Axy recognized, regretfully, that trance mediumship was rife with potentially shameful, licentious, even carnal overtones.

A trance medium must appear before her assembly in a passive, unconscious state. She must surrender to the spirit, be entered by that spirit, seized, and possessed.

Yet there was no other way to carry out her Guardians' commands to deliver "luminous revelations of divine Truth to hitherto darkened eyes," and avoid the ravenous gaze of a merciless public.

"Recipient of Heavenly treasures," her Guardians had advised, "Thou shalt dispense with liberal hand thy God-gifts to the children of Men."

Her mandate was clear.

Our father, more emotionally inaccessible than ever to our family, ridiculed Axy's conversion to Spiritualism. He could not deny her return to health, but he predicted her preposterous path of recovery would threaten the rest of us with disgrace. I advised her to refrain from giving tit for tat (disgrace, indeed!) only because an opportunity might be forthcoming that would allow her to finally break free, as I had, from a father who would not curtail his propensity for drunkenness.

On the evening of July 16, 1854, Achsa W. Sprague made her first public appearance as a lecturing trance medium at the Stone Meeting House in South Reading, Vermont. She was twenty-six years old.

I desperately wanted to be present, but of course that was impossible, so I had to rely upon Axy's explanation of the occasion.

The day had been unusually warm and humid. Those who gathered for the event rested beneath sheltering elms, waiting to be summoned inside. When she arrived, Axy could see our sister Sarah, speaking with an animated Nathaniel Randall. He and Marenda had recently been divorced by decree and Marenda was currently occupied with dividing their property. Axy was not especially happy to see Sarah wearing an expression of fascination while conversing with Mr. Randall, but she reminded herself she must keep her thoughts on loftier subjects and focus on the most important matter at hand.

Everyone was directed indoors. Mr. Wilder called the meeting to order but his initial cries went unheeded. The wooden benches provided insufficient seating and loud complaints were issued by those who had no choice but to stand at the back of the hall.

Axy took her place in a straight chair beside the podium and remained seated while Mr. Wilder was forced to bang with a gavel to quiet the unruly. To keep her gaze from the shuffling audience, she stared down at Sarah's tight shoes that our brother Nathan had painstakingly polished with lampblack and were now hurting her feet. An outburst in a far corner caused Axy to look up.

Women fanned themselves briskly and twisted their heads to see who else was there. Men, red-faced from the sun and the oppressive heat, seemed to be grinning lewdly. Windows had been thrown open but the air was rancid with sweat and other disgusting smells. Axy wore a simple dark sprigged cotton of Sarah's, which felt stiff and confining. In an attempt to help her appear fashionable, our younger sister had stuffed as many petticoats as possible beneath the wide, full skirt, including a stiff crinoline. Sarah had also helped tame Axy's hair, brushing it and parting it in the middle, then severely pulling it back until her scalp hurt, creating cascades of corkscrew ringlets behind the ears with a curling iron.

The starched lace collar scratched her neck and she pulled at it, hoping to loosen the hook and eye. Her breathing was rapid and shallow beneath the stays of her tight corset and she envisioned herself fainting limp as a rag doll in the swelter. Would someone catch her as she fell?

Mr. Wilder led the crowd in singing "Old Hundred" before introducing the speaker for the evening. "Ask and ye shall be given," he announced. "Seek and ye shall find, knock and it shall be opened unto you.

"Miss Sprague," he shouted in stentorian tones, "has risen from a couch of pain to find divine order established in her mind and body. Tonight, out of the stillness, comes her 'still small voice' to speak of this inner knowing. Her strong conviction will carry to the listening heart the assurance that all is well."

Axy had assisted Mr. Wilder by composing the introduction. Now she stood and said a silent prayer, repeating to herself "Underneath are the everlasting arms," hoping those proverbial arms would prop her up along with the invisible "magic staff."

As she described it to me, she allowed her gaze to regard the audience. But then her view expanded, wandered out over their heads and beyond the open door and through the windows where she observed verdant shades of green upon green; her beloved Green Mountains closely shouldering one another. She said the mountains' strength and majesty sustained her. Thank God for mountains.

She stood and closed her eyes, waited for the crowd to settle. Waited for the silence.

In such a quiet setting, I could imagine a dog barking far away. Someone nervously coughing. A child's giggle that proved contagious. A rude person, (surely a man), would flaunt boorish behavior by expressing flatulence. There would be guffaws. Raps and taps of boots against the floor would become an impatient chorus of recurrent thumps.

Axy said she squeezed her eyes shut more tightly and imagined she was alone in the woods. There was a momentary flash of fear—what if she were left uninspired, if nothing came, no words, no spirit—and then she swayed, as if she were going to collapse. She heard a gasp.

Twilight would soon be entering her favorite wooded glen on the mountainside, she told herself. She steadied her balance and wrung her trembling hands. The leafy glade where we played as children would be patterned with long shadows. Squeaks and rustles in the ethereal background would be settling into the corners of evening where fireflies drifted out of the darkness to shimmer and blink.

As Marenda Randall had schooled her, she whispered to the spirits, *I am ready.*

There is a place where you can turn for rest and release from fear and care, she told the crowd. The room quieted. *It is a holy place. Stillness fills that place. The peace of God is in it. There your mind will become like a little child's, lovely, true and pure. There your thoughts are stayed on the things that are good, just and merciful. When you enter that silent place all your troubles drop away and you rise at last, your body healed, your mind stilled, refreshed and restored.*

This place is not far away. It is where we are now. It is inside every one of us.

She continued, speaking about God's healing grace and forgiveness. Her trembling ceased. Words, unbidden, issued from her throat in the new, low voice, unlike her own. This new voice was resolute. It was throaty and urgent, with a power that silenced the restless assembly.

When she ceased to speak, the room was hushed.

Then a callous man rose and shouted, "I am not satisfied with that one test. The subject was a familiar one. Let us hear her speak on another subject! If she is able to treat that one as well and true then we may believe she is indeed what she claims to be."

The crowd shifted.

"Let us hear her recite an original poem!" another man shouted.

"How about *The Life of Perseus!*" an elderly man shrilly barked.

There were scattered cries of agreement. The audience waited, expectant, while Axy composed herself again.

> *Son of a god. Great Jupiter, his sire,* she began;
> *To Danae came in golden shower of fire,*
> *From his Olympus;—Danae captive there,*
> *In brazen tower, and wild in her despair,*

Beneath her cruel father's iron rod.
Ah, wonder not she turned to meet the god,
And gave him love for love. Her heart was riven:
He lit her midnight with the hues of heaven.
Beside his face all else was faint and dim,
And she forgot the world, herself, in him.
Thus Perseus was the offspring of their love.

The inspired poem continued for many stanzas. She closed with these lines:

Old heroes, martyrs, saints, can never die;
Not always visible to the naked eye,
Yet not the less the constellations burn,
Though mortal eyes to see them may not turn.
If <u>souls</u> *could find a telescopic power,*
They'd see them gleam through heaven this very hour...
But like the constellations, when the clouds
Have wrapped them in their darkest midnight shrouds,
They gleam as brightly on the other side,
And gild those clouds that their best power defied.

So truth shall gild old error's clouds of night
Disperse her mists and shades with golden light;
And known at last shall be God's great unknown,
And man unshamed shall claim it as his own.
The truths of God I've found, till then I'll speak,
Though small my power, and though, alas! so weak,
And like the dew upon earth's flowers I'll lie,
Till God's great sun exhales me to the sky.

She ceased speaking, but her attitude and expression remained an embodiment of her closing words. Afterward it was said that many who listened almost involuntarily expected to see her float, exhaled, in a golden mist from their sight.

A written account of her lecture later reported that "Miss Sprague responded with a noble production, showing genius. Her critics, when reminded that by some power she, who had been incurably ill by the judgment of man, had suddenly arisen and gained health by some unknown power, were driven to the old refuge of the bigots: *devils and sacrilege*." A young man in the audience, Merritt Goddard, would later take time from his studies of theology to write of her lecture that evening:

"I shall never forget how your words thrilled my 'heart of youth' when on that first summer, I heard you at the Stone Meetinghouse in South Reading – if I did not first go to scoff, I certainly expected nothing more than to be *amused* for an hour by the then novel sight of a woman preaching. I heard, and went away to pray."

The South Reading lecture encouraged a deluge of requests to speak elsewhere. In Rochester, Vermont, she told me the upstairs room was crowded *"almost to suffication."* Gaysville, South Woodstock, and Cavendish were added to her calendar. That winter she was invited to make South Reading her headquarters and toured Vermont and New Hampshire, lecturing from once to five or six times per week. There was much interest in the subject of Spiritualism, an interest that increased daily. Many who a year before would have scorned the idea of investigation, now stood forth as advocates of my sister. The doors of churches were opened and she was invited to enter.

The call for speaking through mediums was far beyond the supply. There was an awakening interest over the entire country. Though a large class cried blasphemy, infidelity, and even worse, Axy's work proceeded as she wrote to me:

I find many, as I pass, whose lives have never before been cheered by the hope of immortality, now looking to the future with a steady gaze. Many whose tottering limbs are nearing the gate of the tomb and whose hoary hairs and age-dimmed eyes bespeak the end of earth, to whom no future has ever dawned before now listen to the voice of angels as they are cheered on to a brighter home. I have seen many a mourner's heart made glad because they know their loved ones will return.

It is only when I see how little fitted for the work I am that I sometimes falter by the way. I <u>will</u> do good. In view of this, the world's cold scorn, the sound of fame, the scoffing sneer, all pass unheeded. To me they are as naught. <u>I will do good…</u>

Remarkably, within three years of regaining her health, my dear sister was finally on her own. Life was fresh and wonderful. Her letters to me overflowed with exuberance, triggering tears of gratitude.

I have promised to be at a Circle at Mr. Taylor's, South Woodstock, tomorrow evening where among many others I expect to meet Mr. Tewkesbury's people. Wish you were to be of the number as perhaps we might hear from the spirit of Edgar A. Poe. I can almost fancy I hear you say, "Thank my stars that I am at the other side of the country, instead!"

From now on I will name my address as South Reading, as I speak there every other Sabbath for the present, dating from December 25, 1854, and I am there oftener than at our father's home in Plymouth.

It has just occurred to me that this is "New Years Day." That it may be a <u>Happy</u> New Year <u>to you</u>; one which shall have no limit save Eternity, and no measure to its happiness save your capability to receive and enjoy, is the earnest wish of your loving sister,

> *A. W. Sprague*
> *January 1, 1855, Cavendish,*
> *Vermont*

⊰ 5 ⊱

Slave or Butterfly

(1855)

If woman dares to act out of the beaten track
Marked centuries ago for her to tread, straightway
She becomes something out of the course of nature,
A something for the curious to gape at in astonishment...

ACHSA SPRAGUE'S *DIARY*
Monday, December 10, 1855

D EEMING IT IMPRUDENT to divulge to family and townspeople how truly delighted she was to escape, Axy penned an apologetic poem, "Thoughts on Leaving Home," before she left for Boston in the spring of 1855:

For as much as I love home,
Yet I would not stay.
The far-off world calls me.

At the age of twenty-seven, Axy was intoxicated by the freedom to travel beyond the boundaries of her Green Mountains and could not dare to imagine the possibilities of intellectual enrichment that lay in wait.

Her spirit lectures in Vermont and New Hampshire attracted the attention of a Mr. Maynard, who asked to serve as her manager. She promptly declined his proposition and explained,

I go from place to place as a Public Speaking Medium, merely because it is the path pointed out for me by my Spirit Friends who have raised me from a state of helplessness to one of

⊰ 71 ⊱

comparative health…. I wish to make no money speculation out of this affair. If money was my object, I might get four times the amount that I do at the present time without putting myself to any extra trouble. <u>But money is not my object</u>. I would be instrumental in imparting Truth & <u>doing good</u>. If I cannot do this, I have no wish to do any thing. To any proposition of this kind I invariably say No.

At the invitation of Herman Snow, a former Unitarian minister, she traveled by train to Boston. Mr. Snow was the operator of Harmony House, an establishment that welcomed mediums and Spiritualists. Axy was encouraged to reside there during her stay in that city.

The April 7, 1855, edition of *The New England Spiritualist* reported that Boston was highly anticipating the initial visit of "Miss Sprague of Vermont" at the Melodeon, yet lowered readers' expectations by describing her style of address as "more marked by vigor than by eloquence." She scarcely registered that gloomy forecast. All that mattered was stepping off the cars and arriving in a city where the salt air of the sea was exotic. The bustle of crowds, Faneuil Hall, Boston Common, the tall ships in Boston Harbor and fishermen and freighters at the wharf—all were fascinating vistas she had dreamed of seeing but doubted she ever would.

On Sunday, April 15, she lectured at the Melodeon in the afternoon and evening. A. E. Newton, editor and publisher of *New-England Spiritualist*, overlooked his earlier skepticism and pronounced her presentations as most remarkable:

> It is questionable whether her address in the evening, if viewed merely in the light of an extemporaneous effort, was equaled in any of our pulpits on that day. The customary barrenness of *sermons* without "notes" has been forcibly brought to mind to all those who have attended the Melodeon of late, and witnessed the unpremeditated eloquence of Miss Sprague… "trance speaking," at the Melodeon, has evidently reached a high degree of respectability.

Her topic that evening was "The rolling ages of time—the past, the present, and the future." Typically, Axy borrowed her allusions from nature:

> *Nature has no secrets—no darkness—all her children, as they look upon her gaze, can, and do comprehend as much as they are capacitated for…To reach out into the pure fields of spiritual nature, we must become natural ourselves—bring ourselves into <u>harmony with nature</u>.*

Following her lectures at the Melodeon, Mr. Newton requested that Axy compose the lengthy article for his newspaper from which I previously quoted, detailing her years of illness and her miraculous rebirth. The article appeared on May 12, 1855.

According to my sister,

> *Obedient to the voice that calls me from above, I would go forth to speak of comfort to the sorrowing soul, to soothe the aching brow, to bind the bleeding heart, to point the sufferer to a brighter home, and bid the erring ones look up and live. Yet strange as it may seem, the crying ones, those who are steeped in crime and sin, and even in blood—whom though yet in all their sins, the angels still would save,—these erring ones I cannot <u>always</u> reach. For man has been their judge. Man has condemned. And man has barred the massive doors that close them in, perchance, forever in this life. Dark were their hearts perhaps, but yet within those prison walls their hearts grow darker still.*

Mr. Newton followed this with an editor's note, explaining that "Miss Sprague has applied to the necessary authorities to speak to the convicts in the Massachusetts State Prison but she has been refused."

Axy wrote to me, near delirious with elation and enclosing a copy of Mr. Newton's publication. "You will see I have been able to disseminate my story of suffering and deliverance to thousands of readers," she declared, "and my desire for involvement in prison-reform has now been fully revealed."

She seldom returned home to Plymouth during the early months of her travels, still claiming South Reading as her official residence. Father was unceasing in his displeasure with her new occupation. Further family discord reached my ear when, in spite of Axy's voluble pleas to the contrary, I learned that our sister Sarah was to marry Nathaniel Randall, twenty-three years her senior, and notorious for his eccentric behavior. Axy told me she'd warned Sarah, "In two or three years it will get to be an old story." I agreed with Axy that it was a bad match.

Boston welcomed my sister again in June of that year. This time notice in *The New England Spiritualist* attracted even larger crowds to the Melodeon for her three lectures, and yet more eulogiums helped to screen an undercurrent of tittle-tattle that reached her ears: A medium of some authority had been overheard challenging the legitimacy of her Spirit-inspired lectures, implying that her messages were committed to memory before she took the stage.

This new career may have freed her from the punishing confinement of illness, but a lack of rest was now taxing her health. Speaking before crowds of hundreds brought on a severe sore throat—sometimes referred to as "minister's sore throat."

That summer the Abingdon Grove Festival offered an opportunity to consult once more with John Murray Spear. He perhaps appeared wild and frightening to some, with his dark penetrating eyes and apparent disregard of men's fashion, but during a private meeting Axy commented on the strain of her exhausting travels and the punishing demands on her time. Mr. Spear channeled the spirit of his frequent counsel, physician Benjamin Rush. The following instructions were given, which Axy transcribed by phonography.

COMMUNICATION THROUGH JOHN M. SPEAR

Public speaking brings a degree of strain upon the abdominals. If you speak much while the menstrual processes are going forward, that unfavorably affects & somewhat closes up the avenues through which they should & would naturally flow. It would be wise as far as practicable to avoid public speaking at that critical period. This matter being retained in the system which should pass out will as it were choke up other avenues producing a sort of hoarseness or a disposition to cough. The face becomes cold the head too hot & the public effort is less satisfactory.

Now persons who are journeying especially females cannot always regard natures calls, & so, the matter which should pass is reabsorbed & poisons the system. You will need to observe critically these hints, else there is a liability to brain fever unless the avenues are open. If any of the functions are closed the electric matter thrown upon you is retained in the system which should flow through it & pass off… Better always soon after public speaking, take opportunity to pass the urine, so that form of somewhat morbid matter will be excreted. Keep with you figs for laxative purposes when needed. Better also be in habit of chewing either slippery elm or ordinary stick liquorice. Both will help the fermenting process. Be also in the habit of wetting the head freely with coldest water. When in your private apartment unloose the hair, suffer it to flow on the shoulders. … During the peach season eat peaches freely. Peaches are feminine, aid the feminine processes. Thus much of the body. The difficulties below, affect the regions above. When all is right below, no apprehensions need be of those above.

Mr. Spear, like other mediums, believed that when people handled things they left their "spiritual" impressions or residues on them; later, those items could be subsequently "read" through psychometry. By holding the object in one's hand or placing it on one's forehead, one could read the character of the owner. To my sister he presented a gold coin, which she wrapped in a small envelope made from a square of ledger paper. She wrote his name on the outside in ink and below that the date, June 20, 1855. She pledged to carry the coin with her at all times, which she did, until it was stolen.

In August, Axy lectured on "Atonement" during a visit to Burlington, Vermont, where Spiritualism was still in its infancy.

One of those present called her an "inspired evangel, the first woman who has ever spoken in this intensely orthodox city. Curiosity brought men and women of all faiths and no faith to hear. The large hall was densely crowded, and all through the lecture one could have heard a pin drop."

> *All I ever ask is a hearing, and that I received,* she wrote to me, noting that *The audience at the last lecture was estimated at about a thousand, and allowing for the number that would naturally be attracted there by idle curiosity, still there would be left a proportion who <u>wished to hear and judge for themselves</u>.*

The *New England Spiritualist* and related newspapers carried an official announcement of the Spiritual Convention in South Royalton, which would commence on August 31 and continue until September 2. Arrangements had been made with the Vermont Central Railroad to charge half-fare. If the weather was pleasant, they planned to meet in a grove; if rainy, in the church. "We would worship the God of Nature, learn of immortality, and acknowledge that we are brothers."

I'm certain my sister noted the lack of "sisters" in the announcement.

This would be Axy's first appearance at such an exhilarating event. In the audience at the South Royalton Convention was were Mr. and Mrs. J. R. Mettler of Hartford, Connecticut, Samuel Byron Brittan, editor of *The Spiritual Telegraph*, and various other luminaries, including Marenda Randall, who was now living and practicing medicine in Philadelphia. Brittan reported on the gathering in the September 15, 1855, issue of his newspaper and made particular mention of the appearance of Achsa Sprague:

> Miss Sprague was speaking in a state of partial entrancement; her eyes were open, and the whole countenance glowing in the light of her transfiguration. Her manner is earnest and forcible, her utterance remarkably distinct, and she speaks with great apparent ease. Notwithstanding the critical hearer, if so disposed, might occasionally find fault with the want of logical

coherence, and complain of mixed metaphors and other rhetorical defects, it is but simple justice to say that the discourse gave evidence of profound thought; the ideas were, for the most part, clearly conceived and consecutively expressed, while many of her periods were truly eloquent and deeply impressive.

The glowing approbation could not help but further her lecturing career, although in a missive after the convention Axy wrote she was aghast that she was heard to occasionally mix metaphors or lack coherence while entranced!

Mrs. Semantha Mettler, the celebrated clairvoyant and healing physician from Hartford, Connecticut, offered to do a psychometrical delineation. Axy thence provided the woman with a poem in her own handwriting. Mrs. Mettler psychometrized the poem with my sister as her amanuensis.

PSYCHOMETRICAL READING OF CHARACTER

By Mrs. Semantha Mettler

This is a person whose strength & force of character is greatest when aroused to action by opposing sentiment or argument. Thoughts & ideas present themselves more vividly when calmness & quietude surrounds her & it is often aggravating to her when thinking over a subject that she has been discussing, that the arguments could not have presented themselves as strongly while conversing as they do when quiet & alone. The perceptive faculties are exceedingly active, & she grasps a subject as a whole, most readily by the simple outlines or sketches being presented to her interior mind. There is a sense of justice & right which dictates her in all her opinions & expressions. When a truth is substantiated in her mind, no power can cause her to falter or swerve from the path she deems to be right. She is sensitive in the extreme, feels more keenly than she will express. There is a firmness & a pride which prevent her from *demonstrating outwardly her feelings. But when alone, away from the observations of others, will she the more readily give vent to her feelings of injury, her indignation. She is lenient, & sympathises strongly with the afflicted & down trodden. She has considerable originality of thought, inclines to think for herself more than to take others' thoughts & adopt them but likes sociability & the agreeable companionship of agreeable companions. Likes to be an original being. Has a way of her own in almost every thing she does, though is not stubbornly firm. In all the congenial relations of life her affections are active. She has as much fondness for the society of the male as the female, it makes but little difference to her if they are congenial & entertaining. Calculation, order & time are full & active. Acquisitiveness is active. She would not be penurious but she is economical. Experience seems to teach her the necessity of this propensity. Color is fair. Language is <u>very good</u>. Hope is full & her spirits are generally buoyant.*

To Axy's delight, she was requested to join Mrs. Mettler at her home in Hartford that autumn. My sister had first to fulfill an obligation to appear at Newport, Vermont, on September 30. There she was introduced to Warren Chase, the celebrated Spiritualist from Wisconsin, who gave her the impression of being a very kind man. My sister lost no time in telling him that I had recently moved to Fond du Lac County, not far from his adopted home.

Warren Chase had been a senator in the first Wisconsin Senate, and spoke out in favor of women's suffrage in Madison. Axy was deeply moved by his statement that "the men would sooner let the negroes have their rights than the women, and the slavery of women is deeper, and more lasting, than that of negroes in the hearts and the prejudices of the people — and even often and approved and sustained by woman herself." He asked her, "How can she expect the 'lords of creation' to give her her rights, when she does not ask for them?"

I was not aware that Nathaniel Tallmadge, former governor of the Wisconsin Territory, also lived near Fond du Lac. He, too, was a Spiritualist, and his four daughters who became mediums had trained under Semantha Mettler! Due to their influence and the exercise of their highly regarded gifts of seership, trance, musical improvisation, writing, and tongues, the girls had created an immense sensation in New York's fashionable circles. Warren Chase wished Axy the same fortunate prospect.

Originally a Presbyterian and then a Universalist, Mrs. Semantha Beers Mettler of No. 4 Winthrop Street, Hartford, Connecticut, had achieved a wide reputation as a healing clairvoyant and was credited with a great many miraculous cures. After her husband's business ventures soured, Johnson R. Mettler became her public relations agent and booked her many tours.

An advertisement in *The Spiritual Telegraph* touted the curative effects of *Mrs. Mettler's Restorative Syrup*, *Mrs. Mettler's Cholera Elixir*, and *Mrs. Mettler's Celebrated Dysentery Cordial*, all compounded by J. R. Mettler at his wife's direction and readily available by mail order. For an additional 25 cents, one could purchase "The Biography of Mrs. Semantha Mettler, Being a History of Clairvoyant Spiritual Development, and Containing an Account of The Wonderful Cures Performed Through her Agency."

Before accepting Mrs. Mettler's offer, Axy perused the biography and learned of one reason she may have drawn the woman's attention: Her angelic rescue reflected the woman's convictions.

> Every strongly marked character must be unfolded by crises, when there seems to be a concentration of energy to a given point, producing results which, after they are recognized, create land-marks on the life-road, ever showing how the path of the Future was marked by their appearance.

After her arrival in Hartford, Axy wrote detailed letters about Mrs. Mettler and the family's upper-class neighborhood of large Greek Revival and Italianate houses, graciously surrounded by decorative iron fences. Many of Hartford's leading businessmen, physicians, and other professionals were among their neighbors, and Mrs. Mettler seemed to be acquainted with all.

As the state capital of Connecticut, Hartford had a significant influence in the economic life of the entire country, laying claim to the world's largest manufactories of clocks and many other items. Most recently the huge Colt Armory had been completed on the city's South Meadows, where Samuel Colt's popular firearms were produced.

William Henry Burleigh, famed abolitionist, lived in Hartford, as did the celebrated poetess Lydia Howard Sigourney, known as the "Sweet Singer of Hartford." Lovers of fine art could patronize the new Wadsworth Atheneum, which had opened its doors eleven years before.

When she resumed her diary on her twenty-eighth birthday, Saturday, November 17, 1855, Axy was serving a brief apprenticeship under Mrs. Mettler, who exhibited a motherly demeanor. My sister had been assigned a room of her own and later personally confided to me that "it may be prideful of me to acknowledge that deep in my heart I wished also to be recognized one day as someone who created an 'immense sensation in fashionable circles' as well as prisons and poor neighborhoods and other places where I might do good."

While at the Mettlers', Axy chose the larger pages of a ledger to record her thoughts. As Axy languished this past summer, I paged through the Hartford diary. It seemed to reveal not only the reflections of a young woman who was achieving increasing recognition and popularity on the lecture circuit; her writing conveyed a more formal and expository tone, as if it were intended for eventual publication.

1855

Hartford Ct.

Nov. 17th

The pages, both bright & dark, of my former life are left unwritten, save in the great Life Book of Eternity. I came to Hartford one week ago to day to speak under Spirit Influence as I have been doing Publicly for the last year and a half. Having been raised from a bed of sickness, where I suffered the most extreme pain, by Spirit Agency, I have felt it my duty to do that which has been pointed out to me by my Spirit Guides & the result is, that I have felt constrained to take the position which I now occupy, that of a Public Speaking Medium. And in the course of events I am now at Hartford, a place which I have once before visited in the same capacity. I spoke here last Sabbath, at "Union Hall," afternoon and evening. Also spoke at Manchester some eight miles distant last Tuesday Evening. There are very few believers in Spiritualism at that place, but I had a very good audience. I enjoyed it well. Tomorrow (Sabbath) I speak here again at Union Hall. I do not know whether I shall return home to Plymouth, Vermont then, my arrangements are not made.

My liberated sister opened her arms to embrace everything within reach. She was starved for culture, obsessed and almost manic in her desire to compensate for all the years that she had lost. She wished to meet Julia Bruce, the author of children's books and stories she'd read as a child in *Parley's Magazine*, but Miss Bruce was ill and indisposed.

In walking yesterday I passed both the present & former residence of Mrs. Lydia H. Sigourney. Her former residence is the most beautiful place I have seen in Hartford. Just the place for a poet, amid its extensive grounds and beautiful shade trees. It seems a pity that she was obliged to leave it, so well adapted to her mind and taste, although her present home is a very pretty one. I should like very much to see Mrs. Sigourney, for I have always from a child admired her writings, but I have no acquaintances who are friends of hers, so could not get an introduction without being officious.

Each day Mrs. Mettler received suffering and afflicted admirers who were treated with magnetism, psychology and other healing methods including elixirs prescribed while Mrs. Mettler was entranced. Axy observed as much as she was allowed, but when Mrs. Mettler had no need of her my sister was never bored and found time to muse in her journal:

The five hours in which Mrs. Mettler examines her patients I am much alone. I can seem to draw happiness from the resources within, & am not as much dependent upon foreign causes & company on that account. And more than all this and perhaps the hidden cause of it, I feel as though I was <u>not</u> alone. My <u>belief</u> that I am surrounded by Guardian angels and the loved ones gone before seems to people the space around me with living though invisible forms and I cannot seem alone. But the interior evidence I have, the living inspiration welling up in my own soul, the consciousness of their presence not only around me but within myself, my inner self keeps a communion within that satisfies the soul beyond all other communings. This is the most beautiful part of my mediumship, that which others do not see, that which is never spoken, but which is felt in every fibre of my soul, giving a richness to life which it never had before, and a tinge of Heaven to light my path where all before was dim and shadowy… One great thing is taught— Eternal Progression. And the light which this Great Truth casts upon our minds shows us that the changes, the darkness, trials and sorrows through which we pass are but the results or effects of the working of this law as it is refining and purifying our life and soul. With <u>this</u> view I can thank my Creator for the gift of life, but I never could until this light shone upon my mental vision teaching me reality and tangibility of the theory that "all is right."

Axy was developing more finesse and knowledge of her craft that autumn in Hartford, and she was also enjoying Catherine Mettler's companionship. The Mettlers's daughter had inherited her mother's mediumistic ability in a manifestation of unusual musical skills. During congenial evening gatherings Catherine improvised classical music upon the piano, "rendered with wonderful effect," according to those present, all the more remarkable since Catherine had taken only a few lessons before this talent was revealed. As Axy explained, Catherine was laboring to make out the air of a simple song one day when her arms were apparently seized by an unknown power which at once compelled her to commence the most astonishing improvisation, evidencing an extraordinary mastery over the instrument and a thorough knowledge of the science of harmony. Eventually, Catherine performed pieces recognized as those composed by Mozart and Beethoven and executed them equally well in complete darkness or in daylight, even responding to requests, and then closing with an exquisite and pathetic rendering of "Home, Sweet Home."

A healing-specific regimen was drawn up for Axy that included walking, whenever possible, to improve her health. Catherine Mettler sometimes accompanied her but my sister did not mind walking by herself and eventually her outings expanded to surrounding neighborhoods. Cemeteries are as public parks, and their rambling paths provide pleasant settings for a casual stroll. In Hartford, Axy spent many afternoons walking through the Ancient Burial Ground where very old gravestones date back to the 1660s.

Prisons, asylums for the insane and those establishments housing inhabitants known as "deaf and dumb" are also popular tourist destinations because of their size, their architecture, and the so-called unpleasant inhabitants they house. Of course this roused my sister's curiosity and desire "to do good," so with Catherine Mettler's companionship, Axy toured Hartford's "Asylum for Educating the Deaf & Dumb," and was fascinated to observe children from age five to twenty as they were taught sign language.

Saturday, November 17. I was intending to have walked down this afternoon and gather some leaves from "The Charter Oak" to preserve, but it has just commenced raining and I fear I shall not be able to go. When I passed the Oak previously, so remarkable for the interesting incident in our nation's history connected with it, (the local legend in which a cavity within the tree was used in 1687 as a hiding place for the Connecticut Charter of 1662), I found it as nearly like the pictures of it which I have been accustomed to look upon since childhood as any thing could possibly be.

Monday, November 19. This morning after writing a couple of letters I started for a walk, to put them in the Office and also to pay a visit to the "Charter Oak." There it stands, a monument of grandeur even in decay on a bleak cold day with only the dry, rustling leaves to tell the tale of their departed glory. Associations of the past are a sacred spell, linking that old decaying tree with the days of the "Revolution" even farther back than that, and with the deeds of our father's fathers long past away, which this, one of their monuments, still remains. The trunk is hollow to so great an extent that thirty persons have been known to enter this cavity and remain there at the same time. For curiosity and in honor of its age and companionship with the past and the deeds of the past, the good people of Hartford have set a table within its decayed trunk and have dined in its very bosom. It is curious and deeply interesting to see the veneration which man has for these relics of the past. Pieces of tin or zinc are nailed in places all over its trunk to protect it and prolong its life. I love to see such manifestations on the part of those who live in the present age. I looked in vain for leaves to bring away with me, as the winds and the lateness of the season rendered it impossible to find them, till I happened to spy a handful, hidden away in a little crevice of the trunk, like memories of the past, and gathering these carefully from their hiding place I brought them away.

I walked earlier this morning before the rain, a walk of over a mile and a half. Is it possible that I am the same being who three

*years ago lay in a dark room in pain and anguish with no hope
of relief? And all this change wrought by my Spirit Friends. I
must be strangely ungrateful if I am not willing to do and bear
much, yes <u>very</u> much for those who have raised me from
helplessness to comparative strength, from pain and suffering to
happiness, from darkness again to the blessed sunlight of the outer
world.*

Mrs. Mettler's séances were popular with Hartford's avant-garde, especially since it had recently become known that noteworthy individuals such as Harriet Beecher Stowe, William Thackery, the Brownings, Empress Eugenie, and the King of Prussia had revealed their interest in Spiritualism. Catherine confided that her mother occasionally danced around the room while conducting circles, or was moved by the spirits to participate in pantomime, or improvise an impromptu drama that entertained all present with a description of the transition of the soul from this world to the next. Often those around the table participated in such revels—entranced, of course—and afterward no one would have the slightest memory of what had occurred.

It was no wonder, then, that Axy held great anticipation for the séance to be held at Mrs. Mettler's on November 19. It would be conducted by Lottie Bebee, a promising young medium who regularly performed in Hartford and South Boston. Bebee was reputed to give "beautiful specimens of poetry and sometimes has other manifestations."

My sister had never been a slave to fashion and until now had made do with unassuming dresses sewn by our mother or handed down from our sisters. Her wardrobe would always remain fairly modest but for this occasion she felt it appropriate to inaugurate a new gown. Upon her arrival in Hartford, Mrs. Mettler had encouraged her to engage her very own seamstress to produce several dresses for Axy in the new style—with flounces and wide skirts with hoops of fine steel that replaced cumbersome layers of petticoats. Mrs. Mettler insisted it was only prudent to invest some of the income from lectures as one must project a prominent visual image on stage. "Look at little Cora Hatch with her long golden ringlets," she said, reaching out to touch a wayward strand that had already escaped from Axy's bonnet. "Unless, of course, you want to wear the 'American Dress.'"

This was said with gentle sarcasm as the latter referred to a rather defiant, reform-minded outfit resembling a bloomer costume with shortened skirt over loose trousers. Many women claimed it was much healthier to forego corsets and not compress the chest.

For the séance, Axy chose a garnet velvet with matching shawl of garnet velvet and black lace. The bodice fit tightly, so movements above the waist were limited. My sister soon discovered one must take care not to unwittingly overturn small pieces of furniture as one passed by in such a voluminous skirt. Unfortunate as her initial entrance may have been, she felt light and free as she moved, realizing that as she walked, her skirt swayed and tilted provocatively.

There were twenty guests gathered in the Mettler parlor. When she was directed to her place at the table, she was seated between Frank Burr, editor of *The Hartford Daily Times*, and Colonel Samuel Colt, whose invention of the Colt 45 revolver had made him one of the wealthiest men in America. My sister told me she was quite charmed by Colonel Colt, then forty-two; I would judge that *captivated* might have been a more accurate description. He was a handsome man with curly hair and warm brown eyes, a well-trimmed beard. When introduced to Colt by Mrs. Mettler, Axy had been informed of the Colt family motto, "Vincit Qui Patitur," or "He Conquers Who Suffers." Mrs. Mettler assured Colt that Axy had a keen familiarity with suffering and conquering. Colt replied with a laugh that the real family motto his mother had taught him was, "It is better to be the head of a louse than the tail of a lion!"

My dear sister was aware of Colt's indecorous reputation for freely indulging in the pleasures of life, which was recognized by everyone and celebrated by some. Seated at her right, he'd held her hand securely during the séance with a large warm palm that seemed to radiate incredible self-assurance and made her concentration taxing. The British press referred to this man as "Colonel Colt, the Thunderbolt," and Catherine had said that, in order to raise enough money to manufacture his revolver the man had traveled down the Mississippi, billed himself as "Dr. Coult," and staged demonstrations of the ludicrous effects of "laughing gas" on his subjects. Indeed, Axy found him to be a shameless flirt; he was restless during the séance and more than once he squeezed her hand more intimately than she felt was absolutely necessary. But she rather enjoyed his playful demeanor and did not complain. *I thought Col. Colt rather an original, just like nobody else,* she wrote in her diary.

Frank Burr, on her left, was a much more sensitive individual. With his brother, Alfred E. Burr, he was co-editor and publisher of *The Hartford Times*, a Democratic newspaper begun by their father in 1817. This was not Frank Burr's first séance: On March 14 he had attended a circle led by Daniel Douglas Home, one of the final séances held by the British medium prior to his departure for England. Burr had found Home decidedly peculiar, with long hair and effeminate features, but his sensitive hands had caused the most astonishment—perhaps they were Spirit hands.

"I've heard that when a Spirit hand is held, it can melt away in the sitter's grasp," Axy told Burr. He replied that not only had the hand melted, "I pushed my right forefinger entirely through the palm, till it came out an inch or more, visibly, from the back! In other words, I pushed my finger clean through. When I withdrew it, the place closed up, much as a piece of putty would close under the circumstances, leaving a visible mark or scar where the wound was, but not a hole. Then, while I was still looking at it the hand vanished, quick as a lightning flash!"

Axy suspected that Burr hoped for a similar phenomenon to occur with Miss Bebee, whose pale, limp hand was the other one he held that night. Meanwhile, Axy wondered if Mrs. Mettler would get up from the table and dance. It was useless to try and focus on that special, silent place in her mind. She turned her attention to William Burleigh, seated across from her.

Burleigh was a poet and well-known abolitionist and temperance advocate who had recently been appointed as Harbormaster of New

York. Axy described him as "a rather large man with prominent features, large dark eyes and a very prominent forehead. From appearances I should think he might love a good joke, but not as well as Col. Colt."

The group sat for over an hour with very few spirit manifestations, which Axy later blamed on "the different minds and organizations of the Circle, or to the want of quiet passiveness," including her own. Miss Bebee raised few spirits. No pleasing poems were improvised, and no one danced. My sister did not despair, and freely admitted lacking the necessary frame of mind. Instead, she told her diary, *I had plenty of time to read countenances and character.*

In a letter written the next morning, she said that as she sat at the Mettlers' table surrounded by some of Hartford's most notable citizens, she had wondered what had become of the pale, helpless individual who had found her life "a weary, weary way, almost too hard to bear." Now, sitting still was almost a trial.

> *Tuesday, November 20. This morning arose about seven, breakfasted about eight and then went out for my usual walk. Called at a Manufactory where spoons, forks, cups, tea services etc. are made, plated and burnished. I was very much interested in the process of plating. The articles were placed in a solution adapted for the purpose and all around were arranged batteries with poles of silver in this solution. From the peculiar chemical arrangement of the articles, their compound and the solution in which they were dipped, the articles themselves attracted the silver as it was decomposed and thus covered themselves, so to speak, with a garment of silver. Curious, what the ingenuity and invention of man will do.*

> *Wednesday, November 21. This is the first day I have been hindered from walking by the weather since I came to Hartford. In truth, I do not know which way I shall eventually tread. Although this sometimes seems like a wandering life, and the office of a medium a thankless one, I think I can bear much of suffering, much of sorrow for the sake of Truth. I do not wish to be a Fanatic yet I have*

suffered so much with the monotony of a life of inaction, the result of disease, that in my inmost soul I have often cried out, as Byron wrote,

> *Better to stand the lightnings shock*
> *Than moulder piecemeal on the rock.*

Anything but a life of worthlessness, uselessness. A life which is no life.

To help compensate for her room and board, Axy was also acting as an amanuensis while Mrs. Mettler psychometrised letters or objects. This was of interest, she said, since she still carried the coin John M. Spear had given her, imbued with his spiritual residue. Psychometry differed from clairvoyance, Mrs. Mettler explained, in that clairvoyance was spiritual perception and took cognizance of the past, present, and future. Psychometry was impressibility to past or present surroundings or influences.

Friday, November 23. Have been copying this evening as Mrs. Mettler has psychometrised two characters. This she does by placing a paper containing the person's handwriting (who wishes to be psychometrised) upon her forehead, <u>while in the normal state</u> and abstracting herself from other thoughts, she seems to enter the sphere of the person and then speaks her impression. She has given many readings of character in this manner, most of which have been correct, some of them astonishingly so.

Sunday, November 25. Last night at the supper table, the distress of the poor was a subject of discussion and more particularly a poor family of whom Catherine and I spoke. We had stolen away during the afternoon to see in what a state they were in, discovering that the poor man's children had been taken into the Orphan Asylum and the father was left to occupy a little attic, the use of which was given him by people not much better off than himself, no larger than a pantry, partly filled with coal, with a straw tick containing a little straw which they had given him from their scanty store, his only bed, and so poor that he had only the food that he got from door to door and had not even a shirt under his tattered rags. Mrs. Mettler then sent us down with her husband to deliver a good straw bed, a blanket for it, and two old flannel and one cotton shirt of Mr. Mettler's, besides food for the father to eat. When we went in, the tears were running down the father's cheeks. But it was soon turned to joy when he found what presents we had brought him. He seemed very grateful indeed, but the only words he could speak in English were "Good man, Good lady." He shook hands with each of us when we came away and we returned very much elated and happy in that feeling which ever comes to those who do a good action, or make one suffering heart happier than before.

Mr. Frank Burr, one of the Editors of the "Hartford Daily Times" spent the evening here, and just as he was leaving, the above subject was mentioned in his presence. He seemed much interested and said he would see that something was done for the man by first sending a German, who could understand him, to find out his situation and wants, and then by assisting him and putting him in a way to assist himself all possible.

Later, I had a beautiful walk by moonlight. Passed down Main Street, where in passing a shop I caught sight of a painting of a little boy with his head leaning upon his hands in that perfect abandon of childhood's innocence of thought and feeling. I am sometimes tempted to go in and purchase it, if it is not too expensive, but I am divided in the feeling, whether I should make the purchase or give the whole amount to the poor.

<u>Sunday, November 25</u>. Evening. The work of the day is over. Spoke afternoon and evening at Union Hall.

She bade goodbye to her friends in Hartford on Tuesday the 27th and started for Vermont, having been absent four weeks. She paused for the night in Bellows Falls and lost her gold pin, worth two dollars, as she was climbing down from the cars. The next day she purchased a Cameo at the same price, although they sold for three dollars fifty. She liked it better than the other but did not like to lose the gold one and incur an extra expense. Whenever she purchased any thing of that kind she always half felt as though there were poor, suffering people to whom she ought rather to give, yet it was an indispensible article of dress. She felt the same contrition about her new finery, and she did prize her garnet velvet.

From Bellows Falls she went to Ludlow and then to Plymouth Notch, where Father must have remained sober for at least a short period of time.

> *Thursday, December 6. Thanksgiving day, as the world calls it. But if thanksgiving consists in abstaining from all useful labors and "feasting upon fat things," we have had very little of it to day, but if a feeling of gratitude for the comforts of life, health and strength, have anything to do with a thanksgiving, we have had it. And myself in particular. I have spent many of these anniversaries in pain and darkness, without one ray of light to shine upon me either mentally or physically. My whole life ought to be one Thanksgiving.*

> *Sunday, December 9. Vermont snow drifts and Northeasters are not the pleasantest things in the world, particularly to me who so dreads the cold air that unfits me for action. But in a mild, beautiful day, when the sun is shining and the water dropping from the eaves, when the south wind just gives the cheek a redder glow without offering to nip too harshly the nose or fingers, to jump into a sleigh and be closely wrapped in furs and carried swiftly over the snow by a fleet horse whose steps give a merry chime to the "Sleigh Bells" is quite a different thing. If the snow would fall to just that depth to suit our convenience and the Thermometer stand at just the right degree, I should love winter, I should be one of its warmest friends. But its odd freaks and uncertain habit I do not so well relish. It is too unreliable and sometimes too harsh to suit me. I do not much welcome its approach.*

Monday, December 10. Letter from a follower in Rutland. Among other items, she writes it was proposed at the Young Men's Association in Rutland that among other speakers, Reverend Antoinette L. Brown, the first ordained woman minister in the United States who earned a theological degree from Oberlin College and herself an outspoken advocate for woman's rights, having spoken at the first Woman's Rights Convention, should be engaged for a Lecture. But as the Members could not all think alike about inviting a woman it was referred to the Ladies to decide. And what was their decision? A decided negative. So their shame be spoken. It is bad enough to see men who assume the right to occupy the whole platform for Public Speaking, and the undisputable right as Public Teachers, telling and saying what woman shall or shall not do, limiting her sphere of action and shutting her not only from the Temple of Knowledge as a Public Teacher, but also from the Temple of God. But when woman herself, through a false education which has bound her mind in chains, or a want of independence through fear of public opinion, limits her own sphere, and cannot appreciate those who ask a wider field of labor, it is enough to bring the blush of shame upon every woman's cheek who has soul enough or independence enough, to brave the scorn of the world in order to act, to do something for humanity.

Woman must either be a slave or a butterfly, or at least she is so at the present time. And if, following the prompting of the intellectual or philanthropic energies of her mind Woman dares to think, she dares to act out of the beaten track marked centuries ago for her to tread, straightway she becomes something out of the course of nature, a something for the curious to gape at in astonishment, and the world, and particularly her own sex (I speak it with shame) to censure. As if a woman ought not to be firm as well as gentle, energetic as well as yielding in her nature, strong minded as well as pure, and intellectual as well as amiable. Should not all these qualities be combined? And if they are so, what woman can smother these energies and those aspirations till their light shine no further than the fireside?

When will woman learn what it is to be true to herself?

The Day of Small Things

(1855–1856)

This is the day of small things—mediums are imperfect—
conditions unfavorable. We cannot give those things which we would,
and which hereafter will be unfolded. Yet you can see enough to be
able to see that there is more behind.

"Words from the Spirit Life"
ACHSA W. SPRAGUE
The Melodeon, Boston, April 25, 1856

AXY RETURNED TO THE NOTCH in mid-December 1855 and
confided a nagging fear to her diary: *I sometimes think how
long shall I remain a Public speaker, or how long retain the gift of
speaking as I do now?*

Mother and Malvina insisted on serving every meal to her as
though she were an honored guest. Callers and family members
wanted thrilling stories of life beyond the Notch, so Axy described
the attractions (and myriad distractions) of Boston and Hartford,
mentioned prominent people she had met and, when coaxed, read
brief excerpts from newspapers in which her spirit-lectures had
been extolled.

While unpacking her trunk to retrieve trinkets she had purchased,
Achsa said Malvina espied her new garnet dress. Our pitiable eldest
sister pulled the hem to her cheek and cried with pleasure at its softness,
then playfully petted the velvet and purred like Moses, her cat.

Axy explained that the dress was fashioned at the advice of Mrs. Mettler. "A dress of such refinement is necessary when I assume the podium in larger cities, and she anticipates I will soon be addressing colossal crowds."

"Colossal crowds" was intended as a joke, as she had never imagined her audiences would become that overwhelming. Relieved to be home again, she was perhaps unwisely giddy when she implied, again playfully, that the beauty of the garnet dress had caused Colonel Colt, the wealthiest man in America, to warmly clasp her hand in a flirtatious manner.

"Is he a bachelor?" Malvina asked. And Axy nodded, laughing. But Father, listening at the door, abruptly suggested perhaps she had become too worldly to associate with the Spragues and turned his back.

That was not the end of it.

A few days later, when the music of schoolchildren carried over from across the road, their joyful tones reminded Axy of the days when she had her little bevy around her. She wondered again what would happen if her gifts should wane. Would she return to teaching?

She secretly reproached herself for having so thoroughly reveled in her brief whirlwind in Boston and Hartford. But crowds numbering in the thousands *had gathered* to listen to her extemporized messages from the world of Spirits! Prominent members of society had included her as an equal, asked her advice on delicate issues and admired her intelligence. She had witnessed beautiful works of art, rubbed elbows (yes, and held hands!) with illustrious individuals and amiably discussed classic literature with distinguished peers. Moreover, the poor and unfortunate had benefited from her aid.

If her Guardians abandoned her, what would become of this cherished independence?

Father's disdain and bitter winds deepened her vacillating qualms.

For some time now, solely to throw what the spiritualist movement called "progressive ideas" before the public, Axy had been composing miscellaneous pieces for *The Blotter*, a newspaper printed in Ludlow, Vermont. She realized her letters would not be seriously acknowledged if they were signed *Achsa W. Sprague*, so she submitted them half-disguised, under the signature of *Solitarie*, an unknown writer whom no one would suspect. One of the pieces, "Spirit and Matter," was being sharply argued by readers and had recently been reprinted in *The Green Mountain Freeman*, where it was causing further debate. She had wished for discussion and now had that occasion, hence she wanted to amplify the subject and respond to remarks.

Her goal was to argue that utopian thought could actually change the material world. She had proposed, in a sense, "Mind over Matter," listing instances in which Spirit had literally animated matter through such measures as levitation, for example, or other proofs of supra-mundane intelligence that were becoming more and more manifest in the Spiritualist faith.

I had received letters from Axy in which she bemoaned the fact that an inquisitive public was no longer content with simple messages delivered by alphabetical knocks and table tipping. There were demands for even more rousing "tests" and "proofs" of spirit-communication. Some trance mediums conversed fluently in Greek, Latin, and other dialects; others produced writings in Oriental languages, and still others were submitted to eminent scholars who pronounced them to be pure Hebrew, Greek, and Sanskrit.

Even the most caustic skeptics were impressed with mediums adept at Spirit Painting—capturing likenesses of deceased persons utterly unknown to them. To amplify the amazement of their feat, these portraits were, at times, created while blindfolding the medium.

Frank Burr told her in Hartford that he'd held a melting hand. Now she read of séances that boasted of mediums who floated above the floor, of tuneful music issuing from invisible instruments, of water that turned various colors or had become magnetized to give off healing properties. My sister had not yet witnessed such marvels but the spiritualist press celebrated them as being "the most striking proofs" of the relationship between Spirit and Matter. Such were the substantiations she had referred to in the article Solitarie signed, which was now being reprinted in several New England newspapers.

<u>Solitarie</u>. Milton had referred to "those rare and solitarie." Axy originally chose the name because it related to her physical isolation, but it was also appropriate for one who traveled alone, a solitary figure. Hermits or recluses, especially those under a religious vow, lived as solitaries. She often felt (as she had expressed in Hartford) much alone in the world except for her Guardians, so it seemed appropriate and extraordinarily fitting.

As one might imagine, Father was troubled by his daughter's journeys as a single woman. He fumed over her silly, ill-timed jest about Samuel Colt, ruminated on the notion, mulled it over in his mind until, with the aid of strong drink he began to imagine that his daughter was susceptible to all manner of immoral behavior. His ire was further fueled by those who branded Spiritualists morally dissolute, labeling them "Free Lovers." Taking the stage, speaking before the public, he saw her associating with decadent people, a free-loving libertine, almost akin to a prostitute! One night in a drunken rage he accused her of having a Free Love association with Mr. Colt or worse, serving as his mistress.

"I cannot sleep under the same roof as this woman," he announced to the family, and moved his bed to the woodshed after pointing to Axy and shouting, "That's what her so-called 'conversion' has done to our family! You are no longer my daughter!"

The Free Love doctrine of Spiritualism caused many mediums great discomfort. It divided followers of the New Philosophy and brought about troubling complications. In truth, Free Love was a complex, many-hued issue. During her travels, Axy found herself obligated to defend a concept that many (including herself) considered morally perverse.

Many prominent Spiritualist thinkers were promoting Emanuel Swedenborg's theory of correspondences between earthly and spiritual life. Initially, the idea seemed straightforward: Two persons, a male and female, meet and are drawn together by a mutual attraction—a natural feeling unconsciously arising within their natures over which neither has any control. This is denominated love. And it is a matter that concerns these two and no other living soul has any human right to say aye, yes or no, since it is a matter in which none except the two have any right to be involved, and from which it is the duty of these two to exclude every other person since no one can love for another or determine why another loves.

If it were that unambiguous, Free Love would not have raised a questioning glance from Axy. The discrepancy arose over Swedenborg's hypothesis that every man and woman has a soul mate or "spiritual affinity." In other words, a man could conceivably be married to one woman and have a "spiritual affinity" with another. This was seen by the public (and by our father) as "Free Lust" and promiscuity.

To my sister's shame, the doctrine was sometimes exploited by Spiritual leaders who were indeed married, yet believed in total sexual freedom; Spiritualist leaders whose stature she had grown to admire and respect who took advantage of this radical "spiritual affinity" for licentious relationships.

Warren Chase interpreted "Free Love" as meaning that a wife was free to refuse her husband's sexual advances, thus resulting in emancipation and a remedy for an abusive marriage.

To further confuse the issue, yet another definition of Free Love advocated liberalized divorce laws and declared that if spouses did not love one another, then sexual contact, even with one's spouse and within a lawful marriage, became improper. It seemed the definition of Free Love differed, depending on whether it was used as an accusation or a description.

Most Spiritualists did not support Free Love, but most Free Love advocates were Spiritualists. So the term "Free Love" was linked to my sister for better or for worse.

+⸺✳⸺+

Travel in New England can be exceedingly uncomfortable, even dangerous, in the dead of winter, but rather than cope with the prevalent discord at home, Axy accepted invitations to speak in neighboring villages and towns, and Father could move back indoors from the cold woodshed. December 25th had always been a regular working day like any other, in our household. Christmas was considered too "Popish" to be celebrated by Puritans, who associated it with pagan celebrations and occasion for common drunkenness. Even though Father was an atheist, our Puritan ancestry extended back into history on both sides of our family—well before they sailed to this country on the *Mayflower* two hundred years before we were born. But Queen Victoria's marriage to the German Prince Albert in 1840 created new customs in New England and elsewhere. Recent immigrants to America brought Christmas trees and other holiday traditions along with them.

On Christmas Eve, 1855, Axy wrote in her diary:

> *This evening being Christmas Eve, I have been to an illumination at the Episcopal Church at the Randolph Center. I thought it might be pleasing to go as I had never been to an occasion of the kind. The church was trimmed with winter greens of all descriptions from the spruce trees to the unassuming moss. There was much taste displayed in the decorations and in the formations of sentences indicative of their faith. The church was lighted in very pretty and fanciful manners and I liked the reminder of the forest temples and the decorations of Nature. But the forms and ceremonies seemed so without soul to me that I could not sympathize at all in the services. I find no fault, but their ideas and manner of manifesting them are so different from my own, and their teaching, so little allied to original thought that I could not see how they could feel the mind and answer its aspirations better than they can see that which I call beauty in my own. They had a fine organ and the music was beautiful. Taking it in, I came away with that unsatisfied feeling in the soul which ever speaks when unfed, 'Is that all?'*

On Saturday, December 29, the thermometer was fifteen degrees below zero. Axy's energy waned as the thermometer plunged. Perhaps it was the closing out of the old year that caused increasing waves of melancholy. *Even with warm comfortable fires I cannot feel fully how others suffer who have not the comforts of life. God help them and help us to be willing and even* <u>wish</u> *to help them all that possibly lies in our power. Have not finished the "reply"* [to the criticism of her newspaper article "Spirit & Matter"], *I have felt so little like writing.*

> <u>*Monday, December 31.*</u> *I speak at Snowsville tomorrow evening. Company here this evening and as they are now gone I must retire to rest that I may wake refreshed. And as the Old Year counts of its last strokes of time I hope to sleep with Angels around me to guard and protect, and pure and high thoughts struggling for predominance in my mind even in the hours of slumber...*

She spoke at Snowsville but the audience was small and it took an hour and a half to cover four miles afterward, by sleigh.

> *I was perfectly sleigh sick when I got to my home for the night. Anything but such slow riding this cold weather.*

> <u>*Saturday, January 5.*</u> *Started about noon to go to West Bethel where I was to take the stage for Rochester, Vermont. Rode very comfortably with the aid of warm free stones, furs, etc. Took supper at the Bethel House, got my watch fixed and about five o'clock started in the stage for Rochester about eighteen miles distant. The stage was covered and with warm stones at my feet I rode very comfortably without stopping to warm during the whole distance.*

Axy was happy to continue to go wherever the spirits directed her travels but the cold weather aggravated her health.

> *When more mediums are developed, particularly Speaking Mediums, I think I will perhaps be at liberty to stop my public*

labors, or have them changed to some other form. I mean to be content with my mission. I do not want to find fault, but I do not always know what is for the best… for me, as well as for my Spirit friends.

Our cousin Clara Moore was married that winter. She and her husband settled near Plymouth Notch. Clara, twenty-one, was seven years younger than Axy and insisted that she officiate at her wedding. The solemnity of the celebration at our little church was deeply felt. This was the first wedding Axy had conducted and she was caused, once again, to reflect upon her own unmarried state with something like regret, I suppose. And also some relief.

Coincidentally, she had recently informed me that correspondence from Catherine Mettler told of lavish preparations being made in Hartford for the wedding of Samuel Colt and Elizabeth Jarvis arranged to take place the following summer. According to Catherine, it was rumored that Mr. Colt would be presenting his bride with a wedding dress and jewelry worth eight thousand dollars. Axy could not help but wonder how many of Hartford's poor would be able to support their families with such a magnificent sum.

Then there was the Father of Modern Spiritualism, Andrew Jackson Davis, who planned to marry again. His first wife, Catherine De Wolf, had not yet been divorced when she lived with Davis prior to their 1848 marriage. Catherine had been sickly; she died in 1853 and now Davis was attracted by Mary Fenn Robinson, whose husband had abandoned her. Mary Robinson had not yet obtained a legal divorce. Again, Free Love raised its ugly head.

Love and marriage—the subjects arose at every turn. Whenever Axy lectured these days, it seemed, passionate proposals of marriage arrived in the next week's mail—especially from widowers desiring a wife to care for their motherless babes, or perhaps to remove and shelter her from the scandalous lecture circuit. But my sister was beginning to think that perhaps she did not believe in love after all, or if she did, it was the kind of love that existed in Heaven. The only kind of Free Love she wanted to be associated with was the kind that involved the Emancipation of Woman.

In fact, she was more certain than ever that her future as a spirit lecturer depended on remaining true to herself, celibate, dedicated to remaining unmarried. The selection of the name Solitarie was becoming a self-fulfilling prophecy!

> *Thursday, January 1. Yesterday I came to East Middlebury. It is a hard route over the mountain by stage this cold time, but I came much better than I expected. I am to speak in the church at East Middlebury tonight, and tomorrow night there is to be a sort of oyster supper and spiritual gathering at Mr. Farr's at which I suppose I shall have to be present. I don't know whether I think the oyster supper is any addition to a Spiritual gathering. I do not think there is any thing <u>wrong</u> about it particularly, but it seems to me more in accordance with spiritual teaching to dispense with the supper, which will do no one any particular good, and give the same amount to an object, or objects of charity. This I think would be practical Spirituality and we need more of that.*

Over a hundred friends and curiosity seekers from Vergennes and Addison gathered at Mr. Farr's to meet my sister and speak with her.

> *Although we had a very pleasant social and spiritual time, it was less than perfect. If the oysters had been dispensed with and the same amount of money given to those who are needy, I should have liked everything very much.*

She was so incessantly going and receiving visitors that she did not half attend to penning her daily occurrences and her thoughts and feelings with regard to them. Perhaps her lack of notation was sometimes deliberate as she felt she did not write about her life in a very interesting manner. As they were calculated for no eye but hers, she told me, it made very little difference to her.

Comments on her next speaking engagement did include a few personal observations.

> *Before and after the conclusion of my speaking there were sundry rappings and noisy manifestations from a few in the room, but more particularly among the ladies. That won for them the novel and original name of "rowdy ladies." In all the places where I have spoken, I have never before seen anything of the kind. It was no strange thing to see boys and rowdified young men who would like to make some manifestations unworthy of enthusiastic and elevated minds, but to see those of my own sex who would descend to such rowdyism was a new and also an unwelcome sight to me. Well, there are low minded women as well as men, and in some places we must see the effect. I was only semi-conscious, but everything was said to be very still and quiet during my lecture time. I was in hopes there would be better arrangements and entire quiet the following night, but had about the same audience and the same amount of rowdyism. We could not hope for better things where sectarianism and self conceit reigned as triumphantly as they did there in Middlebury.*
>
> *In Salisbury we were unable to obtain the Congregational church, therefore the meeting was held in the schoolhouse which was very large. But such a jam. Every foot of the floor was occupied by persons standing, one complete forest of human forms. I was afraid it might discommode me about speaking, but the room was well ventilated and I did not feel the inconvenience much. The subject was most beautifully chosen. It was almost like a test. "Room, More Room" was the motto and the idea was room for the human soul, more room.*

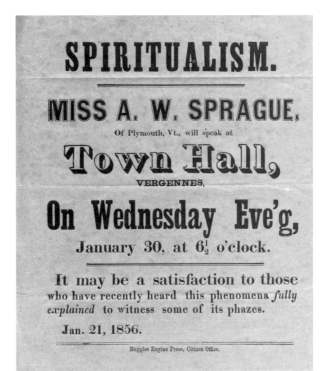

SPIRITUALISM.

MISS A. W. SPRAGUE,

Of Plymouth, Vt., will speak at

Town Hall,

VERGENNES,

On Wednesday Eve'g,

January 30, at 6½ o'clock.

It may be a satisfaction to those who have recently heard this phenomena *fully explained* to witness some of its phazes.

Jan. 21, 1856.

Ruggles Engine Press, Citizen Office.

Handbill heralding
Achsa's lecture
in Vergennes,
January 30, 1856.

Courtesy of Rokeby
Museum, Ferrisburgh,
Vermont.

Vergennes, Addison, North Ferrisburgh, Shelburne, Burlington, Winooski Falls, Williston. When she was not able to speak in churches she spoke in town halls and schools. Keene, New Hampshire, wanted her to lecture, and she was invited to speak at Randolph once a month. She often had invitations to station herself for a lengthy amount of time but did not feel as though she could do so, as her mission seemed to be to go here and there and scatter a few seeds for all to foster and cherish. Many of her travels involved very cold rides, but she told herself: *As I am public property, I must go.*

> *Monday, March 10. I have been sewing today and to prepare for further discussions with Father, have read Thomas Low Nichols' Lecture upon "Free Love as a Central Doctrine of Spiritualism." I found some good ideas in the work as I do in all his writings, but I cannot consider it as a <u>central doctrine</u> of Spiritualism, only so far as Spiritualism tends to liberalise the mind and elevate it*

above all sensual feelings, thus making the law of honor the only law necessary. Nichols claims "God has not mocked man with desires never to be fulfilled," and "that which we can conceive of and desire, must be possible to us."

If Nichols' ideas of "Free Love" are pure and Godlike, he knows very well that the world will not understand and appreciate them as such, therefore it seems to me that he ought to be more definite and explicit in his definitions and use of terms. Perhaps I am not far enough advanced to understand his ideas as being beneficial to the world or to myself, but I shall not bother Father with any of this although I would like to tell him Nichols says those who see "free lust" and promiscuity in the term Free Love should look into their own hearts and lives for the motives of others.

By March of 1856, the Harmony House in Boston had become The Fountain House, and the new proprietor, Dr. H. F. Gardner, welcomed Axy to the same hotel located on the corner of Harrison Avenue and Beach. Mediums were not allowed on the premises of many other hotels or boarding houses in the city but Gardner rented rooms to them at $1.25 per day or by the week "at prices to accord with the times."

Only one year ago I spoke in Boston for the very first time. The glowing accounts of my lectures in The New England Spiritualist in addition to my lengthy essay on my recovery and transformation, have stirred much enthusiasm for this new engagement which is expected to last an entire month. Thanks to Mrs. Mettler, this time I am prepared with several more new dresses in my trunks, all in the latest fashion. I do not like to think of myself as vain, but one must be prepared to put on a good appearance.

This particular engagement found Axy's impression of Boston emphatically mixed. It seemed to be a city affected by a never-ending muddle of growth and construction. Boston Common once held cattle, but with the addition of tree-lined walkways it was now transformed into a public park where one could take a pleasant stroll along former cow paths that twisted hither and yon. In warmer weather, booths would sell gingerbread, candy and lemonade. A fountain would sprout from a little pond. Opposite the Common, some of the city's finest buildings lined Tremont Street. But an untidy waste still remained south of Boylston Street, where a plan had been proposed for filling in the area of mud flats to provide long vistas with a suggestion of French boulevards. She could not envision this massive alteration.

Only hours after her arrival, Axy was rushed off to speak at Music Hall, built in 1852 at the corner of Winter Street and Bumstead Place, described as "a stone's throw from the Common" and home to the Boston Symphony Orchestra. Heavy spring snows had made a mess of the streets. She held her skirts high to avoid contact with the slurry of mud and horse droppings that had been churned up by traffic.

When William and Ephraim had left home for Boston in 1848, Axy and I had dreamed of attending the theater there, or the concert hall, adorned in the stylish attire. Now my opportunities for encountering those idyllic attractions were vicarious, relegated to my sister's descriptive letters, and *her* expectations had been modified: Now she was hoping to visit the Massachusetts State Prison and perhaps attend a lecture by the esteemed Transcendental philosopher Ralph Waldo Emerson.

> *Oh such muddy streets as I have found here, Celia—in some places almost impossible to cross, in others the snow higher than the sidewalks which are quite wet in many places. This makes the city look very disagreeable and if you saw it you should never wish to come again.*
>
> *Notwithstanding the bad walking, it was very pleasant overhead yesterday and Music Hall's Lecture Room was crowded to overflowing in the afternoon and many were obliged to go away for want of seats in the evening when a number of*

Speakers of the House were present. I was introduced to some dozen of them. Providentially, the subject of my speaking in the State's Prison was mentioned by one of my friends and the Speakers seemed quite interested in the idea. Two of them, a Representative and a Senator called upon me this evening to say they would do all they could to bring it about. I do not expect to gain admittance at present, if I ever do, but I like to throw this idea before those in power. The more it is agitated, the more it is brought before the public, the sooner the time will arrive when I shall be able to accomplish my reforms.

I had a well behaved audience of about three hundred in Beverly on Friday evening. They have had no previous lectures on Spiritualism and I think the majority were of the opinion that I had my entire Lecture arranged and committed to memory before leaving Boston. What is it about this locale that will not be convinced otherwise?

The sensational phenomena of physical mediumship was gathering momentum in Boston. Axy's experiences in holding a séance had never proved very fruitful, and the important séance at Mrs. Mettler's (who did not dance or impersonate anyone) was disappointing, so her deep curiosity sent her in search of a séance in this city. She took with her a small piece of lined paper, on which she discreetly noted:

First writing with hand bandaged under the table
Second, opening of a watch
Third throwing the table over the head
with the limbs tied and holding one hand
Then being floated in the air in a circle

She would expand on these details in her diary the following morning:

Tuesday, April 1. Had many callers yesterday and got some tired, but went last evening to Mr. Farrars, No. 14 Hancock Street, to witness some physical manifestations which were very wonderful. I have never been able to see any thing of the kind before, and I think them useful as there are a class of minds to whom this is the strongest evidence of Spirit Power.

First, the table was examined thoroughly to see that there was no sham for trick or fraud, and then after sitting around the table, a piece of paper was placed in the hand of the medium (having been previously marked to preclude the possibility of his changing it) and with a pencil placed under the table, the other hand resting on the table. There was a rustling of the paper and pencil, and in a short time they fell to the floor and on picking them up it was found written upon the paper with the identical marks upon it: "It is so hard we will write no more."

Next the medium held a watch suspended by the chain in his hand, and after having his hand closely bandaged so that he was unable to use his fingers at all, the hand containing the watch was held under the table, while the other hand of the medium rested upon it, and the hands of all the rest were on the table also. The watch was opened and a cap upon the inside of the watch fell to the floor. The medium then raised his hand from which the open watch hung suspended (the cap was picked up from the floor) and the bandage was just as closely confining his fingers as when he placed his hand under the table, this precluding the possibility of his doing it himself.

Then his feet were tied to his chair, he laid one hand upon the table, and I held the other at arm's length from the table. The lights were then extinguished and soon we heard a noise. The door was immediately opened and there lay the table upon a bed behind the medium, bottom side up, having passed completely over his head to get there, and he having no use of his feet and of only one hand. Again, four men took hold to hold the table still. The medium laid his hands upon it, the lights were extinguished. We heard a struggle going on, the table shoving on the floor and the efforts of the men to keep it still. They soon called for light, and there lay the table bottom side up on the floor, utterly setting defiance to those four stout men.

Again we all stood around in a circle in the room, joining hands, myself on one side holding one of the medium's hands and a gentleman on the other, forming a complete circle. Soon the medium began to rise, until our arms (the room being dark) were drawn up to him as far as we could reach, and we could hear his voice speaking to us from near the ceiling. And I and many others touched his feet up in the air. The only thing which he touched, except mid-air, was our two hands, but these so far from supporting him, were by him <u>drawn up</u> until he reached his height.

Many other things were done, which I have not time to mention. But it must prove to a demonstration that there was a <u>power</u> there beyond physical strength. And the fact with all those throwing the table across the room and lifting the medium on his chair upon the top of the table and moving him about, throwing upon the bed, nobody was hurt in the darkness, <u>though it seemed rather careless if done by chance.</u>

And as another proof of power, the medium is a young man, some fifteen or sixteen years of age, delicate and slender, with a girlish look that would not seem to betoken great physical power.

<u>*Wednesday, April 2.*</u> *Yesterday I went to Franklin some twenty-five miles from Boston to speak in the evening. Had a smaller audience (about one hundred and fifty) than I should have had, had it not been for a laughable state of affairs. It chanced to be the first day of April and the people got the idea that the advertisement for the lectures was nothing but a sham. Several circumstances conspired to make it look very much like that, and the people were afraid to come, lest they get "April Fooled." My little audience was very good, but I shall probably remember the circumstances when the anniversary comes around.*

Thursday, April 3. Spoke at Cambridge last evening after which I felt better. They have had only <u>one</u> lecture upon Spiritualism there before, therefore I did not have a large audience but quite as large as I expected. The colleges tend to make the people there worldly-wise and unwilling to hear anything new.

Saturday, April 5. I have sat for my Daguerreotype that the artist might design to some degree from that and relieve the tediousness of sitting. Got a very good one after some trouble. Have had three sittings. Don't know whether the picture will look like me or not.

Axy would have another opportunity to visit with John Murray Spear who had gained an even more eccentric reputation since their last meeting in Woodstock. His daughter Sophronia married an accountant (her father performed the ceremony) who was a boarder at the Spear's house in Boston, after which the couple moved to Melrose, Massachusetts, just north of the city. Perhaps due to his mysterious wanderings and other Free Love preoccupations, John Spear's marriage had begun to flounder, thus Spear often found refuge at his daughter's home.

At the present time, Spear was obsessed with receiving spirit messages from "the Association of Electricizers," who were guiding his construction of an extraordinary perpetual motion machine, known as The New Motor, at High Rock Cottage in Lynn, Massachusetts.

Axy felt sorry for the man, as this latest eccentricity had become a subject of ridicule even among many of his old friends who now sought to distance themselves from him. His "New Motor," meant to influence the control of spirits through the aid of copper and zinc batteries, seemed to be a fizzle for it just sat there in place and did nothing. Now, in the spring of 1856, he was seeking a group of twelve or fifteen believers, "some of the most intelligent and expanded minds of both sexes," to convene for a week of retreat and discussion of his New Motor.

Meanwhile, Sophronia died.

Saturday, April 5. This afternoon went with others up to Melrose to attend the Funeral of Sophronia Spear Butler. She was one of those innocent minded persons, unselfish in her nature like her father, whose goodness is felt by the world more keenly than it is seen or spoken of. It was her request that there should be no clergyman to attend her funeral in the usual manner, but that a few friends should meet, and both those in and those out of the body speak freely. The meeting which was in their house, was opened by singing the beautiful melody so well known, and particularly to Spiritualists, commencing,

> *How cheering the thought that the spirits in bliss*
> *Will bow their bright wings to a world such as this.*

After which her father made some very appropriate remarks, which were followed by others from D. F. Goddard, formerly a Universalist Clergyman but now a firm advocate of the Spiritual faith. A short discourse was then given through myself, other remarks by John Spear when the meeting closed by singing very appropriate words to the tune of Old Hundred.

Saturday, April 12. Eight o'clock P.M. Here I am at the "American House" in Lowell. So it is with me. To day among friends and to morrow among strangers. To day, welcomed and taken in to a pleasant little family with all the cordiality of old friends, and to morrow a stranger in a strange land taking care of myself at a Hotel. But I can get along either way very well. I do not complain for I am always safe.

Lowell, Massachusetts, was a mill town and employed a great many young immigrant women in the textile mills, some as young as ten but the majority between sixteen and twenty-five. They worked from five o'clock in the morning to seven o'clock at night:

Artist's rendering of Achsa Sprague. In Boston on Saturday, April 5, 1856, she wrote in her diary: "I have sat for my Daguerreotype that the artist might design to some degree from that and relieve the tediousness of sitting. Got a very good one after some trouble. Have had three sittings. Don't know whether the picture will look like me or not."

Special Collections, Bailey/Howe Library, University of Vermont.

Coming up in the cars to night from South Danvers, two little ragged dirty children were taken into the cars and the little girl only four years, without any bonnet, and the little boy about six, crying. And I did not wonder when I saw that they were <u>alone</u>. And when the cars stopped at a dreary looking Station to let them off, a lady told me that they were sent there to the Alms House. They looked like Irish children. My heart had bled for them before but the last idea filled their cup full. Thrown out upon the cold charity of the world, with no friend to call forth the better feelings of their nature, and unfold the germs of Divinity within, but only stranger hands to give (and even grudge at that) their scanty lot of bread and harshly bid them to and fro.

I seldom cry at anything. But I could have buried my face among the seats there and cried heartily if it would have done any good, but it takes something besides tears to help such wants as theirs. And this is life. On one side the rich and haughty millionaires, on the other poor suffering children famishing for want of bread, to be trained up to vice and crimes. Poor suffering ones, who will pity them.

Boston author Herman Melville had written a story for the May 1856 issue of *Putnam's Monthly* magazine called "The Apple Tree Table," subtitled "Original Spiritual Manifestations." The story was rife with comic accounts of rappings and ridiculous accounts of Spiritualist attitudes regarding immortality. The narrator of Melville's story recalled Cotton Mather's account, entitled *Magnalia Christi Americana, or the Ecclesiastical History of New England,* originally published in 1702 but recently reprinted. For those skeptics who chose to look upon Spiritualism and rappings as a fresh outbreak of demonism, Cotton Mather's explanation of witchcraft satisfied their needs.

The editor of *The Atlantic Monthly,* James Russell Lowell, went so far as to profess that table-tipping illustrated the durability of popular superstition. "Turning over the yellow leaves of the same copy of *Webster on Witchcraft* which Cotton Mather studied," Lowell claimed, "I thought, 'Well that goblin is laid at last!' And while I mused the tables were turning and the chairs beating the devil's tattoo all over Christendom."

At the same time, *Putnam's* had published an article in May 1856 by Daniel Hoffman, "The Spirits in 1692 and What They Did at Salem," that concluded:

> The misery it may be well to remember, for it grew out of an unwise and superstitious curiosity about devils and spirits, and became cruel and bloody through an epidemic fear – both of which may again recur; indeed, the former belief has been pressed upon us in our own day.... The belief out of which the Salem cruelties grew, is a proof that a false belief is sometimes deadly; and we are bound to protest against any theory of spirits presented on shallow proof.

In the midst of this untidy fray, Axy received a call to speak in Salem, the cradle of American witchcraft. She was expected to remain overnight.

<u>Sunday, April 20</u>. Went to Salem, where I spoke in the evening, Tuesday evening. Had a large audience, much larger than was expected, it being the first Lecture ever given in Salem by a Medium. They were very anxious that I should come again. I shall try to do so if possible. Wednesday morning, Mr. Brown took me around to the Court House to see the relics of the days of the Witches. There I saw pins which were said to have been taken from the bodies of those said to be tormented by the witches, and also records of some of the trials of the so called Witches. I saw one case where a woman by confessing herself a witch escaped hanging, while another who denied to the end was condemned to be hung. It hardly seems possible that there could have been such dark ideas and such strange proceedings. But it is but too well authenticated.

I saw also the house where they tried these witches, but it has been undergoing improvements and now looks quite modern. And I think the people are so too, or they would not have sat and listened so attentively Tuesday evening and listened to <u>one of the</u> <u>Modern Witches</u>, without preparing a gallows for her reception.

By the time she was ready to leave Boston, her recent visit had been as well heralded as the first. *The New England Spiritualist* published a pamphlet, "Words From The Spirit-Life," in which "the substance of two discourses spoken in the Melodeon, Boston, through Miss A. W. SPRAGUE of Plymouth, Vt., purporting to emanate from disembodied spirits… are commended to the reader's candid and serious consideration."

The first lecture closed with these lines:

This is the day of small things—mediums are imperfect— conditions unfavorable—we cannot give those things which we would, and which hereafter will be unfolded… Our happiness is not so much to instruct you, as to teach you to instruct yourselves.

The pamphlet was offered to the public for $1.50 per hundred, 20 cents per dozen, or 2 cents a single copy.

During her first visit to Boston, petty rumors had circulated among cynics and skeptics that Axy's "sermons without notes" seemed so realistic and genuine, they had undoubtedly been memorized before she took the stage. It was insinuated that such acts of cheating were as much the result of avarice or ambition as the acts of the professional trickster. Of course Axy was appalled.

An accusation of fraudulence was a most grievous charge for any medium, and even those who might occasionally practice deception were charged with betraying the most sacred impulses of the heart. To address remaining suspicions or to prevent further doubts from cropping up, A. E. Newton published a glowing account of Axy's 1856 appearances in *The New England Spiritualist,* which Samuel Brittain subsequently reprinted in *The Spiritual Telegraph.* She forwarded a copy of the article to me and it found a home in my scrapbook along with her remark that "if comments were made about inaccuracies spoken by a former schoolteacher, that *must prove without a doubt* that the words she spoke were beyond my control!"

> Miss Sprague's labors in this city closed for the present on Sunday evening last. The interest in the discourses given through her instrumentality was unabated to the end…
>
> The style of Miss Sprague's discourses is usually to some extent argumentative, but simple, and adapted to the ready comprehension of the ordinary mind. Nothing can be more evident to the hearer than that the design

of the intelligence addressing him is, not to astonish and dazzle with novel and brilliant thoughts or eloquent oratory, but to reach and arouse to action the nobler and higher impulses of the soul, and thus to secure his practical spiritual good. No one after listening to her discourse can doubt either the earnestness or the purity and benevolent intent of the speaker. That there are defects, both on the score of clear, methodical arrangement, and form of expression, is also equally obvious; and perhaps no one is more sensible of them than the instrument herself. But we have often had occasion to notice, in endeavoring to make an abstract of discourses given through her, that however disconnected and discursive the successive thoughts might seem to the superficial ear, yet when analyzed and traced in their spiritual relations, there was a unity and coherence readily traceable through the whole.

The mental state of Miss S. during these efforts affords some characteristics, not peculiar perhaps among mediums, but of interest in forming an opinion of their true source. According to her statement, she retains her consciousness complete, so as to be herself a listener to the words spoken through her lips, but her consciousness becomes partially merged into that of the controlling mind, by which she becomes elevated, as it were, and for the time feels herself to be a disembodied spirit addressing mortals. At the same time she is aware that she is not either originating the thoughts or furnishing the words for their expression – nor does she know beforehand the topics of discourse. While speaking she cannot control her organs of speech, for they are moved by another will. Hence she is aware that sometimes ungrammatical sentences and words are employed, much to her mortification, but has no power to restrain or correct them…

> Personally, Miss S. is extremely modest and retiring, possessed of those attractive and amiable qualities of head and heart which at once secure the confidence, respect, and affection of all who come in contact with her. The idea of pretense on her part could be tolerated by no one who enjoys her acquaintance.

The source of the cruel and mystifying rumors of memorization was perplexing. Axy was not aware of having made any "enemies" in Boston, or elsewhere. She did admit, immodestly, that she appreciated Mr. Newton's words describing her "attractive and amiable qualities of head and heart."

Similar scathing rumors were the rage in a satirical book recently published: *Lucy Boston, or Woman's Rights and Spiritualism,* by Fred Folio, surely a pseudonym. Below the subtitle, *The Follies and Delusions of the Nineteenth Century,* there was a slight epigraph from *Don Juan*: "This is the age of oddities let loose." The novel also contained absurd, ugly, burlesque illustrations of women. Axy found the publication disgusting and said it encouraged the worst kinds of doubts of our well-founded beliefs. The novel closed with these lines:

SPIRITUALISM
AND
WOMAN'S RIGHTS

Twins in their birth and ill begot:
Twins in their grave—there let 'em rot.

Then she was off to Portland, Maine, and eventually back to Massachusetts. Referrals went out from everywhere she spoke, and more invitations arrived than my sister—or any medium—could possibly fulfill.

I hardly know when I shall get home now, she wrote to me. *May my works be such and my motives and aims, that I may find a home within myself, if I have one no where else.*

She was setting her sights wherever the spirits dictated and her letters could not contain her pleasure. However, with the press of correspondence and demands upon her time, her once meticulous diary entries became compressed into a digest of days and weeks that had passed. Friends welcomed her back to Hartford, where she spoke before a large crowd at Union Hall on Sunday, May 4th. The following Sunday she was due to speak in Philadelphia. Once she was settled there, she found time to muse upon her curious journey from Hartford by way of the Connecticut River and Long Island Sound.

I took a little steamboat from Hartford to New York on my way to Philadelphia. It rained very hard, therefore I did not enjoy the scenery on the Connecticut River as much as I should have done, but I saw much that was beautiful. The scenery is not particularly grand or striking, but it is pleasingly beautiful, stealing softly into the soul like the melody of song.

We did not enter Long Island Sound until evening, therefore I could enjoy little there, except to go out occasionally in the evening (under cover) and gaze upon the black, angry waters that were very rough that night and listen to the words they spoke, to the lessons they taught me. If the river in its quiet flow speaks, how much more the waters communicate when agitated. If the waters are beautiful when the sunlight rests upon them, they are sublime when the dark clouds are above them and the wild winds tune them to a deep, sounding requiem.

Steamboat travel was preferable to the railroad, as far as my sister was concerned. I have never been on a steamboat, but I concur that trains are crowded with malodorous passengers and floors covered with sticky tobacco juice. In warm weather the smell of rancid beef or mutton tallow used to lubricate the axles is rampant. One must don a linen duster, as soil from the roadbed flies in the windows mixed with cinders that burn holes in one's clothing. Choking soot and fumes from the wood-burning engine can easily cause one's eyes to burn.

Stagecoach travel is miserable at best so the railroads improve upon *that*. But for a very long distances, I can appreciate why Axy much preferred steamboats, even in rainy weather. With their shallow draft and tall funnels for each of the twin engines, steamboats possessed elegance and grace. Flags and pennants snapped above a multi-level superstructure gleaming with fresh white paint, and the river echoed up and down with the boat's cheerful whistles. There was a dining room, brilliantly lighted (thanks to steam), and separate sitting rooms for men and women which were fashionably furnished and comfortable for reading or knitting or needlework.

The little steamer she took in early May 1856, was neither as grand nor as large as those that plied the Mighty Mississippi or any of the Great Lakes, but it gleamed with mirrors, and boasted Brussels carpets and comfortable plush sofas. If she had dared the profligacy, Axy could have retained a private stateroom.

Her trip from Hartford to Philadelphia was not a very long one, yet that little voyage dramatically marked the beginning of an astonishing passage in her life. During that brief journey her soul caught sudden fire with a flame that was never quenched. In the consequence of that evening, she met one whose range of thought, of history, of scholarship and travel, would in due course assist her own by exacting a higher style than she alone could reach; one whose heart would capture her own in ways she had sworn over and over were forbidden.

They met following dinner, when most of the men retired to the men's saloon for cigars and women retreated to their staterooms or the women's cabin to read or embroider. Although it was raining, Axy could not resist the lure of the water and the freshness of the sea air. She wrapped her wool shawls closely and went out upon the deck to weather the storm.

It was glorious.

She said she loved the wash of the waves far below the railing and the easy chatter of the paddlewheel. The rain had let up by then and in the deepening twilight she pretended she was upon the ocean, by herself. Her pleasure bobbed to the surface and she rejoiced by speaking aloud,

"My soul is full of longing
For the secret of the sea"

Her oration was addressed to Long Island Sound and the wet gray distance that seemed to extend forever.

"And the heart of the great ocean
Sends a thrilling pulse through me."

Suddenly she was startled by a deep male voice from the shadows that continued the first verse of the very same Longfellow poem in a strong and certain fashion:

"Ah! What pleasant visions haunt me
As I gaze upon the sea!
All the old romantic legends,
All my dreams, come back to me."

Axy thought it remarkably disrespectful to mock her in such a manner. A polite gentleman would have pretended not to acknowledge her childlike enthusiasm. But the mysterious man continued still, boldly moving closer to where she stood.

"Sails of silk and ropes of sandal,
Such as gleam in ancient lore."

She could see by light cast from lamps inside the boat that he was handsome, a tall man with curly hair, clean shaven, well dressed and distinguished in a waist-length vest and black frock coat with braid trim. Altogether, he seemed to her eyes to be a well-to-do, conservative gentleman, keenly waiting for her to take up the next line. What nerve!

Firmly, and without hesitation, she took a step forward, stared him in the face and boldly picked up the poem.

> *"And the singing of the sailors,*
> *And the answer from the shore!"*

They continued, finishing the poem together, reciting, in tandem, Longfellow's words of longing for the secrets of the sea. Then the two had a sudden, hearty laugh at their daring episode and without pause fell into easy conversation that proved their shared interest in poetry, politics, the California gold rush, and other matters of current significance.

She conceded that it may not have been proper comportment on her part, but she was starving; her appetite was so deprived of intellectual fare that she cast off all pretence of gentility and plunged into what she imagined would be a fleeting confluence of two paths of like-minded dreamers, at only the cost of her own stubborn pride.

On May 12, my sister made a pallid attempt to account for the lapse since her last entry. Her introduction to the man on the steamboat was summarized and almost dismissed with casual indifference.

> *I became interested in conversing with a person on board, and*
> *the night passed on while we talked of Burns, Byron,*
> *Longfellow and countless others; of law, philosophy and religion,*
> *&c. &c. until finally, at dawn, we parted—to drift away on the*
> *billows of time and probably know each other no more. But I*
> *learned much on that sea voyage, I hardly know how. Much that*
> *was beautiful, much that spoke to the soul. Much I will*
> *remember forever.*

I enclose herewith the man's calling card, which I found, worn from handling, and to this day still tucked between the pages of a volume of Longfellow's poems.

There was no way Axy could have realized the enormous influence her nascent feelings for this mysterious gentleman would have upon her future, or the way in which he would cause my cherished sister to reconsider her definition of Free Love.

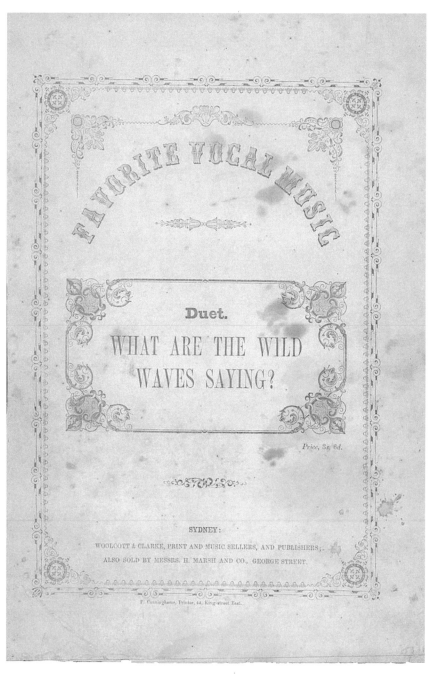

"What are the Wild Waves Saying?" by Stephen Glover, lyrics/poem by Joseph Edwards Carpenter. Achsa and John Crawford delighted in sharing the duet as it evoked their playful personas as wave and sea.

❧PART TWO❧

(1856–1859)

Under every ocean wave
There is still a hidden cave,
With its pearl and shell;
Deep in every human soul
There are powers that ever roll,
Each a potent spell.

"Genii of the Ocean"
The Poet and Other Poems
ACHSA W. SPRAGUE

Floating on the Billows

(1856–1857)

What are the wild waves saying,
Sister, the whole day long,
That ever amid our playing,
I hear but their low, lone song?
Not by the seaside only,
here it sounds wild and free;
But at night, when 'tis dark and lonely,
In dreams it is still with me.

*W*hat are the wild waves saying? Mr. Crawford sang this to Axy on the steamboat that night, although he apologized by saying the lyrics were meant as a conversation duet between brother and sister. When she expressed a desire to learn the sister's part, he printed the verses in a small notebook he carried inside his coat, then tore out the pages so she (as Florence) could respond to the concerns posed by Paul (the man).

Brother, I hear no singing,
'Tis but the rolling wave
Ever its lone course winging
Over some Ocean cave!
'Tis but the noise of water
Dashing again the shore,
And the wind from some bleaker quarter
Mingling with its roar.

Their voices blended in the chorus, which suggested "something greater speaks to the heart alone" and that was the "Voice of the Great Creator." The exchange, Mr. Crawford said, was imagined as a discussion between siblings as suggested by Dickens's novel, *Dombey and Son*, in particular the deathbed scene of Little Paul. Axy had read the novel and said she was dismayed at the way the author depicted cruelty toward children.

Crawford's baritone enthralled her—no man had ever serenaded her like that, and joining him in harmony was an unmatched joy. Long after she had memorized the words she found herself humming the evocative melody and blissfully recalling the enchanting evening. Sometimes she wondered if it had been a dream.

Mr. Crawford had a wife, five children—four daughters and a son—and a home in Ogdensburgh, New York, where he and a partner owned the Northern Transportation Company, a firm with a number of propeller-driven ships that hauled freight on the Great Lakes from there to Chicago and back. The partnership evolved from an earlier venture that shipped goods from Akron, Ohio, on the Erie Canal.

These rudimentary details had been briefly mentioned when Axy inquired of his business interests, but she sloughed off particulars when she later mused on that night. Rather, she preferred to remember he'd said he *had* to live on the water, and that she possessed a truly captivating voice.

Of herself, she had been careful to reveal very little information. When he asked her name, she told him it was Bell. Her home was in the Green Mountains of Vermont, and she was traveling to see friends in Philadelphia.

Inexplicably, they reasoned toward morning, their unison of thought and feeling, their mutual interests in poetry, music, and intellectual pursuits, were so similar as to be almost preordained. It was remarkable to have met under such a circumstance. And poignant, too, Axy offered, as surely their paths would never cross again. (Or if they did, never in such an intimate manner, she privately reasoned.) How fortunate was his wife to have such an agreeable husband—handsome and erudite with a deep longing for knowledge.

I only learned of this happenstance long after the fact, as she claimed it would have been impossible to portray her enigmatic emotions in a letter and waited to reveal her sentiments when we could be together. I appreciated this certainty when I discovered that she had barely mentioned the meeting in her diary. Of that late May evening in on Long Island Sound with Mr. Crawford, she observed:

> *I took a Hack at New York, for the Boat bound to South Amboy, New Jersey, thus making only a <u>post town</u> of the Metropolis, as a traveler once wrote of Rome. Since I had been awake all night and was tired and sleepy—and it rained so that I could not go upon deck of this boat as I did with the other—I did not enjoy the beautiful shores and rolling waters as I had the night before. And oh! The night before.*

All the best spirit mediums and speakers in America were invited to Philadelphia. My sister, no exception, was greeted with generous crowds at Sansom Hall. Marenda Randall, who now resided in the city where she practiced medicine, introduced Axy to admirers that included Philadelphia's most respected citizens. Everyone was eager to entertain Miss Sprague and to be seen in her company. Axy enrolled in the Philanthropian, a new Academy of Music, for two weeks of lessons on the piano.

> *I shall try to retain what I have gained until another opportunity offers, for me to improve upon it.*

She especially wanted to visit the Academy of Fine Arts. The celebrated engraver, Mr. Samuel Sartain, and his wife, gave her a personal tour. Mrs. Sartain pointed out fig leaves that had recently been strategically placed upon the nude figures of statues and sculptures, since separate days for ladies' visits had lately been abolished. Now viewing the statues at any time of day or week would not be upsetting or indiscreet.

Visiting the grave of Benjamin Franklin was another of her desires, but,

> the grave yard is surrounded with so high a wall that we could not see it. I think it is too bad, when they might remedy it so easily and allow the admirers of his genius to see the place where the casket has been buried. Perhaps though the thoughts will sooner turn to seek him Spiritward. There is too great a tendency in the human mind to seek the grave of the mighty dead and follow them no further.
>
> Was intending to go to the Theater in the evening with some friends, but the Spirits through T. L. Harris wished to speak to me, and this hindered my going. I have a strong suspicion that it was a polite hint from my Guardians that they did not wish me to go. I never go to the Theater often.

Wednesday, May 28, she departed Philadelphia for Easton, where she expected to lecture. But upon her arrival she discovered arrangements had not been made. If she went on to her next engagement in Troy, she would arrive there much too soon.

> And as there was no cause for me to stay at Easton, I finally decided to come on as far as New York and stay over night at the Tremont House where Mr. Tarbell of Vermont is Proprietor. Much to my surprise I found himself and daughter there, also Mrs. Mettler and daughter Catherine. I felt myself immediately at home.

The gift of a few free days in New York gave Axy an opportunity to explore:

> I went yesterday into Barnum's Museum where I saw many things wonderful and beautiful, curiosities in nature and art, stuffed lions and tigers and other animals, birds, fish and almost every thing you could think of, including the "Fee Jee Mermaid," and the "Living Sea Serpents." Also saw what they call the Happy Family, consisting of live dogs, cats, rats, anteaters,

monkeys, guinea pigs and different kind of birds, all in a cage together, seeming to enjoy life to the last degree. Lions, tigers &c. &c. I also saw, and to me it was quite interesting. In the afternoon we went into the Crystal Palace which though containing nothing in comparison to what it did in its grand display, yet has many objects of interest, particularly its statuary. Oh, it was beautiful. I have such a passion for <u>marble life</u>, and here were some beautiful specimens.

Had a little Circle at the Tremont House last night as Mr. Tarbell was so anxious. To day we went into Mrs. Rickar's "Humanity School." This is for grimy ragged children whose parents are not able to pay their tuition, or dress them suitable to attend any other. I was very much interested in their dirty little faces. They looked so intelligent, but it must require much sacrifice and much patience to do what Mrs. Rickar is doing. I wish I had the means to assist them more.

This afternoon I have been up in the Observatory and had a view of the city, Hudson River, Long Island Sound and also the Island. I enjoyed it all the more so because I was able to climb all those three hundred steps. I must be very thankful indeed for the strength I've gained.

After one last day in the city she left New York by steamboat and traveled up the Hudson River to Troy where my friends Benjamin Starbuck and his wife welcomed my sister and provided comfortable quarters, as they had, earlier, for me.

There has formerly been much interest at Troy, but owing to inharmonies arising among the people it has been at a very low ebb for the past year. Next week, unless something remarkable should happen, I bend my steps homeward to Vermont.

For regeneration of body and mind, Marenda Randall had recommended a hydrotherapy session at nearby Saratoga Springs. But Axy was convinced that the celebrated watering place catered to frivolous follies of fashion and would be much too commercial for her liking, so she was reticent to comply.

She did agree to an invitation to visit the summer home of Dr. Robert Titus Hallock and his wife, Elizabeth, at neighboring Glens Falls, where she also consented to lecture. Dr. Hallock had been a Quaker during his youth and was now somewhat notorious, having been prosecuted in Philadelphia for "teaching the secrets of maternity to women." Amanda Britt, a strident medium from St. Louis, heard Dr. Hallock's lecture on physiology and told her husband (also a physician) that Hallock ought to be drummed out of the city and was "a bad man to talk of such things as he did."

Axy had heard a great many controversial things about Amanda Britt; The woman seemed to enjoy the spotlight more than was fitting for a medium.

The Hallocks treated Axy to an excursion on Lake George and the awe-inspiring beauty of the Adirondacks:

> *There I found a beautiful Lake, stretching away far beyond where the eye could gaze, sleeping so calmly and peacefully among the mountains that you might almost imagine it the home of the water nymphs and its shores and mountains that for elfin broods and merry spirits and fairies. Its waters are as clear as crystal, and the pebbly bottom, as far as the eye can see it is like some clear magnificent spring.*

Saratoga, "The Queen of Spas," would be a different setting, entirely, and my sister informed the Starbucks that—during her return to Troy—she would step off the train only briefly just to have a look and pay her respects to a friend, yet another female M.D. at the Water Cure.

She was greeted at the early train and given a tour of the facility. The Grand Union (a temperance hotel) and Congress Hall, both enormous buildings with magnificent piazzas, faced one another. The main street, Broadway, extended through the entire village and a leisurely five-minute walk up or down that street took one past all the great houses and the most exclusive shops.

Axy was on schedule to join the morning's promenade to numerous springs where, in exchange for a tip to the dipper-boy, one receives a tumbler of carbonated water (she claimed the odor resembles the stench of rotten eggs). Apparently this observance is the chief amusement of the entire day; afternoons provide leisurely occasions for lawn games, carriage rides, cotillion parties, religious meetings, debates or musical concerts. There is a trotting course just outside the village where horse racing commenced ten years or so ago.

In truth, my sister found Saratoga a much pleasanter place than she expected. It is completely surrounded by groves and has such a combination of beauties of the cultivated and uncultivated that she was thoroughly charmed. She rode and walked around the village, even visiting High Rock Spring where a huge rock, probably caused by the flowing over of the water, surrounds the spring and the water is dipped from an aperture in the rock.

A promise was exacted that Axy would soon undertake a prolonged stay at Saratoga. Meanwhile, the ebullient Mr. Starbuck and his "tribe of Benjamin" had arranged for a "pic-nic" to welcome her back to Troy. The outing was held at a place called Dry River, "a deep ravine a little west of us," as he explained in a letter to me after the event. Fifty Spiritualists were in attendance, and the day was memorable for the joyful songs that poured forth plus a lengthy poem that Axy composed by spirit-inspiration. Starbuck said he believed they could even have have found a tiny space to squeeze me on board. "We left the grounds about 8 o'clock and, Celia, *such a load* as we had in our old Lumber Waggon, you don't often observe. The number was 22 stowed about as close as you see cattle sometimes in a Rail Road Car, and once in a while they made *some* noise. I heard my wife observe during the ride, 'Miss Sprague must indeed think we are a queer set!' The dogs barked at us and the children cheered us as we passed along and we were as 'big children' as any of them and enjoyed it too. Your dear sister says she will never forget her visit to Troy."

Tuesday, June 17. At last I am so near home that I am stopping at Danby among the Green Mountains. Speak here this evening and leave for home tomorrow, after being gone thirteen weeks.

Axy had been absent from the Notch since her journey to Boston three months before, in early March. Everyone seemed to be afflicted with illness, so her healing hands were quickly put to work. She was so busy that she did not pick up her diary again for nearly two months.

Wednesday, August 6. Home again. Home Again. And six weeks have elapsed since I have opened the pages of this Journal. There is almost a life history in that space of time, but like many other life histories—unwritten. Let it remain so. I will write only that my Father was taken sick immediately after I reached home and remains so yet, although he is now some better. Uncle Moore's little boy Ephraim has also been very sick, but is now better.

Father's prospects seemed very grim. He had been failing for the last two years due to consumption and was now suffering from bloody diarrhea. It did not seem probable that he would ever get around the house again and was so weak that he did not protest when it was Axy who smoothed his bedding and spoon-fed his broth.

During her visit, two of Orvilla's stepchildren succumbed to consumption and Axy delivered inspired hymns at the funeral of the little girls. Another great loss, although not as personal: the Charter Oak in Hartford crashed to the ground during a horrendous storm that swept through that city on August 21. Samuel Colt, deeply grieved, sent the Colt Band to the ruined tree where funeral dirges were unfurled over the immense carcass. He ordered his men to carve furniture from resurrected wood. Lydia Sigourney wrote a memorial poem. When the circles in its trunk were counted, the Charter Oak was found to be nearly a thousand years old.

Axy sought escape in Elizabeth Gaskell's new book, *The Life of Charlotte Bronte*. When she had finished with it, she sent me her copy with remarks in the margins. We enjoyed sharing books we'd read with our personal notations; it made us feel closer than the reality of miles.

I am again floating upon the billows of Public Life, Axy would soon note in her journal, for she was called upon to speak again at the annual Spiritualist Convention in South Royalton, Vermont.

Fifteen hundred Spiritualists were in attendance in late August. Warren Chase remarked, "Fifteen hundred people with every chord of their beings beating in harmony and happiness is not a scene often met with in this turbulent world."

But least one medium went home fraught with unease over the so-called harmonious gathering and its disturbing potential for scandal.

Andrew Jackson Davis and his wife Mary proposed a resolution with regard to Free Love. Davis reiterated his belief that women should have co-equal civil and political advantages with men, and his resolution ended by claiming, "in the marriage relation, she shall be fully secured in her natural rights to property, to the legal custody of her children, and to the entire control of her own person, that thereby fewer and better children may be born, and humanity be improved and elevated."

Axy was in total agreement with Davis and his wife in that regard. But Davis and John Spear also offered up their curious doctrine of *divine matehood*. This bizarre concept claimed that an infant was born already married, and that somewhere in the universe the "counterpartal half of his nature was waiting to be united to him." The conclusion then followed naturally that, "while the true marriage was necessarily in-dissoluble and eternal, being in fact not a union, but a reunion, it was lawful and even expedient that other unions should be dissolved as soon as the mutual incompatibility became manifest and intolerable."

This Free Love only encouraged the "Free Lust" association, and further emphasized the characterization of "lunatic fringe" by the public and the press. In addition, if spouses did not love each other, according to Davis and Spear and Warren Chase and other Spiritual leaders, then sexual contact between spouses was considered immoral, even within a lawful marriage.

The amount of the Royalton Convention given over to a discussion of divorce, "spiritual counterparts," and "affinities" sorely tried my sister's patience.

I learned one thing, that as we profess to have a free platform, people and mediums must be allowed to speak and even absurd opinions must be tolerated or at least heard. We must learn to hear all, and try, <u>all</u> of us, to know just when to speak, just what to say and how to say it in order to be in harmony with Truth and with the minds of those who hear us. We must all try to harmonise together before we can ever speak in concert.

Two weeks after the convention, she returned to the lecture circuit but was clearly not herself.

Tuesday, September 16. Saturday I left home intending to be gone several weeks if Father remains as well. I started for South Wallingford, but by accident took the wrong train at Rutland (the first time I have ever made such a mistake) and was carried in an opposite direction of about four miles. I was then obliged to hire a conveyance to take me to Wallingford as the last train had gone, and as I was engaged to speak there on the following day, I was obliged to go. Had a beautiful ride across the country of about sixteen miles, which only cost me <u>four dollars</u>, and upon arrival found that to cap the climax my trunk was nowhere to be found. So I was obliged to appear in Church the next morning in my traveling gear. But as I don't happen to be very proud and was somewhat acquainted in So. Wallingford, I cared very little about it.

Sunday, September 21. It seems as if my evil star has reigned for the past week, for owing to a mistake in time I was left by the Cars at North Wallingford when I was to start for Clarendon and obliged the <u>second</u> <u>time</u> in a <u>week</u> to get a private conveyance. This however, was not as expensive as the first ride, for at the termination of my journey, the man who carried me, unaccountably enough, would take nothing for his trouble. I hope my luck will turn soon for it is a new thing for me to get so many things wrong when traveling. I have always been very fortunate.

<u>Monday, September 22.</u> Last evening, through mistake, both Halls in Clarendon were found to be engaged. We appealed to the Catholics and singularly enough our request was granted. I spoke in their Church last evening to a very large audience. The Church, which was of good size, was crowded very full and good attention was paid by all. A great many Catholics were there. So much is said by the Protestants about Catholic intolerance, I think it is now the Protestants' turn to blush at their own intolerance and the liberality of the Catholics. I don't know what their Priest will say to them however.

<u>Tuesday, September 23.</u> Came last night to Middlebury. Speak at East Middlebury this evening. Coming upon the train, there were two little Irish children put on board going to the Nunnery at Burlington to be educated. The little girl cried and would not be pacified during the route. I tried all I could to comfort her, and her little heart was almost broken. They were in charge of a priest. If I had been going directly home, I would have taken her with me if he would have given her up.

Axy frequently suffered from "minister's sore throat," not an uncommon ailment in those who had to raise their voice to be heard before large crowds. She had tried all manner of nostrums including ingesting a powder made from the dried corms of the

Jack-in-the-Pulpit. It's no wonder that she was intrigued when it was recommended that she try Hydropathy, to "take the waters," be cleansed and refresh her health.

Vincent Priessnitz, an Austrian, had founded a program that relied upon a rigid program of therapy available at his New Graefenberg Water Cure, a thousand feet above the Mohawk River and only five miles from Utica. The proprietor, Dr. R. Holland, was a Spiritualist medium rumored to possess strong healing powers.

Warren Chase had advised, "To a lecturer jaded and worn out by excessive travel and public labors, it is very refreshing to come away from the excitement of public duties, even though these duties be ever so important, useful and agreeable at the time, and to 'lay off' on grassy banks, inhale pure air, pick the fragrant red strawberry and recuperate generally." At New Graefenberg, women were free to wear liberating bathing costumes.

I can vouch for the fact that it is especially exhilarating for women to abandon corset stays, long heavy skirts, and voluminous shawls! In the mountains of Vermont and out here in Wisconsin's farmland we welcome such "rustification." We wear corsets only when that constraint is absolutely necessary, and having become accustomed to the "shimmy," otherwise known as a chemise, and the ever-necessary petticoat, I am always loath to squeeze myself into a corset to obtain a fashionable waist.

According to Axy, the basic water cure costume was remarkably comfortable: a loose-fitting pair of pantaloons and a dress that fell just below the knee, with no tight gatherings or necklines. She was treated at Graefenberg by Dr. Thomas, a native of Wales, who used his faculty of clairvoyance to locate the nature and treatment of diseases that he could discover almost at first sight. Unlike Dr. Gordon, her magnetizing psychologist in Woodstock years ago, Dr. Thomas never laid a hand on her.

I received a letter from her, written there. The rooms were large, clean and airy. *I like to have such establishments smell sweet, the beds clean, the food well cooked, and the general conduct of the house agreeable,* she said. New Graefenberg could accommodate one hundred patients. Exposure to sunshine and fresh air, a simple diet and physical exercise, were prescribed remedies. There were arrangements for the different kinds of baths—for washing, and bathing; for every purpose needed.

The Priessnitz Theory declared cold water efficacious for each and every person. The usual procedure included walking barefoot through morning dew for some ills, plying high-pressure hoses on patients, or wrapping them in sheets wrung out in cold water. Drenched tortures and gooseflesh must be endured. Axy's rigid program of conduct prescribed rising at 4 a.m. for a cold water bath of 15 minutes in length. This was followed by soaking in a wet sheet for at least an hour. After that she took a second plunge bath and then walked outdoors until breakfast at 7 a.m., which was followed by a cold shower. Twelve glasses of water were to be consumed per day, as Priessnitz felt water brought "bad stuff" out of the system.

Axy remained at New Graefenberg for only two numbing days. She said she had never been so cold in her life. Thoroughly cleansed but weak, Axy proceeded to Troy, where the warmth expressed by Benjamin Starbuck's hearty group embraced her with such high esteem that she acquiesced to their appeal for a three-month stay. The comfort and hospitality of the Starbuck home provided a restful headquarters.

Troy seemed to be as good a place as any for Axy to alight that November. Starbuck had earlier told her to "remember Troy and that it is just exactly in the center of the World." To be more exact, Troy had been built along the Hudson River and was connected to Lake Erie by the Erie Canal, which had been opened for business twenty-five years before. In addition to Spiritual interests, Axy was attracted to Troy as it was home to the Emma Willard School, founded in 1814, one of the very first institutions in the country to provide higher education for women. Typically, she wished to learn everything at once and enrolled in a series of classes in fine art.

In the daytime I paint and evenings I knit. I am learning
Grecian and Oriental Painting, also water colors and coloring

*Lithographs. I intend also before I am ready to leave here to
learn to cut paper flowers and to bronze statues.*

Evenings when she was not painting or lecturing she knit stockings
for the poor, did needlework, or composed children's short stories or
philosophical pieces for newspapers. Long hours were spent
responding to requests for future appearances.

Marriage proposals continued to arrive and perhaps imprudently,
she shared a select few with the Starbucks for their amusement:

Madam,

I presume you recollect the subject I introduced to you last Spring.
In continuation of the same I will say, that I wish to
get me a wife in whose bosom I can find a congenial soil,
on which to plant my affections.

The Spiritualists in Troy begged Axy to make Troy her permanent
residence. "You are the only one that can give full satisfaction in our
pulpit," Starbuck claimed. "We have got so used to being well fed
that we can't go back to the precarious and often cold vitals food
dealt out by the majority of those who go around lecturing. I am
sober serious and in earnest now Miss Sprague and want to engage
you for just as long a time as we can, <u>the longer the better</u>."

She had inspired a group of local Spiritualists to gather clothing
and food for delivery to the poor Irish immigrants in that city. "Well,
there is no knowing what you will have to answer for," Starbuck
wrote in his usual jocular style later that month, addressing her as
Achsa the Priestess. "You, Miss Sprague, are the one most to blame
for all this for if it had not been for you all would have gone on
quietly and we would not have been troubled with expending seventy
or eighty dollars for these poor starving wretches and carrying them
as much more value in clothing which has been furnished by others
who have been induced to do so by *your reckless* example."

November 17, 1856, on her 29th birthday, Axy noted in her diary:

> *Here and there like an Oasis in the Desert the green spots of*
> *memory stand forth amid my wanderings, and although some*
> *dark spots are to be seen, some desert wastes, yet summed in one*
> *brief sentence, <u>I have been very happy</u>. I have been much with*
> *strangers, yet I have always found friends. I have been with the*
> *wretched and suffering, but I have <u>tried</u> to soothe their agony. I*
> *have heard many a tale of a broken heart, but I have striven to*
> *bind them and give unto them the balm of consolation.*

By that time I had been away from our Vermont hamlet for two years. I set out from Fond du Lac by railroad on December 11 to join Axy in Troy, where I planned to greet the Starbuck family, and then travel together with my sister to the Notch. My meager teacher's salary barely covered my fare but I was dreadfully homesick and wished to see Father one more time.

> *I have been half-expecting my sister from Wisconsin . . . and*
> *have been going to the cars to meet her and shall do so today, to*
> *go home with me to-morrow as I shall spend a few days at home.*
> *Mother reports that Father is still comfortable.*

I was slowed by a snowstorm in Michigan which delayed my train, but it was agreeable to share my sister's companionship once again and to see our family. Father was still ailing. Axy complained about her sore throat. Still, I learned of more benevolent issues that were competing for her attention. The abominable conditions of prisons had already piqued her interest, but now she was becoming more fervent in her crusade for the cause of Woman's Rights and the plight of the poor slave.

My stay in Vermont lasted only a few short weeks. I had much to discuss with my sister, brought about by gaps in her sometimes less-than-edifying letters.

One snowy afternoon while packing my trunk for my return, Axy sorted through her wardrobe and bestowed upon me several of her dresses. Anything elaborate would be unseemly in my rustic school, but those sewn of sturdy fabrics were prized as my wardrobe was becoming threadbare on my meager salary.

She handed me a folded paisley shawl and when I shook it out to re-fold the garment, a few small slips of paper floated to the floor. I picked them up and began reading aloud, "What are the wild waves saying," when Axy hastily grabbed them from me with unexpected delight and brought the pages to her lips.

"I thought these had been lost," she whispered with tear-brimmed eyes.

I waited silently, not wanting to meddle, but of course awaiting an explanation.

"Let's sit down on the bed," Axy finally said.

Then she told me of her initial meeting with John H. Crawford aboard the little steamship on her way to Philadelphia that rainy evening. Her feelings for him were so favorable, my sister confessed, that she would gladly have given up her earlier pledge to remain single if she had met a man like Mr. Crawford who was unmarried, of course!. I plied her with questions, but she was unable to even tell me the color of his eyes.

"It was dark, my Darling Sister. Rainy and dark. I cannot relate details of his personal appearance, only that he was a perfect gentleman with a calming voice and a most considerate manner."

"And you spent the entire night with him on the deck?"

"Yes, the entire night." Here she smiled an enigmatic smile, and retreated into memory. I thought it best to leave the room and allow her the blessed gift of reverie.

As I bade goodbye to return to Wisconsin, my sister came as far as Troy, where we stayed overnight with the Starbucks. She remained there for much of January and February. In March she was called to lecture again in Boston, where she wrote to Benjamin Starbuck that she was *floating, floating, upon the waves of time*, and that she would *never tire of the world as long as I can make one person happy*. She had already lectured for three Sundays at Music Hall, and made a brief reference to the puzzling accusations of dishonesty that continued to dog her there. As she had protested previously, why would she go through the trouble of memorizing her lectures when they came to her easily and unbidden while entranced?

April found Axy in Portland, Maine, where she had lectured exactly one year before. Her next visit, to Providence, Rhode Island, would be her first of many in that city. She lectured in Providence for five Sundays in May.

We had distant Sprague relations in Providence whom none of us had ever met: The A & W Sprague Manufacturing Company was the largest calico printing textile mill in the world. Our prosperous Sprague cousins also owned the Providence streetcar system, manufacturing and printing plants in the Pawtuxet Valley, and had investments in mills and mill sites all the way from Maine to Georgia. Because of the recent economic depression and since she had no idea how they felt about Spiritualism, we agreed it would be premature for her to introduce herself to our cousins at this time.

But Providence proved truly providential, for Axy was finally able to answer her personal quests for Temperance and Prison Reform:

> <u>*Saturday, May 30*</u>. *I spoke before the Hope Division of the Sons of Temperance one evening and to the women in the States Prison twice. I have long had an earnest desire to speak in the Prison but a way has never before offered. I should like to have spoken to the men as well as women, but thought I would not ask <u>too much</u> at once.*
>
> *The Warden, his mother and the Matron treated me with much kindness. The Warden's answer to me when I asked to be permitted to speak to the prisoners I think is worthy of note. He did not ask me, as many might have, "Do you believe in the Bible, do you acknowledge the atonement, are you a Christian," but simply says these words so greatly important in their meaning, "I suppose you do not intend to say anything to make the prisoners any <u>worse</u>." What want of a <u>longer</u> Catechism? Did*

it not contain the whole Gospel to Humanity? When will the time come that Reformers can enter <u>any</u> <u>where</u> to teach the erring and blind with only this <u>pass word</u>. When will the making people better be the great effort of the world, instead of making them Catholics, Protestants, &c, &c, &c.

It's no wonder that her victory in gaining admittance to the Rhode Island State Prison was a source of such satisfaction. The building, constructed in 1838, had a reputation as a gruesome place that one contemporary newspaper called "of all prisons the most prisonlike in outward show, dreary to see, dreary in history." It was notorious for the stench of sewage and although it was designed for solitary confinement, each 6 x 10-foot cell held two prisoners apiece and reminded my sister of a cage. Many of the prisoners were recent Irish immigrants who had been arrested for petty crimes but punished with harsh sentences. Although women were made to share a cell, they were not housed separately from the men and spent their days mending the male prisoners' clothes.

Her next diary entry, dated a week later, was made in Philadelphia. where she completed her report on Providence. She had previously been denied an opportunity to see the famed actor, Edwin Forrest, but was granted another prospect. Our Puritan background still influenced her observations:

> <u>Monday, June 8</u>. *I went to see Forrest play the Gladiator when in Providence. If everybody played like Forrest and the stage was <u>elevating</u> in its tendency I should enjoy it very much, but as it is I seldom go. I wish it might be different and that it could become an instrument of good, as it is now of evil.*

Dr. Henry Teas Child again hosted my sister during her visit to Philadelphia. He had a large medical practice and a massive personal library.

> <u>Friday, June 12</u>. *There is a beautiful reader in the family where I am stopping, and we have had such glorious evenings reading Shelley, Tennyson, Lowell, &c. But I find that I am <u>public</u>*

> *property, and shall be obliged in great degree to bid goodbye to the quiet happiness of listening to the poets and enter into the realities of life. Well, it is right to mingle in life's realities. Life would have no Ideality were it not for its* <u>real</u>.

Dr. and Mrs. Childs were Abolitionists, united in their radical politics with Philadelphia's Quakers and progressive thinkers. On Thursday afternoon, June 11, Ellen Child escorted my sister to a meeting of the Antislavery Society of Women, where Axy was elated to be introduced to one of our personal heroines, Lucretia Mott. As girls, we had thrilled to read of Mott's role in organizing the Seneca Falls meeting for Woman's Rights in 1848 with Susan B. Anthony and Elizabeth Cady Stanton, so this was truly an especial satisfaction.

> <u>*Friday, June 12*</u>. *I yesterday attended an Antislavery meeting of women, where I met Lucretia Mott. She is a very pleasant looking elderly lady and being of the Society of Friends, dresses in the plain style. Her conversation is very agreeable, and her whole soul seems to be enlisted in the cause of humanity. Their meeting was held at the Antislavery Office, and they reported that for the last two weeks, the fugitive slaves that had come there for help to Canada had averaged two a day. Horrible indeed is the necessity that compels the poor Negro to fly like a hunted deer to the land of Kings, for that freedom which he* <u>*cannot find amid*</u>
> <u>*The land of the free, and the home of the brave*</u>.

Although raised a Quaker, Mott told Axy she now "felt a far greater interest in the moral movements of our age than in any theological discussion," and was active in the Underground Railroad. She had also pledged to abstain as far as possible from slave-grown products and supply her family with "labor-free groceries, and, to some extent, with cotton goods unstained by slavery."

(I later speculated to my sister by mail, that Mott's pledge might exclude the products of our Sprague cousins in Providence with their mammoth calico textile mill which, we knew, utilized massive amounts of slave-picked cotton.)

Also through the efforts of Dr. Child, Axy was able to gain admittance to the Gothic fortress known as Eastern States Penitentiary. The largest building in America, the penitentiary is located within a few blocks of the art museum and its crenellated granite walls encompass a ten-acre site. The European-influenced spoke-and-wheel design of the building is one of America's biggest tourist attractions. Charles Dickens visited there during his 1842 tour of America and wrote of the intense suffering and cruelty he encountered among the inmates. This was the nation's first and only total solitary confinement institution; the Quaker social conscience feels the best way to make "penitent" prisoners is to isolate them from society, so the only personal contact a prisoner has is with the prison physician or the clergy.

On Sunday, June 14, 1857, Axy spoke at Sansom Street Hall in the morning and then went, accompanied by some half dozen friends, to the Prison and spoke in the Women's Department. The Officer treated her with much kindness and gave her the privilege of coming any time and conversing with the prisoners as much as she chose.

Finally entering such a forbidding edifice she felt both both exhilaration and despair in equal measure. The massive Gothic ramparts were designed to deter people from such acts as might land them there, even though women were often jailed for petty street crimes and something called "crimes against chastity or decency," such as lewd and lascivious carriage, stubbornness, vagrancy, and drunkenness.

In addition to prisoners, the thick walls also confined the squalid odor of human waste. At first the stench seemed so unmitigating that Axy doubted she could go any further without becoming sick. Then she thought, what must it be like to be locked up there day in and day out, sometimes for crimes that were no worse than stealing a loaf of bread to feed one's starving children?

The officer guiding them said that all prisoners entering the building were given wool clothing with a number sewn on and each was masked with a hood that resembled a burlap bag so the prisoner would not become familiar with the prison's layout. This also ensured anonymity. No prisoner was ever to see or communicate with another. The guards wore stockings over their shoes when doing their rounds to ensure a stealthy tread. Except for a Bible, inmates were not allowed reading materials, nor were they to make any sound whatsoever. If he or she was caught singing or whistling or talking, the prisoner would be deprived of dinner for an entire week or taken to the dungeon.

"What if I were so confined and you heard me whisper?" Axy asked of the guard.

"It would be the *iron gag* for you, Miss," he said sternly, and proceeded to demonstrate. "This device is placed over your tongue. Then your hands are crossed and tied behind your back as high as your neck. Then the iron gag around your tongue is chained to your hands and it is locked. Miss, I don't believe you'd be of a mind to whisper any more!"

As they were led through the stone labyrinth a most eerie silence festered and the walls were pressing in. Behind each door, Axy knew, there were men who might as well have been buried alive. The women's section was equally deplorable.

Shunned and outcast, women were bestowed a greater stigma than any male prisoner. So-called "decent" women were not normally allowed to speak to them, which gave my sister all the more determination to persist in her pledge. The prison chaplain, who joined them, told her that because a pure nature comes naturally to woman, "the female criminal therefore falls from a higher point of perfection. Thus she sinks to a more profound depth of misery than man."

Axy could not believe what she was hearing and seeing. Each woman was detained in a solitary cell where food and needlework were delivered daily. They would remain in this barren cell for the entire length of their sentence, wearing the same gray wool dress encrusted with grime, and bathing in a single basin of filthy water that was placed in one corner of the room. When the guard introduced her to each he insisted on asking, "Are you happy here?" Each woman solemnly nodded her head.

In the past, an imprisoned woman might look forward to accepting her punishment and being redeemed, but a new moral standard has created this new category that assigns a greater stigma toward them than any male prisoner receives. These "Fallen Women," or "Soiled Doves," are shunned and outcast. Men despise them and decent women are not allowed to speak to them. That did not deter my sister.

Women reformers such as Axy who were brave enough to reach out to female prisoners found that the "fallen" were not necessarily as depraved as one may have been led to believe; instead the prisoner may have been dragged down by a worthless husband or fallen victim to a ruthless employer. Frequently men were indicted for causing their "fall."

Thursday, June 18. I went to the Prison on Monday. I went only into the women's department and did not begin to get among all. It was sad to hear the stories they told, many of them so utterly untruthful. I must confess that I came away from these Sisters of Misery thoroughly disheartened, feeling as though I never wanted to go to a prison again. But the feeling is gone now and I am going again today. Perhaps I can do no good, but I can at least try.

Sunday, June 21. I have to day spoken in the Men's department in the Prison. Several of the Officers were in and several people beside. All this meeting of different orders breaks down prejudice. If I could feel as though one seed was dropped to day that would take root, I should feel very happy. We can't tell. I must rest upon the great law that inevitably brings a good result, from a good effort. This is my hope in such an almost hopeless field as the Prison and Penitentiary.

While passing through the Men's department a few days ago we went to a part of the Prison, the officer told me he called Purgatory. And well was it worthy of its name. Here were kept such as were brought in raving mad with liquor, and those that were suffering from its effects. Some were lying on the floor *asleep from its effects, others half paralyzed, and such gaunt, ghastly looking faces; others were sitting up with such a vacant stare, bruised faces and black eyes, effects of a recent broil, while one young man suffering from delirium tremens was looking in the utmost dread of snakes, and every hideous thing (with handcuffs on) and sometimes such horrible shrieks and yells told the suffering that no tongue can describe. He could not have been over twenty three. Dreadful, dreadful, and yet, though such things are enacted day after day (the very rack and torture of human suffering) still the <u>distiller</u> goes singing at his work, the rum seller tempts his victim, the law says let it be so, and only imprisons the poor sufferer because it has fallen in the snare while the world stands coldly by to <u>condemn</u> the poor victim, and take to the very bosom of society the very men that <u>made them what they</u> are.*

When Axy departed Philadelphia for New York, an admirer wrote, "I could scarcely endure the sight of the carriage as it rolled down the street, bearing you away, without a word passing between us. I returned home with a sad heart reflecting upon your life."

Here my sister's daily journal entries came to an end.

8

A Convention of Moral Lunatics

(1857–1858)

T HE NAME ACHSA W. SPRAGUE began to appear on the masthead of *The World's Paper* in the summer of 1857. It was a new bi-weekly Spiritualist newspaper published in Sandusky, Vermont, by A. C. Estabrook and Daniel Tarbell. She supplied *The World's Paper* with original poems by "Bell," a column "Notes By the Wayside" written under Achsa Sprague, and several anonymous articles on subjects of her choosing. "Bell" also contributed children's stories to The Children's Corner. "Solitarie" had an occasional byline.

In addition to writing for them, Axy was expected to obtain subscriptions. I purchased one at once, and everything I came across that she could have authored was clipped and given a space in my scrapbook. I especially enjoyed personal accounts of her travels, and her thoughts on topics of the day.

At the invitation of Dr. Robert Hallock, the Quaker whose luxurious cottage she had visited in the Adirondacks, Axy attended the weekly gathering of the New York Council of Spiritualists in that city on July 21. Hallock suggested this question for discussion: "What is Mediumship, or wherein do Mediums differ from the rest of us?" The topic was of profound interest to all, including Mr. Whitman, a slender man in his late thirties, seated in the front and dressed in the uniform of a journeyman carpenter. His long legs extended far into the aisle. Dr. Hallock whispered to Axy that Mr. Whitman had just assumed the post of editor of the *Brooklyn Daily Times*.

Whitman confessed that he was fascinated with the phenomenon of trance mediumship, having tried—but failed—for the past twelve months to become a medium himself. He especially wished to get a clear idea of what particular constitution, temperament, quality, or condition was requisite. His physician attributed the combination of a rapidly moving brain in a slow-moving, rather lethargic body to occasional headaches, his only ailment. "I sincerely admire the ability of a trance lecturer to extemporize from a speaker's platform on any subject," he said.

At the urging of Dr. Hallock and Mr. Whitman, Axy took the podium to address the subject in question. Entranced, her words and poem came easily:

> *For years I prayed for speech to tell the thought*
> *That burned within my soul, with beauty fraught;*
> *And though it thrilled my being with a spell,*
> *I could not speak it, had no power to tell.*
> *But in an hour when all was hushed and still,*
> *My soul woke up with strange and sudden thrill;*
> *It seemed, the voice of every greenwood tree,*
> *And rill, and star, and wave, conversed with me.*
> *And Nature stood revealed before me then,*
> *In grandeur that I cannot lose again…*
>
> *And when I stand before thee as to-night,*
> *All round me falls a mantle of delight,*
> *And through my mind there comes a power divine,*
> *As though superior minds were blent with mine.*

Mr. Whitman expressed his gratitude to Axy and wanted to know if the "superior minds" of departed spirits gave her this power. She assured him that she felt they did. The man appeared rather Bohemian and gazed down at her with a sleepy sort of look but seemed markedly entertained by her description of spirit-writing and the fact that she was a published poet. There then ensued between them a lively discussion of spirit versus matter.

"For me," Mr. Whitman said, "I see no object, no expression, no animal, no tree, no art, no book, but I see, from morning to night and from night to morning, the *spiritual*. Bodies are all spiritual. All words are spiritual—nothing is more spiritual than words."

At that point it was late and Dr. Hallock was at Axy's elbow.

"As a gesture of my gratitude, I would like to send you some of my own writings, with your permission," Mr. Whitman said.

The next day, a package addressed to Axy was delivered to the Hallock residence containing *Leaves of Grass*. Tucked inside the book was a printed sheaf of new poems and a note from Mr. Whitman inviting her reactions to his work. He added, the "grass" of the title was slang for the silly things compositors were apt to invent when things at work became stale.

The poems were like none she had ever read before.

Intrigued, Axy purchased another copy of the slender book of poetry before leaving New York. If she found the courage to do so, she would send the new volume to Mr. Crawford. One of Whitman's poems, "Poem of Perfect Miracles," was uniquely relevant, as it mentioned the sea and waves:

> To me, every hour of the light and dark is a miracle,
> Every inch of space is a miracle,
> Every square yard of the surface of the earth is spread with the same...
> To me the sea is a continual miracle,
> The fishes that swim—the rocks—the motion
> Of the waves—the ships, with men in them
> —what stranger miracles are there?

But several of the poems could be read as provocative to some extent ("or sleep in the bed at night with any one I love") and she felt Mr. Crawford or his wife might think her shamefully forward.

Later, she would learn that such esteemed publications as *The Christian Spiritualist* (1856) had spoken highly of Whitman as "a son of the people, rudely, wildly, and with some perversions," yet called

Leaves of Grass "a remarkable volume," advising "our friends who are not too delicately nerved, to study the work as a sign of the times, written as we perceive, under powerful influxes, a prophecy and promise of much that awaits all who are entering with us into the opening doors of a new era."

Axy had not been back to Plymouth Notch for any length of time since the previous February. She seldom complained, but the discomforts of travel, lumpy straw-filled beds, uncertain meals, the problem of laundry, lack of privacy and personal hygiene in the homes where she was put up, continuing problems with her throat, requests for appearances that she was reluctant to turn down—it was definitely time for a brief respite at home.

Consumption continued to plague Father, who was more defenseless than she had ever known him to be. Reversing the roles of our childhood, she sat by his bedside to read to him. Although he drifted in and out of consciousness, she hoped that he could absorb her words of comfort.

September found her lingering there, although she made short forays to Londonderry and to Weston, where brother William and his wife Anne now lived. She wrote to me, praising the October panorama. I became quite wistful for my mountain home and its crazy-quilt autumn of oranges, yellows, and reds.

She spent the remainder of the month in Portland, Maine. Mother forwarded a letter to me:

> *Portland, Maine October 26, 1857*
>
> *Dear Mother,*
>
> *I received your letter & am sorry that father is not so well, but not so sorry as I am that he will not try to live <u>worthy</u> of the <u>light</u> he has.*

How do you feel at the approach of winter? I expect you will enjoy yourself this winter better than usual, with your reading & determination not to depend upon company for happiness. I want when you write, that you should tell me <u>particularly</u> how you get along, & I hope Malvina will do her <u>very best</u> this winter.

I have just closed my engagement at Portland. You may direct my next letter to care of Dr. H. F. Gardner, Fountain House, Boston, Mass. & after that to Providence, R.I. care of Rufus Read No. 74 Pine Street, as I am to be there soon after being at Lowell.

We are having a severe storm today. The rain pours in torrents. I wonder if it reaches you. And the wind blows too. But there will be pleasant days after it, so who cares for a little storm. I am in a comfortable home for the present, & I hope you are as well.

One day last week I rode out through Westbrook Cemetery, a very pleasant place, & then to the Reform School for boys. I think those schools are a great improvement from sending them to prison.

Friday I attended the County Fair that was held here, & saw in the Hall of Display some very pretty fancy articles you would like. The President of the Society (with whom I am acquainted) treated me with a great deal of attention, played me some music from the musical instruments, &tc, & I had quite a pleasant time. I had an invitation from one of the "Members" to attend the "Mechanic's Festival" that evening, but as I was engaged, I could not go

My health is very good; how is yours? I like the people where I am stopping very much indeed. They are very kind to me.

28th. I start for Lowell tomorrow. Our storm is hardly over yet. I wrote to Celia a few days ago. I have sent you each another World's Paper. I don't know as you remember that "Bell" is my signature, and "Solitarie," too. But you need not tell any one else. I shall expect to get a letter from you at Boston, on my way to Providence.

A. W. Sprague

When she was called to appear in a particular city, admirers quarreled among themselves for the privilege of providing her room and board. Typically, her hostess sent in a tray with toast, perhaps a little fruit, as she often rose early to attend to her writing. This also offered her needed privacy; a woman, traveling alone was not expected to join the family at the breakfast table. After a hot water bath (if available), she dressed and if the weather was congenial, went for a morning walk. More correspondence and reading followed, either in her room or another quiet place when one could be found.

Frequently, as in Providence, Axy was expected to give both an afternoon and an evening lecture. She preferred a rest afterward to recoup her strength, but during her November 1857 visit to that city she was besieged by interruptions and well-meaning friends made demands upon nearly every moment of her free time. She had left her comb in New Jersey that summer; when she left Providence she forgot her gloves and scissors.

Somehow she found time to embroider a scarf for me as I braved the advent of Wisconsin's winter, and it was mailed it from Rhode Island with the accompanying note:

Providence, December 10

Dear Sister C.

I send you as a Christmas present this scarf, which is the work of my own hands, those hands that were so long almost helpless.

*   And if these flowers that I have woven from time to time as I have had leisure, remind you of those you made for me when hour by hour you stood beside my pillow and held my head and combed my hair and helped me to try to bear the <u>thorns</u>; if they speak to you anything of my gratitude for those past favors when I had no hope to be able to ever return <u>any</u> of them; I shall not have traced them in vain. I have enjoyed embroidering this scarf very much, for my tears of gratitude to the Great Giver of <u>Spirited Flowers</u> have been like the dew as they have sprung up beneath my fingers. May they be like the cheerful eyes of friends to you this winter when the flowers of earth are dim.*

Your affectionate sister,

A. W. Sprague

P.S. Father was not quite so well when Mother wrote last. Why haven't you answered my last? My address until the middle of Dec. will be 69 Sixth Street, Philadelphia, Pa.

She lectured the first and second Sundays of December in Philadelphia. The Eastern States Penitentiary was paid several more visits and again she was welcomed at the home of Dr. and Mrs. Childs.

On December 19, Axy spoke in the Sewell Street Church, in Salem, Massachusetts. On a whim, which she later humorously blamed on the effect of mischievous witches, she wrapped *Leaves of Grass* and posted it to Mr. Crawford in care of Northern Transportation, Ogdensburgh, New York. She enclosed a card signed only *An Admirer,* and underlined the following:

Of the wave—the ships, with men on them—
—What stranger miracles are there?

When viewed in retrospect, Axy's reunion with John Crawford could be seen as a "stranger miracle" than anything mentioned in Whitman's "Poem of Perfect Miracles." Their paths would cross again in autumn of 1858. The year of our father's death.

Axy had been in Baltimore at the time of Father's final decline, and she was scheduled to speak next in our nation's capital. The Baltimore visit had been arranged by Washington Danskin, who had requested his friend, Dr. Childs of Philadelphia, to "let Miss Sprague come to us." Danskin said he and his wife would entertain her presence at their home, No. 11 North Eaton Street.

Baltimore is the third largest city in the United States and my sister had never traveled so far south. Colonel Danskin, whom Axy described as having a full head of black hair, a long nose, and a black trencher beard that formed a semicircle from ear to ear, greeted her wearing a brilliant red paisley cape (perchance advertising his Gentleman's Furnishing Store). He said had been investigating Spiritualism for three and a half years, during which time he wrote and published a book in which he presented theological ideas that been dictated to him by two "who have long been dwellers in the land of light [and] passed the *thoughts* to my mind; I clothed them with the drapery of language."

From her sober demeanor, Axy initially assumed Mrs. Danskin was more severe than her husband. A large woman, she inevitably wore a dark dress with a white lace collar and a lace cap whose ties hung to her chest beneath a double chin and very long nose. Her small eyes appeared even smaller behind her spectacles. But Sarah Ann Ridgway Danskin had acquired a reputation as a charitable medium with a special talent for contacting those spirits who were "dark" or "undeveloped," meaning criminals, even murderers. She allowed them to return and manifest to earth the deplorable wreckage that crime and ignorance had made of their souls. Friends who had witnessed such events said interviews with such suffering earth-bound beings were often thrilling.

Thrice-weekly circles were held at the Danskin home, at which twelve to fifteen spirits might appear in the space of an hour. At one such sitting, the spirit of Edgar Allan Poe overtook the Colonel and delivered this acrostic poem:

> Earth had no joys for me,
> Dark was my fate below,
> Grief, like the boundless sea,
> And limitless as woe,
> Rolled o'er the poet. —POE

Axy had gone south expecting warmth, only to experience wet snow and a brisk northeast wind. She opened her Baltimore lecture series speaking twice on Sunday, December 19, at the Law Buildings on the corner of Lexington and St. Paul. She spoke there twice again the following Sunday, December 26, and was scheduled to lecture twice more, a week after that.

The Danskins were delighted to comply with Axy's wish for a tour of Washington City landmarks. Our nation's capital was at that time a city in transition but distinctly southern and encircled by slave states. She was appalled to learn that many residents of that city still owned slaves. Moreover, she was disappointed to see that our nation's capital resembled nothing so much as an unsavory swamp populated with office-seekers and hustlers, and pigs that rooted for garbage on mostly unpaved streets. In fact, Washington City reeked so of sewage that she had to press a handkerchief to her nose. Everywhere she saw Negroes lounging, waiting for their masters. She told me afterward she had never witnessed such disturbing sights.

President James Buchanan resided in an imposing White House. From the modest comfort of the Danskins' carriage the couple pointed out the venerable Smithsonian Institution, the Treasury, the General Post Office, and the Library of Congress. But the Capitol Building was still under construction and appeared almost comical without a dome, without columns, surrounded by lumber, blocks of marble, odds and ends and workmen's sheds.

The Washington Monument was also wretched to behold. The obelisk had languished, unfinished since work stopped in 1855, and resembled nothing more than a big white stump. After six years' effort, it now reached a height of only one hundred and seventy-four feet. Chunks of marble contributed by various states had been rudely exposed to the weather, some had been spirited away, and the marble cutting shop was reported to be a downright wreck, too far gone for repair. Despite the hard economic times, Col. Danskin assured Axy, construction would soon resume as only recently the government had placed boxes in Post Offices across the country to receive donations for its completion.

Of course my sister would wonder aloud at the folly and extravagance of such an undertaking, asserting her opinion that perhaps it would have been better to furnish ten or one hundred thousand homes for as many poor families.

Mrs. Danskin patted her hand and suggested she might find Washington City much brighter with the advent of the social season on New Year's Day, when a festive winter reception would be held that afternoon at the Executive Mansion, hosted by President Buchanan (a bachelor), to whom she would be formally presented. His popular niece, Harriet Lane Johnson, would preside as hostess. Despite my sister's protestations of an insufficient wardrobe for such a gala, Mrs. Danskin insisted they'd find a dress in time as she *must* accompany them! After that event the social swing would be in full force; afternoon levees and "at homes," musicales and dinners would clog the weekly calendar with fashionable events.

Baltimore Spiritualists reportedly found Axy's lectures "modest, yet earnest," and requested that her engagement be extended through January 24. My sister was agreeable, and even conceded to attend the White House party on New Years' Day. But an urgent telegram received on New Year's Eve from Uncle Thomas Moore rescued her from that potentially taxing event and plunged her into another: Father was near death. She must return to Vermont.

Axy watched over Father's sick bed for nearly three weeks; Mother had her hands full nursing him while handling Nathan and Malvina, both of whom were disturbed by the anxious concern posed by another death imminent in our household. Orvilla was still in her own state of deep grief over the loss of her two young daughters. I was teaching my winter term and hoped our sister Sarah would be able to join Axy. But she and Nathaniel Randall had moved to St. Johnsbury, where he had opened a jewelry store close to the hotel where they now resided. She wrote that although she had initially decided to come to Plymouth if Father died, "upon more deliberate consideration as it is not possible for the Dr. [Nathaniel] to go, I think it will be *wiser* for me not to go although my inclination would lead me to go but write me immediately upon his departure and as often as you can to let me know how he is."

Nathaniel added a typically rambling postscript with an audacious request of Axy:

> I want you some time to get your "prity face" ambrotyped large size (some of your good friends will see it as a favor) & let us have it, for many of our friends that here speak of you would like a chance to see the picture of the 2nd Madonna. Now don't flatter your self that I think Mary was better looking than my Sister for I do not.

As repugnant as ever, our brother-in-law was most likely again liberally dosing himself with laudanum now that he had abandoned his interest in homeopathy. Marenda Randall had hinted of this tendency and we had warned Sarah. Axy told me she was relieved that he would not be coming to Plymouth Notch with side-effects from a drug that caused extreme salivation and trembling, episodes of dementia. How Sarah tolerated Nathaniel's harangues and drooling we never knew. But her apologies for her husband's loathsome behavior never ceased; "2nd Madonna," indeed!

Charles Sprague, born in Plymouth on October 23, 1794, died on Thursday, January 21, 1858. The editor of *The World's Paper* asked Axy for an obituary.

> **CHARLES SPRAGUE** aged 63 years. His health has been poor for years, and with the slow disease of consumption passed on to a brighter home. It is a beautiful hope that can give to one so skeptical as Mr. S. was, a light in the future; here a man of uncommon talent had discerned plainly that the theories of the churches were not true, had turned away in disgust, and said in his own heart, "There is no God, no hope, no hereafter." But the light given him through his dutiful daughter did give him a gleam of hope and with a loving adieu he passed on. Many are they that loved him for his decision of character, manliness of speech, and often was he the pacifier of broils that might otherwise have been a mar to those around.

Axy mentioned the ordeal in her newspaper column "Notes by the Wayside."

Plymouth Vt. Feb. 8, 1858

I have been LINGERING by the "Wayside" since I wrote to you last at the sick bed of my Father, who on my hasty return from the South I found just
> *"Waiting to take that one step more*
> *That opens the celestial door*
> *And then with sudden splendor blind*
> *Hear the great portals close behind..."*

In a lengthy essay, she spoke of him as a "man of many sorrows" and ended by saying,

There is a <u>Great Within</u> to every human history, and strangely changed would human judgment be could it but read it right. And Invalids—so suffering, yet forgotten—would find their share of human sympathy.

But it was Axy's participation in Father's uncommon funeral service at the Notch church that brought about a fervent debate in *The Green Mountain Freeman,* as the memorial service *was* a far departure from the usual customs. And it was claimed by many who attended, that Axy had refused to cry.

To be fair, most of the mourners at Father's funeral had never experienced Axy's spirit-lectures. Thus they were stunned to be advised by Father (through Axy) that he was yet in their presence and spoke to them, by way of her inspired voice.

Men do not understand Great Nature's laws. Man willfully breaks these laws, trespasses with high hand or through his ignorance sinks deep within the dismal gulf, the noisome cell of sin. Because this Great Nature is something new, he who has not known it answers with sneers and scoffs.

"He" continued, quoting lines from Socrates and Plato.

The skepticism of unbelievers was not foreign to Axy. Nevertheless, the funeral was most peculiar for the Notch and some of Father's friends decried the "strange ceremonies" as being "not only a source of regret and mortification but a subject of general remark."

Mother said that even those who were shocked at Axy's wide departure were yet kind to our family. Many, however, were taken aback because Axy was not observed weeping.

"Spiritualism dries the fountain of tears," Axy explained. "It has not served to harden the heart or eradicate the tender affections of his daughter."

The *Green Mountain Freeman* called her belief "a wild enthusiasm," and "an absurdity that leads to nothing but absurdities." "Nothing is too incredible or absurd for a Spiritualist to believe," one letter to the editor exclaimed. "The greater the absurdity, the stronger his faith. If the *Spirit Power* of which the Spiritualists boast is so powerful a *narcotic* as to steep the affections—to drown the natural feelings of children toward their parents to such a degree that they can, unmoved and unconsciously chant spiritual melodies over their cold remains, have we not a right to call it in question?"

Axy told me she *had* shed many tears over Father's death; albeit in private, not in public. And she told me she cried mostly for herself, as she had not been able to help him see the light. She also wept for herself, that she must yet linger to buffet with the world.

Baltimore hoped for a return to complete her aborted visit, but "the Vermont winter is a mild one," she told friends, "and there is such a call from all parts of the State for lectures, with so few to supply that I have decided to remain for the present."

It is said by many that Spiritualism is "dying," Axy told readers of her column, *But if I were to judge by the audiences I have had in this section since my return and the calls I receive from all parts of the State, I should come to any other conclusion. I think there was never more interest in Vermont than at present and I am glad to see it so.*

With Father gone, our home was now more pleasant than it had been in years. Axy forwarded a clipping to me that had been sent to her by Col. Danskin from a Baltimore newspaper concerning a certain "Major Beale, the chivalrous Vermonter who just returned from his European tour." It seems that while in Paris, Beale challenged a French Colonel, "and the weapons being swords, at the first stroke, the Major's nose was severed close to his face. Hastily picking up and replacing the organ, he tied his handkerchief over it. After leaving the bandage for eleven days he removed it, when to his consternation he found that he had placed it wrong side up and it was now healed. Although it looks ugly, he finds it very convenient for taking snuff."

Unrelated as this was to my scrapbook's theme, it *had* come from my sister and provided a comic element.

She was not amused by receiving yet more letters from men, including one from a Mr. Parker who fantasized about her "in the quiet hours of night when all is hushed and still, when nature's sable curtains are hanging over the resting world and all around is quietly sleeping" including his wife. Mr. Parker admitted he felt love for her, "as 'free love' even? Well I must plead guilty to the last charge in part for all I give is free, perfectly free, without ever a thought of reward, without the least expectation of recompense in any way save the relief I find in revealing it to you."

Axy's said her reply to him was swift and emphatically cool. Eventually she heard from *Mrs.* Parker, to whom she then had to respond that feelings of Free Love for Mr. Parker were in no way mutual.

> *I wish you <u>could</u> know me, Mrs. Parker, you would know me as one who regards the feelings & rights of a wife as sacred. As one who never wishes to set foot upon their territory, or cast one shadow over their path. I never write to a married gentleman anything I am not willing his wife should read, & so vice versa.*

The complexities of Axy's travel arrangements and her itinerary for March and part of April 1858 were indicated in this handwritten schedule I recently came across in her papers:

Tuesday March 9—Swanton

Take Vt. Central Cars at 10 am Tuesday

Thursday March 11—Essex Centre

Leave Swanton morning train for Essex Junction and Seth Butes Esq will meet you at the Depot for Essex Centre.

Take Vt Central Cars Friday pm for Burlington.

Take cars Saturday 9 am for Vergennes

Sunday 14th Addison

Tuesday 16th at Ferrisburgh

Sunday 21st at Leicester

Sunday 28th at Burlington

Sunday 30th at Stowe

Thursday April 1—Waterbury

Friday April 2—Northfield

Our mailbox at the General Store could not hold all her mail, and she was hard-pressed to keep up her correspondence, tucking letters in her valise to answer while on the road.

Now her published writings seemed to be as eagerly sought after as her public appearances. An admirer wrote that she eagerly searched the papers for the words of "Bell," and "how well was I paid in the last issue, finding no less than six contributions." The issue spoken of was *The World's Paper*, March 12, 1858, where Bell's byline was attached to several poems, a children's story, and a lengthy article entitled "A Chapter on Invalids," in which she described sitting "by the side of one dearer than life itself," waiting for death to arrive, which (to me) sounded suspiciously as if Axy were writing about herself:

> *In the spring time of life, she was stricken from all that made life bright and beautiful, and year by year lay in her darkened room a helpless, hopeless Invalid for life.*

When she spoke in public before large crowds, the sore throat that plagued my sister earlier was aggravated and lingered. She kept in close touch with our remaining family at the Notch. Ephraim Moore, young son of Uncle Thomas and Aunt Athelia, wrote to her in late March with a report on events back home.

> Your mother is well she says she enjoys herself as well as any one should expect. The cow gets along well. The hens lay pretty well. I do not have any trouble in finding their nests. I have considerable many letters to carry up, all things are getting along well. It has not snowed much since you went. It looks like planting time, it is raining now very hard. The hills are all bare. We are now just getting out the sap tubs to go sugaring at Mr. Coolidge's sugar place.

Her lectures were delivered with more confidence, but that self-assurance only enhanced cruel rumors of memorization. Amanda Britt, the popular and extremely vocal medium from St. Louis, held forth to friends on Axy's rising popularity and "amazing memory." When Axy wrote to complain to me about this repeated denunciation, I attempted to reply in a jocular manner: "I think you are becoming exceeding giant-like in your physical and mental structure if you can *prepare* your discourses and speak them the same day, and so continue day after day. I think your internal and external woman must blend harmoniously or you would not be able to thus continue."

The remainder of my letter betrayed my own melancholy which I easily fell into, given my family's general disposition. I suppose I was a bit envious of my sister's achievements; I desperately wanted my life to be worthwhile; I yearned to find a purpose for living.

"Axy, you say you 'do not wait until you are a Beecher or a Joan of Arc, etc. etc. before you begin to act, but act that you may become like them.' Let me ask you what it is that causes you to act? Have you not something within that causes you to, and would it not be just as impossible for one who has received this interior propelling force to remain dormant as it is impossible for one to act who has not received it? Perhaps you will say that I ought to cultivate and unfold myself, develop the germ that is capable of being expanded, but as I receive little or no enjoyment in that, it has become a task to me and I feel tired at the thought of having anything to do…You say you try to be happy, etc. etc. Well, *I don't try*—for I have tried so much and find it (happiness) nought but a web of delusion which charms but to 'deceive.'"

My despondent thoughts may have been grist for her column in the next issue of *The World's Paper*, when Axy wrote about the "realities of life," and suggested that life "is almost too real, too hard in its requirements, too severe in its exactions."

I felt better when I began my school term in April, this time in Glen Beulah, a little town not far away. There had been quite a change in the place with a new railroad coming through, one general store, a boarding house, and several dwelling houses. The people intended to have a Post Office, although it was only two miles from the village of Greenbush.

The controversy of Free Love was sometimes alluded to in newspapers that reached Wisconsin. In early July, John M. Spear was quoted in *The Banner of Light* saying, "No set of men, no church, no state, no government shall withhold from me the right to re-beget myself when and under such circumstances as to me and any true woman seems fit and best."

I knew Axy was assisting with preparations for a very special gathering to be held in Rutland in late June. It promised to be an "all reform" convention that would seek ways to join forces among disparate progressive elements, including the Free Love advocates. Almost every prominent Spiritualist of Axy's acquaintance would be in attendance. Even Benjamin Starbuck was coming with his fellow musicians, The Troy Harmonists.

Sarah and husband Nathaniel Randall would be there; Jarius Josselyn and Orvilla, too. The Randalls would bring Mother along to Rutland and invited Axy to join them afterward on a visit to Saratoga. "What say, Achsa? Was you ever their?" Nathaniel wrote, "The season will be the very best & I shall not care to stay longer than one day. I guess you better go, unless you should be ashamed of your relatives."

In fact, The Rutland Free Convention of 1858 would become an historic event. *The Burlington Times* claimed the presence of the "Rutland Reformers" was

> a visitation more to be avoided than war, pestilence or famine, and deeply do we despise its first appearance within the borders of our State...This is the first time in the history of Vermont that her soil has been polluted, and her pure air poisoned, by the orgies of these demoniac men and obscene women from abroad, whose chief and more appropriate head-quarters has hitherto been amid the confusion and indifference of great cities, or in 'communities' or 'passional circles' of their own. We pray that Vermont may forever hereafter be free from their ill-omened visits.

The three-day convention quickly developed a carnival atmosphere. Rutland citizens did not go out of their way to welcome the "radicals," as the optimistic Vermont Spiritualists had hoped; they did not share rooms in their homes as requested, and newspapers rumored that when their prudent papas heard that the "Free-Love" Convention was inevitable in their vicinity, the good-looking young ladies were all sent out of town, "for fear of accidents."

Axy was in the thick of it. Elected one of several vice presidents of the convention, she was present at 10 a.m. for the initial morning session on Friday, June 25.

The Convention is held in a large canvas tent, which is pitched just outside the town," said *The New York Times*.

> The tent, on the east side of Grove Street is one hundred feet in diameter, and capable of holding about 2,500 people, but on the first morning there were not more than 350 or 400 people present. The noon trains, however, brought large reinforcements...The people of Rutland are very much opposed to the whole demonstration, and have recently held a series of prayer meetings, in which they especially besought the almighty to interpose 'the strong arm' to prevent the show.

Although they had signed on to appear at the event, William Lloyd Garrison and Wendell Phillips apparently had second thoughts. Nevertheless, at least twelve hundred people were present on Friday afternoon at what the national press insisted on calling "the radical encampment." The weather was sweltering, the tent stifling, and booths served lemonade, root-beer and ginger-pop to the thirsty crowd. Starbuck and his Harmonial Club steadfastly provided musical interludes.

A reporter for *The New York Daily Tribune* sneered,

> Aside from the speakers and active participators in the exercise, the men who lounge into the big tent, and lazily stretch themselves on the grass and chew straws while they listen with benevolent patience to the tirades from the platform, are as listless, lazy, unshorn and 'shiftless' looking as any set of unfortunates ever gathered into a crowd with the thermometer in a torrid

humor. As for the ladies who grace the assembly with their fair presence, aside from the publicly-known female advocates of Women's Rights and other Utopian luxuries, and who would not thank us to praise their beauty and accomplishments, a single remark will suffice. If any one of them should ever be accused of what people of carnal minds sometimes call 'good-looking,' not a jury in the land but would instantly acquit her of that unfounded charge, even though that jury were composed of a dozen very old bachelors with wigs and false teeth, who would be naturally enthusiastic on the subject of female beauty.

Axy did not speak until Friday evening. The hot summer day dragged tediously and the audience turned restless, freely shouting out interruptions during spirit lectures such as, "How long do you allow these chickens to peep?" and "Put him out!"

The intrepid *Times* reporter acknowledged,

> Miss SPRAGUE, came to the front of the platform. The spirits had a hard time of it to manage this female. She stood perfectly silent for some five minutes; the muscles of her face twitched; her lower limbs were unsteady; her hands moved spasmodically. She presently found the use of her tongue, and began the customary spiritual nonsense. I came away.

Had the twitchy fellow been more patient, he would have heard my sister address the crowd on the subject of prison reform. *The Banner of Light,* a Spiritualist newspaper published in Boston, quoted from her address in its July 3, 1858, issue:

> *Bondage is the fruit of error. Sin is bondage. Out of the grave of darkness and error, truth shall spring forth, and freedom with it. Learn what is great, what is good, and freedom shall follow.*

The much-anticipated subject of Free Love was raised the following day. *The New York Times* correspondent reliably divulged his titillation with his report:

> This has been a great day in the "Free Convention," both inside and outside the tent. In the face of a sun which did its utmost to discourage enthusiastic demonstrations, through the whole ran an under-current of Free-Love. It popped up in the midst of colloquies apparently most foreign to it, and the Free-Lovers, who are as thick as blackberries here, are chuckling to think that they have had the day to themselves, to the intense discomfiture and disgust of the red-hot Abolitionists, who have kept up a running skirmish, unsuccessfully striving to get the whip-hand of the Convention.

On July 29, *The New York Times* devoted its entire front page to the Rutland Convention. By Sunday, the closing day, an enormous crowd of 3,000 swelled the Convention site. When it finally adjourned, the gathering had been ridiculed as "A Convention of Moral Lunatics," by the Portland, Maine, *Advertiser*, and hostility reverberated as far away as Kansas and New Orleans.

The Davenport, Iowa, *Daily Iowa State Democrat* pronounced the convention a sacrilegious gathering of "all that is mean, all that is disgusting, all that is impudent." *The Mississippian Daily Gazette* referred to "masculine females and feminine males," and the Fayetteville, Tennessee, *Observer* titled their coverage, "Female Plug Uglies." Topics discussed were ridiculed by the *Daily Intelligencer* of Wheeling, Virginia: "While their hand is in, why not introduce some resolutions defining the precise position of the Convention on the old hen question, the diagnosis of stump-tail milk, the pathology of pork, and peregrinatory processes of green cheese."

"Right is Might," the theme of the convention, was even mocked by the editor of *The World's Paper*, who called it a "catch penny Convention" to be remembered only for the same old arguments "clothed with the usual degree of oratory, but in our opinion … sectarian in the extreme."

Benjamin Starbuck, who had sung "of the better time coming," called it a "Free Blow Convention." In an editorial, Walt Whitman wrote that at Rutland, "All the mental deformities and intellectual monstrosities of the Union were collected." If Mr. Whitman had, indeed, been present, Axy was thankful for the blessed lack of a personal encounter.

Mother returned to the Notch with the Josselyns, leaving Sarah and her husband with Axy. As proof of her extreme weariness, Axy surrendered to the odious Nathaniel Randall's request to join in their railroad excursion. "I don't blame you a bit for Husband-hunting at these Conventions, Sister Achsa," he teased. "Where *three thousand professed* Reformers get together, what a chance for an Old Maid to choose a partner, or offer *her* charms to the Reformers. Well, make haste, you can't *always* be young and beautiful!"

After the pandemonium in Rutland, Axy's reasons for traveling anywhere in the company of that lout remain an enigma to me so I am blaming it on fatigue. As promised, Nathaniel allowed the women to tour Saratoga, but after only a few sips of vile spring water at Congress Spring (and before Axy could show Sarah any of the luxuries of the grand resort) he anxiously steered them back to the depot to board the train to Brockport, New York, where he had once served as a journeyman watchmaker and where he and Marenda had been wed. Nathaniel was in a rush to introduce his new wife and "famous" sister-in-law to his brother, Myrick Ogilvy Randall.

Free of engagements for the next several weeks, Axy evidently saw no reason to resist a quick tour of Brockport, a village in the northwest corner of New York State on the Erie Canal. Nathaniel's restless agitation did not subside and almost immediately upon their arrival, he insisted on turning Sarah around to go back home with him. Axy stayed on, where she was given to feel very much at home. In her honor, M. O. Randall and family arranged for a spectacular excursion to Niagara Falls.

She would write an account of her first visit to Niagara in "By the Wayside," even though she was aware that *The rainbow hoop, the Maid in the Mist, the stairs, the waterfall, and the Indians, have all been described till no further changes can be rung on them.* Inquisitive readers were grateful for her first-hand impressions of the Suspension Bridge, Cave of the Winds, Table Rock, Horse Shoe Falls and the rainbows over the cataract. The little group arrived by train in time for breakfast at The Monteagle House, a hotel on the American side. Thence they made their way to Cedar Island, where they wandered through a thickly shaded grove of large trees to Street's Pagoda, a fifty-foot tower built of lattice-work that provided a panorama of the American Falls. The distant view was limited, but my sister—even with the encumbrance of her voluminous hoopskirt—made the climb to the top of the tower in triumph!

Myrick Randall later invoked memories of their visit to the Cave of the Winds, the major attraction, "a place that makes one feel his nothingness." His wife was too timid for the adventure but Axy, feeling quite buoyed after her achievement at Street's Pagoda, readily entered what looked like a sentry box at the precipice and descended the spiral staircase, followed by Myrick and his daughter. Only three people were allowed to maneuver the rickety stairs at one time. The roar of water was deafening as they came down three hundred feet to the base where they emerged to bend their course along a slender shelf until they reached an overhanging ledge of more than one hundred feet that produced a mammoth cavern, the famed Cave of the Winds. A rock fall on this very spot had severely injured a group of tourists a year ago. The cave was visible only when the wind blew away the mist. Any vocal expressions of wonderment vanished in dense clouds of spray that left the sightseers thoroughly drenched.

"In spirit, I now stand there with you," Myrick Randall later reminisced by mail, "receiving those things so sublime and beautiful, behold the blue above and the awful chasm beneath into which the liquid element is continually plunging, dancing, foaming, and re-echoing back, the voice of God, in thunderous tones."

Clearly, the man was impressed by Niagara Falls and not so subtly infatuated by my sister. *"Another 'Free Love nuisance,'"* she wrote to me afterward and quoted from the close of his letter where he confessed, "My spirit, having been attracted to Thee, by the powers invisible (over which *I feel* that I have no control), I have followed Thee in thy departure and wanderings, to the present moments," to which Axy added to me in jest, *"I am accursed!"*

Newspapers like *The Boston Courier* now commonly referred to Free Love as "Free Lust." Axy complained that married men were now all too eager to express their fervent affections and their "passional attraction."

July was spent quietly in the Green Mountains with Mother and Malvina. To allay any further comparisons with fallen women, Axy fashioned her garnet velvet dress from Hartford into a soft lap robe for Malvina. The abundance of fabric allowed for a shawl for Mother, too.

One quiet day she reached into her reticule and withdrew Mr. Crawford's business card. She determined that she would find a private corner and *psychometrize* the card to see if she could approximate the owner from his handwriting, as Semantha Mettler did. She softly closed the door to her bedroom and followed Mrs. Mettler's example. Holding the card to her forehead, she squeezed her eyes shut and tried to *see*.

What did she envision? Waves. Upon a great sea. Perhaps it was a trick of memory, referring to the song they had sung together. Waves. Overlapping waves, and the sounds they made when crashing onto a rocky shore.

Disappointed, she tucked the card away again and determined it was just as well. She who had assured many worried wives that she regarded "the feelings and rights of a wife as sacred," and promised

"I take the offered hand of friendship from no man if it is purchased at the expense of his wife's happiness," rebuked herself for trying to summon Mr. Crawford's psychometrical delineation.

Daily walks to the general store found the post office box stuffed with messages from devoted admirers who pronounced their now tedious and barely disguised infatuation. A lugubrious correspondent from Indiana who published *The Truth Seeker,* a Spiritualist newspaper, wrote proposing that she become his wife. An attorney from Montpelier whom Axy had met briefly at the Rutland Convention also sent an outright proposal of marriage. Mother fancied an attorney would possess exemplary husband material for an unmarried woman of thirty, but Axy was not interested, and there were still more proposals to set aside including a recent widower from Portland, Maine, who wrote that his recently departed wife would "rejoice to see one so worthy become the guardian of her loved children."

Benjamin Starbuck wrote from Troy, soliciting Achsa's personal impressions of Niagara. "When I visited there, my wife was by my side and together we rambled that day and drank in of the soul inspiring scenes." Starbuck worried that she was working too hard and advised her to get relaxation and recreation, to mix "occasionally with the gay throng, heartless though they may be."

"The Thing is Done," *The Banner of Light* claimed in tribute when the great Atlantic Cable was completed in early August of 1858. It took only one hour for President Buchanan to receive a cablegram from Queen Victoria expressing her satisfaction at the completion of the work so likely to preserve harmony between England and the

United States. Around the same time, the first overland mail delivered by the Pony Express required twenty-three days to travel from San Francisco to Saint Louis.

But our country had not yet pulled out of the financial panic of 1857, which had overwhelmed everyone with desperate financial unease. The United States Treasury was empty and the overall soundness of the nations' banks was in question. Wisconsin was not immune—undeveloped regions such as ours could not provide economic support for the railroads that had expanded here. Land speculation was collapsing, grain prices falling, rural areas suffering. Up until then we'd seen homes, stores, sawmills, and other businesses enthusiastically sprouting. But when the Panic hit, employees and investors were unable to obtain cash. Teachers were scarce and schools such as the one where I taught in Greenbush were overcrowded.

Tensions between North and South were becoming more and more extreme. Fearful rumors circulating in Wisconsin hinted that slave power might be extended to include German and Irish immigrants. Spiritualists were keeping an eye on Abraham Lincoln, who was debating Senator Douglas for a senate seat in Illinois. Lincoln opened his campaign in Springfield on June 17 by declaring that the Union "can not permanently endure half slave and half free."

⊹—✳—⊹

Axy warned me of her sense of apprehension when Spiritualists called together an assembly even more extravagant and potentially more controversial than the Rutland Free Convention. The gathering, planned for Utica, New York, in September, had been arranged for by Andrew Jackson Davis and his wife, Mary, to discuss "The Causes and Cures of Evil."

On September 11, a crowd of five thousand crammed into Mechanics' Hall. Almost immediately, the mayor of Utica was obliged to summon the sheriff and local police to control unruly mobs who attempted to disrupt the proceedings. The popular press enjoyed ridiculing the "Philanthropic Convention," which, they predicted "will prove considerable of a fizzle." As anticipated, news reports focused on the more sensational aspects, such as Free Love.

With what enthusiasm she could muster, Axy's "Notes by the Wayside" recounted the convention in an early October issue of *The World's Paper*.

> Go where I will I seem to be in a land of Conventions, until now, though not especially an admirer of such gatherings, I have just completed the cabalistic number of "seven" during the last three months, and this seventh will I think be my "last for the season." Now that I go to such places less to enjoy myself and more to learn; to be instructed not only by the speakers but those spoken to, and read mind, motives, etc., I like them better...
>
> I left Rutland on Friday morning last, at six o'clock, in company with several friends from that vicinity and reached Utica in season for the afternoon session. The morning was cool, the air bracing for the first fifty miles, but when the sun had gained the mastery the heat grew intense, and by the time we arrived in Utica we met as "warm" a reception as credited to Vermont at the time of the "Free Convention."...
>
> After meeting a cordial welcome from friends with whom I was to stop, and washing the cinders from my face, I began to think it was best to take the matter coolly, and adjourned to the Hall to see if I could get light upon the all important subject of the "Cause and Cure of Evil."

In her column, Axy referred to "Mrs. Britt." The St. Louis medium, Amanda Britt Spence, was variously referred to in news reports as Mrs. Britt, Mrs. Burtt and Mrs. Butt, although she had recently married Professor Peyton Spence of New York. Whatever name she went by, the insufferable woman monopolized the podium to a vexing degree.

Britt was "a stout, healthy looking matron" in *The New York Herald* and *The New York Tribune* found her "an orator of rare power and accomplishment" whose first speech "was far more eloquent and impressive than any other feminine address to which I ever listened."

Axy was informed by friends that that woman had been overheard spreading malicious rumors that Axy committed her lectures to memory; the very same malevolent gossip that had spread throughout Boston. They marveled that Mrs. Britt Spence could breathe in her dress of dark taffeta with multiple flounces on the capacious skirt. The stout woman's florid face glowed with moisture and she fanned herself dramatically as she spoke in a nasal, flat southern accent. Her heft, plus her riveting voice, gained control of the crowd as she tossed off bold remarks. Britt began with a statement about "the relations between the sexes."

"I know it is a delicate subject, and what I have to say will be heralded through the press of the country" ("Don't she wish!" a woman seated next to Axy muttered impolitely). "For instance, it has been said that women should vote," Britt Spence rolled her eyes. She had studied the matter, she said, and discovered that it was not the number of votes cast, it was the quality. "I could take a barrel of alcohol and get one hundred votes for it." (Laughter) "I cannot see that females can do any good by casting their votes."

Laughter and applause frequently interrupted the speaker, who spouted similarly discordant comments with regard to slavery and Free Love. During her final speech on Friday, the *Tribune* reported that "Mrs. Butt of St. Louis, took the floor for the third time to-day, and…when her period of twenty minutes expired the audience unanimously voted to allow her to proceed as long as she chose."

Axy left the tent soon afterward and walked over to a grove of trees where a heavily perspiring Britt Spence gulped lemonade while speaking with a reporter. Devoted followers shielded the woman with their fringed parasols and delicately whisked the air with their fans.

"Miss Sprague, I'm so pleased to meet in the flesh someone I've heard so much of by reputation," Mrs. Britt Spence said, flashing an imperious smile.

"I have heard that my reputation owes a great deal to your appraisal," Axy replied with a chill that might have allowed the disciples to drop their fans.

After the Utica Convention, my sister confessed to friends, she suffered from "the Blues." To battle her depression she once again visited the Graefenburg Water Cure and Kinesipathic Institute, where she had a fine time in company with friends, including Warren Chase.

Wisely, she opted for a less frigid treatment this time at Graefenburg than she had two years ago. Gritting her teeth, she endured pail douches and half-baths administered by the bath boys. When she had a free moment, she wrote "Who is the Prompter?" for her column in *The World's Paper*, to get that subject into print and out of her system once and for all.

> Shortly after the close of an evening lecture in a very bigoted place where Spiritualism was hardly known, a medium of our acquaintance received a call from a gentleman who said he would like to ask her a question if she would not consider him impertinent.
>
> "Any question that you as a gentleman, think proper to ask me, I am ready to answer," was her reply.
>
> "Well," said the gentleman, "I would like to know if you, this evening, had a prompter in the audience who prompted you in your lectures."
>
> "Yes sir," said the lady with a very grave looking face, "I must confess that I had."
>
> "One that travels with you constantly?"
>
> "Yes sir."
>
> "That is just what they have been saying, and as your friends said it was spirits I tho't I would come and see what you said about it. But as you admit having a

prompter it is decided without further parlay that you commit your lectures, as many believe."

"But," said the lady, "I have not told you that I committed my lectures."

"Not commit them, not commit them, where is the use of a prompter then," said her questioner with an incredible look and tone.

"Simply because I have not committed them, and not knowing a word of my lecture when I commence, it is very necessary that I have a prompter if I speak at all."

The gentleman looked as though he was ready to believe what he had often heard of mediums—that they were all insane.

"Shall I explain to you?" said the lady with a half perceptible smile at his expression. "I have a prompter, but that prompter is invisible; one that prompts me at every word and sentence, one without whom I should never attempt to speak. That prompter I believe to be a departed spirit, and who as I told you, travels with me constantly, and without whom I should never appear in public. Do you understand me?"

Her questioner was a man not devoid of intelligence, and it was impossible for him not to feel his position.

"I am glad you asked the question," continued the lady without seeming to notice his chagrin. "It was far more honorable than unmanly assertion, without giving me an opportunity to defend myself. I thank you for it. Go tell your friends that I have indeed a prompter; invisible to them, yet shining in robes of eternal beauty."

BELL

9

All the World Should Run Nightly Mad

(1858)

I stand upon the shore of the Lake and it is an Ocean to me, for it stretches away, away, and mocks me with its great beyond…And I turn to myself and confess with shame and humiliation that I have capacity in my soul for so little.

"Notes by the Wayside"
November 8, 1858

AXY WAS THEN ENGAGED for a period of time in upstate New York. Utica told her, "Our people have fallen more deeply in love with you than before." Oswego asked her to favor them with her presence through October and November.

On Sunday, September 26, 1858, J. L. Pool of Oswego introduced her to a gathering near the rural seaport of Ogdensburgh, where the gentle Oswegatchie River flows into the majestic St. Lawrence. In the pleasant grove that morning were Elvira Mather Crawford, a Methodist with an interest in Spiritualism, and John, her husband, who had accompanied his wife partly out of duty, and because he had heard that Miss Sprague possessed a remarkable gift.

As usual, Axy closed her lecture by singing a hymn that was inspired by unseen spirits. Then Mr. Pool asked if anyone had a question to ask of her. This uncommon custom had become a tradition for my sister.

"Miss Sprague," Mr. Crawford said, rising and bowing slightly, "Wouldst thou learn the secret of the sea?"

For a brief moment my sister was taken aback. She steadied herself and took a few quavering breaths.

Then she replied, quoting more of the verse by Longfellow they had recited on the steamboat, "Only those who brave its dangers comprehend its mystery."

She found his reaction to be *thoroughly* entertaining.

When she came down from the stage, John Crawford immediately approached her and exclaimed, "You told me your name was *Bell*."

"It is one of several *nom de plumes* I use with my written works," Axy replied with a smile.

Crawford explained to the others that he and Miss Sprague had previously met, "But I was unaware of her charms as an Improvisatrice."

Axy's face glowed crimson. Mr. Crawford's praise was more effusive than she felt was appropriate, under the circumstance. Concerned that such flattery might not meet with his wife's approval, she lowered her eyes and took Mr. Pool's arm as he escorted her toward the awaiting crowd of admirers, leaving Mr. Crawford to his wife's questioning gaze.

Elvira Crawford—plump, soft spoken, and motherly—had reason to be mystified and not a little uneasy at her husband's reaction to Miss Sprague. He had shown almost no interest in Spiritualism before this day.

In order to convey the essence of their unusual attachment as it intensified, I will take leave of my sister's history for a moment and relay, in general, what Axy told me she soon ascertained of this man and his character.

When Axy met him in the grove at Ogdensburgh, John H. Crawford was forty-five years of age and made his home in the city with Elvira, their five children, his aged sister, and several servants. He had been born in Ontario County, New York, one of ten children born to David and Ann Crawford, who farmed there. At the age of sixteen, John was sent to live with an older sister in Detroit, where he attended an academy and clerked at a store. Several years later he spent some time near Green Bay with his sister Sarah, who taught in a Methodist mission school for the Oneida tribe—denominated "The Oneida Mission West"—where portions of their language had been translated and circulated together with hymns especially prepared for the Indians.

At age twenty-two, John entered into the mercantile business in Hudson, Ohio, with William T. Mather as his partner. On December 6, 1835, he married his partner's sister, Elvira R. Mather.

While living in Ohio, John became close friends with John Brown (eventually immortalized with his raid on Harper's Ferry) and Philo Chamberlin, captain of the Summit County Guards and an early mayor of the city of Akron. In the 1840s, Crawford and Chamberlin began transporting goods on barges via the newly completed Erie Canal. Soon after the opening of the Ogdensburgh Railroad, the two men launched their shipping business on the Great Lakes.

Large steamships powered by propellers transited the Welland Canal system more easily than paddle wheelers, and could carry more bulk cargo. Coal and manufactured goods were shipped west to Duluth, Milwaukee, and Chicago, while grain, timber, and iron ore were shipped east to supply the large population centers. Crawford and Chamberlin began with two propeller steamships, the *Boston* and the *Cleveland* (this I gathered from one of the many newspaper articles Axy proferred). In 1855 Crawford and Chamberlin, in partnership with A. H. Hovey and William Mather, became the Northern Transportation Company and added more steamers to their line. *The Oswego Commercial Times* praised their enterprise and expedition in the transportation of freight and passengers. The line became very popular, secured a large amount of business—benefiting largely by the northern lines of railroads—and reaped a very fine profit. John H. Crawford served as secretary-treasurer.

When my sister met him, Mr. Crawford was already a successful and wealthy gentleman. By 1858, the Northern Transportation

Company owned fourteen first-class propeller-driven ships that made daily runs between Ogdensburgh and Oswego, Detroit, and Cleveland, and three times a week sailed to Milwaukee and Chicago to link the Great Lakes to Atlantic ports by way of the St. Lawrence.

The shipping company was especially competitive and bold. They had a reputation for being the first to pass the Straits of Mackinac in spring upon the opening of navigation, and the last to return to Oswego in the fall, risking boats frozen in Detroit, stuck in the Welland Canal, or stopped by ice at the head of the St. Lawrence.

A Morning Lake Scene—The weather was clear and serene yesterday morning, the view upon the Lake was very fine, and the occasional cool zephyrs were peculiarly refreshing. A number of vessels were languidly moving off in the horizon, their sails flapping restlessly in the calm, and the tugs were gallantly escorting others to our harbor. The scene was enlivened by the rising smoke of two propellers approaching from below, which were having a sharp contest in a race for this port.

Soon their hulls loomed up in view, the black smoke and steam rolled out their chimneys in dense volume, floating off gracefully in fantastic and varying forms in the rear; the heavy breathing and panting of the huge racers came first scarcely audible, then more distinct to the ear.

On they came, straining their iron sinews for the mastery, but it seemed a dead heat. Rolling the glittering white spray from their bows, and tearing the crystal waters into a foam at their sterns,—on, on, they ploughed their way, neither apparently gaining an inch upon the other. As they approached, rapid reports of the sharp and struggling cough from their fiery lungs, seemed like the effect of pulmonary convulsions of terrible monsters.

They kept their relative positions, and as they entered the harbor, barely a few rods distance separated them, each as they passed the piers, uttering an ear-piercing shriek of triumph and defiance. They both belonged to Hovey & Crawford's Line, and came up from the St. Lawrence.

Oswego Palladium, JULY 18, 1858

Axy became a frequent guest in the magnificent Crawford home near the banks of the river. The Crawford children: Julia, 21; Lizzie, 20; Jenny, 18; Molly, 12; and George, 6, were captivated by Miss Sprague, who was also afforded special adoration by Pilot, the Crawford's elderly spaniel.

John H. Crawford (far left) and family; c. early 1870s.

According to Axy, only the finest furniture and floral decorations suited Elvira's taste. Informal musicales were commonplace in the household. Everyone soon recognized that Mr. Crawford's baritone harmonized nicely with Axy's sweet soprano. Songs by Henry Russell and Eliza Cook were popular requests, but the two of them especially enjoyed (and were often encouraged to perform) "What Are The Wild Waves Saying?"

Having been raised in the mountains, Axy was fascinated by the rhythm of waves and Crawford, upon learning that she also used "Solitarie" as her pen name, informed her of the *soliton*, or "solitary wave," a recent discovery of Scottish engineer John Scott Russell, who observed a canal boat being pulled by two horses and noticed that after the boat stopped, the water disturbance at the prow continued on and rolled forward with great velocity as a large wave that continued for miles. Such "solitary waves," Crawford explained, could appear in mid-ocean and travel alone over the surface with no diminution of height, dissipating only when they interact with a boundary such as a shoreline.

"Miss Sprague, you are like Russell's 'solitary wave,'" Crawford told her, relating the phenomenon. "He also called it 'the Wave of Translation,' and you translate the words of spirits like a rolling wave."

"If I am a wave," Axy responded with pleasure, "Then you must be the *sea*, Mr. C., for you love it so and have told me you must always live near the water. For me, the sea symbolizes infinite energy, in which human existence is only a tiny part. It is like the boundary between the conscious and the unconscious, a wisdom still unspoken."

He was fascinated by word games. The two would clandestinely argue the merits of their personal symbols, Axy as a *wave* and John Crawford as the *sea*, a genial battle they intended to remain private. Images, metaphors, and similes of wave and sea were repeatedly mentioned in their correspondence and in poems they wrote in concert.

A. W. Sprague.   *JKCrawford*

When I relate Axy's personal memoirs in this manner, I do not mean to imply that my sister spent every moment of every day confined to her sickbed following my arrival in Plymouth Notch of late. In the beginning, she seemed wholly frenzied and spoke obsessively, as if she were thrust by a dire necessity to disencumber herself of the recent past.

Prior to becoming bedridden (seated in the shady garden, for example), her discourse with me was almost entirely related to Mr. Crawford and their mutual affection.

Through her letters and during her visits to Wisconsin I had, by that time, already gleaned many more details of Mr. Crawford's life. Now she pressed even further newspaper and magazine clippings upon me and at last, one day reached beneath her mattress for a hidden sheaf of light blue writing paper.

She had not mentioned her "delicate condition" for over a week when one day she tenderly caressed her abdomen and asked if I thought she should pen a note to Mr. Crawford and enlighten him of her situation.

I was convinced, by then, that this "infant" was only a sad illusion, conceived by her feverish brain. But what benefit would come from destroying her phantom child? And before I could say a word in response, she determined to wait until the day she could appear before him with the astonishing infant.

Initially, the friendship her husband expressed toward Miss Sprague caused some misgivings for Elvira Crawford. She was obliged to ask Lizzie to accompany her to Oswego where, having sent her daughter on a variety of errands, Elvira sought Mr. Pool at his bookstore on Bridge Street, since the man was responsible for issuing the invitation to the Improvisatrice. Mr. Pool assured her that the most trustworthy sources in Knox Corners and Syracuse had given their word that Miss Sprague's moral worth was wholly unblemished and beyond suspicion. Moreover, she was highly esteemed in the entire Spiritualist Community and, by association, the Crawfords would establish an opportunity to dwell in that singular realm.

With Mr. Pool's encouragement, Elvira reached an accommodation: The unique bond between her husband and Miss Sprague was undoubtedly the wish of Spirits. As Elvira's ancestry included Increase and Cotton Mather, Puritan ministers who had been intimately involved in the Salem Witchcraft Trials, a desire for spiritual illumination was a Mather family trait. Miss Sprague may be an attractive woman of thirty, Elvira reasoned, but the young woman dressed modestly, was refined and cultured, and seemed to possess impeccable manners.

Mr. Pool privately notified Axy of Elvira's concerns, so at a convenient time my sister revealed to Mrs. Crawford the scores of Free Love declarations that had been made to her by married men. She assured Elvira, as she had many an apprehensive woman, "I would take the offered hand of friendship from no man if it was purchased at the expense of the happiness of his wife." She then added, "Because Mr. Crawford is man, a husband and a father, is there any reason why he should not be my friend, the same as you?"

That year, Axy lectured and conducted circles in the Ogdensburgh-Oswego area all of October and part of November, with side trips to Utica, Syracuse, and a variety of other towns, where her lectures caused much provocation among the populace of upstate New York.

She forgot her silk gloves in Binghamton, but the woman with whom she'd stayed said she would forward them to her along with copies of *The Republican*. "You would be much amused if not edified at some of the sayings and doings of the villagers; it *is* possible that an angel has alighted here *for the waters are troubled*. May the work of healing follow! Some are rejoicing that the band of Spiritualists is so small that we cannot have trance-speakers very often." She also wanted to know if she ever got chicken to eat, and how was her throat?

A man from Knox Corners said there had been great disturbance, generally, since she left that place. He added, in jest, "The church is still trying to repair the damages that your lectures have caused!"

Owego declared her visit there very successful and "the inquirys are urgent, to know when you will come back." A local minister gave a sermon attacking Axy's lecture, but "the cry is, Where is Miss Sprague? She must be got back here at all considerations. Some say they will give $5.00 apiece and more if necessary. Agitation! Agitation!! Agitation!!! is the cry of the public! We will raise from 50 to 75 to 100 dollars for your labor with us according to the time you tarry with us."

Baltimore. She had left them in the lurch when Father was near death. Washington Danskin inquired if her spirit guides would be able to send her to them this season. "Your former lectures made a deep and favourable impression upon many minds here, and we would be greatly pleased again to listen to the pure and beautiful thoughts which flow from the Angelic Spheres through your mediumship."

For the time being, Axy was quite content to let Baltimore linger. She was happy, traveling by train throughout New York and visiting communities large and small.

One evening that autumn after dinner at the Crawfords, the subject of courageous women was raised. Julia expressed her admiration for the detailed paintings of the Goodridge sisters, Eliza and Sarah, little-known miniaturists. Sarah Goodridge had been in love with Daniel Webster, and after the death of his first wife, the painter presented him with a delicate miniature portrait of her bare breasts.

Elvira swiftly admonished her eldest daughter for mentioning this scandalous anecdote—which caused Mr. Crawford to bring a napkin to his mouth to hide his smile. He knew Julia was fond of tripping close to the borderline of delicacy to tease her mother.

Molly and George were excused from the table.

"I believe Daniel Webster eventually married someone else," Axy offered, "a woman who was wealthy and well connected. Apparently her tiny bosom did not woo the widower!"

This statement caused Mr. Crawford to develop a spluttering cough.

"But she never married," Julia added in all sincerity, "and Sarah Goodridge continued to love him and when Webster died six years ago, the miniature was found among his personal possessions."

"I still live," Axy said. "Those were Webster's last words, *'I Still Live.'*"

Lizzie said that she was an admirer of Harriet Beecher Stowe whose *Uncle Tom's Cabin* had aroused the nation to the plight of the poor slave.

Jennie was fond of the songs and poems of Eliza Cook and subscribed to the weekly periodical, *Eliza Cook's Journal*. She quoted lines from one of Cook's poems:

> "Be kind when you can in the smallest of duties,
> Don't wait for the larger expressions of Love;
> For the heart depends less for its joys and its beauties
> On the flight of the Eagle than coo of the Dove."

Axy agreed with the sentiment. Then she took advantage of the opportunity to tell the girls of a somewhat local story she and I had so loved: Father's tales of the Canadian patriot, Pirate Bill Johnson, and Kate, the pirate's courageous daughter who was known as the Queen of the Thousand Isles. It is a true story of an outlaw who robbed from the rich to aid the poor. We used to beg Father to tell us of bold Kate, who secretly smuggled food and the latest news of his would-be captors to her father while he hid on a tiny island in the St. Lawrence, not far from the dining room where the Crawford family and Axy now sat.

To the utter delight of their honored guest, Mr. Crawford announced he would arrange for an excursion from the St. Lawrence to Lake Ontario, the smallest of the Great Lakes and the gentlest of the inland seas.

A date was set. He and Elvira and Lizzie would accompany Axy and she would be given a tour of the Thousand Islands of our childhood dreams.

I cannot imagine a boat as large, nor as grand as Mr. Crawford's, thus I welcomed my sister's detailed depiction of the vessel. In fact, most people who view the immense freighters would not envision cruising on such a ship as a privileged guest.

Beyond the tall, uninviting exterior, across the narrow plank laid between the dock and the craft itself, beneath huge funnels that emitted dense clouds of smoke, a luxury of travel awaited that was unequalled anywhere in the world except on the largest and finest private yachts.

Axy edged her way with Elvira and Lizzie along the narrow promenade on one side of the ship, stopping only when Mr. Crawford indicated the door labeled "Owners." Through that portal was revealed a vast parlor with rich velvet carpet and lavish upholstered chairs. Brocaded draperies framed the long windows. The luster of mahogany reflected the luxury and wealth of the appointments. From each side of this parlor extended a narrow hall, and on each side of each hall there were large rooms—two guest chambers, bedrooms with brass beds, rich tapestries and curtains, cushioned chairs, more dense velvet carpet.

A velvet covered stairway in the forward superstructure led to the "observation room," a great, richly furnished room with scores of windows from which one could survey the sea from almost every direction. One door led from this room to the captain's quarters, and another door led to a private suite of rooms that the Crawfords and their honored guest were to occupy. The finest hotel in the country could not have afforded finer conveniences. In the seclusion of her passenger quarters, Axy found a unique waterworks system that brought hot and cold water. The guests' private dining room glittered with silver and was decorated with fresh fruit and sparkling urns of fresh flowers.

She wrote to me of her trip on the "aft promenade deck of a Lake Steamer," and further described the outing in her "Notes By the Wayside" column:

I went from Ogdensburgh to Oswego, down the St. Lawrence River and Lake Ontario, and gave two Lectures. I went more for the pleasure of the excursion than for anything else, as Mr. Pool, the gentleman who engaged me, promised slight audiences...but we were happily disappointed. I had audiences of about twelve hundred each, and urgent invitations to come again. Nor was my journey less happy. The two days spent in going and returning upon those waters, I count among the golden journeys of my wanderings. The weather was fine, and there were four of us, besides it was a scene through which I had wished to pass from a child. I remember when I used to sit in my father's lap, of the stories of the French and Indian scenes enacted of the "Thousand Islands," of Johnson & his daughter, "Queen of the Thousand Isles," that he used to tell me, and how, as I grew older, it became from those old associations, as classic ground, and I often did wish that I was an American Walter Scott, that I might write, not the "Lady of the Lake," but the "Queen of the Thousand Isles." Therefore, as we glided over the blue waters, I felt that my Ideal had become Real. As we passed the "Thousand Islands," I almost mechanically looked for the "Queen," with her little skiff. There upon one of the Islands, stands her father's Light House and home, and he still lights the watchfires there, while she, like one of the Pleiades, is seen no more as a star of brightness for she has married a mortal. Ah me! One wants at least a hundred years to pass away, before daring to write a Poem out of real material!

Because he had a formal education, and was so well read, Axy searched for courage to ask Mr. Crawford if he would be so kind as to read her poems-in-progress and assist her with revisions.

"You have such true poetic taste to train and assist my own," she argued. "Your experiences, your range of thought, of history, of fact and scholarship and travel—all this would exact a higher style than I could reach by myself without a mind like yours to teach me.

He readily agreed to read her unfinished works.

"Make suggestions and criticize, tear them into shreds," she insisted. "Tell me what to read. I only want to learn!"

He set about purchasing books by the most esteemed poets of the day for her to explore (including Walt Whitman—he had suspected the copy of *Leaves of Grass* had been sent by Bell), and asked only that she share her opinions of these authors with him in exchange.

They developed a game to entertain guests and themselves, involving the mutual composition of a poem: each took a line or two to continue the quest, which they jokingly referred to as "The Combat." Mr. Crawford averred, "Two heads are better than one."

When she went down to Oswego at the end of October to deliver further lectures there at Mead's Hall, Mr. Crawford accompanied her on one of his finest propellers, *Young America*. Axy was afforded a private chamber in the owner's quarters, but much to her disappointment, her mentor was involved with the demands of paperwork in his office and she saw little of him during their voyage.

"Who is the Prompter?," the article she wrote to address those who accused her of memorizing her lectures, appeared in *The World's Paper* on November 12, 1858. That same day *The Banner of Light* published a letter regarding "The Progress of Spiritualism in Oswego." They'd welcomed a number of Spiritualist speakers, the writer said, including "Miss A. W. Sprague, all of whom have done good service. Of the latter, however, I would speak more particularly, from the fact of her having remained with us some three weeks, during which time her real worth was appreciated. Kind, generous, intelligent and unostentatious in social life; in the desk firm, logical, argumentative, pathetic, eloquent, and truly sublime, she united in one solid phalanx the Friends of Spiritual Freedom; and by her deep-toned inspiration, aroused the slumbering energies of the most stupid and superficial listeners, carrying conviction home to the bigot and the glittering steel of truth to the tyrant's heart."

Axy's published poems began to show signs of Mr. Crawford's influence. He set her words to music he composed, persuaded her to adopt a more lyrical structure for her verses, and encouraged that she discard traditional feminine sentiments she had previously favored. One such example appeared in *The World's Paper* later that autumn, entitled "My Prayer," and signed "Bell":

> *Give me a home where the sun shines clear*
> *And the mountain air is sweet,*
> *Where the birds, uncaged, sing all day long*
> *And the words of love I meet.*
> *Give me a home where the free ones roam,*
> *Where the heart wears never a chain,*
> *Where my soul can be like the breezes free*
> *And I never will pine again.*

Notes by the Wayside
Oswego, N.Y. November 8, 1858

I have just closed my engagement of three Sundays at Oswego and have found the interest in no degree less than at Binghamton, Owego, & other places that I have visited. The audiences steadily increased to the last, notwithstanding the almost superhuman efforts of the Church to prevent. Sermon after sermon was preached against Spiritualism from different pulpits, and the Baptist Church more incensed than the rest, expelled six members during my stay, because they would attend my Lectures. But, unfortunately for the Church, it did not stop many of the others coming also. I could almost pity the Churches for in their blind rage they do but put out their own eyes, instead of the light that annoys others. Two men (one a church member) were talking in the street one day; and because the one who was not a member spoke favorably of the "Spiritualists" and maintained his position, this follower of Christ (?) struck him a severe blow upon his head! The man turned to him coolly, and instead of returning blow for blow, asked him if he thought that a true manifestation of the Christ Principle, that he pretended to advocate. That question was the hardest blow of the two, and the professor then turned away thoroughly ashamed of himself…

The principal charm of Oswego is its water scenery. It sits upon the shores of Lake Ontario and Oswego River, as though in some strange communion, a city of the Ocean King had been washed to the surface and left upon the shore out of pity to man. And I sometimes stood by the lake in awe and listened to the low moaning of the waves, like one in sorrow, or the deep roar when the waters were roused into sudden fury and reached out their great waves to be able to grasp the shore.

I wondered at that great moaning of the sea. As though it had a living, throbbing heart, that vibrated to some great agony. Lake Ontario was an Ocean to me, for it stretched away, away, and mocked me with its great beyond. And it vexed me that when I looked over its blue waves for miles, into the distance that it only seems as one or two! And I turned to myself and confessed with shame and humiliation that I have capacity in my soul for so little.

The Ocean is a great Teacher, and on the shores of Lake Ontario within the last few weeks I have heard sermons, that for grandeur and sublimity, for energy and significance, were never equaled in Cathedral Aisles, and Anthems whose like no choir ever chanted to go up to heaven through the loftiest dome that man ever reared to God…

But here I am lingering by the way again, and I must hasten, lest I worry your patience.

I am engaged at Utica for the 14th and 21st of November, at Syracuse the 28th, at Binghamton Dec. 5th and I expect at Owego on the 12th.

I think some of bending my steps southward then, as the cool airs of this section keep me better supplied with colds than I care to be at present.

As the two of them had been completely at ease with one another on the deck of the little steamboat, Axy felt completely at home in Mr. Crawford's spirit. It seemed the two of them already understood each other fully and completely, as if they'd known each other forever. He also loved "the beautiful, not with a superficial love but with an intense devotion," which she repeated to me more than once. The coincidence of meeting him twice as if by chance, made it seem that her Guardians meant a true friendship should ensue.

He had been away, traveling on business for over a week, and she'd been fulfilling speaking her engagements, when one evening following dinner at the Crawford's Elvira retired early, complaining of a sick headache. The others were engaged with their own pursuits and Axy and Mr. Crawford had found seclusion in the library to discuss her poetry and progress she had made.

"Read to me," he requested, sitting back in his favorite chair. "What gems have you penned while we've been apart?"

She read "Serenade—Good Night," and reached the final stanzas:

But now I know no star for me
In beauty e'er shall rise,
To shine and send a glory through
The midnight of my skies.

For me there shall no morning come,
For me there is no light;
Thou art my sun,—thou risest not,—
And so, beloved, Good-Night!

Mr. Crawford was silent. Axy shuffled the papers in her hands, placed them on a desk, picked them up again.

"The poem is unfinished," she apologized, "it is in need of your expert hand."

"No, it is not the poem," he replied. "It is the poet."

Her breath caught in her throat.

"I can no longer imagine my life without your presence," he admitted.

After another lengthy pause, Axy replied in a voice so soft that her confession could barely be discerned.

"Nor I, you." She turned her back so he would not see the tears welling up in her eyes.

Why weren't her Guardians stepping in to prevent this exchange? She felt no impediment, nothing to prevent her from revealing her innermost thoughts.

"A day or so after our excursion through the Thousand Islands, I found the entire experience could be recalled in blank verse," he said. "I did not record the words, but it seems that your angelic Guardians are affecting me as well. Is that possible?"

"You know my feelings about Free Love," she replied, facing him. The tears she tried so hard to prevent were now trailing down her cheeks. "The Swedenborgians think every man and woman has a soul mate, or spiritual affinity, and that allows us to have unorthodox relationships outside of marriage. I cannot agree with that…"

She spoke quickly, but her voice gave way at the end.

"Oh, my Dearest," he said, rising from his chair and going to her, "I'm not implying that we allow ourselves to become immoral or licentious. Not at all!"

"*Soul mates?*" Axy suggested softly, "Perhaps kindred spirits?"

"As Brother and Sister," he confirmed. "Would your Guardians agree to that?

"I think they may, perhaps," she agreed.

After that evening there were brief opportunities when, in only the most discreet circumstances, Axy allowed him to take her hand and raise it to his lips as he whispered heartfelt endearments. As these avowals of affection represented a "spirit union" between their respective Guardians, she felt they must be essentially pure.

But when he expressed himself thus, she sometimes teased him to "be good," quoting Epictetus: *If you wish to be good, first believe that you are bad*.

"If there is one pure feeling in my heart," he replied, "my love for you is *steadfast, earnest, and sure*. And in your pure soul I can see a ray that burns and brightens. Every look, every word and act, reveals the presence of a power my own spirit cherishes."

"I have craved a soul such as yours that can answer back to mine," Axy confessed, "but finding not, as year by year passed on, my hope to find one such as you was wholly gone."

"Oh, my dear One," he said, holding her so close that she inhaled the scent of Bay Rum and fine cigars.

"After I met you on the little steamship in Long Island Sound, in my heart there burned a living fire that I might still one day find such a love and enshrine it in my heart of hearts," she revealed.

"With adoration undying," Crawford murmured, "like the ceaseless ocean wave."

"And meet return," she replied, her face buried in his collar.

As he had earlier accompanied her to Oswego, John Crawford followed Axy to Utica on the pretext of meeting with Governor Seymour. While in that city, Axy resided at Bagg's Hotel at the foot of Genesee Street and one morning upon her return from her usual morning walk, she found a note waiting for her:

Wednesday morning

Miss Sprague,

Caroline Richings—a singer of much true inspiration—gives a concert this evening at the Utica Opera House. You would be pleased with her. If you cannot accompany me to hear her, I will excuse you and lay no new sins to your charge on that account. But if you can and will go with me, I shall be more than pleased. I will call and see about 7 or ½ past 7. I write this thinking you might not be in.

J. H. Crawford

She *was* pleased with Miss Richings and her English Opera Troupe. The evening was a complete delight. Mr. Crawford especially wanted Axy to hear "I Live for Thee Only," a ballad written and dedicated to Miss Richings by a Philadelphia composer and a song Crawford enjoyed singing in Axy's presence because of its clandestine significance:

> *Like the glimmer of dawn light*
> *That heralds the day*
> *So thy smile is the sunshine*
> *That lightens my way.*
> *Those bright eyes that glisten*
> *My heaven shall be*
> *'Tis for thee I live only,*
> *Ay, only for thee.*

They walked back to her hotel, humming the tune in harmony. Axy felt such pure, unalloyed joy in the presence of this man; her heart sang along with its own "wordless" song. Not even brisk November winds could check her happiness and when he stopped in the lobby of her hotel with the excuse of warming his hands by the fire, she was not surprised when he withdrew a prettily wrapped gift from his pocket. He had known her birthday had been only a few days ago.

"I live for thee only," he whispered softly, so no one could hear.

With reservation, a mixture of pleasure and trepidation, she accepted the gift. An intricate gold ring had been set with a green stone that Axy knew must be an emerald.

When she expressed her reluctance to accept the ring he dismissed its value and said it was merely a "symbolic ring" to represent their spiritual union. Axy hoped it *was* a cheap gemstone. After her condescension of those who failed to differentiate the principled aspects of Free Love, she would not want anyone suspecting she had been seduced by its more contemptible tenets.

There was a moment of brief deliberation when she suggested her Spirit Guardians declared the gift was acceptable if prompted at the urging of Mr. Crawford's Guardians.

Crawford assured Axy that was, indeed, the case.

"Let this ring be proof of my sincerity in our spiritual alliance," he said, clasping her hands.

"Our rapport must exist only on that elevated plane," she reminded him.

"When your doubts arise—as they always seem to do—as to the earnestness of my devotion, Dearest Axy, this symbolic ring will serve as a reminder of my true love."

She knew the ring was an emerald. The sacred stone of Venus, Goddess of Love, the emerald represented love in all its facets.

She would remain in upstate New York until the year was almost out. When he could not reach her in person, Mr. Crawford's letters did. Unlike others in her mail, his letters were immediately recognized by their pale blue stationery. She greedily sought the envelopes in the bundles handed to her by hotel clerks or by hosts in whose homes she had been invited to stay. Then she set his letters aside for reading in solitude. He sometimes signed them with his initials, "JHC," or "Your Brother," or yet another light-hearted reference to their singular relationship, often reminding her to "be good."

The give-and-take of their verbal jousting sometimes carried a sharp edge. She taunted him, repeating that he was her "Evil Genius" because of the strong influence he had, for good or for ill, on her character and conduct. Ever cautious, fearing what others might see as a "Free Lust" association, my sister found opportunities to test his spiritual honesty. A physical relationship must be avoided at all costs: She owed that to her Guardians. John Crawford owed that to Elvira. And to her, as well.

Letter to the Editor:

Why is it all the world should run nightly mad to hear her [Achsa W. Sprague] improvise a "hymn" from a subject selected at random, a hymn that nobody else ever wrote or sung, for the very good reason that it was not worth the while, or why everybody should crowd to hear a woman who is chiefly afflicted with a flow of words, discuss the weightiest questions of social science, religion and metaphysics, is more than I am able to tell.... Whether our intelligent citizens consider a loose, extempore effusion more likely to be thoughtful and truthful than a well considered, carefully prepared lecture or essay, or whether they believe a pretended "trance" to be a genuine indication of inspiration, is difficult to tell. May be they are pleased to see a woman on the platform.

But whatever the motive was, the public were certainly out *en masse*, and judging from the liberal encomiums that went round, and the delighted smile of intelligent comprehension that went from seat to seat as by chance the speaker ventured to express, instead of merely talking about, "the idea," they all went home delighted.

As a woman, Miss Sprague is a pleasant, genial, kind-hearted and intelligent person, of little scholastic education but a good deal of reading. As a speaker, she has a good voice which she will soon spoil, a slightly swaggering gesture, a fair flow of ideas connected with her special themes, a tremendous flow of words, and a tolerable acquaintanceship with the cant phrases of Spiritualistic literature.

As a reasoner, she, like all other verbose orators, is muddy . . . . she does not believe there is rightfully any such thing as punishment . . . . She thinks freedom is a myth. Man is born under, and lives under, inexorable natural laws. He is forever hampered by his surroundings, the sport of circumstances. So he has no merit in doing well, no demerit in doing ill. . . . Criminals instead of being confined in gloomy dungeons . . . . should be surrounded with all the heart could wish . . . . It is a comfortable theory and needs only to be named to catch the general attention of legislators . . . . It is not every itinerant lecturer, whether speaking in a "trance" or in the "natural man," who will make the world wiser.

The Oswego Times,
December 14, 1858

⇥ 10 ⇤

At Darling's Gap

(1858)

*As soon as I get out of school I wish to be alone
so you see of course my society is not courted...*

LETTER FROM CELIA TO ACHSA, May 26, 1858

WHILE AXY WAS CONVENIENTLY crossing paths with Mr. Crawford in Ogdensburgh in 1858, here in Wisconsin we were still enduring hard times brought about by the Panic of '57. In addition, we had suffered from a chilly, wet spring. Rains brutally battered us for a solid two weeks. Desperate farmers wanted to get into their fields. Rivers overflowed; mud tracked everywhere.

This was a harsh environment (and remains so), at the edge of the wilderness, but by 1858 Wisconsin had been a state for a decade. Our wealthiest settlers were Yankees, with household help and farmhands from Germany or Ireland. Yet many immigrants from those countries had been able to establish their own farmsteads. Germans often arrived with funds to build homes, farms, and get a business underway. The area where I live, south of Lake Winnebago, has Germans and Scandinavians who have cleared their land and now grow vast crops of wheat.

We are lacking a single strong leader for woman's rights in Wisconsin, and until recently a married woman's earnings belonged to her husband and she was liable for his debts. Public opinion has been slow to approve of a woman speaking in public. I thought Axy would be prohibited from lecturing here. Although she faced some interdictions, as will become clear, I was eventually proven wrong.

I'm proud that our state's anti-slavery sentiments have always been stalwart. In February of 1858, one of our legislators (whom Southern aristocrats enjoy referring to as a "backwoods hooligan") got into a brawl over the slavery issue on the floor of the U.S. Congress, and when he plucked the wig off a Southern representative he was rewarded with a black eye and an invitation to a duel.

Backwoods is not a term that I cherish, yet we still carry out lynchings, and Indian uprisings remain profoundly feared. Fortunately, when the Wisconsin Constitution was created, this state became a forerunner in utilizing local taxes to provide a free education.

Young women everywhere (including Vermont) are encouraged to think of teaching as a "sacred calling," and are encouraged to consider themselves "educational missionaries." A married woman is not allowed to teach—perhaps because she may become "in a family way," which is a very hush-hush matter and best not shared with the public. Local policy still does not favor retaining teachers for more than one or two years, and there are occasions when a schoolteacher is not rehired because the farmers' wives find her unsatisfactory, which is another way of saying she is not ugly enough.

In truth, teaching school is nothing more than a part-time job for most of us and school officials are more likely to hire a woman teacher because we can be had for half the cost of a man—somewhat dispiriting for a woman who has no adequate means of another profession. We purchase school supplies out of our own meager earnings, are responsible for all eight grades, and give 20 class sessions per day. As attendance is always irregular, due to weather, illness, or work on the farm, our lesson plans must remain flexible.

Most of the one-room schools in rural Wisconsin are built of logs. My first school was a little ten-by-ten structure at the foot of a hill. When the wind blew in winter, snow sifted through the cracks. In summer we had to contend with dust particles flying and landing everywhere. But we were privileged to be furnished with a one-hole privy (some schools had to send their students out back to find a stump) and a well with a pump.

The Madison Female Academy, which is now bankrupt, became The University of Wisconsin in 1857. Classes consisted entirely of men. As I have before stated, I had sincerely hoped to attend school rather than teach. And yet, in June of 1858, when I arose at an early hour that I might prepare to leave the place where I boarded and once more fulfill my duty at the humble post where I was expected to fill for the season, I walked to the schoolhouse and found my scholars anxiously awaiting me with smiles on their young faces and a great many ripe strawberries they'd gathered (which were truly delicious). I felt their affection and once again my mood was lifted. I shared the berries with all.

Most of my students came from poor families. Due to the Panic, many of them survived only on potatoes prepared with salt and a little milk. Those without potatoes were in a bad situation indeed and I could do nothing to help. It had become so costly to ship corn or wheat by freight that I was told farmers were saying it would be more economical to burn their crops for fuel. I wondered why they did not distribute their crops to the poor.

There were only a few women in the area who I considered friends. That summer I lost two of them to what doctors had designated "the seven- or nine-month consumption." One of the women was exceedingly lonesome for her family in the east and I did my best to allay her suffering, but even my most compassionate efforts were not enough to assuage her decline. Following her death, my own melancholy increased, and despite days spent in school I found myself lonelier and more discouraged than ever.

I've heard there are scores of women who moved here from the East and are miserable with their plight. They long to return to New England, but they consented to marry and move West and now have no choice but to contend with their hardships.

Because, contrary to the advice of many, I had boldly set my sovereign hopes on this promised "land of milk and honey," I would be foolish to share my dismay with my family in Vermont. I was discouraged about my situation: twenty-eight years of age with little to look forward to. Somehow I had become the epitome of a sorry backwoods spinnie: the piteous, ubiquitous old-maid school-marm. Unwisely, I suppose, I shared my pensive thoughts with Axy.

May 26, 1858

Dear Sister Axy,

I rec'd your letter in due season & I hastened to my own room to read and weep over it. But alas! I wept in vain as I always do. You asked me to write you when I had learned my wants. I have waited until now hoping I could <u>decide</u> upon <u>something</u> but I cannot tell what I am fitted for. I know no better today than I did five years ago & then I was seeking to know what my mission was. I am always the happiest when I can do something to elevate mankind but then there is so much to contend with & I am not prepared to meet all that comes. I wish I could visit a good phrenologist to tell me what I was fitted to do, but the opportunity has never presented itself. And I have tried to get information from the Spirit world but no, all is a sealed book.

This Spring I have made no efforts to get a living, but yet means have been provided for me. I had so hoped to become a scholar, but my most sanguine hopes have been forced to pass from me and why should I any longer try to act or live? I am now going to submit myself as a creature of circumstance as much as I can for I see that there is but little use for me to try.

I can say with the poet Alexander Pope 'Whatever is, is right,' so henceforth you may expect me to submit to whatever comes & then do as best I can.

Since I came here I have succeeded very well in my schools, yet I know that I do not improve & excel as I ought but as regards anything else except teaching. It was natural for you to write, talk, &tc, from your infancy, therefore you cannot help doing what you do. But I received a different temperament & mind & not being surrounded by conditions suited to me I am obliged to do as I do until obstructions are removed.

I have enjoyed myself better since last fall than any time previous to my coming to this place. I like my school well this summer but the people do lie so about the Spiritualists that it makes me ache. I don't think I am more unhappy than the most of people but I am bold enough to say that sometimes I think perhaps I am not immortal for I had rather become as the dust than to live and rust out.

I know not how to express my gratitude to you for the interest you take in my welfare.

I received a letter from my Catholic friend, Mr. Rausch, who remained in the California gold fields despite not prospering as he'd hoped. I had not had a letter in four years, yet it seemed that neither time nor absence nor distance could remove true friendship—as he termed our affiliation. I was content with that description, also pleased that I had not been forgotten. And I was unreservedly satisfied that I had not consented to become his wife.

Notwithstanding the hot weather, I suffered most of the time from a cold.

I also suffered from teeth ache in June and had two extracted with the instruments put on five times. Never had I undergone such immeasurable pain and I hope to never so endure it again!

Correspondence with my sister had been intermittent and slight, so I became irritated that it had become necessary to glean news of her travels and teachings only from newspapers and letters forwarded by Mother. In my latest correspondence with Axy I expressed my annoyance: "I have received the paper you sent me & was glad to get it for I learned much more about you than I should in half a dozen of your letters."

After spending the day in a suffocating schoolroom with indolent children who seemingly cared nothing about their lessons, the languorous summer nights seemed a perfect waste of daylight. I mentioned to a friend the tedium of working embroidery while the other women of the household tore and sewed carpet rags and discussed the cases of young men who were "waiting on" young women and gauging their prospects for marriage. I was bored with the book I was then reading (so boring I've forgotten the title). Without much effort, she persuaded me to accompany her to a meeting of the local Debate Society, and to brighten my mood I wore a cast-off frock of Axy's. She had felt it was too bright and "lively" for her purposes, but I found the yoked woven plaid silk—too fancy for my schoolroom—perfectly appropriate for such an evening.

The Lincoln-Douglas debates in nearby Illinois were much in the news. Only men were allowed to debate in Debate Clubs, but women were encouraged to cheer from the sidelines and weigh up the arguments. The local Debate Club had already weighed the slavery issue back and forth with trifling disputation since Wisconsin was firmly in favor of abolition and it seemed a challenging assignment to reason in favor of slaveholders, so that evening another subject had been selected for discussion.

The Debate Club met in a back room of the Methodist Church. To my surprise, Anne Steen, my friend and fellow schoolteacher, brought her brother as her companion. Both had been born in the north of Ireland and both were very well-read. I prized Anne's company. She was my age; her brother John Morrison Steen—to whom she referred as "Morris"—was thirty-five, quiet, with dark, friendly eyes and a modest beard. Their grandfather had been a gardener on a large Irish estate and after coming to this country he had acquired a very large farm near Oakfield, which his son Arthur (their father) and several grandchildren continued to operate. Morris, who was unmarried (Anne must have mentioned this a dozen times) also owned his own farm. The family belonged to the Episcopal Church.

Morris, as I also came to refer to him, was skilled at carpentry. When we were introduced, I noticed that his hands were heavily callused. I recalled hard-working Timothy Adams back in Brunswick, New York, with whose family I had boarded, and thought callused hands to be a commendable feature.

The debate commenced. I was prepared to merely sit and watch with the other women, my (uncallused) hands in my lap.

In Milwaukee, women could submit essays to be read aloud at the Debate Club, but they were not even welcome at meetings! As I soon discovered, ours was an unconventional group, an informal association with a wont of amusement. And as they wished for more debaters, Morris and I were urged to each play a part, on opposite sides.

The moderator introduced the subject to be discussed: "Is Phrenology worthy of being deemed a science?"

I found myself on the side of the Affirmative.

I could have announced to all, then and there, that my sister, Achsa W. Sprague, was a highly respected medium in all of the eastern states including Washington City, and she determined phrenology was advisable and accurate. (She had also told me that William Henry Beecher, the brother of Harriet Beecher Stowe, was an advocate of both Spiritualism and Phrenology and had published in *Fowler's Phrenological Journal*.)

I waited for our spokesperson to finish speaking.

"Thousands of traveling phrenologists are touring the country 'reading' character strengths and weaknesses and offering advice on how to overcome personal shortcomings. So here be it resolved: The brain is a mosaic of little organs subserving everything from speech to artistic ability to bashfulness. Each individual is bestowed a fixed measure of his or her faculty according to the luck of birth, and these brain-mind organs may be read by *phrenologists*, according to the bumps on one's head."

Those on our side of the room were expected to follow up with further statements to agree with our spokesman.

"Franz Joseph Gall, a German physician in the late 1700s, developed Phrenology. He measured the skulls of people in prisons, hospitals, and asylums, especially those with odd-shaped heads. He found, when examining the heads of young pickpockets, that many had bumps on their skulls just above their ears that are associated with a tendency to steal, lie, or deceive."

"The brain is composed of as many organs as there are different faculties, propensities and sentiments. The form of the skull represents and reflects the form and development of these brain organs. Those which are used get bigger, and those which are not used, shrink. This causes the skull to rise and fall with organ development."

Those opposed to the concept, responded in kind. Following that we had a rather free-for-all argument, back and forth:

"It has been said these organs on the surface of the brain can be detected by visible inspection of the skull. What if you are not bald-headed?"

"Does the mind run the brain or does the brain run the mind?"

"Then to what extent are we—our experiences, our reactions—shaped, predetermined by our brains, and to what extent do we shape our own brains?"

"This would seem to allow individuals little power of choice, of self-determination or adaptation, in the event of a neurological or perceptual mishap."

"The brains studied in this regard seem to have been only those of dead people, mostly criminals and the insane."

"I've heard there is a 'murder organ' present in murderers.'

"Are we then not the authors, the creators, of our own experiences?"

I volunteered that I was aware of a man named Phineas Gage who, when working on a railroad construction crew near Cavendish, Vermont, experienced—due to an explosion—the insertion of an iron rod over three feet long thrust into his head. After that he became fitful, irreverent, and grossly profane."

(Much laughter here, and the comment, "Well, who would not?")

Another volunteered, "I've heard that Mr. Gage volunteered to display himself as a curiosity at Barnum's American Museum in New York City, where phrenologists explained that his mind had changed so radically that he was 'no longer Gage.'"

"If I gave you a bump on the head, would you become profane? I'd proffer you would!"

The evening continued with more Affirmative and Negative rebuttal comments and conclusions, followed by good-natured squabbles. More frivolity was then encouraged by the addition of cider and cinnamon donuts. I was much pleased that Anne had invited me to share the evening diversion.

Morris appeared again at the next debate, which I also attended, the subject of which was even lighter: "Ought the science of music be taught in our schools?"

Afterward, Morris shyly inquired if he might pay me a call.

He stopped by my residence at Mr. and Mrs. Barnum's on a mild July evening. It had rained earlier in the day and the cooler air was refreshing and crisp, lovely for a casual stroll. Morris was doing finish carpentry for Dr. Samuel Bowers in the city of Fond du Lac. Dr. Bowers, who had received his education in Canada, was a student of the classics and Morris was hungry for further education as was I, which—we decided right off—made us a fitting match. Morris had been freely granted access to the doctor's vast library. "Oh, Miss Sprague, what a feast that is," he confessed. "He has all the ancient poets, original and translated, all the English classics and *The Westminster Review*." He esteemed the latter highly, which gave me a very good impression of the man. *The Westminster Review* is a liberal British publication of philosophical radicals who, in 1859, would see to the publication of Darwin's *On the Origin of Species*. After our leisurely walk we conversed somewhat more, but the evening ended before I was prepared to say goodnight.

Blackberry season began and I anticipated picking a goodly number to dry. One Sunday afternoon, Morris and Anne joined the search. Anne discreetly wandered off with her blackberry basket so Morris and I might speak privately.

As we plucked the plump berries from their vines I happened to catch one of my fingers on a thorn. Without thinking, I brought it to my mouth to catch the blood before it fell upon my dress. Morris tenderly took my hand and brought my blue-stained fingertip to *his* lips. "Miss Sprague," he then said, "I hope this is the sharpest pain you will ever experience while in my company."

I felt myself blush as he continued (as I suspected he might), "Would you consent to become my wife?"

The consequence of our discourse was evident when Anne rejoined us, her basket brimming with berries. Our basket was barely half-full and our faces were flushed.

My school term ended in mid-August. Morris and I joined Anne and other of her friends for a picnic at Darling's Gap, a unique spot of nature near the village of Oakfield that is notable for its attractive and picturesque landscape. .

With its oak-covered woodland, beautiful clear springs, vast domes of disintegrating limestone, and overhanging precipices, Darling's Gap is an especially serene setting. Even before we spread out our picnic lunch, several of our companions sought out the mysterious caverns hidden deep in winding crevices. Anne and her fiancé stayed with Morris and me to arrange the blankets and baskets of picnic fare. Dear Mrs. Barnum, well aware of my lack of culinary skills, kindly supplemented our repast with a delicious apple pie.

After our meal we were treated to some harmonies by one of the couples: He played the violin and she sang. When the musicians had finished, Morris announced to all present that we planned to be married in November. There was much rejoicing. I had scarcely realized how happy I could feel.

My beloved sister must have detected a change from my previously dour outlook when I wrote to Axy from Glen Beulah following the picnic:

> I rec'd your letter a short time since & this warm suffocating morn I will pen a few words in reply. As we have been discussing what avocation I am best fitted for I will first inform you that I have nearly decided what to pursue. The course I am about to adopt will not lead me to the towering heights of fame, neither will it only in a part satisfy the desires

of ambition, it will not bring with it immense wealth, neither will it gather unto me the applause of mankind. But in adopting this course I feel that I shall discharge (if I perform my labors right) the highest and holiest duties that rest upon our race. Therefore increased happiness must be a natural result ~ ~ ~ I am to become a Farmer's Wife ! ! !

Yes, the man I have selected from a <u>vast throng of admirers</u> is simply a farmer, has a good farm & about two thousand out to interest. Oh, now I will be a little sober & tell you what I intend to do. I do not know if I shall commence housekeeping this fall or wait until next spring. I certainly have nothing now towards it, and Mr. Steen has a house to build for us & as he is one of those good practical fellows that will have the "cage before the bird" (& as I have not seen him lately) I cannot tell anything definitely. In the letter I rec'd Thursday he says "I hope we shall soon be on our way to Vermont," so you see he intends to carry out my decisions I made last spring, but as he has to build & I shall have to buy so much & at such exorbitant prices I know not as I shall consent to any arrangements this fall but wait until next.

I anticipated another visit from Morris within the next two weeks and I promised to let Axy know in my next letter of our future travel plans. I begged her *not* to mention anything about it until she heard from me again, except to our Mother.

As I eagerly anticipated a joyful response from my family (I always sent my mail to Axy in care of Mother so she could forward it), I was more than slightly put out when the announcement of my engagement was treated with what I saw as almost indifference. Only nine days after my previous letter I followed it with a note to my sister:

I have this eve rec'd your short note & short letter from Mother. You appear to blame me for not writing positively whether I should be at home or not. How did I know "[and here I quote Axy]—'a creature governed by circumstances,

Greenbush, Aug 17, 1858.

Dear Sister,

I have this even rec'd your short note & a short letter from Mother. You appear to blame me for not writing positively whether I should be at home or not. How did I know a creature governed by circumstances, "knows not to day what the morrow will bring forth," and more than all that, you know you never let me know one of your arrangements, so I knew not that it would make any difference to you, the most I hear from you now is through the Press. I think sisters ought to have a more intimate connection than through the Public Press. & mother writes to me more as she would to a stranger than to a daughter. No wonder that my

On the 17th of August, 1858, a lonely and despondent Celia wrote a censorious letter to Achsa suggesting, "I think sisters ought to have a more intimate connection than through the Public Press, and Mother writes to me more as she would to a stranger than to a daughter." (Letter continues on next page.)

If I can make any such arrangement I have money in the Woodstock Bank that I should wish to pay for them. There is so much cheat in every article that is brought West I dislike to buy silver for fear I shall not get good.

I have gathered ten quarts of blackberries & & I am & going again today. There is an abundance of them.

My health is good and enjoy myself well. Do you get any new styles for dresses? do they wear long or short waists mostly? do they wear short basques? But stop I ought not to trouble you with such worldly affairs, but you can answer them as you see fit.

I hope you will answer this as soon as you can. I shall soon write to Mother. Celia.

Celia's letter to Achsa, asking, "Do you get any new styles for dresses? Do they wear long or short waists mostly? Do they wear short basques? But stop—I ought not to trouble you with such worldly affairs."

knows not to day what the morrow will bring forth,'" and more than all that, you never let me know one of your arrangements, so I knew not that it would make any difference to you. The most I hear from you now is through the Press. I think sisters ought to have a more intimate connection than through the Public Press. And Mother writes to me more as she would to a stranger than to a daughter. Ere this no doubt you have rec'd my last letter which will in part tell you of my intentions. Here again I give confidence but receive nothing in return.

A week later I curtly wrote that I'd decided not to go East that fall as I'd once suggested.

I think I had rather wait until next June or fall, & then have Mother come back with me & stay one year & longer in Wisconsin if she will. I feel disappointed at not going home now yet I think it for the best. I am quite busy sewing, think I shall teach again this winter if I can find a school to suit me.

I opened the letter the next day to add a postscript:

Axy, I don't know but you will think very strange at my asking the favor of you that I am about to ask, but as I wish to get a <u>good</u> article and at the lowest price possible I thought perhaps you and some of your friends who knew the quality of silver might select for me and then send by express.

I wish for a set of silver teaspoons and another set cheaper yet good enough to bear marking, four large spoons, a butter knife and a sugar spoon or whatever is most used to dip sugar with. I want a <u>good</u> quality and style, and all marked with

CS.

If you can or cannot assist me I wish you would let me know as soon as you can, and what said articles would cost. I can make any such arrangement. I have money in the Woodstock Bank that I should wish to pay for them. There is so much cheat in every article that is brought West, I dislike to buy silver for fear I shall not get good quality.

My health is good and I enjoy myself well. Do you get any new styles for dresses? Do they wear long or short waists mostly, and do they wear short basques? But stop—I ought not to trouble you with such worldly affairs. But you can answer them as you see fit. I hope you will answer this as soon as you can. I shall soon write to Mother.

Another quick note then followed, in response to Axy's question about the teaspoons. My sister was lecturing in New York.

I rec'd your letter Thursday eve. Mr. Steen as he came to invite me to his sister's wedding brought it along, so you see here I am at Oakfield visiting the friends of him that I have chosen as a partner for life. Yesterday Anne and myself walked to the spot where my future dwelling is to be. A cellar is now being completed, soon the frame will be up and then John will finish it at his leisure, this winter. I like the country here very well and think I shall like the people.

I think you must have misunderstood my writing before: it was only one set of teaspoons I wanted plated, but think I had better have them silver. They can be sent by an express company to J. M. Steen, Fond du Lac, Wisconsin. A receipt must be taken as the articles are given over to the company. Have them sent to J. M. Steen as he lives near and can see to getting them. I would like to have them sent soon as convenient for I now think of using them in November.

I shall not teach this winter. All expenses can be paid by getting money from the Bank. If anything prevents your getting them let me know immediately so I can send to New York.

Our correspondence promptly continued, as Axy responded with worry that I had "definitely found true love."

September 8, 1858
Greenbush

 Dear Sister Axy,

I have rec'd the last letter you sent (I guess it is the lost one) and dispatched your message to Morris. In reply he says tell her I will be very happy to greet her as a sister. He says that he likes you because you approve of the same principles as himself, "and I admire her for the noble and courageous manner in which she advocates, them, &tc." He has told me I have opened the casket of his soul and taught him to love.

 Yes, Axy, I have every reason to believe that I am now receiving what I have ever desired, viz: First, true & pure love. I believe the <u>whole</u> heart is mine, and you know it is the whole that contents me. You wrote of the manner which I spoke of him. I know I did not speak of love but it was not because it was not there. I feel that I am receiving more than I am able to give yet I believe him worthy of woman's holiest love.

 Morris has not called himself a Spiritualist but has been called an infidel. I call him a Free Thinker. He has let out a portion of his farm that we might visit Mother and all of you the last of next May. This is his planning and not mine, and now I shall see that it is executed <u>without fail</u> so don't engage yourself for the month of June!

 You see I plan as though I were now married. I do so, as Morris never uses the word <u>if</u> since our engagement, neither does he like to have me use it, as I constantly do. Morris expresses an inclination to write to you – he says he would be glad to receive a letter from you. I wish you would write him, he is not afraid to talk about Spiritualism. His address, J. A. Morrison Steen, Oakfield, Wis. I shall have to read much more to keep up with him and I am so glad of it. Axy, what would you think if I should tell you he was born in a foreign country? The next letter I write you, I shall not write entirely about Morris. I hope you will write as often as you can and if you don't place confidence in me, I shall in you.

Axy was away from Ogdensburgh and touring in New York State when she sent me a letter accusing me of attempting to "annihilate" her for asking such a question (regarding my love for Morris). I replied on September 22.

> I know I was unusually severe in my comments but felt so I wrote it still. Yes, Axy, you have offered to give me <u>all</u> I could ask for & you have made me many presents which have been thankfully rec'd, not for the value of the articles alone, but coming from you whom I once never expected would be able to leave your bed and impart unto others & the feelings which I felt always accompanied the presents & have made them doubly cherished.
>
> But in your writing you never speak of your joys or sorrows. I cannot know something of one's troubles of life if I know there is but little confidence. You speak of my taking offense at your writing "<u>definitely</u>." No, Axy, that is not the case. You know I have often asked you to criticize me in writing & everything else but you have never seemed disposed to, only when something drew it from you at certain times. As you have so many letters to write I am sorry I troubled you about the silver, but you know you are not obliged to do anything about it unless you wish to. And you need not trouble yourself to get any patterns for me, either, for I don't know as I shall have anything new. Write when it pleases you.

11

Songs Without Words

(1858)

I am tiring you with personal matters
that ought to be locked forever in the chamber of my heart
and I ought not to write them to you, but …
because you know me better at this moment
than any <u>mortal</u> beside, I write as I do.

Letter to Achsa Sprague,
December 8, 1858
JOHN H. CRAWFORD

MY SISTER WAS IN NEW YORK for most of September, all of October and November, and part of December that year (1858) where she lectured in villages, cities, and towns, always returning to Ogdensburgh or Oswego for a week or more. Her relationship with John Crawford deepened during their moments together and further matured through written correspondence. Their game of "combat" thrived, each initiating a line or stanza for a poem, with the other required to respond with consequential material in turn.

Morris and I were married in Sheboygan County on November 25. Axy had given me an Ogdensburgh address. I mailed a lengthy letter to her from Oakfield in mid-December.

December 12, 1858

Dear Sister Axy,

I am now indebted to you for three letters as you term them and I will call them so too altho' some of them were very short. I should have written you before but I rec'd the letters from you about the time you would leave the place. Now I shall write you a long letter that will be an equivalent to your three in quantity if not in quality.

I did not write again about the silver. I thought "whatever is, is right," so I would make no further effort. I have as yet bought only six teaspoons and three large spoons.

I presume Mother has kept you well informed of my procedure so it will hardly be necessary for me to say to you that I am married and am now housekeeping. Strange it may seem to you that Celia is a married woman, but to be married is not half as strange as to think of it. I feel just as natural and as much at ease in my own household as I ever did in the schoolroom, and it is with a slight degree of satisfaction that I arrange and perform my domestic duties. But I have to murmur to myself because I cannot do more and better. How often I wonder that I was not born to <u>excel</u> in something.

Wednesday, December 15

Sister Axy let me give you a slight description of my labors for this day.

Morris arose between five and six and built a fire. Soon I was seen in the kitchen baking pancakes and broiling beefsteaks, but no simmering of the teakettle was heard or the smell of burnt coffee, but pure cold water stood upon our table; after partaking heartily of wholesome food which was spiced with love, Morris brought to the kitchen wood, water &tc &tc that my labors might be light.

Oh, Axy, if you could get as kind a husband as Morris is to me, I am sure you would enjoy wedded life. But perhaps you think you will have domestics to perform your labor and all you will want in a consort will be superior attainments in Science, Literature, &tc &tc. But now let me tell you domestic men are the best men in the world when they have a good library. But I will go back to my subject. I have set my house in order, baked Graham and fine flour bread, have got a pudding in the oven for dinner and now it is but ten o'clock as I take my paper to write you.

There is something so new and romantic about housekeeping that I enjoy it now, but I keep an eye open to see and a hand open to catch the evil that I expect will meet me. Last Sunday we commenced having a family circle or sitting, call it which you please. We shall now sit every Sunday and Wednesday eve and if it is possible for us to receive more light upon <u>the</u> subject and subjects, we intend to get it. I will leave paper enough for John to write some, but he is so busy today I fear he will not.

Please direct your next to Oakfield, Fond du Lac Co. Wis.

One year from this time I shall expect you out here to see us, and if any thing should prevent our going East next spring, I shall expect you here before. I have not written half I intended to but must leave again and build up more fire or my pumpkin will not get stewed so I can make some pies. Ha, ha, ha.

Celia Sprague Steen

P.S. John thinks he cannot write this time but wishes to be remembered to you. C.S.S.

November and December of that same year witnessed the enthusiastic exchange of letters between my sister and Mr. Crawford. I do not have Axy's text, but as I described earlier, she preserved every sheet of his pale blue communiqués.

Occasionally she teased Mr. Crawford that he was her "evil genius," one who strongly influenced her character, conduct or destiny for good or ill. In turn, he bestowed pet names upon her that possessed private meanings I cannot decipher —for example, addressing her as "Myraj" on December 3, or "Kilmeny" in his letter of December 21.

It is indeed possible (and probable) that my sister would think it ill-mannered and unseemly for me to divulge the following, but herewith I shall include a selection of Mr. Crawford's letters. His depth of feeling and responses to Axy's parrying ripostes will illustrate the exceptional bond of friendship they were commencing to share.

Utica—Wednesday, November 10, 1858

"Just as I expected." I am here and you are away, such is destiny. I arrived here this morning, called on business with Gov. Seymour, but it seems as tho my business here was only half accomplished because I have missed you. I wrote you from New York on Saturday which you probably did not get before leaving...O how I wished it had been practicable for me to be here over Sunday.

I am pleased to hear from your friends here that you spoke of me to them. I hope you said only reasonably good things of me and will save the naughty ones to say to me.

I am quite nervous about your "cold" during this cold unpleasant weather. Your "cold" and the weather's cold had both ought to be "caught" and severely "pun"ished for being "caught" together. Then to have to go away so far in the stage, at such a stage of your cold and in such dreary weather – it makes me doubly nervous. I do hope and pray that you will get no worse. I wish you were snugly housed for the winter at our house in Ogdensburgh. We would keep your room at a temperature of 70 at night and day until you got well. Why won't you go and stay with us until you get well?

I send you the Household Book of Poetry for examination. After you read it all you want to send it back to me by Express. I have glanced at and marked a few passages, but I have only _glanced_. I wish you would fill the margins with _your_ marks, different from mine so I can know your estimate and the _degrees_ of your estimation.

Finish what I have only just begun—I like to see marginal notes in books.

I give you _David Copperfield_ and want you to read it when you have leisure as it contains some firmly drawn characters and many pearls.

I will come here next Saturday & stay over Sunday if practicable, _certainly_ if I don't go home.

Yours in haste and sincerity,

J. H. Crawford

New York,
Saturday, November 13, 1858

My Dear Friend,

I intended, until the morning, to have seen and heard you tomorrow in Utica. This morning I have letters that make it necessary for me to remain in this city until Monday, and of _course_ you will be absent at Oriskany on Monday evening or Tuesday when I get there. If you wanted to see me half as badly as I want to see you, you would be disappointed too, but I cannot flatter myself that such is the case. How I _should_ like to receive Monday or until Tuesday noon at Baggs Hotel a line from you stating your whereabouts and well-being at that particular time. I shall undoubtedly remain over one train on business and If you _should_ be there I could put in a short call, just long enough to say good morning and good bye. That _last_ was a _very_ hard word for me to speak on a certain Monday evening remembered by me, and I _do believe_ a certain person said good bye, "_be good_" to me, almost in the dark to prevent my seeing the smiles that lit up a pair of eyes. I never wanted to see anybody very much, but somehow I would like to see _you_ again long enough to give you an opportunity to say one or two severe things of me because such things said by _you_ are like the storm or whirlwind to me, the most beautiful when most _terrible._

I have been to the Opera and heard _four great stars_, Gazzaniga, Picollomini pronounced pic ol _lom_ inia, Carl Forms and Madame Gihoni. I wished you were there many times.

I have bought Dana's beauties of poetry and there are numerous beauties in it. I have also bought _Miles Standish_, if you want it. I will have a package at Baggs Hotel for you if I don't see you. So you need not flatter yourself that I have been _sincere_ enough to forget you yet.

I really hope Gov. Seymour, to whom I have letters on business, will not be at home when I pass Utica. Then I shall have an excuse for returning there a week from today…

I have much to tell you of my experience in being good, but will omit it now.

Your most earnest and sincere friend,

J. H. Crawford

Oswego, Friday—November 19, 1858

My dear friend,

Fearing the heel of commerce will prevent my seeing you on

Sunday I must beg to plague you with another letter...

I have attended no circles since my return but my experience since I met you has been very interesting indeed, but cannot well be written. Your injunction placed upon me at parting to "be good" has not been unheeded and I am anxiously waiting for the light.

I have a letter from daughter Jenny in which she quotes a portion of the Parson's remarks at church and contrasts them with yours at one of your meetings. The Parson suffers in her hands.

There is much _wishing_ at Ogdensburgh for your return there.

I am fearful you caught an addition to your cold during your country pilgrimage through snows and storms, but I prayed that you might not.

I _did_ see Gov. Seymour at Utica not withstanding I hoped I might not, so I could have an excuse to go there tomorrow. But I don't want an excuse. I will go if I can without doing injury to myself through neglect of business. This bad weather and the lateness of the season requires constant watching and attention. If I get dispatches today requiring my presence at Watertown on Monday, which I some expect, I shall go to Utica to remain over Sunday.

Mrs. Richardson informs me that her church has done nothing towards dismissing the Spiritual element from among them and that she is treated with the utmost kindness. I think the Methodists too sensible to do anything so silly as to imitate their Baptist brethren.

We had sleighing two or three days here but it is all gone now. Your and my "old friend" the sea has been terribly exercised for a few days past and his sad song has been changed unremittingly until _I know_ "what the wild waves are saying" now.

I have already written more than I intended and more than you may have patience over. I have written carelessly at a gallop as I am hurried today. I expect you to find numerous faults but I can't help them now. I hope you will find such because then you shall _read to me_, when I see you, the little fatal poem that got sealed up in your throat so suddenly one day.

Your Earnest Sincere Friend,

J. H. Crawford

Oswego
Friday, December 3, 1858

"Myraj" (or Mirage)

I am sick today with a cold, am in my warm room but inspiration and colds are inharmonious.

The "angel flowers" are falling by my window in beautiful crystal lakes and I fancy not a few of them have tried to stop and look in, as I have noticed them fluttering there for a moment like a humming bird about to light and gather sweetness from the blossom. There's this difference however. The _flutterer_ seeks inspiration of the flower while I seek inspiration in the flake.

I wish my pen could seize upon the snowflakes and give them to you. The offering would _not be more pure_ than these little tributes of my esteem and respect that may seem to annoy you.

Since turning this scrap I discover the blot beneath. I pray God that no "blot" may ever mar your or my future pages in the great unread book that is before us. I trust you will not consider the blot an "emblem," if you do, I wish to construe it myself as I will do when I close.

I have added another verse to the Canto and as 'tis without

merit I have half a mind not to send it, but as you are not very exacting I venture to show it to you. Please bear in mind that the <u>wave</u> is immortal and cannot be annihilated and that as the sea's heart <u>must throb</u> on & its pulse must flow, and <u>the wave and the sea are inseparable</u>, it was better that the wave should rejoice in being the "crown and glory" of the sea than that it should moan, die and sink into an endless sleep. Don't tell me that the wave that can sing such songs, even though some of them may be sad as the requiem of children—will <u>ever die</u>. These songs and the voices that sing them are God's notes and God's instruments and he will keep them in his orchestral and vocal choir until <u>music</u> ceases to please him or elevates his children's souls.

Yours ever, C.   I am <u>above</u> a <u>blot</u>.

✦

Oswego
Monday, December 6, 1858

My Dear Friend

I don't know when I shall send this, probably not until I hear from you so I may know where it may reach you, but I will write it and be ready.

My experience for a few days past has been peculiar. I have times when my brain becomes as light as air, and filled with daydreams of ecstasy and pleasures. I seem in those conditions, to be removed from care, anxiety or trouble, and I seem lost in a kind of mental Elysium—or thought-intoxication…

A day or two since the whole trip made by us from this city across the Lake and down the river was pictured to me in a poem in blank verse – passing indistinctly before me like a moving panorama. Why do these beauties taunt me so? Why can't I give embodiment to them? Is this the budding of the flower that will blossom in Inspiration? Or is it hallucination? #

I have felt something like this before, but never on so high a plane, or never have such pleasurable conditions been attained before. I am impressed that your Guardians have influenced me, as I often feel as when with you.

At this moment I feel that "doughfacedness" spoken of by you when in certain conditions. What a strange life is mine. What will it result in. When end? Good night.

Tuesday morning

As I awoke this morning at my fatal, or regular hour, five o'clock or became partly awake, passing on to the bridge that connects the lands of dreams with the waking state, the cluster of telegraphic wires, or <u>cobwebs</u> passed before my closed eyes and discovering many lines that seemed beautiful I made a spasmodic attempt to grasp the cluster but the effort was too great and I awoke with only a few fragments in my hands which I saw and remembered, regretting exceedingly my inability to remember all I saw. Soon I partly lost myself again and stood upon the "bridge" again and saw the balance of the singular "verse" which follows:

> *These are the dreams my fancy wrought,*
> *And these the Shadows passing by*
> *With garlands from the Realm of Thought,*
> *To crown my brain, and bless mine eye.*
> *Sweet hope to my sad soul is brought*
> *By angels from the azure sky.*
> *This is the Heaven I long have sought*
> *To feel and know that thou art nigh.*

Now I beg to know to whom this is addressed. Is it my language, and addressed to one in the Spirit form? It would seem unreasonable to call it the language of a <u>spirit</u> to me. I may have not fully understood it and may have misstated it. Yet I am confident that I have given nearly the precise reading as I saw it. Were the phraseology changed and the words addressed to me by substituting "thy" for "my" &c it would pass very flowingly until you came to <u>the last two lines</u>. Then this double verse with double rhyme is all a mystery and never thought of by me before.

It really passes but little poetic merit, but it is the manner in which it came that puzzles and pleases me. Can it be the putting words into my mouth to enable me to answer the questions asked upon the preceding pages marked #?

The construction of the fifth and sixth lines in their connection does not please me, and it is possible they may be hereafter corrected. I wish I knew your opinion of my condition and whether you can throw any light upon this mystery. Are these exhalations from the realm of fancy, the higher life, or from my own brain? Then, if from the Spiritual—<u>who is the Spirit</u> that brings me this Heaven? Were she not in the Spiritual Realm as the lines would indicate, I would endeavor to <u>guess</u>, but am quite at a loss to identify her there.

Adieu J.H.C.

Oswego
Wednesday, December 8, 1858

My Dear Friend

Wednesday, and no letter? Well, such is my fate, and perhaps 'tis well that such is my fate…

O, could I have the privilege of _reliving_ the past thirty years, with my present views, yearnings, and longings. I could then shape my destiny and make it glorious, or beautiful at least. But my dear friend, I am tiring you with personal matters that ought to be locked forever in the chamber of my heart and I ought not to write them to you, but as you have seemed, to my mind, to be interested in my development, and because you know me better at this moment than any _mortal_ beside, I write as I do trusting that after you read these lines they will find the oblivion they merit. I will wait until tomorrow before sending this, and perhaps add a word. _Adieu._

Thursday P.M

Your letter and your "Reply" are rec'd. This is the crowning leaf in the "combat" and were I to treat you as you deserve, I should let you "wave," but you cannot have the "last word" yet. What a strange medley you are. You close your letter with the injunction, which you apply to yourself as well as to me, to "_be good_" (and one would suppose three such lines underscored so strongly could constitute a _sure foundation_ for some goodness,) but when any one promises, even impliedly, to be _good_ they should give _some earnest_ of their intentions in starting on the good errand. How is it with you? How does your practice square with your professions? Look at the "Reply," and you will therein find more bitterness, even hate, more evil intent, more malice & more naughtiness than a hundred lines of penance and contrition could atone for. Why you would have to spend ages in confession and prayer before you could begin to "be good." Were I to rejoin by sending you a cask of aloes and a barrel of lemonyice the bitterness and acidity of your "Reply" would _not be_ half answered.

As it is your nature to find fault with me I am not disappointed. Somehow—do what I may, I receive your censure when I endeavor by every possible means to avoid it.

As to your poems, I will return your own original copies if you <u>demand</u> it, which you have not done. (I am now answering your question) but I would prefer to <u>retain them</u>. I think I can see through this matter. Don't you prefer to publish them yourself in some obscure country paper? I would have them published in one of the leading monthlies, or weeklies, where they would be seen and copied far out and wide, while, if published in some "World's Paper" they would die a natural death…

I am requested, in behalf of the Spiritualists of this place, to offer you $1,000 salary for a year or $500 for six months, or if you will not engage for a longer period than three months they will give you $300 for three months. Mr. Robinson and Mr. Pool, Capt. Green and others are amongst the most interested in getting you here. They would be willing to let you select the term for commencing your engagement if within four or five months, but would prefer to have you begin soon. Now you can't say you have not had a "call." I will send my "last word" tomorrow as I have not time today before closing the mail.

Goodbye, may peace be with you whether sleeping or waking and if earnest prayers and wishes for your welfare are of any avail, you <u>will</u> be <u>happy</u>.

Very truly

J. H. Crawford

[Near this date—November/December 1858—my sister was compelled to write a letter to John Crawford regarding an unusual experience. This unfinished draft was found enclosed with the blue letters, obviously an addendum to a letter she had previously composed.]

Axy's Note about "The Mystery"

Before I come near to forgetting what I wished to tell you. Last Thursday I was out spending the evening with a party of friends, when not far from nine o'clock ~~in the evening~~ I was sitting on a sofa beside a gentleman who was a medium and fronting us was a lady who was also a medium. He personates spirits & had at other times previous personated two spirit friends for me that I recognized. The first I noticed that he was influenced, he commenced singing, or rather "humming" "songs without words." So much like <u>your voice</u>, and particularly as ~~it sounded~~ I heard it on Lake Ontario, that I thought I must be dreaming, & turning suddenly round, I saw he was influenced. I cannot begin to tell you anything about it with a pen, but will give you briefly a few things & see if you know what to make of them. You remember I told you that I had a Telegraphic Dispatch from you at Syracuse from Watertown through a medium, don't you?

I said "what spirit is this?" He said, "some one comes from a distance singing a sweet song." I said, "can this spirit sing any song that I may recognize who it is?" Immediately he commenced singing very much in your style, the song commencing with "Come oh come with me." & sang several strains. Then he commenced examining my hands as though he was looking for something & at last missed the ring (my <u>symbolic ring</u>) that you had reset with the green stone which was not on my finger.

I can't begin to tell you. He can talk in that state but very little, yet he made several remarks very like you, among the rest calling me a <u>humbug</u> at some remark that I made. When the lady became influenced, & described the spirit—black eyes, hair, full beard, not a stern looking face, yet emanating power, mirthful yet not mirthless & gave several characteristics that to me were wonderful. Among the rest she said that <u>I doubted the sincerity</u> of the spirit, & made some remarks almost word for word as I have heard you sometimes when you wished to be intelligible to only the person you addressed, each remark leaving me perfectly conscious of their meaning. The spirit staid nearly two hours *(while the rest of the party were playing whist) & <u>would not leave</u> though the lady medium wished to go home & it was the business of the gentleman to go with her. At last she rose to go when the gentleman got up, still partially under the influence, went into the hall, put on his hat and overcoat and then came back and bid me good bye <u>precisely</u> as you did at Mrs. R's (though he expected to see me again that evening). When he paused out at the hall door with the lady, he turned and waved me an adieu as precisely as I have seen you do many times. Your precise gesture. And what was curious, the mediums were left in a perfect fog in regard to the matter, while if you were in the <u>spirit land</u> I should <u>know</u> that it was you.*

I never had a greater test of the presence of spirit than I had of your presence that evening. What am I to think of it? And what do <u>you</u> think of it? Were you thinking of me at all at that time, or were you perfectly engrossed in business?

"There are more mysteries in Heaven & earth than is dreamed of in our philosophy."

As one, the wave & the sea

[From John H. Crawford, regarding the above]

"About the Mystery"

The occurrence you relate, as having taken place on a Thursday evening was very remarkable and strange. I wish I could fully account for it. Why didn't you account for my own experience? Why didn't you furnish reasons for the revelation to me in the cluster of lines which I seemed to see? To whom did the lines refer reading thus:

> *"This is the heaven I long have sought*
> *To feel and know that thou art nigh"*

I cannot explain their meaning, can you? Why were these _lines_ presented before me in this manner so new to me?

I cannot remember _distinctly_ what took place on any Thursday night, perhaps my letter of that date may explain… But I know that one evening _that_ week, and I think twas _Thursday_, I was writing in my room all the evening until near twelve o'clock and about nine I wrote a dispatch to you and laid it on the table asking my Guardians to carry it to you, and if they could not deliver it, to manifest themselves to you in some way so you would know the message was from me. I am therefore not disappointed at your communication, but it takes a different shape from what I expected. But I am none the less pleased.

I _do believe_ I have thought of you with sufficient earnestness, sincerity—truthfulness and purity to impress your Guardians and mine with the same knowledge and I have earnestly desired to be understood and appreciated by you and I know that I have often felt the same influence when alone that I have felt in your society and I know that when under this influence I am a stranger to sorrow and despondency. I also know that I am impressed with the belief that your Guardians try to impress me and I believe when with you that the same influence was often felt by us both.

Now I don't say this out of any motive outside of, and beyond _truth_. You _must know_ if you can read thought, how highly I estimate the casket that holds (sometimes) such beautiful jewels as you have given me and others. You must know that this estimation _has but one name_, which is very nearly allied to adoration, and if _I have not misjudged, you_ have not always considered me the _insincere_ one you have tried to make me, and have to some extent felt the genial impulses of true friendship budding in my direction. If this is not so I have not read correctly. Therefore I can see no reason for a quarrel between your and my Guardians and if they act in concert and harmony, cannot earnest true and noble impulses and desires be sent and manifested in the manner you describe. It is a new phase of intercourse but it may become very interesting. How I wish you felt free to tell me everything that was said or done. You don't say whether your doubts of "sincerity" were either removed or confirmed.

What a strange world. You ask if I am not happy. My life has been a sealed book, scarcely opened or read by myself, much less by another, until you saw me and held the Mirror before me.

I dream of you often. I dreamed of you last night—dreamed of conversing with you. Father respecting you, and he seemed pleased that I appreciated you. I knew he was a <u>spirit</u> too.

Now all this may annoy you. I hope <u>not</u>. I am earnest in writing it and believe every word of it. I think of you earnestly and often and I will not tell you how often or <u>how earnestly</u>. I might tell you some strange experiences when thinking of you, but as you think about Evil Geniuses in connexion with some of my doings, I will not weary you further now. I will gladly do anything reasonable for your Daguerrotype even to sending you one of --- --- why can't you give me one?

Good night—the dearest prayer I can offer is may you be happy and think of me and may angels guide & protect you. <u>Be good</u>. Earnestly, C

New York City
Sunday, December 19, 1858

Dear First Spirit,

You will perceive that my letter is not mailed where 'twas written. The reason for this is I was coming here direct and if mailed here it would reach you as early as it would otherwise. I had a delightfully lonesome trip, without a single acquaintance except for a few newspapers and <u>Hiawatha</u>. (This should be pronounced <u>Hi</u> a <u>wat</u>-ha according to earlier

Historians than Schoolcraft. I have spent considerable time amongst these red brothers and know something of them)...

Your poetry—both the "Song of the Sea" and the "Combat" remind me so strongly and strangely of something undefinable and indistinctly recollected that the reading produces the most strange emotions. They seem a compound of Byron, Shelly and "Songs Without Words." They seem like your eyes and face, to resemble some Spirit or thought seen, felt or heard _before_. Then in some passages in the combat fully equal to anything I ever _saw_ by any author for power, directness, intensity and beauty, viz "I'll call the lightnings from the sky" "I'll bend thy strong ships like a reed," "For I will gather from thy deeps" in short four out of the five, if not the whole five stanzas of the first "Reply" contains as much of the elements above named as any similar number I ever met with.

Now don't get out of patience with me for saying these things for I do know good poetry from bad. Had I not known it I might have written more myself but I feared to pass it through the crucible of my own poor opinion and therefore the gift, if I even possessed any, has died out.

It is no egotism in one to claim to be a judge of poetry and in proof, permit me to refer you to everything I sing. Are not these songs models and gems of power and rhythmical beauty? You have never heard me sing one tenth of the number I do sing, but you will remember some of them enough to show the vein in which my taste runs. Eliza Cook's songs always had peculiar beauties and charms for me and I know I should love her for them could I see her, even were she old and ugly.

I speak thus to prevent you calling me a blockhead for praising you. Your letters do not get "criticized" when they fall into my hands. I like their careless-rattling manners—were they prim and precise I should not dare to reply to them, but their familiar, easy gait gives _me_ courage to write.

Your last "Reply" is capital for the _kind_ and I am so well pleased with the sympathy I find in the condition of the wave that I almost want to let it end where you have left off. I may conclude to give you a specimen of my bitterness in joining in the bouquet & feast of "agony" by & by, but as a woman must always have the "last word" I may rue the day when I arouse the angry wave again.

I have had running through my brain and soul during a part of the time of late sundry "songs without words" which, if you were any ready reader of music I would write out and send you (just the melodies leaving out the arrangement of the harmonies until some future opportunity). Could I hum them to you I would like you to decide upon the respective subjects from impression which I know you could do as easily as I could. I have often thought I would like to write one and pour my spirit so fully into it that it would become a part of myself and then ask you, or the "angels hovering near you," to embody my thoughts in the song or hymn for which the music should be adapted. I can easily get my deepest holiest thoughts on paper in the music and if I could only get poetry that would match prayer with prayer, hope with hope, despair with despair, love with love, beauty with beauty, grandeur & sublimity with the same and so on through all the emotions of the soul, I would then find a boon for which I have long sought. I have sometimes thought I could combine these two graces or gifts but they seem to belong to two distinct realms or departments and the effort to grapple with both might make my brain dizzy—("distrust" I hear you say).

One word about "insincerity." I am not certain that <u>you</u> are not right after all, but I am more insincere towards <u>myself</u> than towards others. This is real truth.

I might add a word about the "mystery" but I may fail to throw any light on the subject. I should like to hear what your solution would be. Perhaps some "Fiend" is practicing a deception on you by my direction, thus establishing the fact that an "Evil Genius" is following you. Did the Spirit claim to be in the Spirit Land? Perhaps 'twas some "counterpart" of myself who really desires to imitate his Earthly Friend and join the "casket" in the world beyond the Stars. Confound the fellow for being like me in this, or any other respect. I am rather pleased, however, at this idea because if he really *is like me* his case is hopeless.

I sometimes think our life is "two fold" and that one spiritual form accompanies our Material one, and does sometimes separate its self, and for a time, leave the Material. This would explain many hitherto inexplicable things connected with dreams, visions and conditions in which our mentality becomes exalted. It would explain many of my conditions from boyhood to which I alluded in a former letter. How provoking it is in you not to even notice a line of my "experience" as given you.

Now please pardon whatever thine eyes may see amiss in my tedious letters. If I say things I ought not to say, consign paper ink and thoughts alike to oblivion (there will be so few of the latter in comparison with the former that they won't make the sparks fly from the grate).

The sparks have been flying from my grate thick and fast. I touched a match (not the one you are going to make) to the paper when paper faggots and coal began to war like a *wave* I know of and soon the sparks flew out like the "bristling of armor" I have seen on me one or two occasions. I did not think a Spirit was there "Reply"ing to anything I had done but it seemed like one. However if "'twas the wave" ending its agony, it has got tired enduring in a snappish way and is as calm as the sea when the wave is hushed and rocked to sleep in the purity and serenity of the transparent waters that sparkle and shimmer in the light of God's Eye.

May Angels be with you when sleeping or awake.

Truly and Earnestly Your *Friend.*

New York City
Tuesday, December 21, 1858

Dear Kilmeny,

I do not propose sending this for a day or two but having a leisure half hour I will write a line or two and send it by & by should I think best. It would hardly be supposed that in the noise and din of this <u>thundering</u> city one could hear the silent whisperings of the soul. I have thought what relief 'twould bring to the weary and tired brain to run away from all this tumult, to the woods and mountains, where you could hear nothing but God and the beatings of your own heart. How can one listen to anything here but the tramp and rumbling of hoof and tire from midnight to midnight? In such clamor and discord I do not wonder people forget they have souls and rush unchecked to destruction.

Oh such a seething, sweltering, foaming, hurrying, swimming whirlpool as is this New York, can only be found here and yet one finds here much that is beautiful, much of beauty in art but nature is almost a sealed book. I have seen nothing beautiful this time but a celebrated painting by Correggio, said to be 298 years old of Venus, Mercury and Cupid. It is very beautiful and is said to be worth $30,000. It is now on exhibition opposite the Metropolitan Hotel and is visited by many of the "Upper Classes." The masses have very little taste in such matters which is a lamentable fact. Bob, Billy, and Philo all prefer to hear Woods Negro Minstrels to paying 25 cents to see such a painting.

Since coming here I have been too much absorbed in business to spend any time in seeing the beautiful. A business engagement this evening prevented my listening to a poem delivered by Oliver Wendell Holmes at the Rutgers Street Church. It was doubtless a rich treat.

I began by saying that one would suppose that nothing but noise could be heard here—but I was going to say, and I will now say it, after all this preliminary babble that a few "Songs without visible words" have been almost constantly ringing in my souls ears ever since my note to you on that subject on Sunday.

I believe my room, which is a very cozy one, is <u>haunted</u>. I feel half the time, when in it, the pressure of another and turn suddenly around to look for them. I never had this feeling before. It does not annoy me but pleases me. At times I feel it very strongly and the influence is gentle and happy and is almost precisely such as I have felt on one or two occasions at Mrs. Richardson's in Oswego when sitting in a circle and being magnetized by you. At such times I have asked and received through a stronger influence in my arm, causing it to ache, and by the unmistakable "dough face"—unmistakable tests of the same influence. Have you not been retaliating for the visit of the Spirit that would stay two hours?

December 28

There has been an "awful pause" in this letter but if you knew how I have been engaged night and day, and Sunday too, with my partner from Cleveland who has been here, and with the President of the New York & Erie Rail Road, you would not wonder.

I had half a mind to not send this, but lest you think the "Spirit" gone, I send it bad as it is.

I start for Ogdensburgh tomorrow to pass "New Years" & shall not be at Oswego until about the 8th of January. Letters that may have gone to Oswego will be sent to me at Ogdensburgh by Saturday next. Where <u>will</u> you be after the 1st?

I shall leave about the 15th of January for Cleveland, Chicago & Milwaukee. So I go.

I want to see you worse than ever. May you continue to be good, and may <u>I</u> get to be <u>good</u>.

Your earnest friend, C

12

The Heart's Dream

(January–June 1859)

*I feel a tone of sadness in some of the letters you write
that tells me you are not as happy as I would have you.*

Letter from Celia
January 22, 1859

B ALTIMORE WAS RAINY AND DAMP, when Axy again accepted the hospitality of the Danskins. They promptly introduced her to the social whirl at the White House on New Year's Day 1859; no excuses permitted. This time she was prepared for the party with her own evening dress of ashes-of-roses silk, fitted by an Oswego seamstress, Miss Phoebe Hewitt. The gown featured garlands of roses and foliage around the skirt, and a smaller crown of matching roses to gracefully encircle Axy's head.

According to Sarah Ann Danskin, the aristocracy in the nation's capital was not distinguished by its residences or carriages, by livings, lodgings, eatings or ridings—because it was not unusual for men to eat and sleep anywhere, and citizens and strangers, rich or poor, all rode in the same public conveyances, for there were few others from which to choose. Sarah Ann's opinion may have been influenced by her husband's haberdashery, but Mrs. Danskin insisted that the male aristocracy of Washington was distinguished by dress, and men who were dressed extravagantly in fashion and folly were to be presumed to belong to the "upper ten." The rest, she claimed with a sniff of disdain, belonged to the "lower million" (which may have explained her husband's red paisley silk cape).

For women, however, there was no excuse or exception to dress, and at the President's Levee, a rush of opulence surrounded Axy like a suffocating mob of butterflies—rich silks and flounces, feathery plumes and loops of pearls, lace fans all aflutter in the swarm. Several women fainted and had to be removed through a window. My sister said she persevered only due to her tight grasp on Col. Daskins' arm. The little orchestra could barely be discerned in the din.

She wished to impress Mr. Crawford by mentioning a personal remark from President Buchanan, but the ensured formal presentation came to naught and no one caught the slightest glimpse of the bachelor president. Her ashes-of-roses frock surrendered a profusion of rose petals and a loop of foliage to the fête.

Perhaps due to late hours of revelry the night before, she spoke to slim audiences on Sunday that were intelligent albeit not very large. She, too, was tired.

On Monday, the Danskins continued with her tour of Washington City. This time they saw military companies marching on Pennsylvania Avenue. The soldiers were trailed by a rag tag group of lads who pretended to march with broomsticks and branches. Axy said she found the sight both precious and pitiful.

A visit to the Smithsonian Institute proved a most fascinating experience, especially a beautiful exhibit of birds' eggs—from that of a hummingbird (like a little bean) to the egg of the ostrich and the eagle, each placed in nests as they would be found in nature. There was also a likeness of Dr. Elisha Kent Kane, the explorer who had ventured into the Arctic regions following his engagement to Margaretta Fox—one of the famed Fox Sisters—in 1853. In a small room, a variety of spirit paintings and drawings were exhibited for the investigation of the public.

The question of Cuba was being discussed when Axy toured the Capitol building. A plan devised by U.S. diplomats proposed adding another slave state to the Union, and the purchase of Cuba from Spain was seen as a possible site for slavery's expansion.

Nonetheless, Axy thought the Senate chamber had a quiet beauty, softly lit from a glass ceiling thirty-five feet above that cast a peculiarly warm glow on senators who were seated in semi-circular rows on a purple carpet clustered with flowers. She thought the Tennessee marble stairways could hardly be surpassed in elegance, and Col. Danskin informed her that elaborate paintings would soon be hung in the unfinished corridors. A workman still labored where panels were filled with the most singular designs, somewhat resembling dancing girls in ungraceful attitudes. Mrs. Danskin declared, "They appear to have failed in their attempts to fly, and are now descending and about to fall upon their backsides!"

By contrast, the House of Representatives seemed gaudy and ornamented in inferior taste. The confusion of the room resembled a disorderly boys' school, with the incessant clapping of hands to call the pages, jumping up and down, moving about and restlessness of the members. Yet amidst the noise and confusion, some House members were soundly asleep on the sofas!

Admirers again pronounced Axy's stay in Baltimore all too brief. "I have no doubt but you have enjoyed a sleigh-ride in Connecticut and had a merry time of it," one of them wrote from Baltimore on January 21st, "quite a change from our damp atmosphere and muddy streets. But since you left us we have had several days of quiet spring weather and I have often wished that you might have been here to have enjoyed it. And what a pity it was that you did not stay here the remainder of the winter as there was such a good prospect for you to do so much good in this place of bigotry and superstition. You would have enjoyed very much to have heard a speech from your old friend Congressman Keitt of So. Carolina on the Cuba question. It is said to be the ablest speech made in the House this winter. I suppose he must have been sober."

The next week she spoke in Cincinnati, where their newspaper reported an annual expenditure of $1,250,000 for attempts to contain prostitution. One woman commented to Axy that it was a sad commentary on the inefficiency of the church in that quarter. The figure *was* appalling, but my sister realized from her experiences with prison reform that prostitution (certainly not to be casually dismissed in itself) often provided a temporary source of income for those poor women, and she politely suggested that not a few women are sometimes branded with that despicable label for a separate subcategory of public order offenses applied almost exclusively to females.

As the subject of Free Love seemed to have been thoroughly debated in that part of the country, Axy was not tortured with further questions of its worth or dignity. Nor was she taunted by malicious whispers from the shadows that implied her lectures were "pre-meditated." For the moment, at least, all was well. She only wanted winter to disappear and warmer weather to arrive at once.

Uncle Thomas Moore wrote from Plymouth Notch to give an account of improvements Axy had directed him to make on Mother's house. The entire production would have been laughable, if it had not been at Axy's expense and Mother's.

> We have raised it up and fixed it so that I think it will stand. We have laid over the cellar wall all that I thought was necessary and I lamed my back doing it and was not able to do any thing for about two weeks, and there fore your Mother at my suggestion engaged Charles Leonard to clean out the cellar and point the wall and he commenced to do it, got sand, lime and all the ingredients together and then he was taken sick with the inflammatory rheumatism and he came to my house three weeks ago last Monday night and has been here ever since and he was very sick for two weeks. It took two and three hands night and day to take care of him and Dr. Holt came to see him six times but he is now able to ride and walk out and appears to be doing well and therefore there has not been as much done to the cellar as would have been under other circumstances."

Uncle Thomas Moore had also purchased two tons of hay for Mother's use and placed it in her barn, furnished her with wood, and "I asked your Mother last night if she had every thing she needed for her comfort and she said she had and was getting along very well and enjoyed herself very well, so much for your enquiries."

In further news from the Notch, Cousin Ephraim wrote to say the two canaries Axy had brought home to keep Malvina and Mother company are smart and sing most every day. Your Mother and Malvina are well. I went in there this morning to take care of the cow. There was to be a wedding over to Mr. Cook's to day. Mother had to make the wedding cake last Friday. Lorinda Ellison was to be married. Mr. Ellison came over to get the cake yesterday and he asked father and mother to come and Mr. and Mrs. Coolidge. And so they went over about 2 o'clock this afternoon. Come to get over there her man had not come. So they waited and took dinner with them. And they cut three loaves of cake. Mother fetched home some to us. Mother said that Lorinda feels very bad. She does not the reason why he did not come. His name is Nikols.

Ordinary accounts of everyday life such as these caused my sister to feel profoundly homesick. She would have to wait for summer to quell any wistful yearnings.

My own letters caught up with her in mid-January when Axy arrived in Philadelphia.

Oakfield, January 22, 1859

Dear Sister,

I did not intend your welcome letter should so long remain unanswered but Time I should think has loosened her swift pinions and one week, yes two weeks pass by without my heeding it. All I will say in my defence is that I will hereafter be more punctual, for I desire to hear from you often.

I have rec'd the papers and the book you were so kind as to send me. A nice New Years gift—"Poets & Poetry" of my own Green Mountain State, edited by Abby Heminway. I was happily surprised to see the book. I knew not that such a work was contemplated; neither did I suppose that there was poetical genius sufficient to produce such a work, but it has made its appearance in good style and talent. Might I not feel a little flattered that I can even be a Sister to one of the Poets of the Day? I liked your piece very much. I took it to be a description of yourself. Please accept my sincere thanks for that beautiful book. Knowing as I do many of its writers, it is more highly valued by me than most any other book.

I have subscribed for the *Green Mountain Sibyl*, thinking you would write for it, have not rec'd a number yet.

Axy, do you enjoy speaking and have as good success as formerly? Is your health good? I feel a tone of sadness in some of the letters you write that tells me you are not as happy as I would have you.

Thank you for your kind wish. We had resolved before marriage to prolong our honeymoon through Eternity. "Bridal tour through the spheres" was not a new idea, but it suited us both and we will endeavor to make it so. Oh, why don't you take some of those fine, brilliant men?

I get along fine with my new duties and am now reading "Gibbon's Decline and Fall of the Roman Empire." Do you read much?

Hoping you will write as soon as convenient and that success may attend you I remain as ever,

Your Sister Celia

Cora Wilburn, a maiden-lady of much delicacy, saw my sister as "blooming, radiant and serenely happy," when she returned to Philadelphia. In *The Banner of Light*, Miss Wilburn spoke of Axy in rapturous terms as my sister had resumed her visits with the imprisoned:

> Miss A. W. Sprague is with us; and angels have blessed
> her life-path with a noble and successful mission; with
> renewed strength, and with untiring effort in the cause
> she has espoused…Miss Sprague bends her willing
> footsteps to the prisons, and cheers the drooping souls
> the world hast cast out from its joys and heritage, by
> words of love and hope, and counsel, long remembered
> by the grateful throng. I am told that the poor prisoners
> listen respectfully, in deep silence, to the spirit-medium.
> God alone knows the upwelling prayer, the faith, the
> aspiration of those longing souls!

Unfortunately, one of that city's more prominent citizens in whose home she had been invited to dine, inferred from a casual conversation with others that Axy was an advocate of Free Love. She called upon him as soon as it was possible to correct his implication.

"Whatever may have been said of me by enemies, those who know nothing of me or my opinions," she told her previous host, "I wish to set you right."

He invited her into the parlor and asked his wife to join them there.

"It certainly is a matter of much surprise to me that you could have found, in either my words or actions, anything that would justify you in the idea that I was an Advocate of Free Love," she protested. "I have only spoken of the injustice of all laws, the laws of marriage, with the rest. But have I said one word to you or anyone else that I thought the marriage law ought to be done away? That I was in favor of or disfavor of any one's marrying if they wished to? Did I even say, concerning myself *personally*, whether I did or did not intend to marry?"

The couple was silent and so she continued, still indignant.

"If I am so careless in my words and manner that you could think this of me, I do not blame the world for anything it may presume."

"Well, we heard from Mrs…" the doctor's wife began, but her husband silenced her with his sour glance.

"I care nothing for myself, but for the sake of Spiritualism," Axy said, knowing only minor discomfort.

All of this, and yet her spirit yearned for the murmur of John Crawford's endearments and the reassurance of his welcoming arms.

A letter from Mary Richardson in Oswego reached Axy in Massachusetts in early February, to say that Mr. Crawford's lame sister, Sarah, had been there for a four-day visit. "I do think a very great deal of that family, Mr. C. in particular." The spiritualist community in Oswego was rejoicing to learn that Axy had agreed to visit there for two whole months the following summer. She reflected upon that whenever she felt blue.

Crawford and his partners now ran thirteen propeller ships on the Great Lakes. *The Lady of the Lake* had gone down off Cleveland in March when its boiler exploded on Lake Erie but they had recently added *The Akron* to their fleet.

Throughout that miserably cold winter, her correspondence with Mr. Crawford had provided a revitalizing pastime. The regularity with which his blue stationery stood out among the white envelopes awaiting her in Connecticut, Massachusetts, and Rhode Island was known only to the two of them.

Watertown
February 3, 1859

Dear Spirit,

On my arrival at Oswego, a day or two since, I found a paper which some Spirit had sent me, containing a song and the music, also an invocation, both having certain characteristic marks to attract my attention; all very beautiful. What heart suggested such a thought to the brain? What brain held the thought? It seemed to me a waif from the land of shadows and mists. I could not make out the post-mark and ruthlessly tore off the envelop destroying the superscription before thinking to recognize in the hand writing some clue to its origin.

Thinking it <u>might</u> have come from you, and <u>sincerely</u> hoping it <u>did</u>; and having been detained at home a few hours waiting for the train; I conjured up from my tired imagination a fragment and hastily writing it down in pothooks, crotchets and quavers—quavering all the while—jumbling together quarter notes (that will receive no <u>quarter</u> from you) leaving out 'Minims' entirely for you will certainly supply their place by placing all in a Minimum position—omitting all <u>rests</u> because I had no time to <u>rest</u>, as darkness came and the cars went ere 'twas completed; not having any piano to try it I could not tell whether it was written too high or too low— 'twill no doubt be low enough when you hear it, and very soon thereafter <u>higher</u> than the <u>kite</u>. I think I shall alter it and raise it half a tone to Bb not because it is for you particularly but because it is from me. I wrote it on ### because 'twas for you—There should have been <u>more</u>, but in music only <u>five</u> are employed, usually, and that would scarcely be a beginning if comparisons are sought. If this is <u>not</u> as nearly original as may be, I do not know it—These breezes blow through our brains and become part of us, we cannot tell from whence they come, but we know they are with us.

You would know were it a "song without words," what the <u>words</u> were if sung properly; I may revise the music or write the song and send you a corrected copy after I sing it. This being my first effort for you, it is very imperfect and I am ashamed of it.

<u>How I do want to see you!</u>

I have nearly concluded to remove to Milwaukee in the spring. If I do, I must live by the shore of the blue Michigan because I cannot lose Ontario without getting another in its place.

I shall remain at Ogdensburgh whither I am bound in about a week—then go west or perhaps to Boston before *going west. Do please write me there at Ogdensburgh and at Oswego where I shall be week after next.*

May Angels while their watchful vigils keeping,
Guard thee from harm when nightly thou art sleeping,
And in thy heart pour sweetest peace while dreaming
Nor leave thee when the light of day is gleaming
But guide thy lonely wandering feet in paths of duty
Showering on all around bright pearls of priceless beauty.

Yours sincerely,

J. H. Crawford

The Heart's Dream

While on my night couch sleeping, While stars are vigils keeping,
And night winds moan along the sky, In shadows dim before me,
Or softly bending o'er me, An angel form seems hovering nigh.
An angel form seems hovering nigh.

Music composed by John Crawford with lyrics he wrote with Achsa: "While on my night couch sleeping / While stars are vigils keeping." But when it was published in a Spiritualist hymnal, the words became "While on my lone couch sleeping / In dreams sweet vigils keeping," and the title became "Mother's Dream," as the song depicts the return of a lifeless child as if in a dream: "No longer am I only / Sad, desolate, and lonely; / My darling lives and comes to me, / My darling comes to me." From *The Spiritual Harp: A Collection of Vocal Music for the Choir, Congregation and Social Circle*, published in 1868.

Ogdensburgh, February 10, 1859

My dear friend,

I enclose you a corrected copy of the "devotion" with piano accomp't. Burn the <u>old</u> one because it is full of faults. This should be sung by most voices in four flats, but as it is, it is better adapted to the <u>person</u> who sung it for me. Pardon me for these repeated inflictions, but as I had begun this I wished to finish it. It is very poorly written and may not <u>please you</u> anyhow, but it <u>rather</u> pleases me so you must forgive me. The "verse" is inferior to the music. The writer must have been less a Poet than a Musician.

If you will show this to Musicians who have soul enough to sing it and they and you condemn it—pray keep its notes a secret and the author will hide for the future. If you <u>do</u> like it, keep its origin a secret known only to yourself and I will <u>let</u> you <u>like</u> it.

Yours very truly,

J. H. Crawford

My sister admired the song (in which she had of course participated) and was eager to sing it in concert with the composer. They were writing yet another ode to the ocean, exchanging lines and friendly insults vis-à-vis the merits of "wave" and "sea," with the usual word puzzles and puns that highlighted their merriment.

She spoke in Quincy, Massachusetts, before a two-week stay in Providence at the end of February. An enticing prospect arose when James H. Blood of St. Louis, Missouri, asked if Axy would consider coming to that city to lecture in September. She was tempted, as she had never been so far west, but Missouri was a slave state.

Oswego, February 24, 1859

Miss Sprague,

I rec'd your letter, a very _short_ one, from Quincy the 18th— and was delighted to hear from you again. O how sorry I am for the "wicked" part of the "reply." Why didn't you refer in detail to the wicked, or offending passages, and I would expunge them at once.

As to my ever being "good," I know not what to say now. I supposed that very reply would settle that vexed question in my favor but you always interpret one wrongfully, always. What a doomed Spirit am I! Always misunderstood, and always misunderstanding. As I recall, _you_ are the one who quoted Epictetus by saying "_If you desire to be good, begin by believing that you are wicked!_" . . .

By the way how are you to get three or four weeks next summer to go around the lakes with Mrs. Crawford within your present engagements? She is making calculations on the trip and often refers to it. You will be "wicked," _very_ wicked if you do not keep that engagement.

I have not yet decided whether Oswego or Milwaukee is to be our future home. Shall decide soon. I expect to be here some of the time and all letters sent here will soon find me elsewhere as I always have them forwarded to me.

Your sincere friend, J. H. Crawford

Oswego, March 2, 1859

Miss Sprague,

I arrived here from Ogdensburgh this morning, leaving all well and in good spirits yesterday morning, and find your short note of February 24 with your "extinguisher." Ah! Me alas! Pain, pain forever. I <u>am</u> extinguished. Snuffed out like a tallow candle when the snuffers dropped too low." "Wick-ed" as I was I'm <u>wicked</u> no longer. Snuffed up too like the last pinch of maccaboy, but so sadly deteriorated that I cannot cause, or provoke even a sneeze. O why did you rage so terribly? Long may you wave, but don't wave so proudly and long. Ah, I never never can sing "There I shall bathe my weary soul, In seas of heavenly rest, And not a <u>wave</u> of <u>trouble</u> roll Across my peaceful (?) breast." I wish I was expunged, let down, "dried up" without the power of remembrance, but here I am chained to my rocky bed, never never to rise. I think I see <u>one</u> gleam, one flickering ray of hope and it peeps through the darkness with bashful eye as though it was not quite sure of kind treatment if it came. Perhaps it shone through the opening of the "door" that is left "ajar" especially for my benefit. Oh you Naughty Spirit to flash such a thought in upon such a dark Sea only to tantalize or torment it, like the sight of oranges and tropical fruits through the glass in a greenhouse.

I send you the fourth verse of my song. I know you don't like it because it is too dark and gloomy for you but you know <u>I cannot</u> make sunshine on both sides of the cloud as you do…

Your friend J. H. Crawford

Meanwhile, here in Wisconsin I had been married to John Morrison Steen for four months and the novelty of being "Mrs.

Steen" and keeping my own house had been thoroughly expended. I loved my husband with all my heart, but I was still despondent for not having distinguished myself in any way. More than anything, I'd hoped by now to be with child. My tendency toward melancholy was prevalent during winter but became even more pronounced with the approach of spring. When Morris was away with his carpentry duties, my daily routine was so wearisome. And when he was home with me, farm chores demanded most of his time.

It startled me, that I missed my students. Housekeeping was tedious and it was never done. There was always sewing and mending. Washing clothes was a huge task I loathed exceedingly, as the process took several days. I had a little flock of chickens to tend daily, and I was planning a large vegetable garden. I could milk the cow, having done so in Vermont, and I churned cream into butter; occasionally I made cheese. Our winter had been a mild one and what little snow we'd received was already gone in early March, a month of mud in Vermont. Here in Wisconsin the fields were bare and had been for several weeks.

Moreover, our part of the country was still seriously reeling from the Panic. This was of deep concern, as Morris had income owed him but those to whom he had made loans were unable to pay. Crops had been inferior the previous year.

My husband tried to cheer me by promising a trip to Vermont in June. I appreciated his kindness, but was disinclined to agree since I realized the severe financial burden this would place upon our lot. Yet I had not been home since December 1856, three years ago. My life had undergone a great many changes since then. I longed to see Mother and Axy. I wished for my family to meet my new husband and for him to gain their approval.

Oakfield, Wisconsin
~~April~~ March 6, 1859

Dear Sister Axy,

Your letter was gladly rec'd and I will leave it for Morris to write whether he felt bad or not regarding your comments. Here I am at the same table and in the same place as when I wrote you before. How strange it seems to me to always be at home when I write but I do believe it to be the happiest place there is, after one has fagged through as much as I have. You speak of my life being happier than formerly. I doubt not but that it will ever be, for I do not grieve over and mourn so bitterly the ills of life, neither do I intend to fill my letters with troubles which I believe are designed for good.

Morris says we will certainly go East this summer and intend to spend the month of June with you, but I dare not anticipate much for fear something will prevent it. I would like to look forward upon our visit, but at the same time I feel that we can scarcely afford it, such hard times, building etc. reminds one of confining the expenses. I expect we will have to go with our parlor unfurnished for a while.

It is next to impossible for Morris to get any of the money which is due him. But you should know by the first of May if anything does prevent our going.

I hope you will be able to soon come out here! Write as often as you can. I will now leave for my Dear Morris to write you.

C.S.S.

Sister, the gentle rebuke that you gave me in your last letter causes me to hasten to let you know that I am not so cold and motionless as a <u>stone</u>. I have often wished to write to you but it is always with reluctance that I commence a correspondence with a person I never saw, although you are well known to me by reputation. I trust we will soon have a personal acquaintance; after that I will be able to write more freely.

I think you might give us more Spiritual news in your letters. I like to hear what progress the Harmonial Philosophy is making in the Eastern States and I think from your extensive acquaintance you are well qualified to inform us. I hope you will yet conclude to come out west on a mission to the <u>heathen</u>. Spiritualism does not seem to increase in numbers in this part of the country, but the mass of the people are being gradually emancipated from Orthodoxy and will soon be prepared to receive something better.

That a brighter day will soon dawn upon us is the earnest prayer of your Brother,

J. M. Steen

I found myself adding a postscript, informing Axy that I had mistakenly substituted "April" for "March," and thus the crossed-out beginning. I also lied by claiming that I *did* take pleasure in housekeeping but there was no use of my writing more about it to her for little did she know or care about it. And I mentioned that Morris had objected to write on the same sheet after reading what I had written to her. "I hope it will not grate so harshly upon your mind."

I made an effort but I could not entirely conceal my pessimistic mood. My sister seemed to move so easily about the country, but for us to even imagine a trip to Vermont was a matter of trepidation and expense that she could scarcely apprehend. Not only were there the crops to be watched over and the livestock to be cared for during our absence, but I argued with Morris that the expense of our journey was prohibitive.

Selfishly, I wanted furnishings for our parlor. I had been hopeful of procuring an upholstered settee.

Our visit was three months away, and Axy expressed her eagerness to meet my new husband. It was my hope that if we made a sacrifice to travel to the Notch, the rest of my family would find a visit agreeable as well. But Axy reported, sadly, that Sarah and Orvilla were not as compliant.

Sarah Randall had demanded of Axy to know why she had ceased writing to Nathaniel so suddenly. Sarah had been sick "almost every minute this winter" and had written only one letter, which was to Mother. Furthermore, she was in a delicate condition and would like to come home in June to see me when I visited, but

"If I feel well enough to go everybody will feel ashamed of me but myself and husband. As regards my feelings, I haven't any scruples of delicacy. Aren't I fortunate to feel so?" She added, "How often have you spoken this winter? Is your throat worse than usual? You must do as I do, think of no one but self and not over do."

We had often said as much about Sarah—that she "thought of no one but herself."

Orvilla decided to answer Axy's long-ago letter, but she admitted in one lengthy sentence, "I have not answered you sooner, I have no excuse but my dislike to writing letters my health is not as good as it was last fall the warm weather does not agree with me the rest of the family are in usual health." Orvilla, her husband, and son had gone to visit Mother the previous Sunday, but she complained that "Mother had been clearing the door yard and was rather tired." She supposed Axy was getting ready "for Celia and Morris I suppose you expect to have a nice time when they come but as I enjoy nothing now a days I do not expect to enjoy a visit with them and unless Celia has changed I cannot enjoy her, she has written to us once and after a long time we answered it." Orvilla's husband said to tell Axy, "you wrote nothing to him and he has nothing to write to you."

⤙ 13 ⤚

Home Again

(June–August 1859)

"You pieface! You thief! You receiver of stolen goods!
You wicked, Naughty Spirit!"

Mr. Crawford would tease Axy like this, writing from Milwaukee in May 1859. The familiarity of his banter would be comforting as she rushed up and down the eastern seaboard that spring, speaking one night here, the next there, smiling graciously at the acceptance of yet another family's offer of bed and hearty board to the popular and pretty "improvisatrice."

Cousin Ephraim wrote to Axy from the Notch to say that school had ended for the season and he was well enough to clean out the barn but if Mother wanted to hire another agent she should, as he had a lame back. And everyone had the mumps. "Your canary bird gets along pretty well, he sings most of the time for I suppose he is lonesome." The second canary had passed on to the Spirit World.

Countless proposals of marriage were still arriving, but Axy was further burdened when Adolph Eiswald, a recent immigrant from Austria, presented himself to her in Providence, head-over-heels in love. The little man's rapidly darting eyes resembled busy water bugs behind round spectacles, and his large black mustache drooped down into a tidy black beard. Eiswald followed her everywhere and seemed to skulk in the shadows. When it was time to quit Providence, she specifically asked him not to come to the depot.

His obsequious letters traced her steps:

Dear Madame,

When last I had the pleasure of seeing you on the day before your departure from this City, and when you left us instead of bidding you good by then, I wished to trust my presence once more upon you the following morning and said so unceremoniously by enquiring from what Depot you were to start. Next morning at 8 o'clock I was at the Depot. As I did not take the hint then, you might have thought that I did not understand it at all…I do not know your reasons, but you must have them and I respect them.

Eiswald closed with a sincere prayer "to be allowed to correspond with you, if it does not interfere with your more important duties."

Portland, Maine, the birthplace of Henry Wadsworth Longfellow, would ever be recalled by Axy as having been marred by an unfortunate event. In the midst of a swirling downtown mid-afternoon crowd, she thought nothing of being jostled; such incidents occurred with frequency on city streets. Then she noticed her purse had been stolen. It carried a considerable amount of money plus the psychometrised coin given to her by John M. Spear—the coin wrapped in paper marked June 20, 1855.

Police apprehended the thief at home, and the purse was found tucked inside the woman's petticoat. "Susan," the pickpocket, pled guilty and was sentenced by the grand jury to one year in the state prison at Thomaston. Axy felt such empathy for the poor woman that she asked if Susan could be given the lightest possible sentence. The judge countered that such cases were now so common, he felt he had a duty to sentence the woman, but as the thief was now behaving well, the governor of the state might agree to assigning Susan one year in the Portland Jail instead. Axy's purse and money were returned by mail. The marshal had considered sending a check, but "probably you may want the same money as a memento of its journey and to refresh your memory of its locality when it was found on her premises, to say nothing of the <u>skirt</u> thus containing the treasure."

All she found missing was the coin given to her by J. M. Spear; the paper it had been wrapped in was still tucked in the purse.

Her long-scheduled visit to Oswego and Ogdensburgh that spring had beamed as brightly as the welcoming lighthouse beacons on Lake Ontario's rocky shores. But the lights had recently dimmed: Due to the exigencies of his shipping business, Mr. Crawford had moved his family to Milwaukee. The Ogdensburgh Spiritualists found it "a serious loss to us not only in number but in money for Mr. C. was the only one of our little band that had the means to do as the will directed. Those of us that are left are not as well off but are willing to do all in our power to have you see us again."

The Sprague/Crawford correspondence continued despite the move. They were now co-writing hymns and argued and teased each other over the stanzas.

Milwaukee, Friday May 15, 1859

Dear Miss Sprague

I have just rec'd your welcome note of the 9th inst with the summing up arguments in the assault and battery case, and it being Sunday and not feeling like going to church this forenoon I will say a word in reply to the note:

You <u>pieface</u>! You thief! You receiver of stolen goods. You wicked, Naughty Spirit! Why did you steal all my thunder, leaving me naught to hang a single fancy on?

What a strange wonder this is. How <u>did</u> this reply come upon you so suddenly and at that time too? What a riddle, what a mystery we are (how <u>completely riddled</u> am <u>I</u>!) One of my omitted stanzas contained very much the same thoughts expressed by you, but I rejected it because I considered it more appropriate for the Next. Now you have opened the argument and according to the practice in some Courts, you have the summing up or closing and I really feel as though nothing more can be said. I will consider it and decide when the fancy comes over me. I have no <u>streams</u> of inner sunlight just now. I shall wait and consult them.

The impressions rec'd by both during this strife have been an earnest lesson to me. I too guessed what <u>your</u> reply would be. I seek no compliment when I tell you that I have shown this quarrel to an old literary friend who <u>insists</u> upon having it published when completed (of course without giving names) as a literary curiosity of great beauty and pays me the undeserved compliment of saying our style and expression are wonderfully similar. You know better. I don't pretend to claim it. Some passages occur in your side of the question that would immortalize me, such as your powers of torture, your endurance &c, and more beautiful than all the rest your waves of "ocean, light, heat electric & thought," so wonderfully compressed that you feel, upon reading them verse by verse, or thought by thought—as though they would expand and bound away from you like a ball of caoutchouc after pressing into a small compass. Then, your bitter vindictive scorn, your "cradle in the sky" and finally your terrible scathing blow at some human mind that might not be "Godlike." Now pray don't call this <u>extravagance</u> as you undoubtedly will. If to admire and love terseness, strength and beauty combined make me extravagant, then I plead guilty.

I thought at first I would say, among the other things thrown in at random

Stay bitter unrelenting wave.
Thou'rt not yet wholly free

For thou art bound, thy fettered feet
  Art chained within the <u>sea</u>.
Why laugh to scorn my earnest words
  And smile in mockery
Thou'rt like a wave of torture dire.
  From Hades' boiling sea.
Thou canst not smile in mockery.
  On hearts with anguish torn
Thy tell-tale eyes may laugh.
  Or weep, but <u>never</u> scorn

These fragments I threw out or modified as before stated, and I only hinted, <u>bitterly</u>, that you might possibly
Go

Below

If you were so naughty as to <u>scorn</u> as you threatened. I think upon the whole that I will keep you upon the rack a little longer, by adding a word by & by when the humor is on me, for fear you will forget me. But I promise you I won't be wicked one moment longer during the strife. I consider an amnesty now exists and you may be sure I will not disgrace my flag for it shall still <u>wave</u> as proudly as before.

Why are you more like a wave now that this strife is over than ever before? "Because in the storm and struggle you have kept the ocean down, lashed it unmercifully, and triumphed by being uppermost."

You don't say a word about a trip to Lake Michigan, but you must come.

I thank you for your notice of the music sent you. I have sung it once or twice and it has been called good. It may be published for your benefit and dedicated to you if you consent, but I wish you would write words for it. I am not ashamed to own the music but the song can be improved vastly…

Do not flatter yourself that you will not hear from me again
for I will write you by and by and either add a word to the
"strife" or tell you I will not.
Then spread thy banner, let it wave.
Unite all hearts as one.
Follow the light that points above,
And errors paths Oh! Shun.

J. H. Crawford

While my sister was more than ready for a restful sojourn in the Green Mountains there was yet one further obligation. The final week of May was "Anniversary Week" in Boston, a time for annual meetings of associations and assemblies. Oliver Wendell Holmes spoke at the Unitarian Festival in Music Hall. The Universalist Association had its own gathering, as did the New England Anti-Slavery Society. Achsa W. Sprague was listed as a speaker at the Spiritual Convention. *The Banner of Light* reported on June 4 that due to pleasant weather "our venerable city was full...We never saw Boston more lively, and even gay and exuberant, than last week. The streets were all the time filled. There were meetings here, meetings there, and meetings everywhere."

Delia Pollard had written to Axy from Plymouth prior to the Boston events, saying she had welcomed spring "by going out onto the side hill and lying down on old dry leaves. And I read a 'Trip to Cuba' from the last *Atlantic*. After tea I walked to the Village and back alone in the dark between eight and nine. I enjoy such lone walks immensely and always come very slow that they may last the longer. I am making great plans for rejuvenating this summer. Going to ride horseback, and do some other wonderful things. Hope you will write to me soon and tell me that you are coming immediately home for I want to see you and tell you lots of things. You seem to think I need a shaking up. Well, I expect those horseback rides will do it with a vengeance."

After her week in Boston, Axy was finally able to head back to the Notch, where she would gladly remain for the entire month of June.

Morris and I took the railroad from Fond du Lac to Vermont. His father would look after our farm in addition to his own, and care for our cow, our pigs, our horses, and my chickens. Crops had been planted and the steer was no longer fattening in our pasture: When Morris butchered him the steer dressed out at nearly six hundred pounds and the twelve dollars he brought was put toward our railroad fare.

I had last visited the Notch before Father's death, and I anticipated much difference in the aspect of my home. My nerves could have been blamed on my excitement in introducing Morris to my family, or apprehension over how much everyone else may have changed. I knew marriage had altered me considerably for the better (I hoped) and I was anxious to show my partner where I was born, have him meet Axy, and walk the trails in the mountains that we loved.

As I said previously, Wisconsin had enjoyed an early spring. Early June was already as warm as mid-summer. During our journey we were obliged to change trains several times. The cars seemed unusually hot and close, and much too thunderous for sleep. The stink of unwashed bodies, filthy clothing, the sulphurous smoke, caused me to feel unwell. When we disembarked for hasty meals, my appetite was poor.

Thus I found the pure mountain air doubly refreshing. Morris was warmly welcomed. He was especially intrigued by the farm of Galusha Coolidge and his prize-winning Arabians. Aunt Mede brought over a ham for us to serve at our family pic-nic and Mother invited the Coolidges to join us. Aunt Mede took me aside and said Mother had so looked forward to this day when her children would be together again.

Mother looked much older than her sixty-one years, although she was still able to handle the few remaining farm chores with cousin

Ephraim's help. Nathan had moved to Weston, Vermont, where he was living with brother William and his wife, Ann. They were not able to join us for our reunion, nor were Sarah and Nathaniel Randall, as Sarah was in a family way.

Sadly, I found Axy much changed. Her countenance seemed less accommodating, as if by seeing more of the world she had become unyielding. I could read this in her face and while observing her interaction with others. With me she was warm and loving as ever, and she extended that same sincerity toward Morris. But the demands that had been placed upon her had, I thought, caused her to develop a sense of remove, of detachment. At times she seemed preoccupied with intruding thoughts and was not always in the present.

A more perfect June day could not have been created for our family pic-nic on Tuesday, June 7. We were pleasantly surprised that it was to be a celebration of our marriage! As it turned out, Orvilla and husband Jarius Josselyn came up from Tyson Furnace. Uncle Thomas Moore and Aunt Athelia were there with their son Ephraim. All the family brought hearty contributions to our afternoon meal.

The men set up a long table in the dooryard with sawhorses and planks that the women covered with gay tablecloths and vases of flowers. Chairs were brought out from indoors and the Coolidges donated several of theirs. A good many children were present (some from the village), running around, playing tag, getting under foot. I did not mind the children nor did Axy, as their joyful laughter added to the festive mood.

By one o'clock we sat down to a table laden with the usual pic-nic fare: smoked ham, fried chicken, potato salad, fresh bread, fresh churned butter, pickles, cheese, crisp lettuce from Mother's kitchen garden, cider vinegar, horseradish, mustard...and (because Vermont had also enjoyed an early spring) Mother had baked our favorite strawberry pies.

Axy led us in a prayer that invited our guardian angels to always watch over us. Then we began passing the dishes around.

I spotted Eiswald first, a debonair little man climbing Schoolhouse Hill. He was overdressed for the summer day, with a showy blue and yellow silk vest and a horizontal cravat beneath his frock coat. He paused often to dab his brow with a white handkerchief. Women were clearing the table, preparing for dessert, by the time he stopped at our gate.

"Excuse me?" he called out, "Is this the Sprague residence?"

He was obliged to repeat himself several times, as our family was enjoying a relaxed and unusually animated visit.

"Mr. Eiswald," Axy exclaimed with surprise. She replaced the bowl she carried and approached the gate. "Whatever are you doing here? Our family is celebrating the recent marriage of my sister from Wisconsin."

Everyone then became subdued with curiosity, including the Coolidges.

"But I sent you a letter only a few days ago, to inform you I would be in your neighborhood on this date." Mr. Eiswald's tone was disdainful.

"I apologize, Mr. Eiswald! With the demands on my time, the excitement of welcoming Celia and Morris, I may have forgotten," Axy said. "Do come in and partake of our pic-nic fare. The ham and chicken have gone back into the kitchen but someone will be happy to fix you a plate."

He entered the dooryard, then with flamboyant gestures of refusal he would not take a seat at the table. What an odd little man, I thought; he apologized many times for interrupting our meal and insisted on sitting down in a patch of green clover, where he asked for the vinegar, pepper and salt.

"I'll just have a bit of salad," he said haughtily, plucking clover and sprinkling it before popping the flavored greenery between his little red lips between moustache and beard.

Children giggled and some of the women covered their mouths with their hands.

"Mr. Eiswald, what brings you to this secluded part of Vermont?" Morris asked. "Do you have business nearby?"

"As I enlightened Miss Achsa Sprague in my letter, which she obviously ignored," Eiswald nodded at her in a haughty manner, "It was suddenly necessary for me to take a trip north which would lead me to her neighborhood and thence to her gracious presence. I had gleaned from her letters to me that she had not always been as happy as she persuaded herself to be, and hoped that my consoling attendance might help cheer her."

This was met with an uneasy silence as he concentrated on chewing his clover. He continued, after a gulp.

"Miss Sprague was informed some time ago that I take great delight in criticizing others. Naturally, I benefit from her instinctive penetration and analytical conclusions, as applied to me, or in the criticism of me. When she is in any nearby city—I come from Providence—you may find me closely at her side."

"Not entirely with my approval," Axy snapped, and we were all taken aback at her sharp retort.

Eiswald turned and lay casually on his side to speak to my sister, picking idly at the lawn.

"Some lady in town had asked me once whether I did not think you a little bigoted. After a short reflection I said yes. I repeated this to you, because firstly I wanted you should know what I had said behind your back of you, and secondly I expected you would clear yourself immediately of the imputation of an argument and clear away the misunderstanding. But you did not please to take it as a question for decision, but a critical assertion."

Eiswald sat up, then once more sprinkled salt, pepper, and vinegar on more clover leaves and examined them in his palm. "Thus you misunderstood me, Miss Sprague, as I have, no doubt, sometimes misunderstood you."

I could see Orvilla rolling her eyes. I was tempted to do so as well, but reached for Morris, fearing he might respond to Mr. Eiswald's rude comments.

"Let there be no misunderstanding *me* now," Axy said, as she grabbed hold of Eiswald's arm with what we all regarded as unusual strength, to disengage him from his clover patch and lead him behind a grove of lilacs where we could easily listen in on their conversation.

Even the children were silent, fascinated by the eccentric's ill-timed interruption. Axy detested confrontation of any kind, so the unusual nature of her thinly lilac-sheltered encounter with Eiswald was a novelty, indeed.

"Mr. Eiswald, I must ask you to leave," we could hear her say. "I have no idea what you anticipated from me during this unwelcome call, but I suspect the reason for the 'necessity of your northern trip' was to continue to dog my footsteps. Perhaps my directive in Providence was not clear, so let there be no misinterpretation: I am *not* pleased with your unremitting attention. I have *no interest* in developing a relationship of *any* kind with you. If you are indeed a gentleman and possess any manners, you will understand that the polite action at this time would be to *please go away.*"

Eiswald apparently could or would not take her advice. Rather, his hackles were raised and he replied, "I do not fear to stimulate your love of approbation, which you, no doubt, have held under command for many years. Now, however, you are wounding my self-esteem by censuring me for merely wanting to be by your side! You are gravely impairing my sense of worth. "

"I care not that you feel censured," Axy replied. "This is a very special day for my family and I will not have you spoiling it."

"Surely you realize, Miss Sprague, that I am quick in perception but slow in interpreting what I hear. When you said 'Do not come,' when I wished to accompany you to the station in Providence, your remarks appeared to me to be an envelope of the meaning. As I did not take the hint then, you might have thought that I did not understand it at all because I understood you to say, 'it is not agreeable,' although you permitted it."

"That is in the past, Mr. Eiswald," Axy responded, "and this is now. *You must go.*"

"I ought to know by this time that it is dangerous to find fault with and contradict ladies—particularly when they have been feasted and praised and applauded for several years."

"Mr. Eiswald…" Axy interrupted. But he went on.

"I will only leave if you promise to send me your daguerreotype.

THE BENNETT GAZETTE

APRIL 9, 1885　　　　KILBOURN CITY, WISCONSIN　　　　VOLUME XXIV NO 3

KIDS FOLLOW NEWPORT BAND DOWN STREET

When the sonorous strains of Vanderpool's Newport band was heard at Kilbourn City, every kid in school jumped from his seat and followed the band down the street.

REMEMBERING OUR HONORED DEAD

It has been twenty years since the end of the Civil War and today we recognize an important figure for the Union, Private Truman Head, commonly known as California Joe, who passed away almost ten years ago.

Immortalized here in an illustration by Larkin Mead, California Joe is pictured positioned as he often was to fulfill his sharpshooting duties. This illustration was first a photograph taken by George H. Houghton.

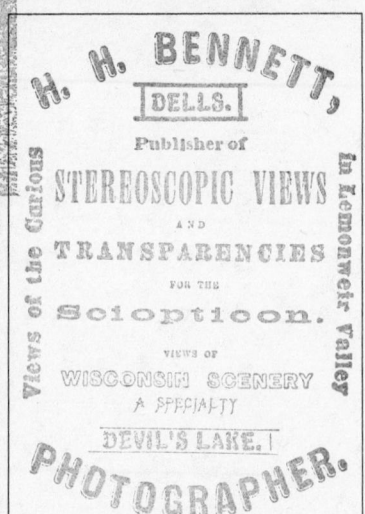
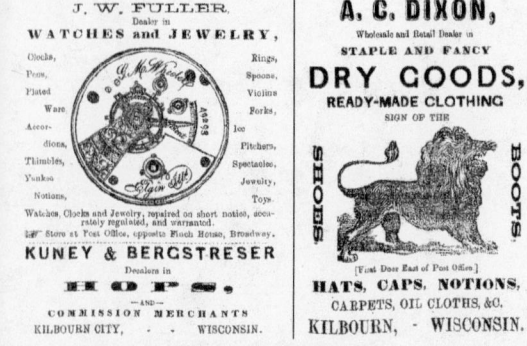
THOMPSON DISPOSES THE MIRROR (OF KILBOURN) TO DAVIS, WRIGHT & DAVIS

Mr. T. O. Thompson, finding it rather difficult to carry on a paper at Berlin and Kilbourn City at the same time, has disposed of the Mirror (of Kilbourn) to the firm Davis, Wright & Davis, the latter a lady, who are highly commended as fully capable of making a good paper. In their salutatory they say the paper will labor for the interests of its locality, making hop reports abroad and home a speciality.

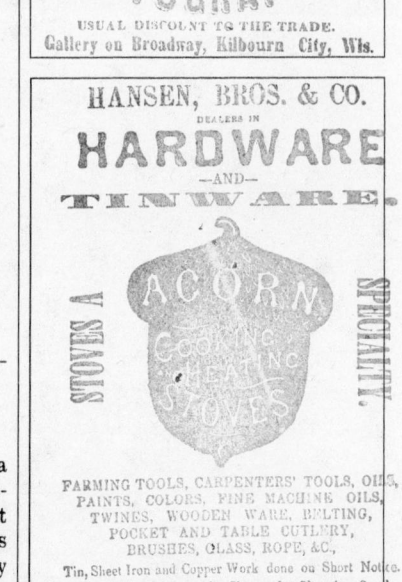

As a great favor would I receive it, but not as a sacrifice. Next to the original, I would naturally appreciate the copy and if you will have one taken for me at your earliest opportunity, and trust it to me, you shall never have occasion to complain of the use I will make of it."

Morris had left the table, and now I could hear his voice booming over Eiswald's timid plea.

"You will leave the premises, Mr. Eiswald," Morris said, "and you will leave *straightaway!*"

We watched, open-mouthed, as Morris escorted Eiswald to the gate, the collar of Eiswald's frock coat held firmly in Morris's strong fist. Eiswald's polished shoes dangled, barely touching the ground.

"There is a hotel in Plymouth Union," Morris informed the obsequious little man. "The road there is all downhill. Please make use of it and do not call upon my sister again."

"I hope, Miss Sprague, that you will forgive my temerity," Eiswald feebly cried back to Axy as he fairly stumbled in his haste, but she had resumed her place at the table and was motionless. We watched as she sat lost in thought, all awaiting her direction. Then she raised her head, clapped her hands, and advised, "Now, strawberry pie!"

We cheered. Whether it was a cheer for Axy and relief that the little drama had been resolved, or for Morris's heroic action, or the prospect of delicious strawberry pie, I never knew. But soon merriment resumed.

That was not the end of Eiswald, however. His letters to Axy continued to arrive daily until eventually he said he was moving west.

> As I left Plymouth so abruptly without taking leave from the good people whose acquaintance I made at your home please, tell them that I had to leave so and therefore present my excuses; and to your mother, oh! Kiss her hand most affectionately for me, for having carried under her bosom a child like you. To Mr. Steen, you will please not reproach him

for having spoken to me as he did because his motive was pure and generous and his manner very kind. I would never forgive myself for having been the cause of even a slight annoyance in any, particularly, in a young family.

Then he added,

> I have shaved off my mustache. I look a good deal milder and I think more confidence inspiring to children and not dandylike.

He sent Axy a four-leaf clover which, he suggested, she put over the door and await the result. Or perhaps make a salad of it, as he did with the clover he found in Vermont, taking the salt, pepper, and vinegar afterward. All his letters were lengthy and filled with such twaddle. I wondered at her ability to respond with her usual civility but she said she considered it an obligation, recalling her initial promise to her Guardians.

I had so wanted to make a difference with my life, to elevate mankind. But meeting Mr. Eiswald taught me not to be envious of my sister's given role.

During our stay at the Notch, Morris and I were issued more invitations to call upon others than we could accommodate. One day while he was off with Uncle Thomas, Axy and I went for a stroll through the hamlet and found ourselves near the burial grounds, where we visited the graves of ancestors and our father and our brother Ephraim.

"I, too, shall be buried here," Axy mused.

I had no words to respond, as I could not allow myself to realize such a somber thought.

So I commented on the beauty of the location: the curving dry stone wall that surrounded the area as if embracing the earliest settlers; the abundance of colorful phlox in bloom. In that setting we were held close by the shoulders of the verdant Green Mountains and encircled by the sweetest breath of summer. But my sister's mind was somewhere else.

"In autumn, if all goes well, I shall be visiting the West and will enjoy a brief stay with you, Celia. I hope that is convenient for you and Morris. Spiritualists in Milwaukee have issued an invitation for me to speak."

I believe I may have hazarded a dance step in the graveyard, so pleased was I by the possibility of her visit to our farm. Axy laughed at my exuberance.

"I can't wait to share the news with Morris," I exclaimed, tugging at her sleeve. "Surely there will be other towns besides Milwaukee that will want you to lecture! How brave you are, to venture so far west by yourself on a speaking tour."

She had already shared a good deal of information with me about her "Evil Genius," so I added, "Aren't your friends, the Crawfords, living in Milwaukee, now? Will you stay with them?"

The glance she gave me was inscrutable, as if my question was imprudent.

"I only thought," I muttered, "because you speak of him so often..."

"Shall we go?" Axy said then, leading me by hand, through the maze of tombstones. "I want that you should contact the Spiritualists in Fond du Lac and see if they, too, would like me to lecture."

I mentioned this peculiar exchange to Morris in seclusion, and he suggested that as my mention of *Crawford* may have proven disconcerting, there may be more to the bonds of friendship between Axy and Mr. Crawford than those about which we were aware. I alluded to the intricate ring she wore and remarked that I had never known Axy to wear jewelry.

"I have not dared to ask," I confessed. "It must carry a profound meaning for her."

"And perhaps someone else," Morris proffered, reaching for me. "If your sister is happy, we will be happy for her."

I was relieved to say our goodbyes the following day. Morris and I were traveling to St. Johnsbury, as he wished to see the northeast part of Vermont and meet Sarah and Nathaniel Randall. From there we would travel to Ludlow, and thence to Wisconsin in early July.

"Your friends are all waiting with delightful expectation of your coming,"

J. C. Pool had written to Axy from Oswego in June 1859; this would be her first prolonged stay in that city, but she felt melancholy toward the locale, which lacked appeal without the presence of Mr. Crawford; they had bade farewell in Ogdensburgh eight months ago.

She was there when Morris and I wrote to let her know of our safe return home.

Oakfield, July 24, 1859

Sister Axy,

I have repeatedly asked myself this question for the last two weeks, "if you spare a few moments of your active life, to think of your friends in the west," and I always receive a flattering answer. Do not think that we forget you if we are dilatory in writing. The truth is that we have been so busy since we got back, and it has been such excessive hot weather that it requires some effort to write a letter. But the last few days have been cool and pleasant and we are resting ourselves today by writing to our friends.

I hope you enjoy yourself in the busy active bustle of City Life but I presume you have many a ramble through wood and wold, mountain and glen, excursions by land and water, "moonlight evenings on the vasty deep" intermixed with your favourite game of literary chessplaying. I suppose ere this your opponent has been obliged to take refuge in his castle. When you take him prisoner (as a matter of course you will) I hope you will give him no quarter.

We had an excellent visit to St. Johns. I was much pleased with Sarah and the Dr. They did all they could to make us happy. Then the fine scenery on the Connecticut River, even the river itself rendered classic by so many events historical, traditional and romantic, will make it a visit never to be forgotten.

We started from Ludlow the afternoon of the 5th and arrived here the 7th. Had a very quick and pleasant passage. Celia was much better on her return trip than on her outward one, but the hot weather since she got back was rather severe for her. I hope we will not have any more this season. Please write soon and let us know all that has happened to you since we parted.

Yours truly, J. M. Steen

Dear Sister,

It is now past tea time but I must spend a few more minutes to write you although I have nothing to interest. My Dear Morris has stepped so far into the land of romance and classic allusions that I feel it will be but a blight to your mind to once more arrive at a kitchen chit-chat, but come with me and upon my table behold a vase of flowers that only a short time ago were culled from the fields where they grew in beauty without the assistance of man. But do not stop there too long, for I wish you to look upon my noble cooking stove and to have your own face reflected in its own, and then cast your eye upon the white woodwork and then say if you can there is not that which is refining and ennobling even in kitchen work.

But in came our friend Mr. Orvis (to collect the mail) when I first began this, so I will bid you good bye and say write often.

Celia

Mr. Pool had met Axy's train from Syracuse on Friday, July 1. Her first lecture was on Sunday, July 3. She had previously found Oswego to be a friendly city and a desirable place of residence, with a population of 20,000.

A room could be had at The Doolittle House Hotel for $3 per day, where the famous "Deep Rock Spring" on its premises advertised "most salubrious" waters. Doolittle Hall, a popular meeting place on Water Street, provided a large room illuminated by gas light and equipped with a platform upon which entertainers appeared. Prior to Axy's presence that summer, the Davenport Boys were arrested for "jugglery without a license" after a performance where they caused a guitar, violin, and tambourine to play music in the darkness as if by spirit hands while the Davenport Boys themselves remained in chairs to which they had been previously tied by a member of the audience. After serving time in the Oswego jail they moved on to perform "spiritual" manifestations in other venues.

Axy looked forward to Oswego's Independence Day Celebration on Monday, but when she awoke that morning she was reminded of the observance of "The Glorious Fourth" in the Notch, where there would be the usual pitched battle for possession of the cannon, patriotic music from the little band, and Chinese fireworks spraying brilliant sparks above the mountains as darkness fell. Nine years had passed since she wrote in her diary, *Independence Day, so they term it. It may be so to some but it certainly is not to me. I only feel more deeply my own dependence, my own misery.*

The afternoon was sunny and mild, with billowing sails of sailboats and schooners that blessed Lake Ontario's undulating waves. She was surveying that broad expanse of blue from a lakeshore park and feeling wistful for Mr. Crawford's presence, when he startled her by appearing at the Fourth of July pic-nic just as it was about to commence! She had fully expected him to be absent. They had not seen each other since the previous November.

At times, during her travels, she had wondered if her feelings for him were fantasy. That was when, in her mind and in her letters, she challenged his devotion for her. But now, spying him with Captain and Mrs. Richardson in the midst of pic-nic preparations, there was no misunderstanding in her heart and she lifted her skirt to make her way to his side as quickly as she could, to clasp his hand.

"Miss Sprague," he said with mock seriousness, "fancy finding you near the water again. I wonder that you did not wave!"

"Mr. Crawford, I am similarly startled to see you near the 'C.'"

The Richardsons stood aside, beaming with joy at the reunion.

To Axy's delight, he would be in Oswego for several weeks to make arrangements for the Northern Transportation Line to run a fleet of canal boats from Oswego to New York City. The offices of Northern Transportation were located on the Oswego Canal, a thirty-eight-mile extension of the Erie Canal that connected that waterway to Lake Ontario. Their ships docked at a wharf in front of the stone building within the city limits, and not very far from the Doolittle Hotel.

Arm in arm they wandered away from the pic-nic site, imparting details of the eight months they'd been apart. It was not until they were well away from others that Axy thought to ask, "Is Mrs. Crawford here with you?"

"She remains in Milwaukee," he said, squeezing her hand.

Then followed Axy's questions about their new home, the children, all in an effort to demonstrate she was not head-over-heels with delight.

Although their shared joy was almost too much to conceal, their encounters after that afternoon were obliged to be necessarily discreet. As Axy had a room at the Doolittle House, any further meetings had to be clandestine since she was almost always in the public's view.

Further proof of the risk of their close association was evidenced when a letter arrived from Benjamin Starbuck, who sent along a short piece of doggerel that he'd recently come across, "a sublime apostrophy to the beautiful Lake upon whose shores you are now located. Take it where the waves come rolling in, and as the sun descends in glory then seat yourself upon a great big large stone and read. And then, and then, Oh think of me. God Bless you." He added a postscript: "I wish you would come to Troy to disprove Mrs.

Britt Spence who had the desk last week and pronounced that 'Miss Sprague has become a Free Lover like all the rest.' I presume she was insinuating the scandalous 'Free Lust' variety. You know I have never been fond of 'Mrs. Butt.'"

Axy wrote off the report to Mrs. Butt's green-eyed monster, but such a tiresome charge was not a revelation anymore. The few times that she accompanied John Crawford to concerts or other social gatherings in Oswego, even as part of a group, well-meaning friends reported of hearing talk of indecorous behavior spread by skeptics who were all too eager to apply degenerate labels.

Her conscience was clear. She and Mr. C. had never gone beyond whispered endearments and a few brief, stolen kisses that had been influenced, and indeed, supervised, by their respective Guardians.

One summer day Axy was invited to join a group of "Excursionists" for a trip to Little Sodus with three hundred others. Crawford had provided the ships for their convenience and would regret that he had remained in town and not joined the gathering, as *The Oswego Palladium* reported that the pic-nic was

> an exceedingly pleasant affair...The elements were highly propitious and the company enjoyed the passage up and back in social conversation, singing and dancing. Disembarking at Sodus in a pleasant grove, the company partook of refreshments of which there was great abundance, and those who were deficient were amply supplied by others. During the day on the grounds, Miss Sprague delivered a very eloquent discourse, which was predicated upon a bird's nest, picked up and presented her just before she spoke. The beautiful and practical thoughts she uttered upon the simple object are said to have been touchingly interesting.

Captain Richardson of the ship *The Ogdensburgh* was again in port when Axy was invited to dinner at the Richardson's home. It was a warm summer evening, most appropriate for relaxing on the broad veranda with dessert: a luscious gooseberry pie.

"I presume you are anticipating Mrs. Crawford's arrival tomorrow on *The Prairie State*," Captain Richardson commented to John as the golden twilight began to gild that hour. "Williams will be looking after your wife first rate. After this trip she will have no qualms about journeying on her own."

Axy attempted to catch his glance, but Mr. Crawford looked away. She suddenly felt warm and reached in her reticule for a handkerchief.

"Oh, but I travel by myself all the time," she told Captain Richardson. "I have seldom had an opportunity to be fearful, especially on a ship! I cannot imagine why she would be afraid."

This had been spoken too quickly and too critically, she knew. Axy excused herself and went into the kitchen for a glass of water. When she returned to the veranda she found John taking his leave.

"I'll be working at my office tonight," Mr. Crawford apologized. The sun had gone down and the sky dispersed a tangerine afterglow. "Another excellent dinner as usual, Mrs. Richardson." He offered a formal bow and Mary Richardson fluttered her fan to conceal her generous smile.

Axy rushed to his side and offered to walk part way with him.

"It's been such a pleasant evening," she called back to the Richardsons, adding that she felt a need to exercise after eating such a sizeable slice of pie!

When they were out of earshot, Mr. Crawford apologized for the awkward announcement of Elvira's impending arrival, which had seriously discomfited my sister.

"I realize the ridiculousness of my response," Axy told him, "but you'd said she was staying in Milwaukee. Why was this information not shared with me before this evening?"

He had no response beyond a deep and ragged sigh.

A dark mood descended over my sister with the unanticipated news. It caused her to doubt the earnestness of *her own* devotion of thought and feeling toward the *spiritual realm*, rather than the *material*. Instead of blaming herself (for such was her state of mind), she twisted her discouragement into the familiar accusation of John Crawford's insincerity. Thus ensued once again the tiresome arguments they had already endlessly examined.

Elvira arrived, and in order to face what she saw as a growing ambiguity of her own fondness for Elvira's husband, Axy altered her behavior and began to behave politely but coldly toward him.

For this change in conduct, he called her an "iceberg" and "an actress," and accused her of pulling back because of fear of scandal.

Axy admitted to his face that in this instance, he was unquestionably right.

⊰ 14 ⊱

Darkeyed Lass

(July–December 1859)

W ord of Axy's impending visit to Milwaukee that autumn resulted in requests for her to lecture in many other Wisconsin locations. I corresponded with her in late August.

We received your letter the twentieth inst. Are very glad you are coming out to see us. We have ascertained that it will be very satisfactory to have you lecture in Fond du Lac the Sundays you mentioned. The Friends of Progress are also making calculations to have you speak during the week. Axy, I wish you to write immediately when you receive this stating your lecturing places during the month of October and whether you intend going to St. Louis from Milwaukee or would you like to remain in this state for a month or two?

We wish you to come here as early in October as you can. Know I wish you to go to Greenbush and I think you would be wanted at Sheboygan Falls. As soon as we hear from you again, public notice will be given of your lectures.

You ask about our house. It has been very silent since we returned—the noise of the plane or hammer has scarcely been heard, but as the wheat harvest is now over Morris will soon commence to work with renewed courage.

Life passes as usual.

Morris added a postscript:

Dear Sister,

I suppose you will think we have hard times out west when we can only use half a sheet of paper to write a letter on. I am glad you are enjoying yourself so well and that you have concluded to come and see us. I wish you could arrange it as to lecture in Milwaukee first, then you would have more time to spend with us. I would like to have you stay through the holidays.

I have been harvesting for the last four weeks but will commence on our house today so you must excuse this short letter. Please write soon and let us know your arrangements for the fall.

John M. Steen

If you were to stay through the Holidays I would fear you would think them dull days.   C.S.S.

For all of July and most of August, Axy lectured in Oswego to enormous crowds. Two weekends in September were spent in Ogdensburgh, but she returned to Oswego for the final two Sundays. In my scrapbook, I pasted this letter sent to *The Banner of Light*—a Boston newspaper to which we now subscribed. It was strong praise for my sister from a supporter in Euclid, New York. As I had never witnessed my sister "at the desk," as they referred to a medium standing upon the stage, I was intensely eager to attend one or two of her lectures. I felt very proud.

> On the evening of the 17th August I listened to one of the most sublime discourses I ever heard through the organism of Miss A. W. Sprague, now of Oswego, New

York... Miss Sprague is doing a permanent and lasting good wherever she goes. She is a medium of the first class through whom the spirits of the highest circles communicate. Hers was the first spiritual lecture ever given in Euclid. I confess my surprise in seeing so large a house. The seats were all full; and a more attentive audience never congregated.

Friday night, September 2, Axy was asleep in in her room at Oswego's Doolittle Hotel when the Richardsons called for her, citing an emergency. They hurried her out, concerned that the manifestation may be fleeting, and dissuaded her from getting dressed. Axy climbed into their carriage wearing only a dressing gown over her nightgown. Mrs. Richardson still wore her lace nightcap tied in a bow beneath her chin.

A miraculous phenomenon was occurring in the heavens during that first week in September. Against the northern sky, a remarkable display of the Aurora Borealis provided a dazzling light show so curiously powerful that telegraph wires in the United States and Europe short circuited. Gold miners in the Rocky Mountains began preparing breakfast because the glow was so brilliant they thought it was morning. Here in Wisconsin, Morris and I were awakened by our roosters crowing! Neighbors said they were able to read a newspaper outdoors at midnight. In New York City, Boston, and Chicago streets were filled with thousands gazing skyward, astonished by the sensational spectacle. So it was not a surprise that Axy would be roused from sleep to behold it, too.

Residents of Oswego seemed all to have come directly from bed, as a crowd gathered on the shore of Lake Ontario sporting various manner of nightclothes. No one appeared disturbed by the mass dishabille as all eyes focused heavenward, mesmerized by the alluring dance of colors on a black palette dazzled with stars.

A curious music accompanied the activity—a kind of whoosh or swish. Some claimed they heard this sound and others complained they could not.

Captain Richardson hailed the Crawfords in the crowd. Together the little group marveled at the astonishing revelation. Axy shared A. J. Davis's explanation that Northern Lights were produced by the discharge of electric fluid from the North Pole as it darted into the atmosphere.

The spectacle was like magic: One part of the Heavens would be a cat-eye green, and then tentacles like those of a celestial jellyfish seemed to grow in pinks and gold, uniting the thrilling green rays. A man in the crowd declared the exhibit an "I've-been-to-heaven, let-me-join-the-church" sort of encounter, which provoked laughter. Generally, people were completely silent except for exclamations of awe.

After an hour or so, Elvira complained of a cramp in her neck and a sick headache. The Richardsons kindly offered to see her to her room; John and Axy were urged to remain at the park.

They had not spoken in their usual fashion for several weeks, so their conversation was terse, even though they were essentially alone. When the celestial display became most dramatic (at its height the aurora would be described as the color of blood, a deep crimson so bright Morris could tell the time on his timepiece by its scarlet light), they saw this as an auspicious energy akin to their etheric exchange of souls.

Everyone knew Spirit existed as electrical energy, and here was energy from the North Pole in capricious veils of indescribable shimmering colors, shifting and flickering as if the significance of their Spirit-love was written overhead, with God's own hand.

Northern Lights can blur the border between dream world and waking life, but any lingering doubt between the two of them dissolved that night. The phenomenon must signify their relationship was sanctioned by the Heavens; a divine endorsement.

Here was proof, as if proof had been requested.

"What does all this mean?" John asked.

"Is it coincidence that we are together this extraordinary moment?"

"Can this marvel be a precursor of the hereafter? Is it a foretelling of our future?"

Axy closed her eyes as he placed his arm discreetly around her waist, then pulled her close to him and whispered, "Oh, that this may be prophetic, my darling. If a symbol of my hereafter, I thank God for it. And I will bear and wait until it arrives."

Only a few hours later, Axy boarded one of Mr. Crawford's propeller ships for Ogdensburgh. Her fare was covered by a special "pass."

> *Dear darkeyed Lass*
> *Receive this "pass"*
> *Across the foaming Sea*
> *'Twill safely keep*
> *Thee, for the <u>deep</u>*
> <u>*Will always take thee free.*</u>
>
> *Be strong of heart*
> *When rocked thou art,*
> <u>*And feel thy brother nigh.*</u>
> *No fear betide*
> *My <u>hazel-eyed</u>*
> <u>*Whose cradle is the sky.*</u>
>
> *May angels bright*
> *Guard thee tonight,*
> *Secure from care or pain*
> *And God above*
> *Keep thee in love*
> *Till we shall meet again.*
>
> *Sep 2nd 1859   <u>Thy Brother</u>*

A pale blue envelope was delivered to her in Ogdensburgh the next day. Mr. Crawford commented on the seasickness she had feared, and the night before, which seemed to signify a confirmation of their rapport and reassurance of their future attachment in the Spirit-world:

Oswego Sep. 3, 1859

A.W. ...I suppose you did get a _little_ sick last night, but I hope not much. How could you after getting such a view of Heaven? That was an hour long to be remembered by me, such transcendent beauty, such splendor, such a manifestation of _passional and emotional Nature._ Such gleams of soul passion, such seen yearnings, such true hymns of devotion. I gave no vent to inspiration last night because I was too full for expression, but oh my soul's dream _will come again_ when I will give it form if possible.

This desolation, apparent and intensified, is only the more fearful each repetition. The chasm between having you near me and then gone seems widening, the contrast daily becoming greater.

How stupid I was not to provide you with a room and leave you as I did to the tender mercies of snorers, to grope your way to sleep – but such a Manager as you must have known enough to lie down if you were very tired. How much I did want to go along. O _such_ a day you must have had among the Islands— all in the day time too. Oh dear, such is my fate.

Mrs. C. is quite recovered—we all took tea at the Judsons this morning.

The Prairie State leaves there Tuesday evening and if you don't come Monday night by Steamer, you must come here Tuesday night on your pass. You remember Capt. Williams and you must come with him to atone for the evils you brought upon him when you went down before.

Do come and stay two whole days when you return. What _will_ become of me when you turn your back on us for the last time?

Did you keep your promise?

Oh pray for me when evening's sun is setting,
And night her mantle spreads o'er land and sea,
When on thy couch life's cares thou art forgetting
And thy soul yearns for Heaven; then pray for me.

When morning beams and mists are on the meadow
And birds sing songs of love, I'll pray for thee.
But when my soul is dark, and sorrow's shadow
Hangs o'er my fainting heart; Oh, pray for me.

More anon
Yours as ever…

Axy returned to Oswego accompanied by Jenny Crawford, who had been staying with friends in Ogdensburgh. After that, my sister would head toward unknown territory and fresh audiences. Her schedule had her lecturing in Milwaukee, where the Crawfords were now settled, and requests had been made and assurances vowed (albeit with her trepidation) to stay with their family while she was in that city. Still, farewells were painful. Crawford sent an anguished note to her by messenger just as her train was about to pull away from the station at five o'clock:

September 29, 1859—Thursday.

"Five o'clock"

If these two words had been bars of hot iron they could not
have burned deeper than now. "Five o'clock" ! ! ! !
Can it be possible that I shall not see you again, or at least
for many weeks?

Time is a great soother of woes but the eight months we were apart brought no change to me. I fear the woe is eternal unless I find a better philosophy or – but I shall make you unhappy and rather than do that I would bear this agony & desolation alone. <u>Do be happy</u>—but pray for and think of your

Brother

The power emanating from the thundering waters of Niagara Falls was energizing for Spiritualists, who were drawn there by the electrical charge built up by the roaring cascades. This time Axy politely declined to stay with Nathaniel Randall's brother Myrick, who had declared his Free Love after her earlier visit to nearby Brockport with Nathaniel and Sarah.

By coincidence, in late October 1859, a French "funambulist" who called himself "The Great Blondin" skimmed across the vast chasm of Niagara on a specially made rope three inches in diameter and 1,100 feet long. When she told me about the feat, I wished I could have stood next to Axy, crammed with others on a wooden platform overlooking the gorge, to watch The Great Blondin perform this breathtaking exploit. The tight-rope walk had been promoted for some time and newspapers all over the country complained of accidents due to the *Blondin mania* among boys. Axy said she might have tried such an act herself if she were younger, running a rope over Pinney Creek instead of Niagara, which would have caused less damage to her fingernails, now chewed to the quick in her anxiety over Blondin's daring.

Many such events, including notices of lectures she delivered then, were eclipsed due to radical actions taken by John Brown, Mr. Crawford's long-time friend from Akron. On Sunday, October 16, Brown seized the United States Arsenal at Harpers Ferry, Virginia, with twenty-one of his followers. The armed invaders kidnapped several prominent residents to hold as hostages in an attempt to cause insurrection among Virginia's slaves. The slaves did not revolt as hoped, but Brown was regarded as a martyr by those who sympathized with his aspirations.

Oswego missed their favorite lecturer, and Mr. Crawford's frequent letters professed that when she was away she "loomed up more and more with the masses here," as she receded and disappeared. It was an outlandish notion but completely comprehensible, as the further away she traveled, *her* thoughts of *him* seemed more affectionate and more frequent.

For weeks she had been working on a poem, "Sky Dream," that he wished to read. Their verbal joust resumed. Crawford claimed,

> *You see only evil and "insincerity" in some people. May it not be that your shadow looms up before you distinctly at such times? You may theorize, speculate and accuse, but can you assert that I ever took, by ruthless force, a single unread manuscript out of your hands after handing it you to read? Did I ever begin sentences to you, then stop abruptly with the single addition of "No matter," "I won't say what I intended," &c—dash your expectations to the ground in less than a twinkling, leaving you feverish with excitement? Ah! My Sister, does your conscience speak?*
>
> *But, I have resolved to forgive you in advance for all your short comings, long-comings and stay-awayings, because you have promised to send me the Sky Dream when finished. Of course I am not unreasonable enough to expect it until it is finished, but please don't delay too long. Now let us be good, but until I am satisfied of your sincerity, how can I be more or less than "doubtfully" &c.*

What a pity it is that you could not have been in the balloon with La Mountain during his recent trip in the clouds, then you could have joined your fancies with the reality…How I would like to lie, in soft amber leaves on some beautiful hillside and look up in the sky and watch for you today. I would fair entice you to stop and descend long enough to give me a description of your new home, and perhaps I too might be transformed sufficiently to enable me to float…

God be praised for such institutions as Indian Summers. I get on tip toe every time I think of them.

Fearing your patience may weary I will conclude with the little I have said. God bless you my sister.

Beyond doubt—

Your Brother

He had hoped to meet up with her at the Spiritualist convention in Penn Yan, or at Niagara Falls so they could to travel together by ship to Chicago; or he would meet her in Chicago, or perhaps later in Milwaukee. But a letter received in Niagara Falls explained the futility of those plans:

October 15, 1859—Oswego

My Dear Sister,

As I expect to be permitted to write you at least one more letter, I will begin now and finish by degrees….

I wrote you at Binghamton on Wednesday last and presume you rec'd it before leaving for Penn Yan. I fear I shall have to remain here closely all the fall, and may not see you in Chicago or Milwaukee—which will be my luck or fate. I always manage, or my fate is always managed, so I am a victim of inevitable or unavoidable circumstances,—doing everything as I <u>must</u> and not as I <u>would</u>….

    Sunday evening

    …I have had one of my awful headaches today & have lain in bed half the day. The spirits have promised to cure me. I must eat only twice a day—meat only at breakfast, drink <u>nothing</u> but a cup of milk at each meal—only think, no <u>water</u> ! ! Do you believe in this? They say I must abstain from all <u>liquids</u> except as before stated.

    What does this dreadful feeling in the head mean? It seems compressed, bound, held as it were between two strong hands part of the time, sometimes it is clear, bright, light as air—full of ethereal thoughts and inspiration—Is it development? Have you ever felt it?

    I dreamed a prayer this morning in a singular metre—if I ever get it on paper will send it to you. I have no <u>time</u> out of my office to fix up your music, but will do it by and by. I am very busy—have to steal short moments to write this—with any number of interruptions. You know music <u>won't</u> be arranged, or <u>rhyme</u> written under such circumstances…

    I would so much love to see you at the Falls and go west with you, but tis <u>impossible</u>. That one word explains all. I hope you will see all the beauties and see it in part for your Brother who will send his spirit to join you in your rambles and prayers at that great shrine of beauty. Please go over by Table Rock and while standing there look at and feel the Spirit of Almightiness that so spoke to my soul when I first stood there—Think of <u>me, too</u>, if your thoughts are not wholly filled by the Great Spirit.

    Write to me. Tell me to whose care to write in Chicago. When you go to Milwaukee, don't fail to go <u>direct</u> to our house at the corner of Martin Street and the Lake—former residence of Col. Grant. If you do fail to go without further *invitation, don't expect Elvira to hear you lecture at Milwaukee. Or me to* <u>*remember*</u> *you one hour after I learn the fact.*

Yours in hope,

Your Brother

In October, Cousin Ephraim Moore, now 14, had written one of his characteristically edifying letters about life at the Notch: He suffered from "the tooth ache" since the Plymouth Town Fair.

> I guess there was about 2000 and a half of folks here. Oh! What a crowd there was here. There was 24 yoke of oxen came up from the south part of the town with a big cart full of folks. The Ludlow Band came up in it; they got in between here and the Furnace. James Brown and Augustus Slack and two or three others had up a tent to sell vituals and they had oysters and lots of other things. There was a tent show come out here, fellows that blacked themselves up to perform. We had a company here on Sunday. A lot of young men and boys got together a week ago last Friday eve and talked it over. Alfred and myself and we drilled a little that night and then we met again Monday night and drilled some more. We dressed as bad as we could some had old dresses on & others old caps and shirts and most every thing that you could think of. We had a grand time I tell you. The fair was Tuesday. You ought to have been here, you would enjoyed it so much. Our folks are all well. We have got all of our potatoes all dug and apples all picked. It snowed here yesterday and this morning the hills are all white. It is cold as winter most. We had about two hundred and twenty five bushels of grand great potatoes.

We are not going to have but little corn this year. We had about 35 bushels of apples.

It distressed her to imagine the children of Plymouth Notch, her former students, pretending to drill like soldiers as if it were a game! Ephraim's letter brought an ache to Axy's heart. The prospect of war was on everyone's mind.

Warren Chase had recommended that she visit Chicago, calling it "the most remarkable city of our nation." Compared with the more settled and civilized cities of the northeast, she certainly found Chicago *remarkable*—and rawboned, ugly, and sprawling. Early structures had been built directly on swampy ground only a few feet above the level of Lake Michigan, which did not allow for either cellars or sewers and caused impassable roads. When he first visited there in 1838, Chase had found the sidewalks deep in mud and vehicles constantly getting stuck on the streets, but during his most recent visit, in July 1859, he found that everything had been raised about two stories in height.

Chicago was approaching a population of 120,000. Axy arrived at the home of Thomas Richmond, a wealthy railroad financier and investor, who had arranged for lectures the next day and the following Sunday, with visits in between to Waukegan and Libertyville. She confirmed Chase's report that Spiritualism was flourishing.

Mr. Richardson was a committed spiritualist and deeply involved in economic projects which, he was convinced, the spirits had conceived. Her host had advised Axy to prepare for a city "like New York with the heart left in," but she found Chicago to be a city of commerce and commotion, of brisk winds rushing off Lake Michigan to meet prairie winds blowing in from the flat lands to the west. One day Mr. and Mrs. Richmond took her for a carriage ride out into the country, where she was shown a wheat field of several thousand acres. It seemed as much a symbol of the "infinite" as the ocean.

After her visit, Richmond wrote to say their short acquaintance "has begotten a love friendship and sympathy for you that makes me

feel happy, at your recollection, and excites a deep interest in you."
She was grateful he did not refer more explicitly to Free Love.

On her way to see us on our farm near Oakfield, Axy stopped in
Libertyville and Waukegan, Illinois, and Evansville, Wisconsin.
Estimates claimed there were already 80,000 Spiritualists in our
state. By train, she witnessed our heavily forested countryside and
settlements that appeared much shoddier and more plain-looking
than those in New England. Farm people dressed differently out
here, too—many wore crude, peasant clothing made of coarse
homespun. The women tied colorful kerchiefs on their heads instead
of bonnets, and the spoken language was sometimes heavy with a
gutteral resonance. Upon learning this was her first trip west, a
fellow passenger pointed out Indian villages where the wigwams of
the "Menomonees" or "Wild Rice Eaters," consisted of poles bent
over and united at the top, then covered with hides. She was amazed
to learn the Indians had sugar houses, too, built of split logs. Twice,
Axy noticed scaffolds made of crotched sticks supporting poles laid
horizontally against one or more trees. These were for Indians to lie
in wait for the approach of deer, she was advised, but another
passenger said that the bodies of distinguished Indians were placed
on the platforms after death.

She later confessed that she had wondered at my courage to endure
such a raw wilderness, but upon her arrival on November 5 she
climbed down from the cars with a broad smile in response to our
cordial reception. Morris placed Axy's trunk in our wagon and she
was carried back to our farm.

I was understandably proud of my husband and his carpentry skills
and, as I'd hoped, the sturdy farm house Morris had provided for me
impressed my sister as spacious and beautiful with modern conveniences
(although I apologized for the lack of furnishings in the parlor).

I know she felt very much at home, with the opportunity to be
herself, in need of respite from the strain of travel and those who
demanded so much of her. Off came her corset and crinolines: I
gave her clean, comfortable dresses of mine to increase her ease in

our household. She did insist on dressing more formally one day when we had a pleasant walk over to Morris's parents' farm to join Mrs. Steen and neighbors for afternoon tea.

Her trunk of winter clothing had been sent on ahead so Axy reviewed her garments. She gave me two of her dresses that she no longer wanted: The cream wool printed in green, brown, and purple lace, was in need of cleaning and the pink printed calico had a button missing. After she left, I certainly would not lack for time to launder, mend, and sew.

Morris suggested investing some of her money, perhaps buying up mortgages. He drew up, and they signed, a business arrangement so he could manage her increasing funds.

Axy spoke to me in an enthusiastic manner about her feelings for Mr. Crawford. She spent an inordinate amount of time explaining why theirs was not a "Free Lust" association—the term meant little to me. She seemed determined to have me understand that their respective Guardian Spirits wished for them to be together in a "spiritual" and altogether acceptable manner. I finally comprehended that their physical relationship had not resulted in a conjugal engagement, but, rather, the holding of hands and an occasional secret kiss.

I had no way of knowing what any of this truly entailed, except that the Axy I'd seen in Vermont during our summer visit was not this same Axy. Here was an enlivened, blushing woman who was, doubtless, deeply in love.

Her mood changed considerably after receiving the following letter. She explained later that she'd hoped Mr. Crawford would be at home in Milwaukee during her stay, but now he expressed his regrets.

November 8, 1859—Oswego

My dear friend,

I write this to confess my usual stupidity, nothing more nothing less. I wrote you last week-end, forgetting you were at Oakfield—directed my letter to "Fond du Lac."

I trust you are having a nice time with your relatives, and hope you will soon have a pleasant time with mine. I am glad for your sake that I shall not be at home because I like to have every-body pleasant and happy if possible.

Daughter Jenny is still here with me and I think she'll remain until I go west in Dec. or 1st Jan'y. I cannot go before the last of December...

I think the wave tried to give me your message a day or two since, but being unusually stupid I couldn't understand it.

Have you read Wendell Phillips' speech at Plymouth Church? It is as much a study as one of Emerson's essays. His remark that "every Virginian had a 'John Brown' in his conscience" was awful,—But I must not incite rebellion in you, as you will soon be in a slave state. Your favorite City, Baltimore, is at her usual killing amusement again.

With wishes and prayers for your success and happiness, I remain

Yours truly JH Crawford

Her two-week visit to Oakfield was interrupted by many requests for Axy's public presence, which drew her away from us. Morris and I accompanied her to Fond du Lac.

The city is easily accessible from here by rail. Its name is French for "bottom of the lake," as it is located on the southern end of Lake Winnebago, Fond du Lac now boasts numerous industries that produce agricultural implements and machinery. "Hunter's Magic Fountain" is visited by thousands of invalids, many of whom claim to receive remarkable benefit from its waters.

On Sunday, November 6, Axy spoke at the First Congregational Church, which was packed wall to wall. Morris and I found seats toward the front as we had arrived early, accompanying my sister. In the gathering audience I observed many murmurs. My sister had predicted there would be skeptics whose sole purpose would be to test or refute her message.

I had already described to Morris the spirit lecture I'd attended in Troy, with the Starbucks, and warned him that rousing controversy might prevail.

Soon the lights were dimmed and Axy appeared before us. Only a few hours before I had fastened the tiny buttons on the back of her emerald silk dress with my own trembling fingers. I'd brushed and helped fasten her hair. She'd joked that I was welcome to join in her travels, as it would be pleasant to have an assistant who understood her needs and served as a companion since her task was often lonely.

"I could help you memorize your lectures," I added with a friendly jab of my elbow.

"Indeed," she replied with amusement, "I am in dire need of fresh sermons to replace the threadbare ones."

Now the Axy who stood before us seemed a wholly different person. Her eyes were focused somewhere other than within the sanctuary where we convened. Conversations quieted and from the silence arose a voice that could have belonged to a stranger. She began by singing a hymn. She had assured me she knew not what it would entail, but she was confident that spirits would inspire the necessary words and music:

> *I seek no homage from the crowd,*
> *Though hushed in silence long;*
> *I sing at last because my soul*
> *Will pour itself in song;*
> *Because a fountain leaps within,*
> *Whose ever-dashing spray*
> *Can catch the light, and bear it back,*
> *Like golden beams of day.*

After several verses of the hymn she spoke of an invisible cord that entwined from every human mind and reached to the great beyond to provide power and strength for our own inspiration. "When I'm alone with this deep unknown," she said, "this power is strongest. When my thoughts are pure, this power showers my soul with nature's essence;

the spirits of the beautiful and free. There are brighter things to come, before whose beauty the earth shall sit dumb."

A man in the audience asked brusquely, "Miss Sprague, do you truly believe departed spirits give you power?"

Axy nodded. "God's truth has ever been unknown to earth. And while searching for its light, doubting eyes have seen it pass and called it Cloud of Night. For this, the True of earth have been defamed, their teachings have been proclaimed false and they have been declared infidels. Men do not understand Great Nature's laws; they break them willfully, trespass with high hand or sink deep within the noisome cell of sin. But the soul that wins one gleam of light from heaven, and from those waiting there, can bear the sneers of many a scornful face. So I stand tonight, with waves of joy sweeping through my soul. None can destroy the angel Peace that sits with radiant wings within me and ever sweetly sings."

Since my sister sang and spoke in such a manner, and with a deep and strident voice that emanated from some mysterious source, I knew she must be inspired by essences that employed her as an instrument. It seemed curious, yet beautiful. Curious only because this was *my sister*, my *dearest friend*, who had been chosen to impart wisdom and assurance as I'd never heard from her lips.

She spoke in Fond du Lac again the following Sunday. Morris and I once more accompanied her. A report was sent to *The Banner of Light* by a man who had journeyed there with eight others and said, "We were well paid for going, for such a lecture as was given through Miss Sprague's organism, was truly a feast. She spoke over an hour, and the lecture throughout was replete with beauty and sound logic. This is her first appearance in this county, and, allowing me to be the judge, she has made a lasting impression."

From my scrapbook:
Fond du Lac Nov. 16, 1859

FOND DU LAC COMMONWEALTH

LOCAL MATTERS

MISS SPRAGUE—Our citizens have been listening, at four different times, during the past week, to the Lectures of Miss. SPRAGUE, a noted Trance speaker, who advocates Harmonial Philosophy. We heard the first and last lectures only. She professes to be influenced by a circle of Spirits in another Sphere, and takes the words as they are put into her mouth without any knowledge of the subject she is treating upon, only further than she hears the sound of her own voice. The Lecture she gave in Amory Hall last Sunday afternoon, whether dictated by spirits in an off-hand manner, or made by her own unaided powers, or written out by others and committed to memory was a brilliant majestic, and logical discourse on True Devotion. We know not, and care not where it came from for the purpose of judging of it as a production by itself; as it rolled from her tongue it was a great discourse. If she does it by her own unaided powers, then the keenest logicians, the most eloquent divines, and the best States-men can take lessons from her with profit. If it is the Spirits let them have the credit. If it is the Devil give the devil his due, for one good job at least.

She spoke at Greenbush for two nights, and also in Sheboygan Falls. We were pleased with the high regard paid to Axy, although we'd hoped to share more private time. During her next visit, she promised, she would allow for a longer stay.

It was a rare treat to host a party for to celebrate my sister's thirty-second birthday. She was astonished when I (who had never before demonstrated any aptitude for homemaking skills) produced the most remarkable apple cake made with our own apples and butternuts. The cake was shared with friends from Oakfield and neighboring farms who stopped by to meet Axy and wish her well. Her birthday gift from Morris was truly extraordinary: He had traded with neighboring Winnebago Indians for a delicate pouch fashioned from deerskin and decorated with feathers. It may have been intended for carrying tobacco, but Axy said she could easily find another use. I had knit and embroidered a pair of thick woolen slippers, knowing of the aches and pains Axy suffered in winter. She would soon be traveling in extremely frigid weather so I hoped she would be comforted by my gift and then reminded of me.

The fortnight passed all too quickly, and long before any of us were ready, Axy left the tranquility of Oakfield for the emotional chaos of Milwaukee. She was met there as promised, by the Crawfords' carriage pulled by Bobb and Charlie, their matched black geldings.

Milwaukee is even more wild and wooly than Chicago. It consists of three individual and citified villages lying near each other but separated by rivers over which several bridges span. The distinct entities are known as Walker's Point, Kilbourn-Town, and The East Side. The populace is a conglomeration of immigrants from all over the world, especially Germany, as this is a common destination for emigration. The newly arrived can easily be determined by their clothing and seeming sense of disorientation, although Axy commented later, the "disorientation" could as easily be blamed on their enormous consumption of beer.

The Crawfords' impressive home was then in the choice residential district of Yankee Hill on the East Side, at the corner of Martin and Lake Streets. The house, of Italianate design, boasted two stories and three bays, built of the pale yellow cream brick so prevalent in that city, and very pleasing to the eye. Almost at their doorstep was Lake Michigan, a belligerent body of water, much more boisterous than Lake Ontario.

Mr. Crawford had requested of his wife Elvira and daughter Lizzie that Miss Sprague be shown their utmost hospitality. He did this in his usual mirthful way, relating Axy's identification with "the waves." Of course that disclosure caused his fun-loving family to relentlessly tease her for her association with Lake Michigan and its relentless surf. My sister found this unexpectedly annoying, as she had grown to believe the expressive personal symbols (the *wave* and *sea*) were meant only for the two of them, and the lack of his regard was yet more substantiation of his insincerity.

To Axy's relief, Elvira was much involved in the activities of the local Friends of Progress, a Quaker society that observed the tenets of Spiritualism. Having boasted to someone of her distinguished background as a "Mather," someone commented on the Salem Witchcraft trials in which her ancestors were involved. Elvira found solace in a book about Spiritualism that claimed "the history of Salem Witchcraft is but an account of spiritual manifestations, and of man's incapacity to understand them."

Mrs. Crawford invited Axy to join her when she attended her meetings or went calling, but when my sister was not visiting spiritualists she preferred to stay home with Sarah, John's spinster sister, and the children—Lizzie, now 21; Julia, 19; George, 7; and Molly, 13. The older girls had beaux who took them for rides in carriages or called upon them in evenings, so Axy was occasionally asked to serve as chaperone. Sarah Crawford appreciated Axy's companionship and Axy found a stout friend in the highly intelligent woman whose pleasant countenance resembled her brother's. Sarah also shared his hunger for knowledge and his dry sense of humor.

It felt absurdly awkward, to be a guest in John's home with his presence so evident among his family, yet physically absent from her side. She asked George to write her a poem but he could not manage anything beyond "My dear Miss Sprague, You are a terrible plague, To ask me to write you a poem."

Windows in her bed chamber overlooked the water, where she had a view of the Port of Milwaukee and large steamers that docked there. With the onset of winter the water traffic was slowing.

"The Lake prospect is rather gloomy just now," Sarah Crawford remarked one afternoon, "No sails, no steamers to enhance the scene, and the *waves* have to recoil on themselves. At times the waves can be very boisterous."

Although Sarah meant to be humorous, Axy frowned over her needlework yet managed to cast her friend a weak smile to account for the wretchedness of her little joke.

"I cannot see why you should liken yourself to anything so capricious, Miss Sprague," Sarah continued, "but really you have made *something* out of it."

One of the few truly devout Spiritualists in Milwaukee, Enos Hall, warned Axy that a Presbyterian minister had preached a sermon against Spiritualism a few weeks prior to her arrival with an omen that had already been repeated three or four times in different parts of the city. In the course of his remarks the minister warned, "When God has any great truth to give to the world, he invariably employs men, but when the Devil has anything to be done, he always employs women."

In spite of this (or perhaps *because* of Hall's sermon?), Axy's public debut in Milwaukee drew overwhelming attendance. All seats were occupied. Elvira and Sarah Crawford thought her address was well delivered, but one disgruntled reviewer published a censorious account in *The Milwaukee Sentinel* which I grimly but dutifully pasted onto a blank scrapbook page:

> We listened...to a declamation by Miss Sprague at Good Templars Hall...She is not by any means a prepossessing young lady. Her "human face divine" promised us no superior intellectual treat. We thought she was haggard, as though the "trance state" in which she spent part of her existence, was not congenial with the corporal system; and we were disappointed at the outset, for we knew that the magic of a woman's tongue is scarcely effective with a mixed audience, unless there is the important adjunct of personal beauty.

Miss Sprague seated herself upon the platform and commenced what Tom Hood has called—

The washing of hands with invisible soap
In imperceptible water.

After wringing her palms, and passing them slowly over her face for a few moments, she rose with her eyes closed, and commenced her lecture. It was spoken in a clear, distinct, but not by any means pleasant voice. Her articulation was perfect, and not a word was uttered but might be understood in any part of the room. But the subject was the same pointless collection of beautiful abstractions which it has ever been our misfortune to listen to when Trance Speaking was announced.…To the honest listener, who went with the desire of learning something, it was profound twaddle from beginning to end.…The clever arrangement of words descriptive of beautiful things—the speaker's acquired knowledge, or clairvoyant perception of musical beauty, and the fervid flow of stolen poetry, produced a pleasing sensation for the time being— much after the manner of one of our own rivulets.

Stolen poetry! Profound twaddle! It was bad enough to be accused of appearing haggard and lacking "personal beauty," but to imply she had delivered a *memorized* lecture, and a boring one at that! Axy was mortified. The Crawfords were extremely gracious and brushed it off, saying it was merely more evidence of the struggles of Spiritualism in the West, but my sister worried that her stay in their home might prove to be an embarrassment to them.

The ten days scheduled for Milwaukee were dragging by. She also spoke in nearby Racine and again in Waukegan, Illinois.

That year, 1859, thirty States and three Territories held Thanksgiving on the same day—the last Thursday in November. Axy celebrated the holiday with a sumptuous meal at the Crawford home and gave thanks as always for her return to health and the gifts bestowed by her Guardians. She also expressed her deep gratitude for family and for special friends, including those gathered around the table.

On the 29th, Axy again fled Milwaukee for Waukegan. After a quick stop in Chicago on Friday and after her evening lecture on Saturday, she caught the 9 o'clock p.m. train to St. Louis. It was a brief, hurried launch southward with little time to tarry, catch her breath, or nurse her sore throat.

Since May, James H. Blood had been beseeching her to lecture in St. Louis, where Spiritualism was thriving and where Blood served as secretary of the Friends of Progress. She might have gone to St. Louis for that reason alone, but the city was also the home town of Axy's nemesis, Amanda Britt Spence, who had developed her powers in some of the city's earliest séances. Axy *would* go to St. Louis to demonstrate her truthfulness and her resolve!

Indeed, Axy found a heavy demand for private circles in St. Louis. Some of the country's finest lecturers had been welcomed there, despite the distance from what they considered the "constellated intellectual centers of the East." Their visits were mostly due to the generosity of the same James H. Blood, a director of the St. Louis Railroad and a respected accountant who was also a strong advocate of Free Love—the scandalous, "Free Lust" kind.

Although Mr. and Mrs. Blood endeavored to make her stay in their home a pleasant one, Axy was uncomfortable in a slave state with the prospect of war growing ever closer. She also was made to feel uneasy in Blood's presence, by his own immodest actions. Despite assurances that he was a gentleman and "gallant alike with pen and sword," the man was incapable of understanding that she did not want to entertain any intimacies of his Free Love affinity no matter how extravagantly he praised her attributes nor how frequently he suggested otherwise, even whispering lurid comments in her ear!

After Axy left St. Louis, Blood wrote to her: "Not that I entertain any doubts in regard to the matter, but to satisfy Mrs. Blood. When you left us you bid us all Good Bye, excepting my wife. I know it was not intentional unless indeed she may have said or done something to offend you. She feels badly about it and wishes to know if she did offend you in any manner. I, myself, noticed a change just before you left and could not account for it. If there was anything done or said in our house unbecoming on our part I desire to make most ample and earnest apology as entirely unintended and the furthest from our feelings. We all regard you with most affectionate respect and should be very sorry to have you entertain any other feelings toward us."

Poor Mrs. Blood (who would remain his wife for only a very short time afterward); if Axy had felt compelled to respond, she could have reminded him of his unseemly advances and additionally informed him of Mary Ann Blood's casual comment, "Miss Sprague, I certainly do agree with my dear friend, Mrs. Britt Spence. She says she possesses nothing but the utmost admiration for *your remarkable memory*."

Axy had completed her poem about the "Sky at Rest." It included mention of a "sky dream," a topic that tantalized Mr. Crawford. But she withheld the poem for reasons that are not altogether clear to me except for their repetitive cat-and-mouse routine and her wish to provoke him for the untimely "wave" revelation in Milwaukee.

After the nuisance of Mr. Blood, she struck out (by mail) at John with complaints about the West in general, saying she was unable to find poetic inspiration in such a harsh landscape. He was sympathetic and replied in his usual manner:

Oswego, December 1, 1859

My Dear Sister,

Your letter of the 26th came in the same mail with Lizzie's, reaching me last evening. I begin my reply this evening only because I am indebted to a slight neuralgia and headache for keeping me in my room all day. I have played being sick until

I am out of patience with my head—have read until I considered myself sufficiently punished in that way and now out of sheer fatigue by exhausting every means of making myself happy I have begun to annoy you on paper. If you precognetize this you will perceive all these elements readily. I hope you will fail to get the infection as I would by no means give my aches and pains to _you_, even though the giving might bring me relief. If this letter is in bad taste, you must regard it as a confession of a culprit in the stocks, not entitled to full credit.

I am so sorry I wrote Lizzie a word about you or the _wave_ as I did. I never could say the most harmless words of my friends without hurting them especially when endeavoring to be witty. Now if you will only imagine those words spoken in our mirthful moods, you cannot lay up anything against me. I am right glad you did not write the stinging reply you thought of.

Now my dear Sister, pray do forgive me, and trust me for the future.

Now that I have made my apology, let me ask you to analyze the milk of such sentences as "it is a fine thing to have a brother &c especially when that brother is away." Again, "I got Mrs. C's ambrotype when I was gone"—"and _that_ is all I care for" (this last sentence I think perfectly _true_). "I am to return in Feby or March—I shall look out for a new stopping place" &c. "Some one will be at home part of the time" &etc. "and he does not like to be identified with Spiritualists" &c. I "have disgraced his house already" &c.

Now if I were not the coolest mortal in the world, my pen would tremble in _very rage_. Among all the mean things ever said by a brother to a sister or a sister to a brother, I have never said anything like this. My offences are thin effluences, shadows compared with these. Can it be possible that my _sincere_ hazel eyed Sister (they say hazel eyes are always sincere) said this? Did not some evil spirit have undivided control of her pen when these words were written? I believe it, and will therefore not hold her responsible...

I regret exceedingly that I could not be at home when you were there, but I trust you gave much pleasure to Mrs. C. and the children. I get homesick at times, but then I am full of perplexity and trouble on account of business and those things blunt the homesick feeling and fill my cup.

I don't wonder the lake was angry at you. That lake from that bank would resent an insult on unkind words aimed at me with as much spirit and promptness as would my friend Minerva whom you saw here, and that lake knows one well, and knows my friends and <u>enemies</u>, too. There are hallowed associations connected with that spot. There I beheld the moon rise from her bath of blue &c. There I have talked with the waves and I repeat I don't wonder they were angry. When you return there, they will be reconciled if you will only tell them you were <u>not</u> in earnest. They (always) had no thought of finding any "Sky of rest" under your guidance, so long as you harbored ill thoughts or said naughty things of <u>their</u> brother.

A sky of rest, how beautiful is this thought, that we shall one day rest in the sky, where there shall be no more sorrow, pain, disease and longing... I used to think when looking at the moon and stars, apparently in the sweetest repose, how much I longed to be at rest with them but then the thought that notwithstanding all their seeming tranquility and rest, they were whirling and reeling through space at an inconceivable velocity, and that really there was nothing but the wildest unrest even in the skies. I concluded there was no rest but in the grave, and in an endless sleep... In my revolutions on the wheels of trade, <u>these</u> are my periods of rest, when I go to my room and shut out the noise of steam, smoke and the hum of revolving wheels, and write lovingly to a Sister or friend – when the inner life is manifested and spirits hold communion. Were it not for this unfolding of the inner Nature, life would be little better than a perpetual public execution of John Brown.

Poor dear old man; tomorrow the black tyrant that rules our goodly land will murder him. He was infatuated, insane and impracticable. I have known him personally twenty four years. Misguided, injured, persecuted, but honest man. He should have used only the word of the spirit, but in his insane moods he imagined himself chosen by the _God of Wrath_ to punish guilty slaveholders. His Presbyterian God taught him that the wrongdoer must be unrelentingly punished, not believing as I do that the chains of the slaves must first be broken in the hearts of their masters & then they will fall off — as the frost falls from the branches of the trees before the morning sun.

John Brown may be hung tomorrow, but not _die_. He will live in fire in Northern hearts, and his Spectre will haunt slaveholders at their bedsides—till they shall grow haggard and pale. His spirit will arouse them to deeds of _kindness_ when he finds God is _Love_, and like Samson, he will slay more in his death than in his life...

If you desire it I will release you from your promise to send me the Sky Dream, but you must in that case look out for the consequences. I can easily open the subject again, and though no inspiration has touched my pen since you left Oswego, I can get some few drops of burning fluid and mix with this ink just sufficient to send you a small sprinkling of terror.

And as to finding some other place when you return to Milwaukee, I beg of you not to think of it—for rather than have you ill treat your friend Mrs. Crawford in this way, I will stay away altogether and not molest you.

As I have written my headache all way, I think it may be in the letter, but I hope you'll not get it. I hope your sore throat is well, if not you may wrap this letter about it. I do believe I could magnetize a band and send it to some people to wear around their throat with good results, but perhaps not with such results with _you_.

Don't wait until next spring before answering this.

Sincerely, your brother,

John H.

Friday morning

I have looked over my letter and have half a mind not to send it because it looks like a headache production, but I will send it with the understanding that it is to be considered a very <u>poor article</u>. I am better this morning but not quite well yet. I don't think I have had a day of poetic inspiration since you left. Where do you think it has gone? Musical Moods too are very scarce, but I must not omit stating a little matter. I was at Mrs. Stewarts a few evenings since. They have a fine piano. I sang a song at Nettie's request—Nettie plays the Melodeon at the Hall—and Nettie and another person present assured me that they distinctly heard <u>two voices all through the song</u>.

    Several things were sung by those present – and just before coming away I sang another and while singing was full of inspiration. During this time Mrs. Dodge was entranced and after singing, Nettie and the other person aid they heard <u>four voices</u> or the four parts distinctly. Mrs. Dodge still entranced – spoke and described two females on my right and one male on my left – all singing the same piece.

    The piece happened to be the melody of a quartette, sung many times by me in days of yore, with three singers <u>all this side</u> now still, but my niece, now <u>beyond</u> had often sung it with me. Somehow, when singing, I remember now to have felt a beautiful sweet influence around me for years – one in which I was so fascinated that I wanted to live and die in it. I have often felt it when alone than otherwise. This it is which makes being alone so pleasant to me at times, but there are a few spirits in this Sphere that give me <u>the same</u> emotions when in their presence—<u>but they are very few</u>.

      I am interrupted.   Good bye

Poetry had been a convenient excuse for isolating themselves from others while they pored over a writing project, in subdued whispers. One poem they refined was Axy's "Devotion," for which Crawford wrote music and sang to her, then sang for others to her profound pleasure. Within two weeks of the above letter he revealed to her that he had submitted "Devotion" for publication in *The Banner of Light*. It would appear in the December 17, 1859, issue:

Devotion

I worship at great Nature's shrine,
    Devout as any saint
That bows before the "great white throne,"
    The past has loved to paint.
My temple is the Universe,
    Its dome the arching sky,
Its lamps the glorious burning stars,
    The clouds its imagery.

The ocean my baptismal fount,
    The "holy water" there;
The fruits of earth God's sacrament,
    And all may in it share;
The earth my Virgin Mother pure,
    To whom I kneel and pray;
Ave Maria! Says my soul—
    She answers me always.

The crucifix to which I bend
    Is God's own Bow of Light,
I count the stars, like Catholics
    That tell their beads at night;
The morning mist that graceful floats,
    And lingers on the hill,
Makes e'en the mountain seem to me
    A nun, white-veiled and still

And, oh! The mighty organ grand,
    Whose countless thousand keys
Are scattered through the universe,
    And swept by every breeze;
How does my inmost spirit thrill—
    Spell-bound with magic wand—
Beneath those grand and solemn strains,
    Waked by the Master Hand!

I join the hymn of Nature's choir,
    That binds me as a spell;
With Nature's Beautiful in prayer
    I whisper, "All is well:"
'Tis always Sabbath unto me,
    And hallowed is the sod;
Our priest is at the altar there—
    That Priest the living God!

❧ PART THREE ❧

(1860–1862)

. . .Let the future go
But live the present—that the future makes—
And into beauty all the world awakes.

"I Still Live, A Poem for the Times"
MISS A. W. SPRAGUE, 1862

☙ 15 ☙

Misanthrope

(JANUARY–FEBRUARY 1860)

I F JAMES HARVEY BLOOD thought Axy was in a bad mood when she left St. Louis the day after Christmas, he should have observed her not long afterward: quarrelsome and lonely, sick at heart for being so foolish as to venture west in winter. Or (excepting Wisconsin), perhaps to venture west at all. Although she had been invited to lecture in Atchison, Kansas Territory—a prospect thrilling in theory—she would not dream of entering that rambunctious terrain. Her sore throat was worse than ever and her wrists and ankles ached *all* the time.

Seeing us happily situated on our farm had been very pleasant, she allowed. In her travels she found few opportunities to laugh as freely as she did with us, unburdened by the need to project a public image that must be reserved, polite yet contrived. She and I had played with different hairstyles, studied the latest fashions in *Godey's Lady's Book*, and shared family gossip and confidences. She admired all facets of my new house, built by my loving husband, but said she had no need for a house of her own as *her* home would always be back in Plymouth Notch with Mother. And any material possessions not carried with her still resided in her childhood room.

Oakfield, Wisconsin December 26, 1859

Dear Achsa,

I hasten to write you so that you will receive it in Davenport. You did not give us any information in respect to your address, so Celia and I concluded I would send it to the place above mentioned, where you will speak. I supposed you would like to know how I disposed of your money.

Well, on the 26th day of November I bought a mortgage from William A. Smith of Oakfield, on twenty acres of land whereon there is a good water privilege, sawmill and a log dwelling house. The place is only two miles from here and is valued at one thousand dollars, so you may rest satisfied that it is well secured. The principal is three hundred dollars, the interest due on it at the time I bought it $22.90. There was a five dollar bill on the International bank of Canada that is uncurrent here. I will send that and the assignment of the Mortgage to you when you will tell me where to direct to. The balance of the money ($22.10) I will pay you interest on until I get some more to put out with it. There will be thirty six dollars interest due you on the mortgage in April, so if you have any more money to spare and choose to send it here, I can let it all out together, but I suppose I am taxing your patience so I will drop the subject.

I am now finishing off a house a mile and a half from here. I leave home before daylight and do not return till after dark. It will take me about three weeks longer to finish it. I board out so Celia has the house to herself.

I have got my horse nearly broke so the next time you come here we will not have to depend on our neighbors.

We have had a very mild and open winter so far, not enough snow to make sleighing. I had a letter from Mr. Josselyn last week. He and Orvilla thought we must have had a good time when you were here, sleeping on the floor in a <u>small</u> house.

Write soon, J. Morris Steen

Home. Monday. 1 o'clock p.m.

Dear Sister,

As my housework is all done up and no babies to cry I can sit down unmolested and write. I see by your last letter that you keep on the move, and daily there is something new presented for your eye, ear and tongue. Life with you I think means action—never ceasing motion—but do you not sometimes weary? Would you not like a quiet and happy home to shelter you at night? Ah no, you little realize the comforts of home so do not miss them; so go on and labor for the good of mankind.

We received a letter from Mother written December 13th. She was then to start the next day for St. Johnsbury to see our sister Sarah as she was daily failing, bloats all over and lungs painful and sore. I presume you know it all, so I will write no more particulars. Mother seemed to look upon the journey as a greater undertaking than you would to sail around the world.

Can it be that January is the fated month to carry all our family away? Ephraim and Father passed from us in Jan. and Sarah expects to, but yet she may not. Will you go home if she continues to fail? It does seem too bad that more of her relatives cannot be with her. She is nearly as bad off as I should be if sick.

From the same

Celia

Axy could barely conceal her irritation with James Thompson for begging her to visit Iowa in his letter the previous fall, and was upset with herself for consenting, although he apologized for Davenport's brutal temperatures and impassable snow drifts. He also expressed regret for the area's defiant public opinion toward Spiritualism, and, out of shame, shared a clipping torn from the *Daily Iowa State Democrat:* A reporter at last year's Rutland Convention had found it "a happy meeting of all that is mean, all that is disgusting, all that is impudent, all that is sacrilegious."

When she presented a lecture on New Years' Eve in neighboring Genesco, Illinois, Axy was prepared for adversity, but the event attracted only a few curiosity seekers due to severe weather conditions and problems in heating the lecture room.

The next day was no better. On New Years Day 1860 she delivered a sparsely attended morning lecture in Davenport, where bitter winds blew through the building's walls and disturbed dust that Axy thought would have been too fraught with frost to stir.

The steamboat *Illinois* would carry her south on the Mississippi, and she felt greatly relieved with the promise of more temperate weather. By the time she reached Memphis her aching joints would surely be thawed and her mettle strengthened to meet the challenges of that city. With reckless extravagance, she took a private stateroom. She had no desire to mingle with other travelers, only to conceal herself in a heaping featherbed and create an envelope of comforting warmth.

One hundred and fifty travelers were jam-packed on the paddlewheeler. Probably that many cattle were stowed on the lowest level. The vessel was also transporting a great amount of flour to be unloaded in New Orleans.

For much of the first day she dozed, aware only of the clunk of ice floes against the side of the boat and a soothing, rocking motion. When she arose, still weary but warmer, and dressed for dinner, she was seated next to the daughter of a cotton planter from Tennessee. "You must visit our home," the young woman urged with a gracious Southern drawl when she learned Axy had never been to Memphis or viewed a cotton plantation.

After the meal Axy excused herself, preferring the isolation of her stateroom. A fat bundle of mail had been collected at Davenport but she had been too busy, too cold, and her swollen hands too sore, to respond to any of them.

Here was a rare letter from our brother, Nathan Sprague. He had *never* written a letter to her, and she could envision his shoulders hunched over the table as he laboriously composed the brief note.

He had been working in Weston, he said, staying with brother William and his wife Anne. Nathan wanted her to know that Sarah's baby was dead.

"My health is quite miserable this fall," Nathan wrote. He was going back to Plymouth but "I shall not enjoy myself when at home. Far better would it be for me to be some whare else. I was glad to get a letter from you. I have nothing to write of interest or I would write more."

Anne Sprague, William's wife, added a brief note to Nathan's. Buoyant with news of her own healthy children, she expressed concern over what Mother would do with Nathan upon his return to the Notch.

Cousin Ephraim then reported, "Nathan has got home last Monday with his clothes. We had grand times Thanksgiving, George and Clara came down and we went over to Mr. Coolidge's and took supper we had a baked Goose and a Chicken Pie and some chickens and two kinds of pudding rice and cracker and three or four kinds of pie we had a grand time in the forenoon…Friday Eve the next day Hiram had a ball and they had a nice company of them there was about twenty five couple there."

She had been away from her mountain home since June and did not want to yield to self-pity, but Axy, who seldom cried, experienced a rush of tears prompted by homely reminders of our family's love and concern. Soon she was weeping into her pillows without restraint.

Nathaniel Randall had written from St. Johnsbury, as had Sarah. They were devastated over the loss of their baby daughter. Sarah, who sometimes exaggerated her suffering, seemed unusually distraught: "That beautiful embroidered waist you presented her she never wore; that with all my other bright plans have vanished unless you or through you there can be something done to save me. I do not feel as you did when sick, I am not willing to die."

Also troubling was a lengthy letter from one of Axy's East Coast admirers who added, "Wonder if you are among the excited elements of the John Brown affair? The people here are expecting a war as the final effect of that, and many other things under process of development now. The military are found mustering in every town and city."

A prophecy had been published in *The New England Spiritualist* not long ago, and her friend conjectured that perhaps it would be fulfilled: The Catholics would unite with the South, the land would be deluged in blood, an obscure child would be brought into the presidency, famine and all horrible things would prevail. "Oh! Dear!! I wish you had a real good, kind, loving, <u>forgiving</u> husband with you, and then I should think you was made as perfect as this world admits of. Now don't you go and marry anybody who will take you into 'Western or Southern lands to dwell,' for you belong to the Eastern States, and I fear would meet a Sad fate on other soil."

A great stretch of the imagination was required to think of Axy marrying and settling way out here! All the same, plentiful offers of Free Love were tendered in practically every city and town she visited and at least four letters in this very bundle proffered similar pleas. A man from Philadelphia who had physically followed her all the way to Springfield, Illinois, expressed his disbelief: "You say you do not wish to correspond with anyone on a certain subject I referred to and say you do not think I would if more acquainted. I should like an explanation on this point and hope you will write again and at length."

Such tedious subjects of "Affinities" and "Congenials" and "Free Love" were exasperating, and Axy feared her western audiences were more interested in the lurid and sensational aspects of Spiritualism than the promise of everlasting life. Her messages of reform (she didn't dare touch on abolition and hoped her Spirit Guides would stay silent on the subject for the next several weeks) seemed overlooked and ignored.

Benjamin Starbuck, the dear man, teased her about enjoying the rigors of a New England winter while she was in St. Louis. "I would think that you would get tired being road on a rail and yet after all as you say it ain't half as bad as having to pay notes or staying where you ain't wanted. And so you are going to Memphis are you? I hope you won't get into any trouble in these exciting times amongst our Southern brothers and sisters. But I don't fear for you, for I know you will at all times mind your own business and as a general thing that insures a safe passage in most any kind of a storm."

She recognized the deliberate advice to "mind her own business" and Memphis's welcome of another well-known medium was in her thoughts. Emma Hardinge, a highly respected trance-lecturer, had been subject to unmistakable hostility there. The Memphis *Inquirer* voiced antagonism toward Hardinge and insulted her with allegations that she was an "infidel lecturer" from the "Free Love Party," and a "New England Abolitionist." At the Sabbath lecture, Mrs. Hardinge had spoken for half an hour when a large stone was thrown through a window exactly opposite, shattering glass and landing directly at her feet.

Thankfully, Axy was only going to Memphis, not Alabama where, just this week, newspapers reported that the Alabama legislature had passed a bill declaring that any person or persons giving public spiritual manifestations in that state should be subject to a penalty of five hundred dollars.

Tied with ribbon in a separate bundle of mail were pale blue envelopes holding letters from John Crawford that Axy already knew by heart. Here was a new one! She would set it aside unopened, in an attempt to look forward to his trademark stationery for one more day.

As she put out the flame on her lamp she could hear the reassuring whap-whap-whap of the paddlewheel and the seemingly more insistent thump of floating slabs of ice.

The Woman's Salon proved to be a comfortable place to write. The next afternoon Axy sat at a writing desk, where she gazed out at a woodland riverbank choked with new snow. Other women were intent upon their needlework, caring for babies, reading, oblivious to the tedious landscape. In one corner a group played whist. A family of concert singers, the Riley Family, lifted their voices in song around the upright piano and their music almost brightened the room.

She had mistakenly bound a new note from Sarah Crawford in Milwaukee with the latest from John. Her brother was expected to arrive in Milwaukee by the first of February, "very consoling," Sarah remarked dryly, "while we were expecting him soon after the first of January."

> I don't see wherein John can be likened to the sea, which is always stationary. If he had chosen the wind for his cognomen it would in my opinion be far more appropriate. I can find many resemblances between him and that fickle element. Your appellation is far more to the point than his, as given in your late explanation. The "waves" on our side were all last week in obeisance to the strong hands of the Ice King, but they have at last succeeded in bursting their prison doors, shaken off their chains and spent their fury…We have had some bitter cold weather. Last week the ice in the Lake extended as far as the eye could penetrate but now there is only an occasional float to remind us that it has been and today I saw a sail vessel gliding as smoothly as in mid summer.
>
> We have had delightful sleighing for sometime but not a sleigh have I been in this winter as our three sleighs by some unaccountable caprice of their owner are in Oswego. I never in my whole life passed my time in such utter loneliness as I have thus far this winter. Whenever you have a stray thought to devote to me, you can see me in my room and for variety gazing on the broad waters of Lake Michigan. The Lake is my company. Were it not for that I think my winter here would be unendurable.

Sarah Crawford enclosed loving sentiments from Elvira and the children with a comment that Axy was taking a wide range from St. Louis to Davenport, from there to Cincinnati and so all round the Western states.

And how in the world did you find time while at St. Louis to deliver a course of lectures at Springfield in Ill? You are a regular chain of lightning. You may thank God for the lightning speed with which you can travel. What would become of you if you had to travel by the old fashioned stage coach?

Axy visualized Sarah Crawford staring out at Lake Michigan while at the same time she was observing the impenetrable wilderness beyond the Mississippi River's steep banks.

John's note, which she'd saved to read, had been peremptory.

> *I am very sorry you have found such a cold climate. It must be milder ere this. I trust you have thawed by this time. How unkind it is in you to intimate that I do not feel interested in your appointments and success. I wish you would tell me more in detail about your lectures. People begin to refer to you now, and say "Nobody" &etc.——you know I never flatter you.*
> *I fully agree, and sympathize with you as regards society and their demands. We'll never quarrel about that, but don't get misanthropic over it. There's yet virtue enough in mankind to leaven some small portion of society, and small seeds produce in God's good time great results.*

Axy addressed an envelope to John Crawford in care of his Oswego address and inserted the "Sky Poem." With the colorful cynicism he so enjoyed, she would begin by telling him about this steamboat, the *Illinois*; how it differed from his massive propeller ships with its garish décor, the swaggering riverboat gamblers, the Southern planters, the cattle traders, and the cows. Of her scheduled time in St. Louis she would say little; he would be perturbed with James H. Blood if she mentioned the man's brazen advances. But she would tell him of the series of lectures she delivered at Springfield during those weeks and the comfortable home of Mr. and Mrs. Worthen (the Illinois State Geologist, Director of the Illinois Geological Survey). Sarah Worthen speculated that the wife of Mr.

Abraham Lincoln may have been present at her lectures, both in Springfield and St. Louis. Mrs. Lincoln, who had lost a son, Eddy, in Springfield in 1850, was known to use the alias "Mrs. Tundall" when attending Spiritualist events.

The effort of capturing all this on paper for Mr. Crawford took an entire afternoon. There was barely time to retire to her stateroom to prepare for dinner, even though the letter remained unfinished. Again, she was seated next to the cotton farmer and his beautifully adorned daughter. And again she was issued an invitation to call upon them during her Memphis stay.

"Do you have slaves on your estate?" Axy asked, with what she hoped sounded like innocent curiosity. "Of course," the father replied with a chuckle, and he assured Axy that his three hundred Negroes had a kind overseer, they were well fed and well clad and well paid, and all their wants were cared for. "They seem as happy as the cotton spinners in your New England," he added, "although perhaps not as intelligent." He also added, to Axy's relief, that he actually felt Tennessee as a state might have her interests advanced by abandoning slavery. Many in Kentucky, Virginia, and Missouri agreed with that assessment, he said, but not those in Louisiana or Mississippi.

After dinner the Riley Family entertained, and a comic by the name of Connor from New Hampshire told jokes. The *Illinois* docked at St. Louis around ten o'clock. By that time Axy was in her stateroom, asleep.

She was awakened by a shudder and jolt of motion when the boat was on its way again. It was not until just before daylight that she woke again, this time with a sense that everything was much too quiet.

When she emerged from her stateroom for breakfast she found the boat was marooned in the middle of nowhere and could not move. Only thirty miles out of Memphis, where she was expected to lecture the following evening, they were stranded, completely surrounded by ice. Warren Chase had mentioned that last January, he had similarly been held up for over a week!

The prospect of glacial imprisonment did not seem to bother the others, who carried on with their card games and other leisure pursuits. But Axy's schedule was rigidly prearranged, with little time to spare. She paced the salon until it became obvious that her impatience was attracting undue attention. Then she resumed her place at the writing desk and continued her letter to Mr. Crawford with a personal postscript. Now that she had an opportunity to think it through and plenty of time to address it, once and for all she wanted to confront a troubling issue.

There were times when she agonized over her feelings for this man. If her Guardians disapproved of her actions, if they were not sufficiently "of spirit-to-spirit," might she risk the loss of their benefaction, or of her renewed health or Spirit-rapport? Could all be lost? She had asked for their response, but no message was received.

> *This last is not of the least importance, but of the greatest. You say, "write me often." I want to say a great many things, for we ought to understand each other fully. Shall I say them? Have I your full permission? I seem to hear you say "yes," so I will write unreservedly.*
>
> *When I first made your acquaintance, perhaps the third time I saw you, (at the Lake) I heard you make remarks upon certain movements of the day, & criticisms upon certain individuals, that led me to suppose, in your present condition you could never regard any one (no matter how sacredly) in any light but as a friend. It set me perfectly at ease & at home with you. I found a spirit that like mine loved the beautiful, not with a superficial love but with an intense devotion & thrilled beneath the touch of Genius & Intellectual, conscious when touched by master hands; & I thought I have at last found a friend & a brother. You remember the month that succeeded. You doubtless remember saying things to me that you ought not to have said. Because they were not said from the material plane, were they the <u>less</u> a wrong? Situated as you are, where the material self is recognized by law as appropriated—& the Spiritual & Mental as a matter of course—is not the gift of the spirit to another ten thousand times more unlawful than of the body, for is not the spirit of*

countless times far greater worth? And were I the other party, it were to me ten thousand times the greater wrong. But you will say, as you sometimes do in moments of passion, perhaps the spirit may not always obey the will. But the language *should, & that would assist in the subjection of the other. But I need not reason farther upon this, you know the subject in all its bearings as well as I do, but turn rather to the effect it has produced upon myself and the fact that out of this has grown nearly all our quarrels.*

You wrote me after I left. Your letters were mystical, doubly *just like yourself. There was just enough of the intellectual & of the friend in them to make them interesting, but enough of the wicked to make me distrust your friendship & distrust yourself. Therefore I wrote but seldom & then usually briefly, yet did not drop entirely the correspondence, for I wished you to be my friend, & trusting to what I thought to be the changeability of your nature, I believed you would in time be that or indifferent.*

I came back to Oswego last summer, because I felt that duty & my mission called me. When I found your business compelled you to be there, I determined not to meet you in loving spirit until I met you positively and definitely as a friend in spiritual agreement.

You, having heard insinuations, supposed I treated you coldly because the eye of the world was upon me. What is the world to me, weighed in the balance with a true *friend? I would not treat one coldly for* ten *worlds unless mutually understood, & then 'twould be no coldness.*

As it was, I became what you called me—an iceberg, *& so you said I was an actress, when to be true to myself, to you and to* yours, *I felt that I could not be otherwise, & I should have remained so if Mrs. C. had not come, & then I found it a difficult matter to be cordial to one & cool to the other, & when I thought about it more I said, "I will let things take their course, perhaps I shall sooner arrive at the result I wish." I did so, & am on the whole glad that I did. The day before I left, you spoke* more definitely upon the subject than ever before, & asked my opinion as you recollect, & so I feel justified in giving it now.

If you do care at all for me which I often doubt, I believe your word, that it is of the spirit. If I believed, or even suspected it otherwise, I should cast aside your memory as a thing too worthless to be even despised. You know you have <u>no right</u> to be anything else, that you cannot be. Intellectually, poetically & musically, I am at home in your spirit, will you thrust me from it by unlawful thoughts & feelings that you have no right to give? And again, would you wish me to respond to the feeling, when you know it could only result in my wretchedness?

If you really cared for me, would you not rather that I should escape such agony, even though your own spirit was desolate?

Forgive me in that I have spoken plainly. I have not meant it unkindly. Don't say that I take a severe, a worldly, or a precis view of the matter. I only look at it as connected with right & wrong, with the happiness or unhappiness of <u>three</u> individuals. I have the world & their decisions entirely out of the matter.

I should prise your correspondence. I should prise your friendship, for few spirits respond to mine, intellectually, poetically, devotionally & musically as yours. To me we are so naturally brother & sister. Our unison of thought & feeling in so many things decides the question. To me there is no doubt about the relationship. Why can it not be so, not <u>superficially</u> but really & wholly of the spirit? Just when I think I have found a real friend & brother, some strange fancy enters their brain & destroys it all. I know this <u>is</u> a <u>fancy</u> with you, & you <u>will</u> have it, will you not, Like an "Ignus Fatuus," & be generous & noble as you know how to be? When you said to the poor wave, "go rest in the sky & be my sister," I took it as an earnest of our destiny. And shall it not be so?

Shall I ever write to you again? It rests with you.

That gloomy January afternoon, welcome rain began to fall. The steamboat's officers assured their passengers the rain would soon soften the ice. In the dark of night, as Axy heard reverberations of booming and breaking, the boat began to drift with the ice and current. When the next day dawned, Axy saw five or six boats waiting to make their way up river through the open path made through the ice by the *Illinois*.

Her stay in Memphis was necessarily brief, and unremarkable. No rocks were thrown by angry crowds, and no occasions for tours of cotton plantations with three hundred happy Negroes singing in the fields, which was just as well. Axy soon boarded another boat and went up the Ohio River to Cincinnati where she lectured for two weekends, then took the train to Terre Haute, Indiana, where she lectured on January 22 and 29.

I added the reviews of her lectures to my scrapbook when Mother sent them to me:

> Large audiences greet, on every occasion, the eloquent and powerful discourses of Miss Sprague who, in "thoughts that breathe and words that burn," teaches the truths of Spiritualism. It is surprising how a lady, with less than the educational advantages of the clergyman or the lawyer, can pour forth, for an hour and a half or more, such beautiful sentences with such eloquent and impressive elocution, as no clergyman or lawyer, of our acquaintance, can equal. Miss Sprague's exordial singing, last night, was melodious, appropriate and beautiful.
>
> She lectures again to-night, and those who would enjoy what is great in sentiment, and enchanting in language and mode of speech, should attend.
>
> *Terre Haute Daily Evening Journal*
> January 25, 1860

Crawford responded to Axy's questions of his sincerity by whimsically addressing her as "My Misanthropic Sister":

I duly rec'd yours and was made "misanthropic" too—was turned to an immense "icicle"—then thawed slightly—just enough to get moist and then rolled in snow until I fancied myself an elongated snowball of large dimensions, so large that it was impossible for me to enter any known door and I became too much paralyzed to even crawl to the sunny side of the house—and all by catching the infection contained in your blue freezing icy letter, you gave me the headache. And I began in earnest to hate (through sympathy) all the ones who passed my window. Now, don't you see the power of your pen or your own power through the pen? I shall never never provoke a quarrel with you by letter. Why who could estimate the results if the letter being only as you say "unamicable" produces such effects.

Ah! My Sister how cruel it was in you to lead me on in this way, like a lamb to the slaughter, or hang me on the gallows I erected for another.

Time, they say is a great consoler of the afflicted. If it bring no balm to me, I shall never never write another line of poetry.

I cannot criticize your "Skyrocket" it until I read and study it further, it is now so far above my criticism that I shall not attempt it. If I could only be up there with you to assist in driving your steed. Or even harness him for you. And hand you the whip, when you start, I would be your courier when you were worn and weary—your lieutenant or counselor. Then, too, having once held a prominent position in the county militia, I might assist in marching and countermarching the clouds if they happened to fall into confusion. I repeat I shall forbear criticism until some other time.

But Oh! My dear Sister—true to your tantalizing spirit you make these # - # x x x x x to show me that you had some fancies too good for me! I would willingly give all the rest for these

<u>omitted</u> verses. I shall die a thousand deaths if I don't get them.

While in some things I like you exceedingly, you do mix in some of the very worst elements—but if you'll send the missing verses I'll——I was going to make another promise but concluded to let you fill up the blank to suit yourself ! !!

Oh! What shadows me, and what shadows we are pursuing? May Angels sing to your spirit until all trouble shall be dissolved in peace and joy.

As ever, J. H. Crawford.

Friday morning postscript

In reading the Sky dream I find a little error in a verse or two.

> And when their tears cannot allay
> Her thirst, her anguish "<u>still</u>"
> But like a feverish child she calls
> For "water" water "<u>still</u>"

You certainly did not intend to make <u>still</u> rhyme with <u>still</u>.

The following may be all correct, still I dislike to see words so nearly alike as <u>rest</u> and <u>unrest</u> used in rhymes when they can as well be avoided.

> This is my sleep and these my dreams
> And this my nightly rest,
> Compared with these all dreams of Earth
> Are sorrow and unrest.

Since you commenced this sky dream I have not had one <u>hour's</u> inspiration and I fear no glory will ever shine through to me again.

...But I am tiring your patience. You know I can never stop when quarreling with you.

J.H.C.

The wintry weather did not subside during February, and Chicago's winds were bitterly cold. Axy again resided with the Richmonds while lecturing there and in neighboring towns. Her January travels had noticeably affected her health; she was suffering from sick headaches and almost daily there was a throbbing and flickering of bright light behind her left eye. More mail caught up with her. One letter was from Madison, requesting her to lecture in Wisconsin's capital.

Morris and I had written to her in late January:

Oakfield, Wisconsin 28th January 1860

Celia and I received your letter of the 13th December on the 19th of January. I suppose it was the size of the letter that retarded its movements as "large ladies move slow." I am much indebted to you for such an excellent letter and for your kind solicitude about my bodily welfare, and here let me urge you to not forget yourself in your anxiety for the happiness of others. I take it for granted that you enjoy good health else you could not endure the fatigue of so much travel. For myself, I think work is necessary for me as food and I enjoy it much better. In fact there is a stimulus in work that invigorates my entire system.

I have just finished the job that I have been engaged on, and will soon commence on our own house, hoping this time to finish it.

I am getting along very well breaking my horse, will have him in a short time so that we can both ride after him. I used him last Sunday to draw ice for washing. He is a fine looking animal and very gentle. I hope some day to have the pleasure of taking you out riding. Celia is going to drive him.

I can let out money for you any time you wish, and get real estate security, although our legislature is discussing the subject of abolishing all laws for the collection of debts. Abstractedly I am in favor of the movement but I think the present state of society in Wisconsin would not admit of it. I hope you will not consider yourself under any obligation to me for any trifling act I can do for you. Such things between friends "grate harshly on mine ear."

I wish you could come and see us when you are next in Milwaukee; I have never yet had half a visit with you.

We are having very pleasant weather. Celia is getting breakfast ready so I must close. I send you that bill in this letter. I hope we shall hear from you as soon as possible.

29 January 1860 Oakfield

I am alone today so you see I can do just as I please but as the wind whistles around the house and the dust flies in every direction I think I shall be forced to stay indoors and spend my time in sewing or writing. I am having a very easy time this winter, have no more work to do than I like.

I will now talk about your visit with us in March! Axy, you know how we are situated and you see at a glance that we cannot visit you near as well as you can us, and if we were to go to Milwaukee you have no place to receive us for a couple of days, while we, you know have ample house-room (if it's not finished) and a new horse and wagon to take you out riding. And then you know you make money fast and can afford to come; and it's not likely you will be near us again for years. So I think you must decide to come up here on Monday and stay till Saturday and rest during the week.

Before you come I would like to know it in season. Send your word and get me a few articles out of the store as they trade cheaper there than here.

I expect ere long to hear that you have eloped with some of these distinguished characters that you so often meet with, but if you do not I will give in that you are a "strong minded woman."

Well, how do you like western people now? I hope better than when here before. Write as often as convenient.

C. S. Steen

Orvilla wrote of Sarah's continued illness; Mr. Josselyn added, "I see by your letter you are not exactly <u>captivated</u> with <u>western life</u>. I did not much expect you would be. There is a sort of <u>bruskness</u> (or if I might be allowed the expression) a sort of <u>Buccaneerism</u> in the Western peoples manners that does not take with one accustomed to the manners of the Eastern cities. So I shall not expect you to bring a Western Husband home with you."

With a stable base in the Richmond's Chicago household, Axy's outlook improved, but it may also have been that her good humor returned with the promise of spring. She placed a notice in *The Banner of Light* to facilitate engagements on her way back east in April and May. Letters demanding her presence began to arrive from Michigan, Indiana, Ohio, Massachusetts, and Oswego, New York.

She had been asked to visit Iowa City, but she responded with the query, "Will it pay?" They only expected an audience of around two hundred, so she decided to pass. But she took pity on James Thompson in Davenport and made a quick trip there by train on February 14.

Sarah Worthen in Springfield missed her terribly. "My heart was sick with <u>loneliness</u> for a week, after you left. When I came home from the depot and entered the parlor, where I had seen you so often, I could not refrain from tears…I gazed on your picture—no gentle tones greeted my ear to cheer me in my sadness—yet as my eyes rested on those lifelike features I could not but hope that your <u>spirit</u> might still be lingering near me—'tho I felt that <u>you</u> were <u>gone</u>.'"

Sister Sarah, still malingering and convinced of her impending death, was in Plymouth Notch and commented, "I have always said I would not burden Mother with my last sickness. She has all her life had much more than her share and I hardly think it is well for me to be with Mother as I am very low spirited and cannot overcome it… Mother is going to write the news and I will cease this murmuring letter by saying again do not come home any sooner on account of Sarah."

Meanwhile, Axy's correspondence with John Crawford had turned playful again. He had a way of teasing her out of despondency and since his arrival in Milwaukee the week before he had written to her twice. She had been presented with a bright scarlet bonnet by a well-meaning but misguided milliner in Terre Haute; the outlandish red concoction was trimmed with bunches of yellow grass and black lace over a maize-colored silk cape. She confessed to Crawford, she could not imagine an occasion where she would wear such a ridiculous hat, nor could she fathom why the milliner was inclined to fabricate such a tasteless production for *her* because she always endeavored to refrain from drawing attention to herself. Crawford replied, tongue firmly in cheek:

Milwaukee, February 3, 1860

My Worthy Sister,

I ought not to trouble you again so soon, but having forgotten to compliment or congratulate you in my last for your progress in the realm of taste, in getting a new red bonnet, I am beginning to think there is some hope for woman. If you could reform in some other respects, such as wearing innumerable flashy ribbons on your wrists—flapping and dangling in the air like tattered sails after a gale of wind, and have your dresses made to fit your form instead of being thrown at you and barely caught and held—like sheets on a swaying currant bush. I almost despair of ever reforming you. If I could make your taste over I should have some hope of you.

There, if you are not angry now, I have failed of my purpose.

I suppose you know that the Oswego Speakers are all engaged up to Sept. much to the chagrin of many of your warmest friends. Were it not that we are going to move back there in May, I should hope you would refuse to go there at all, because you are not on the bills for some of the summer months.

If you should consider my letters worthy of a reply, it would find me here for a few days.

Very truly &c,

J. H. Crawford

Two weeks later Axy heard from Sarah Crawford, who reported on her brother's three-week visit to Milwaukee, "but he is off again today, Monday, February 20. I presume you will see him in Chicago. I am quite sure he will call on you if he can find the time to spare from his business."

There had been many adjustments in the Crawford family: "Miss Julie is now Mrs. Barclay. She was married last Tuesday noon and left on the 1:40 train for Virginia via Pittsburgh, Philadelphia and Washington."

Axy was scheduled to visit Milwaukee in March, and Sarah wrote:

> Mrs. Crawford bids me say to you that she could not afford to go to Chicago to hear you, but that she wishes you to come directly here with your trunks. If you will let us know what day you will be here the ponies will again meet you at the depot. So now I will join my entreaties to her. I shall be delighted with another visit from you and should feel very much hurt to have you go any where else to make your home. We will make it just as pleasant for you as we possibly can and I shall consider it a special favor to me to have you here. Your visit here was to me like an oasis to the traveler in the desert.

In addition to the romances of the eldest daughters, Sarah Crawford echoed John's announcement that the entire family was moving to Oswego in the spring. Sarah admitted that she was not sorry to leave Milwaukee and didn't think Elvira would regret it very much. Julie would be left to represent the family there and *appearances* seemed to indicate some prospect of Lizzie making Milwaukee her place of abode, as well.

Lizzie Crawford added a personal note of her own:

> My Dearest "Axy,"
>
> I write particularly to tell you tell you that you <u>must</u> come here to this house, when you come to Milwaukee next

week—I didn't know that there was any doubt on the subject, until a little while ago Mother said "I wonder if Miss Sprague won't come and stay with us, when she comes"—Well, I wish to put all doubt to flight, & so, here I am, to ask you to come—& you shall have a room that looks out on the lake—& you can talk as much as you like to the "waves"—and who knows what may come of it?

Now that I am done about your coming to our house—I will proceed to other subjects. You know I wrote you a letter at St. Louis—perhaps it was just as well you did not get it—it wasn't worth much—It failed to accomplish the only purpose for which it was written—i.e. bring a reply from you. Now you must write & let us know what day you are coming.

I expect you have seen father; he was to have been in Chicago three or four days—He made a long visit here on, Long for him—he is such a "bird of passage."

Jule is married & gone. We had a very quiet wedding. But I have saved some of their cake for you, for withal its quietness it had cake. When you come, maybe it will seem more like home, for Jenny is here now. It is more like home to me with her, than with Jule.

It is dreadfully dull & lonely without father, he was funnier and happier than I have known him in years, during his last visit. We get up in the morning & go through the same performance, eat, sew, eat—& go to bed, without anything to disturb this monotony of "single blessedness"—for we are not all women? …

My dear Miss Sprague, will this letter produce the effect intended bring you to stay with us during your sojourn in this city? If so, I am your most truly & affectionately,

Lizzie Crawford

⪧ 16 ⪦

Birds of Passage

(February–May 1860)

…Those sounds that flow
In murmurs of delight and woe
  Come not from wings of birds…

"Birds of Passage"
Henry W. Longfellow

THIS WAS HOW IT HAPPENED, as Axy later confided to me. She had completed her third lecture in Chicago on Sunday evening February 19, 1860, with the usual inspired hymn. Then, after a period of polite silence, the moderator asked if anyone had further inquiries of Miss Sprague.

Statements were made by the usual disbelievers, and familiar challenges were launched on the topic of "Free Lust." Another man firmly declared that he'd heard from "good authority" that Miss Sprague was known to commit her lectures to memory, as well as her songs. Could she prove to them that what she'd preached tonight from the podium originated in the world of Spirits?

A subdued mumble passed throughout the hall. Axy began to speak of the wealth of thought and hidden powers provided her from the deep unknown, but her response was interrupted by a tall gentleman in the back row who silenced her all present with his strong and powerful voice:

"Now, it is reasonable for you to suppose that Miss Sprague is artful. And you may suppose that because she knows Men love the marvelous, she takes this novel way to hold sway over thousands.

But I have attended Miss Sprague's improvised lectures in many cities and towns, and the words I heard her recite tonight were fresh and new, unheard until this evening. Miss Sprague has always borne the stamp of virtue and of truth. Like you, I know not why she possesses this mysterious link between the dwellers of the earth and sky, but my own doubts on that point have long been put to rest. I am certain in my belief that no power has framed this medium's message until this present hour, and that her message was doubtless inspired by Spirit-influence."

The gentleman bowed slightly toward my sister, "Miss Sprague, you are truly blessed."

Axy had to breathe slowly to calm her galloping heart. She made a show of coughing slightly and then cleared her throat so her voice would not waver in her grateful response to the statement by John Crawford.

"I *am*...blessed," she stuttered, her face glowing warm with his praise, "Blessed by Spirit, and blessed that even one of you recognizes this power and deems me truthful. I have no motive to deceive or stoop to sin merely to win homage. Some of you may wish to condemn me because you believe a public hall is not the place for a woman to speak. Others may cast reproach unkindly on my name because you know not *what* to think. And yet others, still doubting, may nevertheless look upon me and my art with benevolence. I hope my words of revelation will reach your hearts."

Her emotions were still befuddled when Crawford arrived by carriage at the Richmond residence on Monday morning with an invitation for Axy to accompany him to a toy and fancy store at No. 40 Clark Street. The store was operated by the son of Captain and Mary Richardson of Oswego, and was the only one of its kind in the city. Mrs. Richardson had written that her son would be expecting Axy to say hello.

The visitors made a few small purchases. Then Crawford coaxed Axy to accept his invitation for a midday meal at the Sherman House, the finest hotel in Chicago.

"How truly remarkable, that we have not yet quarreled," Crawford said as they were escorted to a private dining room.

"I had not thought particularly about it," Axy replied, playfully aloof, taking a seat in the velvet upholstered chair held for her.

"You are a strange woman, Miss Sprague. A perfect enigma. Naughty as ever, despite the miles you have traveled and the millions you leave hanging on your every word."

She demurely placed the starched linen napkin in her lap. "I've found the world is much the same as society, although on a larger scale and with a different name."

Crawford perused the menu. "My Dear, I cannot help but love you for your very spirit of 'don't caritiveness' if for nothing else."

The waiter took Crawford's order—scalloped oysters for each.

"You realize that I cannot help but love you, no matter how peevish or disagreeable," he added with a smile.

"Your testimonial at the close of my lecture last evening was gratifying, but I believe any conversation about love, spiritual or otherwise, is inappropriate for this public setting."

"Shall we then seek a clandestine location?"

"Once again, you insist on perplexing me," Axy sputtered.

"Ah, the combat returns in earnest," Crawford sighed. "I knew your harmonious attitude was too sublime to endure."

They launched into their cat and mouse routine, vis-à-vis his feelings for her and her misgivings regarding their "spiritual" nature. The jousting had a sharp edge, but was couched in affectionate wordplay. He seldom acknowledged Axy's more serious arguments with anything more than an expression of amused indulgence.

At the close of the meal, Crawford insisted that despite the snowy afternoon, she may never again have the opportunity to view the city from the heights of the new courthouse tower with one who desires to exist with her spirit in the sky.

How could she posit an argument against that line of reasoning? Axy informed him, with what serious demeanor she could muster, that this ascent to the cupola may be his only opportunity to be *skyward bound* in her company.

The Chicago courthouse dominated the city and the cupola was the only truly tall object in sight. Since arriving in Chicago she had experienced the hourly clang of the massive bell, widely depended upon by residents to guide them through their day.

Challenged by his mockery and eager to show her tenacity, Axy began the slow and tedious climb. The circular balcony ringing the amazing cupola was designed exclusively for sightseeing and even on a wintry day in late February she was impressed with the panoramic view. Crawford said the hills of Michigan, thirty miles to the east, would be visible across the icy lake were it not for blowing snow. Below them, broad stretches of trees on Wabash and Michigan Avenues evidenced the city's reputation as "The Garden City." Chicago University, founded by Stephen A. Douglas (who owned much of the land in the vicinity) was in evidence, too, and to the north there seemed to be nothing but woodland in a vast unbroken stretch.

Breathless from the long flight of stairs and unsettled by scrambled emotions, my sister remained uncharacteristically silent. Wind spun around the cupola, tugged at the hood of her cape and her voluminous hoopskirt and petticoats. Within moments they were enveloped in a vortex of blinding snow.

"I long to know for certain that one day we will look down upon the earth in just such a way," John remarked, drawing her close in his familiar, protective fashion to shelter her from the wind, "There we will have no more quarrels, no more pain or unreasonable longings. It may be far, very distant. But the anticipation of loving you there, free and openly, is such a source of pleasure. Together in the clouds— that is a truly beautiful thought."

Axy allowed herself to lean comfortably into his shoulder and shielded her eyes with gloved hands against the snow and all she knew was almost certainly honorable and proper. So far above the city, concealed by a flurry of white, she lacked the earnestness to carry on the battle just now.

"Apply your remarks to yourself," he had said in a letter, *"May it not be that your shadow looms up before you? Does your conscience speak?"*

She wondered if she felt compelled to continuously instigate this quarrel because she was constantly admonishing herself to *keep her own* fondness for John on a Spiritual, not physical, level. If fear of disgrace did not conspire the very core of her discontent, how would her Guardians interpret her weakness for this man? Way back in Woodstock, when John and Sophronia Spear initially spoke to her through Spirits in the Randalls' kitchen, it was resolved, *When she sees that the path of wrong is open before her she will not walk therein, though worldly honor, riches and prosperity are presented to her view… she has a strength of character, a balance of intellect.*

Did loving Mr. Crawford represent "the path of wrong?" What had become of her "strength of character," and the "virtue" he had publicly spoken of last night?

As if he were reading her thoughts, a coincidence that happened so frequently between them, Crawford bent to kiss her forehead, then softly brushed her lips with his. Caught in the cloud of swirling snow, she surprised them both by returning his kiss passionately, lifting her face to meet his far above the city of Chicago; a joyous kiss, encircled in his arms of sweet repose.

"I deem that a holy kiss," Crawford murmured, "completely approved by your Guardians and mine."

"Here is their seal of approval," she said, placing her warm lips softly upon his once again. And yet again.

She chanced a risk and trusted that her Guardians were imparting their consent.

If there had been a gracious way to avoid the Crawford family, Axy would have gladly taken a room in a modest boarding house in

Milwaukee. But on the first of March, the Crawford carriage and matched pair of black ponies again met her train from Chicago and the fulsome warmth of their family enveloped Axy despite her reticence. She was regaled with descriptions of Julie's wedding and served crumbs of desiccated wedding cake. When she parted for bed, Axy hoped her remoteness would be blamed on exhaustion.

She certainly was not feeling well. From her room the next morning she studied the broad expanse of black waves as they cut across Lake Michigan to collide, again and again, crashing upon the breakers and the jagged shelf of ice. The thunder of their incessant surging was endured in her very core as she called herself duplicitous, disloyal, hypocritical, false hearted, deceitful, untrustworthy, worthless, contemptible, and unfit to sleep beneath this family's roof.

Elvira kept the house on the corner of Martin and Lake Street as quiet as possible while their houseguest rested. Axy's reserve was obvious to Jenny and Lizzie; their typically vivacious guest no longer seemed capable of the enthusiasm the girls cherished in her companionship.

Molly, fourteen, was home from school with a cough. George, now eight, was home due to a cut lip incurred during a sledding accident. He had completed his poem:

> My dear Miss Sprague
> You make a terrible plague
> To want me to write you a poem.
> You know I am but eight
> And that I must skate
> As long as there is ice for me to go on.

Pilot, their spaniel, and the youngest Crawford children followed Axy everywhere. George begged her to play "Muggins" with him. Molly had endless questions about her travels. Axy took pleasure in the presence of the children, as it gave her an opportunity to avoid interacting with Elvira, although Mrs. Crawford was consumed with household affairs and organizing the family's impending move back east. John was not expected back in Milwaukee until mid-April, yet the family would depart for Oswego soon thereafter, and this plus the usual social obligations took up much of Elvira's time.

Lizzie begged to accompany Axy by train to Madison for lectures on March 5th and 6th and my sister relented. It was pleasant to have a travel companion while travelling through the desolate landscape. The train from Milwaukee went only as far as Sun Prairie, where they disembarked and caught a stagecoach to the capital.

There they were welcomed in Madison by Thomas P. Bovee and his wife, Susan, who had recently relocated from New York.

Only a few years before, Horace Greeley had visited the city and declared in his *New York Tribune* that Madison "has the most magnificent site of any inland town I ever saw...The University crowns a beautiful eminence a mile west of the Capitol with a main street connecting them *a la* Pennsylvania Avenue. There are more comfortable private mansions now in progress in Madison than in any other place I have visited."

The women shared a room at The Capital House, on Main Street. Axy's lectures took place at the First Baptist Church, across the Capital Square. The new Historical Society had its library in the church basement and the director, Lyman Copeland Draper, was curious about Spiritualism, as were many leading citizens of Madison who had no doubt been impressed by Nathaniel Tallmadge, Wisconsin's territorial governor, still an exceedingly influential Spiritualist advocate on the national stage.

The day after her first lecture, the women were given a tour of the young city which had seen much construction. The new City Hall had opened in 1858. The area known as "Mansion Hill" contained luxurious new residences. The state capitol had just been enlarged and Forest Hill Cemetery provided a lovely prospect, overlooking the city and surrounding four lakes. On the southeast side of the cemetery they were shown an effigy mound in the shape of a goose. Apparently there were several such locations in Madison, sculpted from earth in the shape of spirit animals such as bear, birds, deer and others, perhaps by Indians, nearly 3,000 years ago. They were told a very large mound in the shape of a panther had been demolished to make room for construction of Central Hall, a large building upon a hill known as "the park" on the University of Wisconsin campus. Their carriage took them down Park Street, where they could see the school, and the women would have enjoyed a stroll on the board sidewalk if it had not been sunken in mud.

Streets in the city were rutted; pigs seemed to roam everywhere. Two miles out of town stood the now-vacant Lakeside Water Cure on Lake Monona. The cream-colored estate had provided steam heat and an elevation with a beautiful view of the city, but a squabble had resulted in trenches dug across the road by an adjacent landowner who resented the traffic and the resort had failed in the 1857 panic. During the drive back to their hotel, Axy entertained her companions with the frigid trials she'd endured at the Graefenburg cure in New York. Later that afternoon, a circle was held at the home of Joseph Osgood Barrett, a spiritualist lecturer, author, and forestry expert, prior to her final lecture that evening.

Lizzie enjoyed every minute, as the visit to Madison with Axy gave her an intimate illustration of the life of a traveling medium. It was as informative as it was fatiguing.

Requests had come in for visits to Palmyra, Whitewater, and other neighboring small towns. Despite her weariness, Axy accepted these engagements, as they removed her from Milwaukee and the Crawfords' overheated parlor. She had not heard from Mr. C. since their Chicago rendezvous.

Then, to her great embarrassment, Axy's Milwaukee lectures were imperiled by a stand taken by Caleb Wall, a native of Baltimore and currently Milwaukee's city auctioneer. He owned a two-story wooden building on Wisconsin Avenue that held a meeting hall above. Spiritualists wished to hire this hall for Axy's Sunday lectures. But Wall refused, on grounds that caused an uproar so loud that it reached the *New York Tribune* and Boston's *Independent*; both newspapers commented on rights of free speech that were infringed upon, but Wall said he declined to rent his hall for the performances of a trance medium upon the Sabbath because he regarded *such an* exhibition as tending to irreligion and immorality. He protested that he had not violated the rights of conscience and free speech, for those were his honest convictions; he was responsible for his own public acts and, "believing as I do, that these exhibitions are a desecration of the Sabbath, I cannot do otherwise than I have."

The newspapers determined that Wall's *actual* objection was either because (1) Axy was a woman; or (2) because she professed to be a medium and was not; or (3) because she actually *was* a trance-speaker and spirits, not Miss Sprague, were responsible for what she said.

A satisfactory venue was found, and *The Herald of Progress* reported in April that Miss Sprague "lectured in Milwaukee, Wisconsin, during the month of March to large and constantly increasing audiences." Some may have attended out of curiosity arising from the Wall incident, but Axy hoped everyone went home enlightened.

This entire episode proved enormously distressing. Had it transpired anywhere besides Milwaukee, where she was known to be residing with the family of John H. Crawford, the weight of Wall's charge of "immorality" may not have wielded such a keen blow. Now she was convinced that she had again cast a negative light on their family.

"Put it out of your mind, Miss Sprague," Elvira assured her. "We are only sorry that you were treated so rudely by those poor souls who do not share our convictions."

"I have dealt much with both critics and flatterers," Axy assured them, her hoarse voice nearly breaking, "and I've discovered that it gives the soul a broader view of life to be thrown out to mingle with crowds. I know I have become stronger by meeting the world's denigration, but I shall be sick at heart if this scorn reflects on you!"

A spring retreat on our farm near Oakfield could not have arrived at a better time. But our merry plans dimmed when Morris and I noted Axy's altered appearance. She seemed unusually weary and her face was pale and gaunt. She was scheduled to speak in Fond du Lac on following Sunday, but she agreed that afterward her time would be given over entirely for convalescence.

I had so looked forward to driving our new horse and showing

Axy the beauties of Darling's Gap, but she could not withstand the jostling of the wagon. After we had traveled less than half a mile, I turned the horse around and headed home.

For two days afterward, Axy lay in bed tormented by a wrenching pain behind her left eye, complaining of dizziness and occasional double vision. I offered to read to her, but she said she wanted quiet.

The reality (she confided to me later) was this: By herself, in the darkened bed chamber of our silent farmhouse, she could not escape the truth of intense emotions she had been attempting to suppress. When she accompanied John Crawford in Chicago *she had enjoyed being mistaken by onlookers as his wife.* She had taken his arm proudly as they walked down the street. To behave in such a manner with anyone's husband, she said, was sinful, dishonest behavior.

"I rejoiced in his affections and returned his kisses! If not for the meager amount of time we were able to devote to our rendezvous, Celia, I may well have succumbed to a physical union!"

I may have gasped at that, for she continued, "I am ashamed to admit, Dear Sister, that even now I am thrilled to imagine it."

Naturally I was shocked, but the room was lit only by a single candle so Axy could not distinguish my reaction.

"I have assured countless women that I took the offered hand of friendship from no man if it was purchased at the expense of his wife's happiness," she confessed. "I even reiterated that pledge to Mrs. Crawford, after we met in Ogdensburgh."

Self-recrimination engulfed Axy during her revelation. What if her Guardians abandoned her, or were, even now, with this headache, reprimanding her by bidding her dreaded illness to return?

I held her in my arms and cradled her fragile body as I had when we were girls. In the bleak silence I heard the howls of wolves, and hoped Morris had sheltered our new calf inside the barn. But of course he had; Axy's anxiety was proving contagious.

"My first loyalty must be to my Guardians," she wept. "I despise my weakness of character. I despise myself!"

She pried herself from my arms and pounded her pillow until feathers began to fly.

As soon as her strength and vision allowed, she drafted a letter to John Crawford. She copied it over in a steadier hand and gave it to Morris to hand to Mr. Orvis when he came with the mail. I found the initial draft crumpled beneath her bed after she had gone.

Their mutual love, friendship, and lighthearted correspondence, their creative partnership, their intellectual discussions and compositions of poetry and music—all of which had granted both such deep rewards throughout their companionship and even their good-natured quarrels—she was ready to disavow, due to her guilty conscience. All association must vanish, along with any and all expressions of affection or remorse.

> *Sir,*
>
> *I told you I was not going to write you any more ~~letters~~ and therefore I have not, until now. I write this note simply to tell you that I was and am in earnest. ~~I have determined~~ My unjust feelings for you have ultimately caused me to become untrue to myself and to the trust of my Guardians.*
>
> *You will say our mutual behavior was of the Spirit, yet I, who have had cause to doubt the sincerity of <u>your</u> actions, now doubt <u>my own</u>. I, who have always regarded the feelings and rights of a wife as <u>sacred</u>. As one who never wished to set foot upon their territory, or cast one shadow over their path.*
>
> *We cannot be friends, for you are always giving me occasion to quarrel with you (I know you deny this, nevertheless it is true) and I never saw a person that I would take the trouble to be a downright enemy to, therefore I prefer the middle ground, careless acquaintanceship, or better yet, total indifference, and the word stranger would suit me better than all.*
>
> *So I relieve you from all obligations of friendship and all claims to remembrance and what I will be hereafter, and sign myself in the character we are both best suited to maintain ~~toward each other~~.*
>
> *A Stranger*

It could be that she felt this letter of dismissal would reclaim her Guardians' approval, if it had ever been abandoned. Perhaps she hoped this would rouse them to heal her again, if they had chosen to punish her. But after the letter was mailed, she remained in her room, suffering from what I perceived was profound misery.

If her health had not been so poor, we would have had a wild time the following day.

From the beginning, I had withheld from Axy the fact that an Indian trail was located near our farm. It led from Milwaukee to Lake Superior. Sometimes the Indians stopped by to ask for food, which frightened me terribly at first! But Morris assured me the Winnebago were a peaceful tribe, grateful for a cup of water, or slice of homemade bread with butter and a little jam, if I had it. They would eat near the house while seated on the ground.

Eventually we traded eggs and butter with the Winnebago for maple sugar that we used throughout the year. But no Indians had shown up during Axy's initial visit or this one, for which I was grateful. She didn't need to be unduly frightened.

That summer Morris had taken on an itinerant carpenter, Robinson Kreutznauer, to assist with farm duties and the completion of a new house not far away. The day after Axy sent off her letter to Mr. Crawford, we heard a commotion at our back door and Mr. Kreutznauer calling out, "Help! Help! The Indians are coming!"

Of course he was not from the area, so *any* Indians may well have frightened the young German, even the good-natured Winnebago. The poor man was so terrified he could barely speak. The Indians were coming, he said, and a fellow was riding through the countryside at full speed, warning everyone to flee for their lives!

I could hear Axy moving around upstairs, so I went to tend to her even though I was desperate to hear the terrible tales related by Kreutz, as we called him. While quieting Axy (and not mentioning the alarm),

I glanced out the window of her bedroom to see families crowding the road that led into Oakfield. Teams of oxen pulled wagons piled with stoves, beds, and other possessions, women and children. One elderly grandmother, whom I knew had been bedridden for a year, had been hastily dumped into a wheelbarrow and was being trundled into town, clutching a teakettle. I was sorely tempted to laugh.

Morris went out to the road and spoke with some who were fleeing. They said Indians were burning, destroying, and laying waste the whole country! Manitowoc was in ashes! Fifteen hundred Indians were at Horicon! Sheboygan was plundered and burning! The red devils were thundering on to Chilton and Greenbush! Soon, *very soon*, the Indians would be *here!* One man claimed at least two thousand witnesses reported to have seen bloodthirsty savages in all the surrounding towns, and others had beheld grain stacks, barns, houses, and mills in ashes. Men were purchasing firearms. Every hotel was crowded to the roof!

Morris came back to the house and reported the above to me.

"I cannot say the alarm is not valid," he stated, holding me close, "but I have my sincere doubts about the source of this chaos. If you would feel more secure by taking your sister into town, I'll hitch the horse and wagon. Kreutz and I will remain on the farm and protect our property."

I believe the hired man would rather have high-tailed it into Oakfield rather than grab a pitchfork and stand at the ready, awaiting rioting Indians who never arrived. I refused to leave Morris, remaining at home with them and my sister, and attempted to knit. It helped to stay busy.

Morris and I were awake the entire night. The scarf became a sorry mess with dropped stitches and knots but I knit and purled and paced the floor and stared out the window anticipating the bloody onslaught. All I saw was Kreutz out by the road with his pitchfork, alert and watching for the ambush.

The Indian Scare Spectacle was blazoned far and wide in the Wisconsin press. By the time it was old news, I shared it with Axy and we had a good laugh. By that time, the sun's welcome gift reminded us spring was close at hand. On the final day of her Oakfield visit, my sister and I shielded our faces with straw bonnets and strolled in the kitchen garden behind the house, where we found asparagus beginning to sprout, rhubarb plants unfurling. We agreed this was a good sign.

I had begun a flower bed but I wanted to start a rose garden to remind me of Mother's dooryard in Vermont. Morris placed two chairs beneath the leafless apple tree where we could drink in the sun's healing, refreshing rays, and we loosened our shawls to absorb as much as we could.

It was agreed that the situation back in Plymouth Notch was troubling. Sarah, who had gone home to the Notch in mid-February to convalesce with Mother, yet remained there. Sarah had written to Axy, "I do not want you to make any different arrangements on my account as you say, after I had seen you a short time I should be satisfied, and it would be all that you could do."

We did not wonder that Sarah was much discouraged, for she had lost her baby. But everything seemed to ail her and she was a malingerer. Nursing her would unquestionably be taking a toll on our poor Mother.

Axy commented, "I may have to return home sooner than I had planned."

In Milwaukee for her final week of lectures, Axy felt stronger in body but I knew her mind must be agitated. She counted down the days until she would leave for parts East.

In the meantime, she lectured in Milwaukee on Sunday evening, March 25. On Monday before dinner, after leading a circle for a neighboring family, she sat in the parlor to sew with the Crawford women. She was embroidering a paisley shawl for Julie, a belated wedding gift. Pilot sprawled over her feet, comfortably warming them. She loved that old dog, probably because he was referred to by the family as being devoted to John.

Lizzie had received a letter from Julie in Virginia, who told of her new husband's relatives and his gracious ancestral home. Julie hoped to return to Milwaukee with her new husband in April.

Lizzie sighed as she put down her sister's letter, "I fear I am resigned to a lifetime of *single blessedness*."

"You know I am a warm advocate of matrimony, Lizzie Dear," Sarah Crawford admitted to her niece. "I believe with all its disagreeables, its crotchets and all its trials, that marriage has more happiness, more advantages than *single blessedness*. Celibacy will answer a very good purpose when one has plenty of money and is not dependent on friends for their bread and butter."

Axy was startled by Sarah's comment. Was that a callous observation that *she* was dependent on the Crawford's hospitality? She blushed more deeply than before and Elvira quickly spoke up.

"Of course, Miss Sprague, we know you are serving a greater good. You are wedded to your art. Perhaps that's just as well, and yet some noble mind might find great happiness as your husband."

"You must excuse me, Mrs. Crawford, as I know I'm far from perfect."

Axy was recalling her latest self-recriminations.

"In fact, there are times when I am quite dissatisfied with myself! There is so much passion expressed through false love, so much pretense, so much deception, that I am determined to evade it. And even if there were one that I *could* love, he would be as much dissatisfied with me, too. When there's a *perfect* man, and *I am perfect, too*, then I think perhaps I might find happiness. But never until then."

Relieved of the burden of Sarah's remark, Axy continued, "I believe *I'm* the one who must be reconciled to *single blessedness*, Lizzie. I *must* believe in marriage, of course; let others marry—my sympathy is theirs—but no marriage for me, thank you. Anyone I might marry would surely be tormented through all his life!"

She attempted to laugh while saying this, but it sounded more like a deep sigh.

"Well, I hope you will lay by in store sufficient for old age," Sarah prompted. "You know old age will come upon us unless we anticipate it by dying young, and I fear I have already grown too old for that!" She sighed amiably, "I now regret not having married young, but that is only one of the mistakes of my life which cannot be retrieved, so I will not make myself unhappy with vain and useless regrets."

Elvira brought up the subject of the Married Woman's Property Act, which had been adopted in New York only a few days ago. Now married women would no longer be legally required to give all of their property, including any goods they had inherited, to their husbands.

Lizzie, who had been listening patiently, interrupted. "Axy, forgive me if I seem too forward, but have you *never* loved?"

"Lizzie, *Dear*," Elvira warned her daughter, "you are behaving like a *perfect* busybody!"

Axy put down her needlework.

"If I were not in a home where love is in such evidence I might say I did not believe in love."

Lizzie was astonished.

"Perhaps it would be more accurate to say that if I did believe in true love, that it must exist only in the kind of love angels have for heaven," she continued. "Yet I honor those women who fulfill that most important mission of wife and mother. For myself, I will be content to fulfill my own mission, to help undo others' wrongs and mistakes, or to rescue someone who has sunk into the deepest sin."

There was an uncomfortable silence. Axy took up her needle again. "Forgive me, I may seem outspoken. Yet I speak these words less strongly than I might somewhere else where the semblance of such love is not expressed. Then I could pour out my soul with a strain that I now cannot, for it would be too painful for you to hear. Here and now I say, God bless all lovers! But I wish fate not to portion one to me."

She forced a tremulous smile, hoping the other women in the parlor were more convinced than she.

Before Axy left Milwaukee, news arrived of a tragedy that had befallen one of Northern Transportation's propeller ships. On March 24, *The Lady of the Lake*, with Captain Sisson, bound for Dunkirk from Ogdensburgh, experienced a boiler explosion and sank in a very short time. Nineteen men had been on board, one was killed, several were badly injured, and the cook could not be found. According to reports, the craft carried 1,070 barrels of flour, 100 barrels of pork, 83 tierces of hams and shoulders, 200 sacks of wheat, 60 barrels of high wines, and several barrels of eggs. Some of the freight was salvaged, most of it was insured.

"Mr. Crawford takes the loss of his ships very personally," Elvira commented. "He will be mourning this devastation for months."

The Cleveland Plain Dealer carried a lengthy notice of Axy's lecture in late April. Spiritualist newspapers rejoiced that the secular publishers were finally opening their columns to progressive and spiritual discourse.

During the entire month of April there had been a flurry of letter writing between Axy and Vermont. She was scheduled to lecture in Toledo, Ohio, in May, and she was looking forward to a lengthy stopover at the Starbuck home in Troy before heading back to the Notch.

As feared, Mother had fallen ill, caring for Sarah.

"I am a great sufferer," Sarah wrote, "It is a great job to take care of me. I do not feel as though I had any right to have you come home on my account, but I desire it so much I cannot say, do not come. It is said April is a short month but it will seem so long to me. Mr. Randall has been confined to his bed at home, I have not seen him since he was sick. We have not heard anything particular about him and I sometimes fear he is not out of danger. Mother I guess will write the news. I am to weary to write. I do not allow myself to write only to Mr. R. May the blessed Angels give me strength until you come is my most fervent prayer. Sarah S. Randall."

Axy cancelled her second lecture in Cleveland and the long-awaited reunion with the Starbucks in Troy. She even cancelled her August appearance in Connecticut and sent her railroad ticket to Toledo for a refund. A note was mailed to Oswego to have the trunk she had stored there shipped back to Plymouth Notch. Warren Chase, lecturing in Oswego, mailed her the key.

With ominous preparations for a war gripping the country, less attraction toward spiritual matters was evident everywhere. Axy found herself speaking so frequently on the subject of "Freedom" that she feared she might be repeating herself and did not want to reinvigorate the old charge that her lectures were memorized. Besides, her audiences were smaller than usual and those who showed up demanded lurid details of "Congenials" and "Affinities."

The United States was still recovering from the Panic, and embroiled in an uneasy transition: A presidential campaign underway. Stephen A. Douglas had been nominated in April for the Democrats. Abraham Lincoln of Illinois was expected be nominated for the Republicans in May. The secession of Southern states from the Union seemed inevitable.

The Banner of Light was informed that all of Axy's Sundays were engaged until the following January, 1861.

When the propeller *Maple Leaf* docked at Port Huron during the last week in April, she boarded the steamship and displayed her free pass. A young medium in that city later sorrowfully recalled the "whistling steamer that bore you away from us."

ᘿ 17 ᘾ

No Unholy Kiss

(June–December 1860)

Have mediums for thyself,
those who shall speak for thee,
those who shall give to earth the lessons
thou hast taught in word and deed.

—Axy's Guardians, 1860

DURING THE SUMMER OF 1860 the inevitability of war preoccupied everyone. We all followed and discussed the looming peril. John Crawford would have educated opinions based on his interactions with the world of business, and Axy wanted to speak with him. When she sorted through her mail at the Notch she searched for his pale blue envelopes, but he seemed to have taken her last letter to heart, having been "relieved of all obligations of friendship."

Instead, a woman in New Jersey wrote that she liked to imagine Axy "tracing the winding paths around and up those dear old mountains." Another mentioned, "You ask what I think about the war. I think as you say, that it is inevitable, although so terrible; and sometimes I wish it was over, but then I shrink from the thought of how many noble souls are doomed to fall on the battlefield."

By mid-July our sister Sarah finally felt strong enough to return to her drug-addled husband, Nathaniel Randall. Mother's health had improved so Malvina could return from Aunt Augusta Moore's where she had been looked after. Brother Nathan had been doing what little he could to help out with the remains of the Sprague family farm, namely our old cow and a few chickens. Axy's beloved horse had been sold.

When she found private time for reflection, old fears resurfaced. Five years earlier Axy had written in her journal, *"I sometimes think, how long shall I remain a Public speaker, or how long retain the gift of speaking as I do now?"* Doubts had besieged her for the past two years. The uncertainty of her health—the ubiquitous sore throat, vision problems, violent headaches, extreme fatigue—were her Guardians displeased with her?

She appealed to them, imploring a message. After a time, automatic writing revealed the following:

> *And now to you who are doubting forever the power of those who are around you, we would speak. Nerve thyself to bear and also to do, for thou hast much to do. Why look back and when so steep the way and thou dost feel the hands that ever help thee on, why dost look back upon the darkened hours and say they shall return? Say the power is almost fled? From thee it shalt not flee. Nay, and when thine hour to pass away shall come thoult feel it strongest then.*
>
> *What, doubting still? And yet we do not blame. It were well to doubt at times, as on to walk and think no lurking foe. There shall be snares, there shall be foes. But when thou doubtest most we shall be near.*
>
> *For thine own acts thou art responsible but not for ours. Go as thy debt is paid. We set thee free and cancel all.*
>
> *Have mediums for thyself, those who shall speak for thee, those who shall give to earth the lessons thou hast taught in word and deed.*
>
> *Go, and linger not for great must be thy way and great thy toil. And let it be thine own free will for unto us thy debt is paid.*
>
> *Thy Guardians*

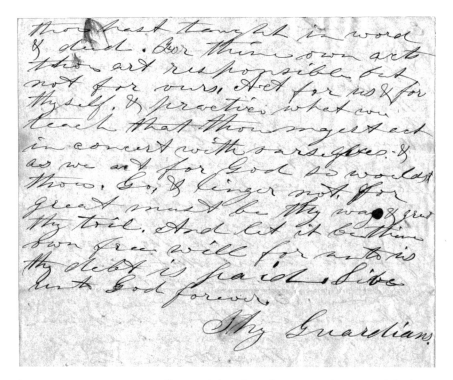

Automatic writing message, freeing Achsa from her required mission: The letter begins, "And now to you who are doubting forever the power of those who are around you, we would speak," and concludes, "For thine own acts thou art responsible but not for ours…for unto us thy debt is paid. Live unto God forever. Thy Guardians."

Her "debt was paid." Her debt was paid! Wondrous news. She no longer owed her Guardians for her recovery from illness, seven years ago. She was liberated at last.

Requests to schedule lectures continued to arrive. Axy declined them all, including Oswego, where they offered to pay her $75 plus board if she would come for five Sundays in December, "two lectures, afternoon and evening as usual."

In a mid-June letter she wrote to us that Adolph Eiswald, now in faraway Texas, had begun a school near the town of LaGrange. He said he had developed some healing influences and was known by his students as the "Wunder Doctor." Morris and I had a good laugh at that.

James H. Blood begged Axy to return to St. Louis and added, "Please do not let any previous circumstances predetermine against us as a whole."

Out of loyalty to Vermont friends, she attended the Quarterly Convention of Vermont Spiritualists, in Burlington, on June 16 and 17, where she heard concerns about political unrest affecting the cause. Someone said a medium in Georgia had been confined to an insane asylum because she tore off her clothes and ran naked through the streets of Macon.

In late July a newspaper item mentioned a fire on another of John Crawford's propellers, *The Prairie State.* It had been fully loaded and bound for Chicago but burned in port at Oswego, *the very dock* whereupon she had embarked upon many enjoyable voyages, and *upon that very ship.* She could envision the rampaging blaze mirrored in the water and Mr. C. illumined by the flames. The Oswego Fire Department battled bravely but the boat had to be scuttled. Holes were bored in the sides of *The Prairie State* and she was left partially sunken, in a greatly damaged condition.

The ruined image seemed a symbol of her relationship with John Crawford: a scuttled ship beneath the waves.

After much meditation, she decided to entrust her Guardians with her affections for him, and his for her. If her Guardians intended for the wave and the sea to meet again, an opportunity *would* arise.

A Spiritualist Convention was to be held in Providence in August, but even Axy's fondest supporters warned, "We do not think the people are worth your killing yourself for them." She should have heeded their warning: A clambake there left Axy with a stomach upset following an attack of seasickness. Another friend opined that her queasiness was provoked by the nauseating presence of Amanda Britt Spence.

From Providence she journeyed to New Jersey, but her outlook was waning. She awoke each morning feeling despondent and retired even more disheartened.

There was a request to speak in Boston for all the Sundays in September, as a splendid new hall had been built on the site of the old Melodeon that could comfortably seat nine hundred with ease. Instead, Axy consented to return to Niagara Falls, with conviction that jovial crowds at that festive location would improve her sinking morale. Another elderly widower there had made a touching proposal of marriage: "I have no evle design in caressing you in the way I do it comes from the Bottom of my heart. I have told you I loved you and so I do better than I do all woman kind, you will Excuse my weekness if you deem it such. I hope the time will come when I can freely clasp you to my Bosom as my own how happy would I be to have you go South with me this winter."

She had barely settled in Niagara when she received a tantalizing request from J. D. Pool, leader of the Oswego Spiritualists, who asked her to accompany them on "an excursion to take place next Tuesday per Hand Bill enclosed, as no Lecturer is so popular in this region as yourself."

The objective of the excursion would be Sackett's Harbor, a small port city at the entrance to the Thousand Islands. The spiritualists could not promise much remuneration, but all her expenses would be paid and her comfort would be assured. "Hundreds have asked repeatedly why don't Miss Sprague come to us again. We have most intensely wished to hear that eloquent voice of thine."

Indeed, they had a splendid outing planned. If he were not away on business, might it be possible to find John Crawford in attendance? Elvira would surely be one of the excursionists.

Could this be a twist of fate arranged by her Guardians now that *her debt was paid?* She hoped Elvira would insist that she stay with them in their new Oswego home; she longed to tell John that her Guardians' obligations had been fulfilled, and she was *free.*

My sister arrived in Oswego harbor on Monday night and stepped off the boat into an enthusiastic crowd of well-wishers. Indeed, Elvira was among those who rushed forth to welcome her with a warm embrace, and Axy caught a brief glimpse of John standing next to Captain Richardson on the edge of the gathering. Mary Richardson revealed that Axy was to be given a room at their home. The issue seemed to have been agreed upon ahead of time.

Thunderstorms rumbled over the lake on Tuesday morning, the appointed day for the excursion. A lavishly decorated reception room—actually the owner's quarters—had been arranged for Axy's personal use on *The Bay State,* with Captain Brown at the helm of the propeller. Despite the inclement weather, she was present at an early hour to welcome prospective voyagers.

Mr. Crawford made a brief appearance with Elvira and daughters Jenny and Lizzie. He inquired about her health and her family, then excused himself, due to pressing business. Elvira later confided that her husband had contributed both ships, and made a generous donation to help cover expenses. She seemed determined to ensure that Axy enjoyed the day.

The skies cleared in mid-morning and at ten-thirty *The Bay State* and *The Akron* set sail. *The Bay State* carried The Mechanic's Sax Horn Band, and the *Akron* featured a fine quadrille orchestra. The waters were smooth all the way to Sackett's Harbor while everyone was musically entertained.

Watertown newspapers estimated the crowd at between two and three thousand. A hickory grove on the edge of the bay had been appropriated, where a carpet of fine grass provided ample seating for everyone. Trees had been hung with banners and suitable mottoes especially prepared for the event.

The Oswego Palladium sent a reporter along, who found the excursion very congenial.

> Upon arriving at Sackett's Harbor at three o'clock, the excursionists were cordially received by a large concourse of people. A procession was immediately formed, preceded by the band, and marched to a grove about a mile south of the village where they proceeded to dispatch sundry edibles in the original pic nic style, for which their morning ride in the cool, invigorating

air had given them a keen relish. This over, addresses were made by Dr. D. S. Kimball of Sackett's harbor, and Miss Sprague, from Niagara Falls.

Axy was buoyed by the occasion. She spoke on the subject of "Freedom" for more than 75 minutes and advised listeners, "instead of tearing down others' standards of freedom, you should go to work and erect a better criterion." According to the reporter, her lecture astonished "those who had never heard speaking by <u>inspiration</u> before."

After the lecture, a procession formed to march back into the village. During their walk, D. S. Kimball remarked to Axy, "As orthodoxy claims that you often have your lecture well committed to memory, *en passant*, I will just say if you will furnish me a lot of such lectures, I will go about delivering them!"

The group of excursionists dispersed in the village and rambled about for an hour or so, then re-embarked at half past six for home, highly gratified with their reception.

> The homeward passage was equally as pleasant as the one down, and was enlivened by the excellent music of the band, dancing, vocal exercises by several "glee clubs," and the display of fireworks from the deck of the Akron on the approach to this city, which was about half past ten p.m.

Elvira Crawford was thrilled to flaunt her personal friendship with the much-loved Miss Sprague. Several times she apologized for not being able to give her a room but said their home on Lake Ontario was filled with summer houseguests at present, and Sarah Crawford sent her regrets for not being able to join the outing.

The next morning, Mrs. Crawford and daughters were at the boat to see her off. Compared with the abundant crowd that had welcomed Axy on Monday night, the farewell celebration was diminished. Her reception room was furnished with tea and fancy cakes for those who gathered to bid her goodbye.

"I'm going to be married," Lizzie Crawford whispered, "I so wish, Dear Axy, that you would return for my wedding."

"So much for being consigned to *single blessedness*," Axy teased. "I could not be happier for you, Lizzie! May you and your new husband experience all things beautiful and fair and bright. God bless you both."

"Don't be a stranger, now," Mrs. Richardson warned.

Apparently there was some embarrassment regarding the lack of fanfare over Axy's departure. Back in Niagara Falls, she would receive a letter hastily sent by J. D. Pool with his apology (the Sackett's Harbor excursion must have included spirits of another kind):

> I regret very much that I did not reach the boat yesterday AM in time to bid you good bye. I awoke at 5 o'clock and oh! What a sick headache I had. I could scarcely move. I did however reach the wharf to see you in the distance. Lest you should obtain the idea that I cared not to bid you farewell, I drop you this letter. And to the Spirits who said come, give my best regards. I trust they will tell you to come again to Oswego. With ten thousand good wishes for your prosperity and happiness.

Much to Axy's astonishment she received a pale blue letter that closed with two lines she had often previously shot back at Mr. Crawford when annoyed:

Aug. 20 1860

Dear Minister

I will begin this note by saying I don't owe you a <u>letter</u> *or anything else but good will (sometimes) but as Mrs. C. has severely censured me and your friend Captain Richardson is astonished, I will explain. Mrs. C. censures me for not saluting you with (of course) an unholy kiss even in light of so many friends (This shocked me because none but your friends* are, I presume, permitted to perpetrate so delectable a thing), And besides, I was fearful Mrs. C. would become as jealous of me as I am of her in regard to you. Captain Richardson is astonished that I was not at your "reception room" on the boat to say goodbye to you.

Now in regard to this let me say I <u>was there</u> until 9 o'clock by my time. When thinking you had concluded to stay over a day and also expecting my partner on the nine o'clock train I could not consistently remain longer, therefore I spared you the infliction and astonished Capt. R. I suppose you will ask "what is all this for?" I reply, "for what it is worth."

Really I should have been delighted to have seen you more, but t'was impossible. I was a witness before the Court, and had a large day's work on hand, so I couldn't go to the pix nix, and we could not ask you home with us because we <u>were</u> full.

I hope you are enjoying your self <u>immensely</u> at the Falls.

I wish you would return this way to visit us, because I would like to see you again. I expect this is the last letter you will ever receive from me, therefore I will make it short.

I have been unfortunate, very, in losing what little grace I had ever found in your estimation—which was doubtless always small, but I do not "mourn as one without hope." "I never let trouble trouble me..."

Yours Sincerely (as ever), JHC

Here in Wisconsin, the summer of 1860 was an eventful one, albeit not that joyous. During a plentiful grain harvest, Morris sustained an injury to his head and was bedridden for several months. He had hired two young Irish men to help on the farm and they managed to complete the reaping. I was near collapse with worry and nursing Morris and feeding two very hungry hands. Morris's mother and I took turns sitting at his bedside while he suffered a bilious fever. Family and friends came by often to help see to his needs.

I wrote to Axy on August 26, as we had not had a word from her in a very long time.

> It is half past eight and all is quiet. Morris is in bed as he has been for the most of the time for three weeks, but as he thinks he will be able to write some tomorrow. I will not state the particulars. We had several callers this morning before nine o'clock. The house has been nearly filled the most of the day but I have just put my bread to spring and think my day's work is over and that people yet possess some good.
>
> Thursday, August 30 Morris has just written a few lines but he is not able to bear but a little exercise of either body or mind, yet it is hard for him to be still. We will expect a letter from you soon. C.S. Steen

> Dear Sister. I have been laid up with sickness for the last four weeks. I was taken with a bilious fever then a very severe pain in the head proceeding from the hurt I got in July. I am now able to be up but my physician thinks it will be several weeks before I will be able to resume my business. It is hard to be confined to the house so long. I had got about half through harvest when I was taken. The crops are very good all over the state. My head aches severely so I must stop. Write soon. J. M. Steen

Wisconsin was embroiled in debates over states' rights, fueled by the slavery question. One of our state legislators introduced a motion that directed Wisconsin to declare war against the United States unless slavery was abolished by the federal government. Governor Randall went so far as to suggest that if the government did not end slavery, Wisconsin would secede from the Union.

While Morris convalesced, I read to him from a Madison newspaper only just published by the recently organized "Wide Awakes," a company of young partisans who dressed in shiny uniforms and formed a volunteer militia of sorts. They were known for raucous midnight rallies and competed with other Wide Awakes across the country with a fresh and youthful spirit in their support of Abraham Lincoln's election. Republican newspapers printed announcements of their parades and meetings. In Madison, the Democratic paper accused the local Wide Awakes of stealing its editor's hat.

Also campaigning for Lincoln (since losing his party's nomination), William Seward visited Madison in September and stayed at the Capital House hotel. Mrs. Seward said she would not want to venture out alone in the evening due to the noisy Wide Awakes in the streets.

For Axy, the summer of 1860 also provided unusual diversions. Traveling under the name of "Baron Renfew," the Prince of Wales arrived in North America for a two-month tour. It had been hoped that Queen Victoria would pay a visit to Canada to inaugurate a new bridge across the St. Lawrence River, but the Queen claimed her nerves were too stressed to endure such a trip. She and Albert had their doubts that Bertie was equal to the occasion, although at last it was settled that their eldest son would represent her on this first Royal Tour.

The prince landed in Halifax and during the second week of August he sailed through the St. Lawrence River to Quebec, where he received a rapturous reception referred to in the press as "Albertmania."

In honor of Bertie's visit, the Falls was illuminated for the first time in history with two hundred Bengal Lights—blue flares that burned with a sustained brilliance. Sixty lights were aimed at the American Falls, sixty under Table Rock, and eighty behind the sheet of water at Horseshoe Falls, a magnificent sight.

Axy witnessed the illumination spectacle with her hosts. They decided among themselves that the prince must be the fine-looking man dressed in ceremonial garb, but *he* turned out to be the Duke of Newcastle. The prince, only eighteen, was the young, timid lad at his side who clutched an umbrella and a cigar.

The Great Blondin was in Niagara Falls for his second season of daring feats. One of his acts included pushing a wheelbarrow over the tightrope as he crossed the gorge; others involved drinking a bottle of wine while crossing, standing on his head, walking blindfolded, hanging by his feet, lying down, and walking on stilts.

The prince presented Blondin with a purse of gold coins. In turn, Blondin offered to carry the prince across the Falls. The prince begged to be excused.

Axy made a side trip to Buffalo, but after Niagara Falls, Portland, Maine, was her next intended destination. She utilized her steamship pass and paused in Montreal where she lectured several times. When she enquired about *The Prairie State*, the captain reported that the propeller was again seaworthy, thoroughly repaired and refitted with handsome upper cabins and beautiful ornamentation. As before, it would carry both passengers and freight between Oswego and Chicago. Steerage passengers, given their own cooking apparatus, could sail to Chicago for $4 with their own provisions. For $11, cabin passengers were given meals and staterooms.

The captain inquired, "Do you have plans to sail to Chicago, Miss Sprague?"

"Perhaps next year," she replied, "if we do not have a war."

That autumn she forwarded a letter to us that she had received from Nathaniel Randall. Axy was not at all pleased with his rude remark that she "could never love nor be loved," &c.

Dear Sister Acssie, This is a glorious morning & you are such a glorious girl that we are ever mindful of you. We

read in the Banner of your whereabout, and whatabout—
<u>drown</u> in Oswego as <u>usual</u>. Some great Humanity must live
there. No. No! We go by opposites. Some little infernal
deformity, must reside there—that is <u>your</u> magnet…Where
one the female like yourself, possesses the female, & <u>nearly</u>
all the male (as you claim to do) it takes but a very <u>inferior</u>
man to make you a unit—a whole individual. Now ain't
this good philosoph? & how is the agreeability to you? We
feel <u>bad</u> about it for we are <u>inclined</u> to be <u>proud</u> of our
relations…This discovery flashed upon my mind once I took
the pen to write to you. Now our idols vanish, when we
allow our thoughts free flight, or follow their wanderings.
Your <u>womanly greatness, & perfection has changed to</u>
monstrous <u>imperfection</u>. You can never love nor be loved
like a <u>whole</u> woman in this life. I wonder if you ever saw
yourself in this light before? Do write us, how you feel in
this <u>unfortunate</u> position…Excuse the pencil, the tremor of
my hand causes me to use it.

Yours N. Randall

Maine hosted Axy for the remainder of September; October
found her in New Hampshire and she was in Putnam, Massachusetts,
on November 6, when Abraham Lincoln was elected president of
the United States.

As an odd coincidence, that was the day she lost the "symbolic
ring" with the green stone. She searched her room in the home
where she was staying and enlisted the help of the entire household.
But the ring could not be found.

The letter John Crawford had sent to Niagara Falls had been
pored over so many times that the creases in the paper were softly
pulling apart.

*"I wish you would return this way to visit us, because I would
like to see you again…"*
He did not *"mourn as one without hope."*

Giving her a kiss was *"so delectable a thing."*

She had not anticipated that she would miss their quarrels every bit as much as their easy banter. No matter how many lectures she scheduled to fill her calendar, nor how close to Oswego she might find herself drifting from time to time, a gulf existed that caused a miserable ache in her heart.

"You can never love nor be loved like a whole woman in this life."

Nathaniel Randall would be stunned if he realized how deeply she had *loved* and *been loved like a whole woman.*

Only two days after Lincoln's election, the first flag of Southern independence was flown in Savannah, Georgia. South Carolina passed an ordinance of secession and other states in the Deep South prepared to follow her lead. Axy composed a poem for *The Banner of Light* and related it to the sea.

> *All, all is dark! Ten thousand clouds*
> *Make pall-like all my soul,*
> *And through its dreary, dismal depths*
> *The awful thunders roll…*
>
> *I'll stand a martyr on the shore*
> *Of time, my little day,*
> *And bravely meet the surging waves*
> *That bear my life away.*

Sarah Crawford wrote to comment that the poem in *The Banner* about the sea was very beautiful.

John knew immediately that it emanated from your prolific poetical pen, but I can't think you quite so despondent and so tired of the world as that would seem to indicate. Still as you are such a devoted worshipper at the shrine of Mr. Neptune perhaps you may wish to be entombed in the mighty deep. There is something awfully grand and sublime to me in a regular burial at sea although it has never been my lot to witness one and if we could only be sure of resting in the bottom of the deep it would be a burial to be coveted. But the idea of one being a dinner for a great half-famished shark destroys all the romance.

The Crawfords were quite content with their new Oswego home on Lake Ontario's shore. Sarah said, "It is a pleasant little town and our locality is delightful. It seems so homelike to be able to look out on the broad waters of the Lake and to compare the almost hourly changes of life's fitful phases. It is a source of pleasure to me and atones in a great measure for the absence of other society."

Lizzie had been married shortly after the Sackett's Harbor excursion and moved back to Milwaukee, where Julie was also living. Sarah Crawford said their house was awfully quiet, and their hitherto large family was quite reduced, only eight including servants. The last of their summer company had left on Friday morning, and "Jennie goes about like a dove who has lost her mate. Poor girl, she is so lonely she hardly knows what to do with her dear little self."

Julie, Sarah reported, was "in a <u>condition</u>, and she seems very happy in the prospect…She is very anxious to have her mother with her at the approaching crisis which is looked for in December, but Mrs. Crawford is not willing to be absent all winter from home though Julie and Lizzie would be delighted to have her in Milwaukee until Spring."

Sarah and Elvira and were embroidering flannel shirts for the expected Tommy, as Lizzie called him, and she was also knitting fancy socks for the little fellow. "I can't make John say anything about it," Sarah wrote. "I showed the socks to him and all he said was 'how do you know they will fit.' We do not tease him with the prospect of being grandpa. I don't know as he will ever forgive either of the girls for getting married. I believe he opposed Lizzie about as much as he did Julie."

Axy's symbolic ring was returned by mail, her hosts noting that it had been found soon after she left.

With so many distractions, other personal items had gone astray. Friends from Worcester, Massachusetts, found her veil and had wrapped it in newspaper to send on the Marlboro Stage. "If you have not received it, you can make enquiries of the driver for it…Aunty says 'give my love to Axy…tell her I wish she was here tonight to talk with her or read Walt Whitman.'"

She spent Thanksgiving Day in Providence, where she gave a lecture late that morning. Only four days earlier President Lincoln had been seen at an evening lecture given by Miss Belle Scougall, the spirit-medium from Rockford, Illinois. This was reported to Axy by a friend from Chagrin Falls, Ohio. "So much towards Lincoln being a Spiritualist as is asserted," he said.

Her obligation in Providence would run through the month of December, and she invited Mother to visit her when she moved on to Boston. It would be a thrilling opportunity for Betsey Moore Sprague, involving much preparation at Axy's direction:

> *You may carry the box you speak of to Uncle Thomases. I wish you would rip the trimming off my black brocade silk dress sleeves and bring to me. Don't forget it. I want Mr. Josselyn to carry you to Ludlow and put you on board the cars and ask the conductor to see to you at Bellows Falls where you can change cars. You can ask him if he does not tell you where you can find the cars for Boston. Perhaps you had better wear your straw bonnet, as I shall have my soft straw fitted for you when you get here. Don't forget to take your cap and furs. And wear your thick shawl and I guess you had better wear your debage dress and bring your lioness, and you know what other things to bring. You write me as soon as you get this. I should want you to come the Saturday after Christmas. I suppose I do not need to send you money to come with. Tell Uncle Thomas if he knows any __good__ place for that money or any more. I would like to dispose of it.*

Providence, R.I. December 15, 1860

Dear Mother,

I have already written seven letters without rising. I shall expect you at Boston when I send for you. I don't want to compel you to come if you don't want to, but you like to travel and see things so well that I thought you would enjoy it so much and I should too. You must dress very warm. Wear those gray snow boots on the cars, and bring your rubbers. You can wear my sandals if it is not too muddy. I shall write you about it when I get to Boston.

Who cares if you are looked at. I want you should be, and it won't trouble you half as much as it would Orvilla. I wish Uncle Thomas and Aunt Athelia were coming, too. Wouldn't you rather come than go to William's this winter? Perhaps you will not have another chance to see Boston, and I shall write all directions, besides meeting you just before you get into the city.

I am well as usual, and hope you all are. You don't want to bring much work. If you have some nice knitting you can bring that and some nice small sewing.

I'm in a great hurry, so good bye to you and Malvina.

A. W. Sprague

Before she left Providence, my sister was invited to the governor's mansion to dine with our Sprague cousins who, as it turned out, were Spiritualists. "They sent their carriage and driver for me," she wrote. "I have not entirely lost my position in society."

William Sprague, then twenty-nine years old, was the youngest governor in the Union and sometimes referred to as the Boy Governor of Rhode Island. Always interested in politics, he had been elected governor in 1860 (and would be re-elected in 1861). Governor Sprague had already assured President-elect Lincoln that in case of war, Rhode Island would immediately furnish an infantry regiment and a battery of light artillery.

When she queried Governor Sprague regarding the chances of war, he strongly assured her that the war, if it actually happened, would last no longer than 48 hours, for that's how long it would take the North to whip the South.

⤞ 18 ⤝

Angry & Sorry By Turns

(January–July 1861)

"To Arms! To Arms!" The electric wires
Flashed forth the summons o'er the land:
Fort Sumter's lost! Our nation's flag
Insulted by the Rebel's hand!

"Last Words of the Dying Soldier"
Solitarie, *Herald of Progress*, July 1861

U NIFORMED SOLDIERS WERE MUSTERING on Boston
Common; militiamen surrounded the ports where tall-masted
ships departed daily with supplies and reinforcements for the federal
forts at Charleston and Fort Sumter, and Axy was speaking at
Allston Hall when Mother journeyed to Boston in early January. *The
Banner of Light* told its readers, "Miss Sprague's old friends and new
ones welcome her with pleasure…She was one of the first, and is one
of the best trance speakers in the Spiritual field."

My sister took Mother on a thrilling shopping spree. Axy
purchased gifts to send along back home: A lace collar for Aunt
Athelia, a book for Uncle Thomas, necktie for Alfred, little doll for
Clara's baby, writing paper for cousin Ephraim and books for Louise
and Charlie, the children of our brother William and wife, Ann.
Mother would also deliver a deep blue scarf for Malvina and Nathan
would receive a model ship in a bottle that would fascinate him.

Ralph Waldo Emerson spoke on "Domestic Life" at Music Hall.
Axy and Mother were in attendance, but Mother chose to stay at the
hotel rather than hear famed orator Wendell Phillips at the same

SEVEN YEARS OF GRACE

location on January 15. His address to the Massachusetts Anti-Slavery Society urged, "Let the slave states go!"

Axy had long been a staunch fan of Phillips, a deep-chested, broad-shouldered man, six feet tall with reddish-brown hair that waved back from a regal, high forehead. Some called him beautiful, "a young Apollo." Phillips believed the government owed the Negroes not only their freedom, but land, education, and full civil rights as well.

A crowd of five thousand rampaged outside Music Hall that night, calling Phillips "treasonous," and accused the radical abolitionists of making an "Unholy Alliance" with the slave states. Thankfully, Mother was not there to witness the frightening mob scene and later Axy noted:

> *And then what if they did get into a row in the back part of the hall and rush out into the street in order to have room to show their patriotic spirit and manliness and then make mighty* (make right?) history with their yells *raise their cries of "fire" which they succeeded in getting the halls vacated and the firing shots (just as they intended) and also <u>two thirds of the audience out of the hall</u> just as their favorite speaker came on the stage amid uproarious applause. "That was nothing, a mere common occurrence," as the gentleman who went with me said when I made the remark that I might perhaps have enjoyed the evening quite as well at my hotel. However, I considered the evening very profitably spent for it was a fine study of human nature as it is and it is necessary to know something of the true state of society in order to be able to better know its wants and needs and supply them. It seemed very much to me as though they cheered vociferously many a trifling anecdote and strangely enough sometimes forgot to cheer at all.*

Several weeks later Axy would dedicate a poem to Wendell Phillips, call him a "noble, almost god-like form," and comment on his speech:

> *But when our Northern blood had stained the street*
> *of Baltimore – foul Treason's work complete;*
> *When Massachusetts sprang to avenge the stain,*
> *Then WENDELL PHILLIPS could be heard again!*
> *They pressed to hear,—the mob of weeks ago,—*
> *Their hearts with patriot fire at last aglow.*

The Banner of Light soon published Axy's poem, "Voices," which she deliberately filled with rich imagery and lines meant for John Crawford.

> *I stood, today, where at my feet the Ocean billows rolled,*
> *And hushed my breath to hear the grand, deep mysteries they told.*
> *How well it wears the Prophet's robe, through ages has that tone*
> *Pealed forth the solemn mysteries of all the Great Unknown;*
> *But only they that listen close—as to the sea shell pressed*
> *The ear detects the murmuring, the sound of its unrest—*
> *Shall hear prophetic words that break in every billows roll*
> *And understand its solemn Voice as speaking soul to soul.*

Sarah Randall sent a note to Boston advising Axy to take Mother "a-cousining every where among the relation and have her stay a good while," but after Mother went home it was left to Aunt Athelia Moore to catch up with family gossip.

> You say you hope I did not get talked to death—why Malvina says she is no talker at all compared with you, what do you think of that? I think you will not say anything more about large talkers, do you?
>
> I want to write a little about Sarah Randall. I was out to see her the first of December. Well there is strange things in the world, he has got her in a family way again. He thinks if she can have a babe and nurse it she will get her health back…she is in hope you will be with her the first of July.
>
> Ephraim has been up to your house and spent it with your Mother. She and Malvina are well as usual. They dare not keep much fire for fear the chimney will burn. Your mother was highly pleased with her visit to Boston. I suppose it will satisfy her for the rest of the Winter.

After Mother left her and returned to Vermont, Axy's calendar bulged with obligations. She was wearing the symbolic ring and lost the emerald stone in Willimantic, Connecticut. She assured the family with whom she was staying that it was a valueless little stone with only sentimental value, but everyone searched for the seemingly contrary gem.

Paradoxically, she heard just then from Sarah Crawford in Oswego:

> The very day I got your letter, I read it to Jennie and Mrs.
> Crawford. When I read what you said about <u>not</u> coming here,
> Jennie said 'Tell Miss Sprague to go to grass.' She felt quite
> indignant that you should say 'you would not stay with us, if
> you could find any one else to keep you, and you thought you
> could as it was for so short a time.' You know Mrs. Crawford
> well enough to know she would never write you if she did not
> want you, and all I have to say about it is, that it would be no
> pleasure to me to have you come against <u>your will</u>. A pleasure
> to be enjoyed must be <u>reciprocal</u> and if you can't be as happy
> here as elsewhere I say go where you will be happiest. You
> know we all love you too much to wish to make you feel at all
> <u>uncomfortable</u>. If it is only from motives of delicacy or
> because you are afraid of being burdensome, then let me tell
> you that you are <u>never burdensome</u> to any member of our
> family, and no one of our present family feels at all afraid of
> being lowered by associating with <u>Spiritualists.</u>

The Crawford children were ill with diphtheria, but Sarah confided,

> I am far more contented here in Oswego than I was at
> Milwaukee. We all spend our evenings and indeed most of our
> time together in the sitting room downstairs. We don't find
> time to read much but newspapers this winter. We read the
> news aloud to each other, discuss political matters and even
> Mrs. Crawford is much interested in the <u>all absorbing</u> question
> which is now agitating our country. Do any of your <u>guardians</u>
> give you any clue to the future? Can't you raise up Patrick

Henry or some other good old Patriot to speak through you? I wish some good old orator would take possession of me. I would <u>stump</u> the length and breadth of the land…But I will not weary you with political matters. We are having fine sleighing here now and we are enjoying it. Wish you could have one ride with us behind Bobb and Charley. They go like lightning with a strong arm to guide them.

The letter closed with, "All send their love. John says, 'tell her that I send her <u>all my love</u> without any reservations and that I don't want her to come here if she doesn't want to come, but that I shan't go to hear her lecture if she doesn't come.' I have thus given his message <u>verbatim</u>."

Axy would not be visiting Oswego until August, six months away, so she had plenty of time to consider her lodgings. But John *had* sent *all his love, without any reservations.*

Benjamin Starbuck's family expected her in Troy the last Sunday in June, when they would pic-nic and camp and vacation together with friends. Starbuck sounded like his usual jolly self in his letter, but then backtracked:

Just as sure as the South fires the first guns, the echo will break the chain of every slave upon the American Continent—War in its worst phase, civil or rather <u>un civil</u> war, will spread over the entire country, but the Slave States will be the principal battle grounds. The slaves will rise against their masters and pay off a long unsettled account. Their wives and daughters will be parceled out amongst the blacks, desolation and destruction will be the inevitable doom of every Slave State. Oh! My heart sickens at the contemplation.

The appearance of more poems and reviews of her lectures in the popular *Banner* caused Axy to be even more sought after than ever, but severe headaches and blurred vision—which she blamed on extreme fatigue—were taking a toll. She attempted to cancel another trip to Providence but an urgent telegram insisted, "Must come wont excuse you. Can rest here come Monday without fail."

While she was in Providence, her upcoming visit to New Haven was cancelled: "New Haven feels the Panic the severest of any place in the country…it is the darkest time now we have seen yet."

A letter from cousin Ephraim back in the Notch discussed school and an exhibition at the meeting house. He'd tapped five trees and sugared off twice and had half a bowl of maple sugar that he was saving for his oldest sister, who was coming home to visit. Everyone was sick with colds. "Tomorrow I suppose Mr. Lincoln takes his seat in Washington. I should like to be there. We are going to put up our flag tomorrow if everything is right."

Axy liked to imagine little Plymouth Notch draped in patriotic bunting.

Abraham Lincoln was inaugurated on Monday, March 4. Benjamin Starbuck, never at a loss for words, wrote,

> Well the 4th of March is here and honest Old Abe is our Chief …I hope Lincoln will prove himself a true man with a good strong back bone. But I don't like the way he run from Harrisburgh to Washington. I would have gone through Baltimore openly and in the day time if I had known there were ten thousand there, sworn to kill me. But that is past and I hope for the future that he will always face the music and show his face when need of it, if it ain't verry handsome.

Axy had told Starbuck she was "waiting for the summer to rest and be glad," although Chicago wanted her for the next six months.

On April 5, she received a letter with the green stone from her ring inside:

While cleaning your room this morning we found the little missing stone which I herewith enclose. All ages have had more or less to do with stones, mystic stones, the fortune teller's stone which reveals all hearts of past and future, etc. etc. I hope the temporary absence of this (apparently valueless little stone) will not damage your mediumship, for fear I dispatch it to you at the earliest opportunity.

She took the ring to a jeweler in Connecticut and had the stone firmly secured so it would not be lost again.

On April 12, Fort Sumter was fired upon. The War Between the States had begun.

Everywhere, uniformed troops were marching toward the battlefields. Spiritualists were sought as recruits, even by those who had no sympathy with their belief, for it was believed true Spiritualists lacked a fear of death which promised to make them the bravest of soldiers.

With the country at war and the nation in such an unsettled state, Axy cancelled all her engagements to return to the Notch. She was there on May 4 when her poem, "Voices of Home," appeared on the front page of *The Banner of Light*.

I hear the sound of the tinkling rills,
The rush of the mountain streams;
They mingle with every waking thought,
And they haunt me in my dreams....

I'm weary of wrestling with sin and wrong,
It needeth a stronger than me;
My hills, my streams, and my mountain air,
World weary, I turn to thee.

Neither Morris nor I had heard from our sister in a very long time. I wrote to ask, "How did you find Sarah? Is her condition arising from choice or from mistake, as they say?"

I mentioned that we had noticed Axy's articles in the *Herald*, and asked why she did not use her true name in that paper instead of "Solitarie," as there were letters to the editor from those who wished to know who Solitarie was.

> There is much said here about war; I think the people here are now having the pleasant side of it, pole-raisings and presenting flags accompanied by pic-nics are not very savage, but I am getting tired of them.
>
> Has Mother broke up housekeeping or does she have so much of it to do that she cannot write us? Months have passed since she last wrote.

And Morris added,

> Amid the troubles of Civil War I hope we will not neglect to keep up our correspondence. I would have written to you sooner but I was waiting to arrange your money matters. Well, last week I put out $100 for you in your name, to go on what we owe you. I have not got the interest from Mr. Hubbard yet, expect it soon and will dispose of it as quickly as possible. Upwards of 40 Wisconsin banks have failed and more expected to every day. We have a new banking law which goes into effect the first day of December, after that I hope we will have a safe currency.
>
> We are having very dry weather now, crops look fair though in much need of rain. How do you enjoy yourself this summer? I am busy as usual. We drill every Saturday. Does the war enthusiasm continue in the New England States?

Axy sent letters to friends and repeated that "sex alone prevents Uncle Sam from having one more General in the field!" Her letters were sealed in envelopes boldly printed with the motto, "Stand by the Flag."

She managed to deliver two lectures in Bethel, Vermont, but after that increased problems with her vision left my sister feverish, nauseated, and wild with frustration when she could not read. One day Mother remarked that Axy's left eye seemed to be protruding a bit and Axy realized she had been deliberately avoiding mirrors.

Eventually, her visit to Troy in late June was dispensed with, as were all of her July lectures.

But the National Convention of Spiritualists scheduled for Oswego was fast approaching. Rather than endure a grueling railroad trip in hot, humid weather, Axy hoped to travel by steamboat from Montreal. She checked with the Lake Ontario Steamboat Company regarding her "free pass." Unfortunately, the company had reorganized and the free pass was no longer recognized.

Meanwhile, the Richardsons greatly anticipated Axy's arrival. They had won the competition with Elvira Crawford and others for her company: "Of course we have not forgotten your <u>promise</u> to make our house your home during your stay in this city," Mary Richardson wrote, enquiring what day and by what route she would arrive. "The last train of cars leave Syracuse at 5:45 and arrive here at 7½ PM and unless I hear from you to the contrary shall expect you by that train. I think <u>we</u> shall be better <u>able</u> to <u>withstand</u> the <u>great</u> amount of trouble to which you put your friends than any one else. I believe it is generally admitted that <u>we are entitled</u> to be honored with your company. We are sorry to hear that your throat is again troubling you."

The question of where she would stay and with whom in Oswego erupted like a volcano when Axy received an unexpected dispatch from John Crawford.

Oswego, July 25, 1861

Miss Sprague,

I must ask your indulgence for a few moments while I say my say in reference to the hotel you are to "put up" at while you remain here. Mrs. Crawford and myself were angry and sorry by turns when you almost or wholly declined her first invitation. I attributed it to the fact that I was expected to be home during the time, while Mrs. C. supposed you actually thought you would be too great a burden, and rather than break Mrs. Richardson's heart she had become partly reconciled to let you go to Mrs. R's. I didn't care a copper for Mrs. Richardson but inwardly affirmed that if you preferred stopping with Mrs. R. to coming over to our haunt by the lake you might do it and be ___hanged. That I wouldn't visit you or go to hear you preach, but as that would be no punishment to you, but a pleasure, I changed my tactics and thought I could make a martyr of you soonest by writing you this note and laying down several propositions.

1st. Mrs. C. has gone with her sister and niece to visit Mrs. Bronson, a relative, in New York. Mrs. C. says she will be back the last of next week as she cannot miss your lectures and the convention. I shall expect her Friday or Saturday. If she stays there a week longer than she anticipates she'll still be home a week before you leave. Now suppose you come and stay with us, provided Mrs. C. gets home next week. If you do, you will disappoint fewer persons than would be the case if you stopped elsewhere, and you would make less trouble because we would not put on airs or make any extra exertion on your account. We certainly should not kill you with kindness, preserves or elderberry wine. You would doubtless be happy with the R's, but you couldn't inhale so many cubic feet of lake air as you could over on the shore with us. Mrs. R. will nearly kill herself and you with efforts to please you, as you are her Deity, and if you stop with her, it will be because of your large approbativeness and love of adoration. I confess I have none of it. I had a little formerly, but I soon found others were traveling that road in such numbers that I could not consistently with my nature go with the crowd as I like to be unlike others, wherefore I positively do not adore you one whit.

Nevertheless as I am grown so old and so grave I should

like very much to have an opportunity to talk soberly and religiously with you again without being compelled to go to a Fourth of July celebration to do it. If Mrs. C. doesn't get back the first week of your tarry here, she doubtless will the second, when you must divide yourself and be with us the last half of the time...

My Sister Sarah goes to command the orphans on the first of August. You know she's not in her element unless she is commanding. She has been so long a General that she is quite unlike herself in a private sphere. She, too, is one of your admirers but she will not be with you at our home if you come.

So look out for impressment when you arrive. You will most certainly be taken somewhere. Remember me especially to your dear Mother and believe me as ever

J. K. Crawford

My Burning Thought Leaps Up

(August 1861–May 1862)

We've, thank God, a standing army
In the heroes of our land.
Farmer, merchant and mechanic,
Lawyer, millionaire, divine,
These shall make our Stripes a terror,
These shall make our Stars to shine.

"*The People*"
From *The Poet and Other Poems*
Achsa W. Sprague

In July 1861, Sarah Crawford wrote to Axy from Oswego and wanted to know if her "lodge in the mountains" excluded the din of battle. "As we have not received a letter from you in some time, we must conclude you are either buried in the mountains or gone to war."

My sister personally knew of several instances where spirits warned Spiritualist officers of the proximity of danger. And only days before, our cousin Governor William Sprague had participated in the Battle of Bull Run. Although the Confederate troops were ultimately victorious, Governor Sprague was said to have performed conspicuous and gallant service with the Rhode Island Militia. He had ridden a white horse into combat with a yellow plume streaming from his hat (truly "conspicuous"), and when his horse was shot out from beneath him, Gov. Sprague quickly mounted another and rode on.

Axy struggled to read Miss Crawford's letter to Mother, who puffed her little clay pipe, content to sit and get pleasure from the twilight.

Yellow roses in the dooryard were so fragrant that Axy's head was throbbing, and the evening sky, a luminous red stain behind the mountains, seemed much too bright, even as it faded to pink.

> You ought to have been here to eat strawberries and cream. We have two cows and you had better believe we revel in cream. Mrs. Crawford has bought a churn and is going into the butter making business now that strawberries are gone. She says 'give my love to Miss Sprague, I expect to see her soon.'

Lizzie and Julie were home with Julie's new baby, now eight months old, but the girls were soon leaving for Milwaukee by propeller ship. Lizzie expected to give birth in August. Elvira had been invited to accompany them to Milwaukee but would wait until after Axy's Oswego lectures. Before she left for New York to visit her cousin, Mrs. Crawford sent her love and wished Axy to know that she desired her "to come here for your home in Oswego." She said, "I would not be satisfied to have you go anywhere else to put up." Sarah concluded:

> If you are still determined not to make your home here, go your own way, but if you have thought better of it and conclude to accept the invitation given through me just write and let us know when to meet you at the Depot, and you will find the little black ponies there and you shall have a room where you can look out on the brave waters of Lake Ontario and derive all the inspiration you can possibly digest from its never failing source.

Axy still had difficulty reading, but she could write, and her poems spoke of the solemn perils faced by our country. "The People" quoted a message of praise for the common soldiers from Abraham Lincoln ("It is worthy of note that while in this, the government's hour of trial"), and the poem had been accepted for publication by *The Herald of Progress*. She would see that Sarah Crawford received a copy.

In a burst of patriotic zeal, Axy had also written "Emancipation in the District of Columbia," and her boldest and most vivid poem yet in its partisan comments about the war, "The American Eagle."

The Eagle sits with drooping wing upon the Southern coast,
With soiled and broken shield, the arrows from his talons lost,
The stars from his blue banner fled, the lightning from his eye;—
Old Eagle, by thy sons betrayed, doest think it time to die?

She was scheduled to lecture in Oswego for two Sundays in early August, prior to the National Convention of Spiritualists in that city. Before leaving home she completed a poem of a more personal nature. She called it "Sermon on the Mount" and mailed it to *The Banner of Light*.

Today I stood upon a grand old mountain
  That lifts its forehead, broad, sublime and high,
Where oft I gazed in dreamy hours of childhood
  And thought if at its height, I'd touch the sky—
But now, though landscapes spread in beauty round me,
  Though sunset hues shed glory o'er the place,
I stood alone, the sky as far beyond me,
And not one glimpse of Heaven could I trace.
My childish dreams through knowledge had departed,
  As other dreams had faded, too, away,
I had ascended to my child-heart's temple—
  The answer to my prayer still further lay.
I sat me down upon the mountain's summit,
  And could have wept at those old dreams of bliss,
To think how oft the child's first grand ideal
  Must end in cold reality like this.

Mother could not comprehend why her ailing daughter would insist on going to Oswego when she had cancelled almost everything before and after. Axy could not find a convincing response.

It was not as though her Guardians insisted that she carry on her ministry for their sake; her debts were paid. The most honest motive was, she missed her Evil Genius. She *had* to see him. His comment, "I positively do not adore you one whit," resurrected long-repressed joy in such mirthful remarks.

The Oswego Convention was slated to debate "What are the special demands of the age upon us as Spiritual teachers, and how can we best become fitted to meet those demands?" No one doubted that Mrs. Britt Spence would boldly and reprehensibly take the opportunity to push her own pet agendas. Axy had confided to a friend that the woman's "Low Libelous Tongue is too foul and meddlesome to meet in a public assemblage."

Captain and Mrs. Richardson met her train but they barely recognized the woman who stepped from the cars. Axy, shivering, was draped in shawls and shielding her eyes in the warm summer dusk. She hailed them with a cheery greeting and they responded in kind, albeit taken aback by her pale, pinched features and an eye that protruded in an unsightly fashion. The effect of her altered appearance was not lost on my sister. She knew she looked a little different and saw, in the countenance of her friends, their dazed response.

Friends who gathered at the Richardson home to welcome Axy later that night were privately urged to linger only briefly. The Crawfords were not among the callers: Sarah had gone to her new position as head of the Oswego Orphan Asylum, Elvira was still visiting relatives, and John had a business meeting in Ogdensburgh that kept him away. After Axy retired, the Richardsons resolved to send a telegram to Mr. Crawford. Yes, she had warned them that she had not been well, but her affliction was alarming beyond anyone's imagination. All who loved her expressed their grave concern to her hosts.

Despite a stiff neck and mild headache, she managed to carry out her early lecture on the first Sunday afternoon in August. Standing before the outdoor gathering, her new dress of black bombazine (she was mourning the horrors of war) was a weighty cloak on her thin frame and she had to cling to the back of a straight chair to steady herself. At some point she found herself seated, but she could not say when that occurred. She was later informed that her voice was very weak and the audience, leaning forward, strained to hear her words.

When he arrived in Oswego later that day, John immediately reported to the Richardsons' house. Axy was attempting to restore her stamina for the evening lecture when his fury shook her from her nap. She emerged from her room to confront them, intending to prove her confidence, but her legs buckled and she was betrayed by her fragility. John sternly ordered her evening lecture cancelled and the next Sunday's lecture as well.

"You weigh no more than a bundle of twigs," he muttered as he swept her in his arms and took her to his carriage. "How could such a small bundle cause me such a monstrous heartache?"

Dizzy with fatigue, Axy could only murmur a vague reply.

Thus, with little fanfare, she was moved from the Richardsons' residence to the splendid refuge of Lakeside View, where, it was hoped, she would be energized by cool breezes while reclining on the gracious veranda that overlooked Lake Ontario.

No one could have foreseen that the Crawfords' Gothic Revival mansion at West Lake and Eighth would become her sole residence from August 1861 until the middle of April the following year.

The account of her illness in Oswego and subsequent recuperation—such as it was—consists of pieced-together convictions from my sister's fogged brain, an article that she penned, and those details that John Crawford divulged to her.

The National Convention of Spiritualists began their four-day meeting at Music Hall on August 18. Axy was entertained by accounts of the proceedings delivered by friends who paused at the Crawfords' home with words of consolation. As feared, Amanda Britt Spence monopolized the gathering.

Elvira, now returned from her visit, joked that her need to nurse Axy kept her from the lake excursion to Canada planned for Thursday. Two of John's steamers had been chartered by the Convention and were to embark at precisely half-past seven in the morning. Music would be provided; fruits and ice cream would be for sale. By midnight the Spiritualists would be returned to the Oswego dock.

The gala was fraught with unforeseen tribulations. Due to a storm on Thursday, the excursion was scheduled for Saturday instead. Spiritualists and skeptics registered so much interest that three boats, *The Michigan*, *The Buckeye* and *The Jefferson*, had to be hired. According to idyllic accounts in *The Banner of Light*, the boats were jam-packed and everything proceeded as planned with music, dancing, and agreeable good humor. "Daylight shot up in the east over the bosom of the Ontario as they landed back in Oswego, and the contented and satisfied mortals were soon scattered around the city, hurrying through a short Sunday morning nap."

Axy and Elvira determined the account must have been written in advance.

The Oswego newspapers captured a less virtuous rendering of the outing: At Picton, an excursion party from Kingston, Ontario, joined the Oswego party and a dozen drunken rowdies started a fight, then tried to wreck the Globe Hotel. Police fought a pitched battle with the rioters that landed five of the leaders in jail. There was talk of detaining the boats to search them for liquor, at which point the ships' captains were prompted to make a hurried departure. In their haste several of the "more worthy passengers" were left behind, including "the distinguished medium, Mrs. Amanda Britt Spence."

Despite the sweet lake air and the soothing ministrations of the Crawfords and their servants, Axy was deemed much too frail to travel back to Plymouth Notch. As her health declined, she was confined to her bed, where a high fever and convulsions brought about episodes of delirium.

Meanwhile, Lizzie Crawford Brown telegraphed that her doctor had ordered strict bed rest and she needed her mother in Milwaukee. Elvira desperately wished to be with Lizzie and John assured his wife that her responsibilities rested on the side of their daughter. The very dependable Miss Phoebe Hewitt, a steadfast Spiritualist, seamstress, and middle-aged spinster who sometimes cared for bedridden patients, was hired as Axy's private nurse; she had fitted and sewn the exquisite ashes-of-roses dress that my sister wore to the event at the White House. Due to her own poor health, Jenny Crawford, now twenty-one, was back in Ogdensburgh with friends. The youngest Crawford children, Molly, fifteen, and George, nine, were left at home in Oswego under the guidance of their father and the care of the servants.

Phoebe Hewitt was quiet and efficient. Sarah Crawford, who occasionally came over from the Orphan Asylum to visit Axy, declared that Miss Hewitt "seems to be a good homely sort of body," and added in confidence, "They used to tell me when I was a child that homely persons were always clever, which in common parlance wasn't good, but my experience shows as many bad persons with repulsive features as otherwise, though I do really think Miss Hewitt a very good sort of person."

Morris and I wrote to Axy in care of Plymouth Notch; Mother forwarded the letter to Oswego. Phoebe Hewitt read Axy's mail to her.

1 September 1861

Dear Sister,

"The summer is past and the harvest has ended," and here I am the same as ever, nothing gained or lost as I see when making an estimate of the varied scenes of life. But in these times of war and commotion I know not as there is to be much gained only by the brave soldiers who would gladly gain freedom for the enslaved and union for the nation. But our rulers are so slow to act and speak forth, that the object of this war is not only to put down rebellion but to destroy slavery and in that I fear a long siege is before us.

Your last letter was directed to me no doubt, thinking Morris was away, but as the Oakfield Guards disbanded a short time previous to being called into camp, Morris yet remains and I hope will do so as long as there are men sufficient.

Thank you for the pattern you sent. Oh! I must tell you of my plaid silk (or rather yours) it is still in existence, but only fit for home dress up but I have worn it more than fifty times; it became me so well it was always first chosen and I am loath to give it up even now.

I suppose you have had a joyous and instructive time at Oswego. Write us about it if you do not post in the Herald. Mother wrote that you were intending to return in a few weeks so I shall direct this to Vermont. Can't you get help for your throat? What is it, a "minister's sore throat" again?

I will leave now for Morris to write when he finds time but he appears to be perfectly well and has as much work to do as ever.
Good Night, C.S.S.

9 September 1861

Dear Sister,

I suppose when you wrote your last letter you thought I would be in the army before this time. Well I am here yet and likely to remain here. The company quarreled about the selection of officers and were disbanded. Still, I hold myself in readiness to go if I am needed. At present there seem to be enough of the non-producing class to fill up the ranks and make food for powder. If I go I would like to join Fremont's division as there is more action there than in the army around Washington. I have got through harvesting. Crops are rather light. Business is very dull and a great cry of hard times although I do not see that it makes much difference so long as we have an abundance to live on.

I hope you will take good care of your health so as to be able to come out here next spring. We enjoy as good health as usual. Write soon and let us know all the news.

Throughout September, October, and well into November, my sister was confined to her bedchamber, where the heavy draperies were drawn. Furnishings she so admired in her room in Milwaukee had been transferred to Lakeside but in the dim light she could not appreciate the carved wooden inlays of the rosewood suite. In reality, she would recall little of the earliest days, as sleep-inducing draughts were administered to dull her pain.

A swelling behind her left eye caused it to protrude so that she was unable to completely close her eyelid. She moaned, "I must look like a gargoyle!"

At her request, mirrors in her room were covered so she did not have to behold how grotesque she had become. She asked that no one else be allowed to witness it either.

Doctor Goodnight made daily visits, and determined that she suffered from inflammation of the brain. He expressed regret that very little could be done for such a serious condition in scrofulous individuals. The disease, he confided to Mr. Crawford in private, usually varied in duration from one to four weeks and prospects for Axy's recovery were slight.

Pilot lay next to her bed, keeping faithful watch over his friend. The dog's devoted presence calmed her with his deep sighs and snuffling snores.

Lizzie and her new baby were doing well, but Elvira elected not to return home to Oswego from Milwaukee alone, by railroad, preferring to remain in the west until spring when the ships were running again. Her husband assured her this was wise.

Axy was aware of very little, but she did prize those rare afternoons when she heard John excuse Miss Hewitt and knew he would then sit at her bedside to hold her hand in his. He soothed her brow with a cold compress and tenderly spoke of his affection.

"Sing to me," she begged so pathetically one evening that he did, softly, lovingly — "Devotion," her poem that he had set to music, and "What are the Wild Waves Saying," melodies they had sung together in the past; "I Live For Thee Only," and "The Heart That's True," songs by Henry Russell and Eliza Cook that he knew were her favorites, music meant only for her.

On a tempestuous night in early November when thunder crashed and lightning revealed snow blustering in from the north over Ontario's angry surf, Axy experienced a soaring fever that resulted in agonizing convulsions. Miss Hewitt, alarmed by my sister's delirium, woke Mr. Crawford who ordered her to fetch Doctor Goodnight.

My sister was now so feeble that her whispers could scarcely be perceived. In torment, she tossed upon her bed and agonized, hallucinating, over the turmoil of the waves and haunting cries of lost souls. Terrors caused by the waves crashing against the rocks, crashed over her. She was bitterly cold. Later, she would recall this event for *The Banner of Light:*

> *During my illness the past winter in Oswego, N. Y., the home of the friends where I was entertained was upon the banks of Lake Ontario, only the street intervening between their residence and the waters, and I used to lie and listen to the rushing of the waves, until their wild unrest seemed almost a part of my own. Night after night, when the storm had swept over the waters, dashing them against the rocks until they moaned and shrieked like my childish idea of lost souls, or sighed and sobbed themselves to sleep after the fury of the storm had passed; when I lay burning with fever, my brain scorched and tortured with most intense pain, I used to mingle the sound of the surges with my own agony, until I could hardly tell whether it was the wave, or me, that was thrown upon the rocks and then sent back, only to return again with the same wailing tone, to meet inevitably the same fate.*

One night, when much worse than usual, although I was watched with the kindest care and affection, and although I was perfectly conscious of the presence of my friends, and of being in my room surrounded by every comfort, yet this fancy kept wandering through my tortured brain, and at last became almost a reality. It seemed as though I was lying out in the grounds, wrapped in the thinnest possible covering, with the cold rain falling heavily upon me, and the winds howling in every direction through the trees, while now and then the great waves rolled over me, and then swept coldly back, as if in scorn at my sufferings. There are no words to tell the strange painfulness of the sensations that crept over me, mingled with a thousand nameless fancies. Only those who have wandered in a fever to the very brink of consciousness, and live to remember their vague, shadowy visions, can have any idea of their wild, fantastic agony.

Miss Hewitt returned with Dr. Goodnight who insisted on waking the cook: Pounded ice chips would be placed in India-rubber bags and then positioned around Axy's head.

"But first," he disclosed to Crawford when Miss Hewitt had left the room, "We must shave the patient's scalp."

Grateful that she appeared insensible and unaware of the humiliating procedure, John Crawford found his razor and strop and a bar of shaving soap. He gently untied Axy's lace night cap and removed it with the utmost tenderness. Then he supported Axy in his arms while the doctor cropped her hair close to her scalp with a scissors, and proceeded to use the razor.

Miss Hewitt burst into tears when she returned with the ice and saw her patient's altered appearance. John clutched locks of Axy's dark lustrous hair to his breast. His eyes were damp.

"The ice bags must be placed so the cold influence is distributed evenly over the entire head," Dr. Goodnight advised as he arranged the apparatus. "Miss Hewitt, if ice cannot eventually be procured you must wring a cloth in cold water and apply it to her head every five or ten minutes or the cloth will become warm and useless.

Light mustard plasters can be applied to her calves and the soles of her feet. This encourages the blood to circulate in her feet and limbs, rather than in her head. Immersing her in a warm bath may also produce similar results, but there is the essential matter of the ice around her scalp."

"Is Miss Sprague going to die?" Miss Hewitt asked timidly.

"The most that can be done is to relieve the patient's suffering," Dr. Goodnight replied after a pause. "If the delirium becomes a prominent symptom, the patient may be rendered insane. But in my experience, tuberculous meningitis is invariably fatal. I am sorry."

By the time the doctor left, Miss Hewitt was hysterical.

John saw the doctor to the front door and helped himself to a stiff whiskey. Then he heated some milk, added a goodly amount of spirits, and carried the warm cup upstairs.

Pallid and distraught, Miss Hewitt gulped her warm milk and was soon snoring on her cot just outside her patient's door.

John kneeled at Axy's bedside. He brought her lifeless hand to his lips as he recalled her poem, "The Inspired," in which she had described standing on a mountaintop with her lustrous dark hair "floating in the breeze." He remembered their first meeting on the steamboat near Long Island Sound; she had been as innocent as a young girl then, untouched by the world's evils, with so much radiance and trust in her hazel eyes. He had loved her at once. Certain he would never meet this remarkable woman again, he bade farewell on that little steamboat with great reluctance. He was not ready, now, to say goodbye again. He would never be!

"Please, Guardians! Please don't take my love," he wept.

Shuddering chills rocked her body and her teeth chattered as again she raved about ice hurtling over the rocks, smothering her.

John moved the ice packs slightly away from Axy's head and gently placed her sleeping cap back on her poor, shorn, blood-flecked scalp. Then he tore off his dressing gown and pulled back the quilts to lie at her side. With Axy cradled firmly in his arms he rocked her and murmured, *"This is the Heaven I long have sought, to feel and* *know that thou art nigh...*I will never let you go, *never! Nevermore, my darling!*" and other loving sentiments, soothing her, calming her, warming her with his body, lamenting that he could not bear for her to be so deathly ill. He would pass his own strength on to her, magnetize her, *give anything* if only she would get well enough to quarrel with him once again!

John clasped Axy until morning and her fearsome trembling had ceased. When he heard Miss Hewitt stir he kissed Axy lightly, then dressed and left the room before the nurse was fully awake.

Dr. Goodnight returned to paint Axy's scalp with iodine. She was not as delirious as before, though attempts at conversation resulted in incoherent and imperfect speech. Miss Hewitt was advised, "All her wants must be supplied without waiting for her to express them."

During the remaining weeks of Axy's worst suffering, John would ask Miss Hewitt before he retired if there was anything he could get for her. "I wouldn't mind a cup of that warm milk like you fixed for me before," she would say, inclining her head to one side and shyly glancing away. Then he would join Axy in bed and hold her as Miss Hewitt slept. Slowly Axy became conscious of his presence, but she was much too weak to protest.

"We are truly meant to be together," she whispered in his ear one night, to his astonishment. They conversed softly, so as not to wake Miss Hewitt.

"You must not die!" John declared.

"I do not fear death," she replied faintly. The effort of speaking drained all her strength. "I shall wait for you. I give you my solemn promise."

"I want us to be together in *this* world," John answered, "ask your Guardians for their approval."

"I see that you have not discarded your usual argument," Axy managed a faint smile.

"I rejoice that you are well enough to argue."

For the first time in many weeks, John felt an enormous sense of relief.

From her labyrinth of vague dreams Axy wanted to say that she was now able to act according to her own free will; that her Guardians had set her free. But she lacked the strength to form the words.

Dr. Goodnight felt her disease had reached a "stage of oppression." He claimed that an exudation had taken place from the membranes of the brain, whereby the organ had been compressed. The result could cause impairment of several of the brain's functions and although the pain in her head had decreased and extreme sensitiveness to light, sound and movement had ceased, a paralysis of various parts of the body might occur. If she recovered fully, there was a chance this would gradually disappear, yet some paralysis was apt to persist.

In truth, the physician was somewhat stupefied. In the majority of such cases, death would have occurred in eight to ten days.

John and Axy clandestinely attributed her increasing recovery to a transfer of his magnetism.

With compassionate care and exacting attention, Axy began to gain even further, taking warm broth and then solid foods. Mother forwarded letters to her from friends who inquired about her welfare. Phoebe Hewitt read them aloud to comfort Axy as she lay half asleep although decidedly growing in strength.

It seemed useless to expect a response, yet I wanted Axy to be aware of our concern. Morris and I felt quite alienated, so far away in Wisconsin.

10 November 1861

Dear Sister

I take my pen now to ask why you do not write or get some one to write and let us know how you are. I saw in the Herald in August that you were not able to speak. I supposed you were then suffering from your throat. But Mother wrote in October to say you were sick and similar to your first sickness and since then I have heard nothing!

I would like to hear from you as often as convenient. What restoratives do you resort to, and is your complaint similar to that awful sickness? It seems hard that you must be sick away from home. I have thought perhaps you were with the family you stopped with in Milwaukee and, if so, kindness and the best of care would be yours. Morris and I are well as usual. Please answer soon.

C. S. Steen

By early December, Axy was walking the length of her room, unaided, and bored with Miss Hewitt's uninspired rendition of *Silas Marner.*

Elvira sent several dear little caps of fine, soft wool that she had crocheted in Milwaukee to cover Axy's shorn head. But even after her curls began to grow back Axy refused to leave her chamber, claiming she would frighten the children with the daunting visage she observed one day when, out of extreme curiosity she uncovered a mirror and ventured a peek at herself.

"I think you are beautiful," John told her. "Have I not always said you were beautiful?"

Axy replied, "Have I not called you a blockhead when praising me?"

"I wish I had seen this earlier." He pulled a clipping from a pocket inside his frock coat, "I have here an article from a recent *London Times* which offers a cure for "Clergyman's Sore Throat." He began to read:

> Medical men recommend all public speakers who have a tendency to 'relaxed uvula, clergyman's sore throat,' or 'aphoniaclericoreum,' to let the beard grow under the chin, and I cannot recall any one case of this complaint where this treatment was adopted…

His account was interrupted by the blow of a pillow.

Sarah Crawford, Miss Hewitt, and the Crawford children tried to tempt Axy to join them in the parlor with an honored position by the fire, but there was no budging her from the second floor. George sent word upstairs that she must come down to play Muggins with him. Molly wished to read a new poem she had composed especially for her.

Then Mr. Crawford returned from a business trip to New York City with a specially made pair of spectacles — the right side had a clear glass lens but the left would conceal Axy's bad eye with a lens of smoked glass.

She had become so slight that her dresses no longer fit. Sarah Crawford raised a skeptical eyebrow at Miss Hewitt's romantic notion of an invalid's attire: The heavy silk dressing gown lovingly stitched for her patient was beribboned and dense with flounces of lace. Finally, wearing her unusual spectacles, a wool cap, and a white cashmere gown lined with quilted rose silk over which was drawn a robe of fine embroidered cambric, Axy conceded to wander downstairs for brief periods and eventually joined the family during evenings by the fire.

Everyone knew her health was gaining when she asked to be informed of what was happening in the war.

As Axy's health slowly returned, her yearning to compose new poems became paramount. *Oh take me home!* she wrote in secret:

> *Oh take me home! I cannot bear*
>   *In this strange land to die,*
> *With stranger hands to smooth my brow,*
>   *And close my dying eye…*
>
> *The tones I hear are strangers' tones;—*
>   *Familiar sounds and dear*
> *Seem far away,— so far away*
>   *They cannot reach me here.*

Why, far away from that loved spot,
Dear kindred, did I roam?
I cannot die in this strange land,—
Oh, take me, take me home!

She was easily drained and could not begin to put down the words as swiftly as they appeared to her. Although Phoebe Hewitt was skillful with a needle and thread, she was abysmal as an amanuensis. Axy much preferred working with her old partner. When he could spare the time, John endeavored to commit the lines to paper as rapidly as Axy spoke them.

Exceptionally sustained poems were the result of those intense winter sessions. One of the earliest of her new compositions, "I Still Live, a Poem for the Times," was a moving, didactic piece in pentameter couplets with the subtitle,

To the Brave and Loyal Hearts,
Offering Their Lives at the Shrine of Liberty,
Is this Little Voice For
Freedom Dedicated with the Deepest
Gratitude and
Earnest Prayers of its
Author

The poem referred to Civil War as "a house divided against itself." It was a vigorous denunciation of slavery and oppression that extolled the names of Washington, Adams and Jefferson. She began the pentameter couplets by celebrating Daniel Webster's dying words ("I Still Live"), and applied the statement to the current situation of our ineffectual government and the crisis of civil war, denouncing "a house divided against itself," oppression and slavery.

John thought the poem of such great consequence that he arranged to have it printed as a pamphlet of nineteen pages by Oliphant & Brother, Steam Job Printers in Oswego and sold at the local bookstore.

In January of 1862 she composed "The Poet," a play in verse, featuring the plain, sensible Miss Raymond (an Improvisatrice who strongly resembled Achsa W. Sprague) and two idyllic lovers, Ida Seymour, a beautiful young woman who was striving to be a poet; and Ida's father's friend Henry Bruce, "a man of intellect, travel, and liberal views," clearly based on John Crawford. It was reported by the Crawfords that the 4,600 line piece was completed within three weeks from the time of its commencement. The play began with the Poet proclaiming, "My burning thought leaps up," and closed with Henry Bruce's declaration to Ida,

> *...oh, to think that thou wilt be my bride,*
> *And beam the day-star ever at my side...*
> *That side by side, ay, ever hand in hand,*
> *We'll journey toward the sunny, summer land,*
> *Fills all my soul with such a peace and rest;*
> *For all my wandering, now I'm more than blest.*

The chaste Miss Raymond, however, who had pledged never to marry, claimed she would be happy to open a good place on Oxford Street for "those poor creatures who are sunk in sin, and see if something cannot tempt them in." She promised to improvise for them in song and speak to them of sin and wrong, working with "Mr. Bell," a character never actually introduced in the play but who had known Miss Raymond since she was a child.

Samuel Colt's death in Hartford was reported in the newspapers. He was only forty-seven years old. Prior to the war, Colt had helped the South build up its armory, but now that the war was raging he had become the Union Army's biggest supplier of handguns. His final words, unlike Webster's, were, "It is all over now." Axy, although saddened by this news, entertained her hosts by recounting the colorful details of her introduction to Colt at Semantha Mettler's home seven years ago, and the thwarted séance during which she was unable to clearly concentrate as her hand was held and squeezed by wealthiest bachelor in the United States.

The Northern Transportation Company now had twenty-one propellers shipping goods between Ogdensburgh and Chicago, and John Crawford and partner Philo Chamberlin were currently overseeing the establishment of the New Oswego Line of canal boats that would run between Oswego and New York City. The purchase, involving forty-three boats and over two hundred horses, would ensure their control of the passage of goods from the West all the way to the Atlantic ports.

The Banner of Light mentioned that the public labors of Achsa W. Sprague had been suspended due to disease, but Portland, Maine, undaunted, begged her for two, three or four Sundays the following summer; Lowell, Massachusetts, asked for the first two Sundays in May; and Philadelphia wanted to know if she could lecture for a month between October 1862 and May 1863. A meeting of speakers was scheduled for Boston in mid-June. Her correspondent said she was expected to be at that convention "for certain."

Orvilla wrote in March to say, "I think but what you write to Mother you are with a very kind family, but I should be very glad if you were where I could run in and see you. I hope you will be able to come home as soon as it is warm weather for if you do not come soon I am afraid you will think there is your home."

Sarah Randall said, "You have been sick O so long and such a sufferer I cannot bear to think of it or have it so – but what a blessing that you are where you are. I feel it so at least and I can never be grateful enough to Mr. Crawford's people for doing for you what ought to have been my privilege to have done."

Axy thought she might be strong enough to return to Vermont in March, but bad weather precluded that possibility and she was directed to put it out of her mind.

Publication of "I Still Live" presented its own responsibilities. She mailed copies to friends who might be able to place them in their local bookstores, and the response was encouraging. A. H. Worthen, with whom she stayed in Springfield, Illinois, replied, "I found the little pamphlet you were so kind as to send me, and I can assure you that I was right glad to hear that you were still able to wield the pen in the cause of the true and the right." Friends in Providence were glad to receive the poem if only because they feared she had been unable to read or write. Benjamin Starbuck, who had lost his house, clothing and furnishings to fire (everyone escaped in time) sent two dollars for 50 copies of "I Still Live" to distribute to friends.

When Axy suggested that she might be well enough in April to take the train to Vermont, John insisted that Doctor Goodnight be consulted. The doctor continued to be astonished at Axy's recovery but insisted that she wait for warmer weather, when travel would not be so treacherous. Vermont roads were still very poor.

A tentative accord was reached: Mr. Crawford planned to travel to Rutland in June for a meeting with Vermont railroad officials. At that time, he would guarantee her safe delivery back to Plymouth Notch.

The Great Lakes opened, shipping commenced, and Elvira returned to Oswego. Easter Sunday, April 20, Axy was well enough to join the Crawford family for dinner with Captain and Mary Richardson. The weather did not lend itself to gay spring fashions— dark skies and blustery north winds blew in over Lake Ontario's tempestuous waves, lashing anyone who ventured out of doors with pellets of sleet and freezing rain.

Since last summer, Captain Richardson had been in command of the new propeller, *The Empire*, the most splendid ship in the Northern Transportation Line. Axy had not yet seen it, but Sarah Crawford had sailed to Ogdensburgh on *The Empire* last autumn and claimed it was absolutely elegant.

My sister was yet in a weakened state, but determined. Whenever she left Lakeview (and whenever she left the privacy of her room) she wore her new spectacles or tied a silk scarf over her bad eye. Her equilibrium was uncertain, so when standing she often requested the stability of someone's arm.

Not until after dinner had concluded did talk turn to the recent battle at Shiloh, near Pittsburg Landing, Tennessee. The greatest battle thus far in the war, Shiloh would go down in history recording thirteen thousand casualties for the Union and ten thousand for the South. Axy's thoughts turned to the Memphis cotton farmer and his daughter whom she had met while on the riverboat *Illinois*, and wondered if they or their property had been caught up in the bloodbath.

The men went off to converse, while the women got up a game of whist. Axy, now sleepy, declined to play and sat apart, enjoying their tête-à-tête. Away from her orphans for the day, Sarah Crawford was talkative.

"When I decided to take charge of the Orphan Asylum I felt I had been idle quite as long as I could afford. You know the poet says, 'Satan finds some mischief still for idle hands to do,' and those are my sentiments. I believe I am *less pious* – in thought, at least – when I am underplayed, than when I have plenty to do. My vocation seems to be among children. I believe I am good for nothing else. Do you think that specification will accompany me to the Spirit level, Miss Sprague?"

Axy replied that she believed Miss Crawford was wise to utilize her gifts, as children were the bedrock upon which this world would one day depend, and added that she, herself, had greatly enjoyed her days as a schoolteacher.

During a lull in Miss Crawford's chatter, Axy overheard Captain Richardson in the next room make mention of the wind being from the south. She excused herself on the pretext of needing to retrieve a handkerchief from her reticule, and boldly eavesdropped on the men. One had only to venture away from the fire to realize the wind whistling past the eaves was from the north. She knew the men were discussing the Underground Railroad: code words in their conversation meant fugitive slaves were nearby.

After they returned to Lakeside, Elvira went upstairs to check on Jenny, who had returned from Ogdensburgh suffering from a severe recurrence of consumption. Axy asked John if his ships ever carried fleeing slaves.

"From time to time," he replied. "The Underground Railroad is active here because of Gerrit Smith's support, and my ships frequently sail to Kingston harbor."

This was a side of him she had never suspected. "Mr. Crawford, *you* would take that risk?"

"Several of our captains are sympathizers," he shrugged. "And early spring sees a lot of traffic. There's a saying down south, 'When the sun comes back and the first quail calls...'"

"And if 'the wind blows from the South,' that means there are fugitive slaves in the area?"

"Soon such maneuvers will be unnecessary," he responded, changing the subject. "I'm only doing my small part to see that the blood of our cherished dead will not be shed in vain."

Startled by this disclosure, Axy shivered as though chilled.

"*Soldiers lying upon the battlefield, their foreheads to the sky...*I've had these words echoing in my head all day. I must be writing."

They hastened to John's library, where Axy paced back and forth on the Persian carpet and haltingly dictated "The Soldier's Shroud." She paused to regain her balance whenever dizziness threatened to overwhelm her. John watched over her closely, and copied the words as she spoke:

> *He lay upon the battle-field,*
> *His forehead to the sky,*
> *The death-damp in his matted hair,*
> *And dim his glazing eye;*
> *Embalmed within his own heart's blood*
> *At Freedom's altar shed,*
> *Among the heroes of that strife,*
> *The dying and the dead...*
>
> *He lay upon the battle-field,*
> *No friend nor loved one nigh;*
> *He wrapped his banner round his form,*
> *Most royally to die...*

Elvira looked in upon them and recognized the necessity of not breaking Axy's concentration. She retired to her room.

After the lengthy poem was completed, John read it aloud. It reflected the depth of pain felt upon losing so many valiant young men to battle, and their devotion to Liberty. He suggested a few minor changes, such as swapping "royally" for something else – perhaps *daringly? fearlessly?*

Axy barely heard him. She leaned against the window to gaze at the fierce night. Now accustomed to seeing with only one eye due to the smoked lens of her spectacles, she removed the eyeglasses so she could more fully catch sight of the tumultuous waves as lightning illuminated the scene. The window-glass rattled, buffeted by powerful gusts. She placed her fingers on a pane, to absorb the strength of the storm. She felt enormously drained and extraordinarily sad.

John's footsteps sounded behind her. He would surely catch her if she faltered; had he not been there to support her through her darkest days and nights? She had been helpless as a babe in her illness, yet his love never wavered, even during her most perilous hours.

"This night reminds me of my freezing nightmare," she said, "when I was washed by wild waves."

"That was one of the most frightening nights of my life," John said quietly. "I nearly lost you."

He took her in his arms. "I must be with you. You know your place is by my side. One night, not long after that dreadful dream, you pledged that we were truly meant to be together. This has given me profound pleasure, but I am not a patient man."

"I have promised that I will wait for you."

"I want you with me, *always*, not just in the spirit world! I will not gamble on losing you again!" His voice grew louder and Axy was afraid Elvira might hear.

"You will *not lose me*," she calmly insisted, holding his face in her hands, "You have my promise. I am yours! We will be together in the Summerland!"

She drew him toward her for a reassuring kiss.

"My darling, if only I could be as convinced as you are about the Hereafter," he said as he pulled away. "But even with your guarantee, I lack the equanimity to wait until then. I want to share my life with you *now*, show you the world, converse about fine literature, write music and poems together and sing and travel; I can bestow every luxury upon you. All the good things *in this life* can be ours! Surely your Guardians and mine can agree. I'm convinced it's what they had in mind when we met, our selves are so similar. Surely they will approve!"

Axy turned away only slightly, and took a few hesitant steps. In an emotional and unguarded rush of words she explained that nearly two years ago her Guardians absolved her of all responsibility to them. "*Unto us thy debt is paid*, they said. And since then my Guardians have acted as guides and assistants, but any work I do is of my own free will. I no longer need their permission."

"Then you are free to marry," he reasoned.

"*But you are not!*" She turned back to face him and now *her* voice had risen, underscoring the seriousness of her resolve. "I *cannot* marry you, John! We have discussed this so many times. I have always said I could *never* come between a husband and a wife. And Elvira has shown nothing but kindness toward me."

"Elvira and I have had twenty-seven years together. Five children."

"And grandchildren," Axy reminded him.

John groaned, "And I am nearly fifty. How many more years will I have left? How many years will either of us have? There is no telling. Your illness is proof . What if I had lost you? Everything is so uncertain, with this diabolical war and our economic plight! Whatever time I have, I want to spend it with you."

Never had she supposed that he might divorce his wife. Elvira had been so considerate throughout her illness; imagine the shame that good woman would have to endure with such disgrace. And Axy would gain notoriety for having brought even more dishonor upon this family — all her years of public efforts for reform and other beneficial causes, the conviction of her Guardians, her Spiritualist friends — she would be shunned by everyone (think of Amanda Butt!) — all her labors would be judged by this bold action. *Free Lust*!

No, she could not marry him. She loved this man, that truth she could not deny. She could not imagine ever loving anyone more. But she would sacrifice her love, or wait until Eternity. *Three lives* would be placed in jeopardy if she agreed to his request.

"If you truly loved," she began, then groped clumsily for balance. She feared she would faint with the effort of what she must affirm, and her good eye was blind with tears.

"Surely you know how wretched this makes me."

Axy, who seldom cried, was now weeping profusely.

"Once again I must ask, If you truly do love me, John, would you not rather that I escape such unyielding anguish even though your spirit may be inconsolable?"

John placed a clean handkerchief from the pocket of his waistcoat in her hand. "How can I convince you that I love you, here and now, with all my heart!"

"True love is void of self! It seeks another's happiness before its own," she whispered hoarsely.

John would have continued the discussion, but for an insistent knock at the front door. It was an agent from Philo Chamberlin with an urgent message.

"The Bay State," Axy heard, "all hands gone..."

"This is not the end of our debate," he told her, returning briefly to give her forehead a hurried but tender good night kiss. "An emergency has arisen. Sleep on what we have said, and may kind angels bring you soothing dreams..."

Elvira informed her the next morning that *The Bay State*, under Captain Marshall, had foundered off Oswego on her way to Lake Erie and gone down during the gales of the night before. "A man from Vermont was in the cabin, and a woman and a little child," Elvira added sadly, "and four passengers in steerage." Officers and crew, sixteen in all, had also drowned. Mr. Crawford would be away for several days, as there was much business to be settled when a ship with travelers and merchandise experienced a tragic end.

Ironically, the day had dawned sunny and calm. Axy wrapped a woolen shawl around her shoulders, tied a scarf around her eye, and went for a faltering stroll along the lake. Wreckage was already washing up on shore. Debris rocked in the waves, as if comforted by the pulsing motion. She was disturbed to note that residents of Oswego were eagerly gathering merchandise and other items from the wreckage and loading them in carts, but when she came upon the remains of a China doll, she fell to her knees to retrieve it.

The Bay State had carried her to Sackett's Harbor with the Oswego Spiritualists, and she held fond memories of that joyous excursion.

She must leave this place before she left only ruin behind.

That afternoon while Elvira was out, Axy packed her things. She paid the Irish stable boy, James McDonnall, to smuggle her trunks out to the carriage barn and have them at the ready for her stealthy departure the next morning at dawn.

After dinner she finished a poem she had been writing for Elvira, "Ye Have Done It Unto Me."

Then she sat at the desk in her bedchamber to begin one last letter:

You asked me never again to speak to you of remuneration for my long stay this winter. I have <u>done</u> as you <u>wished</u>. I have not <u>spoken</u>.

⇥ 20 ⇤

Like Some Bright Evening Star

(April–July 1862)

There are but few such souls; they cannot tread
The path that others mark; their course seems led
By some strange destiny to earth unknown;
Like some bright evening star they stand alone.

The Poet, p. 186
Achsa W. Sprague

HER TRIP FROM OSWEGO WAS ARDUOUS, and because Axy had not made preparations in advance it involved tiresome delays at railroad depots while connections were arranged. By the time she reached the Notch she very nearly tumbled from the stagecoach and started up the hill with no thought for her trunks, which were being unloaded.

Brief refuge was sought in the comfort of the Notch church for what she intended would be only a moment, then she slumped in a box pew like a bored parishioner. A tan mutt that had trailed her eventually began to whimper. She awoke and discovered Amos Butler standing beside the dog.

"Miss Axy, your trunks're outside," he said shyly. The young man stammered and blushed like the backward schoolboy who'd squirmed in her classroom over a decade ago. "I got your trunks," he repeated, "they said at the store you was here."

Amos expressed no reaction to her peculiar appearance. She repositioned her spectacles, placed the heavy veil and bonnet over her soft dark curls, and took care to arrange her velvet cloak over her shoulders. Getting to her feet, however, seemed to be an insurmountable task, as her swollen ankles had turned to lead. She fumbled for Amos's arm.

He helped her to the church door where, with a sinking heart, she saw that he indeed had her trunks. Her belongings were piled in his cart and the cart was harnessed to the red spotted heifer that Amos had trained to drive like a horse.

So the final lap of her arduous journey was completed in this slow, plodding manner, over a deeply rutted road that caused gobs of mud and muck to be propelled from the rear of the cart with each revolution of the wheels in rude-sounding splats.

If only John Crawford could see her now; he would find this scene immensely entertaining. She pictured his usual gusto, head thrown back, his deep laugh, merry dark eyes, black beard, gold watch chain looped from his waistcoat pocket swinging as he guffawed. The vision of his amusement was so real that she had to shake her head to dismiss the image and expunge the lines she was composing to compare the irony of escaping Lakeside View yesterday morning behind Bobb and Charlie with this ignominious arrival at the Notch courtesy of Amos Butler's red-spotted cow.

Still dazed, she did not realize how lifeless the farmhouse appeared at their approach. She even overlooked the pain in her legs as Amos brought the cart to a stop. Home again!

> *Weary wanderer, sad and lonely,*
> *We will bear thee to thy home.*

She removed her bonnet with a smile of greeting that quickly faded as she made her way to the front door. The darkened rooms smelled damp and echoed suspiciously of abandonment. Ashes in the cookstove were dead cold.

Axy investigated the remaining rooms and called out for Mother with a note of increasing dismay. Amos deposited her trunks in the parlor, set her valise on top, and left without a word.

She made her way out to the barn, the chicken coop, and the dairy, but even the cow was gone; an inauspicious omen. She had come all this way to find no exclamations of joy from her mother, no wild grin from Malvina, no welcoming embrace to pull her back into the fold.

The bonnet and veil in her tortured hands were wrung shapeless with exasperation. She threw the disguise at the kitchen wall with a wail of despair.

At least a few pieces of kindling remained in the woodbox. She lit a fire in the cookstove to take off the chill. How quaint the kitchen seemed, after such a lengthy absence: Near the sink, a rack of linen towels her mother had woven, some slightly stained; dented pots and pans she knew by heart; oil lamps with sooty chimneys; the cracked butter churn; Malvina's stitched sampler of ABCs still hanging, crooked, on the plaster wall.

Kindling snapped and caught while Axy pulled her velvet cloak to her throat.

Amos Butler opened the front door again and held out a plump loaf of crusty bread, a round of cheese, and a small crock of butter.

"Mrs. Coolidge says your ma's gone calling."

Axy sent a silent blessing upon their kind neighbor, Aunt Mede.

"Up to Woodstock."

"Thank you, Amos."

"Malvina's with Thomas Moore and the Coolidges got your cow."

For his kindness, Axy reached into her valise and gave Amos a copy of the pamphlet, *I Still Live*. He would probably not be able to read a word of it, but she had nothing else to offer.

In years past she had often found the lack of anonymity in the small hamlet exasperating, but today Axy was relieved that her arrival had not escaped notice. Mrs. Coolidge would see that word was sent to Mother. Aunt Mede was a saint.

Her bedroom had been kept exactly as it was when Axy left for Oswego last summer. The paintings on the walls had been done in Philadelphia when she studied Grecian art. Little mementos given to her by devoted followers throughout her travels were carefully arranged on a curio shelf along with a collection of stones she had collected from the Mississippi River, Atlantic Ocean, and the shores of various Great Lakes. Leaves from the now-vanished Charter Oak peeked out from between the pages of a book.

Her books! Her precious books: *Lallah Rookh*, the poems of Lydia Sigourney, Poe and Longfellow, *Leaves of Grass*, *Jane Eyre*, *Wuthering Heights*. In a separate bookcase were *David Copperfield*, *Miles Standish*, *The Household Book of Poetry*, *Hiawatha*, and others that John Crawford had purchased especially for her.

She could hear the teakettle whistling in the kitchen, but curiosity drove her to rummage for her diaries. Twelve years ago today she had written:

> *Wednesday, April 24, 1850: What a strange thing is life! To one it lifts the cup of happiness filled to the brim, which they may drink and know no sorrow; to another it is ushered in amid storm clouds, and gives but bitterness and anguish to the desolate hearts as if it mocked their yearnings for happiness.*

That had been an almost prescient entry: *What a strange thing is life*, indeed. Since then she had known more than her share of astonishing happiness and unfathomable despair.

> *She comes once more to visit*
> *Her early girlhood's home,*
> *And once again to listen*
> *To soft affection's tone.*
>
> *But where are they—the loved ones,*
> *For which her spirit craves?*
> *Oh, some are scattered far away,*
> *And some sleep in their graves.*
> *No father's voice shall greet her,*
> *No brother's tender tone,*
> *The green grass waves above them,*
> *And she is all alone.*

Of course Mother was shaken by Axy's appearance when she returned. She brought warm greetings from Sarah and a promise to call with her babe as soon as Axy was strong enough for visitors. Malvina and her cat, Moses, came home from Uncle Thomas Moore's. Although the weather was now pleasant, mounds of snow waned in the shadows and mud tracked everywhere.

Initially, it seemed that Axy prospered under Mother's care. Friends and relatives celebrated her return to the mountains. Delia Pollard wrote, "I hoped you would come fully restored to health, and with leisure enough on your hands to make me a long visit; but I hear that you are far from well and my wishes are that you may immediately recover."

Writing furiously during almost every waking moment, new poems of Axy's had been accepted for publication by *The Banner of Light*.

Her longest poem, "The Mountains," consisted of 155 lines, and fulfilled her desire to pay homage to the natural setting she so loved.

> *Teach me, sublime old mount,*
> *To stand like thee, defying clouds and storms,*
> *And wrap the snow-white mantle of a calm*
> *And holy resignation round my soul,*
> *When sorrow's dreary winter-time shall come!*
> *And when 'tis past, like thee reclothe myself*
> *In life's fresh verdure, till the hour shall come*
> *To be reclothed in Higher Worlds, in robes*
> *That young immortals wear, to lose their light*
> *No more forever.*

The poem was completed on May 24, 1862.

The Banner also accepted an article she wrote about her illness in Oswego and incorporated a perfected revision of the poem she wrote there, "Nevermore and Evermore," with Axy's explanation that the poem was given to her "A few days after I commenced my recitations… embodying that peculiar state or phase of mind more nearly than words of mine can. Doubtless some who read it may recognize their own feelings, though given in the words of another."

She knew the Crawfords would see the piece about her stay in Oswego, and witness her public acknowledgment of gratitude for their care. Never far from her mind was the fact that Mr. C. had often expressed a desire to visit her home. He would have, if she had consented to wait and accompany him on his visit to Rutland in June. When she sat in the dooryard encircled by her cherished Green Mountains, she imagined him sitting next to her. She could have shown him the little schoolhouse, walked the mountain trails...

Like everyone else, she closely followed the progress of the war: the sinking of the *Merrimack* by the Confederates on May 11; the Battle of Winchester later that month, when Stonewall Jackson's Confederate troops defeated the Union soldiers in Virginia. The bloodshed unnerved her. She composed yet more poems, articles, and letters to express her profound anguish. She could not sit idle.

On the tenth of June she wrote to a friend that her health was decidedly better. She was much engaged with her writing, she said, which rested her, and it was an enjoyable pastime. In fact, she continued to write even though her physical strength seemed to wane, sometimes completing five hundred lines per day.

That Axy was "decidedly better" was an obvious falsehood to all who saw my sister, and the restless euphoria did little to mask her weakening condition. She had been emaciated upon her arrival at the Notch; now the frailty of her frame and her fanatical obsession were such that Mother dispatched the urgent telegram alerting me to *come home*. Axy seemed impelled by an irresistible power, an "inflamed intellectualism" that some claimed was scarcely less than madness for her to attempt when her health had been so reduced.

It must surely have seemed like madness when, toward the end of June, Axy asked Uncle Thomas to drive her to Rutland in his carriage, twenty miles over mountain roads. Uncle Thomas had been mowing and raking hay. The weather had been clear with no rain for a week, but there was very little he could do for his niece these days. She asked little from him and was so sick.

Mother, who was in the midst of making soap, tried in vain to discourage my stubborn sister. "If you won't stay at home, then I will have no choice but to go along," she told Axy. They left at dawn and arrived at Rutland late in the day.

Axy had not revealed that this was the day John Crawford would be meeting with directors of the Rutland & Washington Railroad, which extended from Ogdensburgh, New York, to Burlington, Vermont. Crawford and Chamberlin leased some of their vessels to the Rutland line. The reason given for her urgent trip was Axy's delivery of *I Still Live* pamphlets to Tuttle's Book Shop, where they would be offered for sale.

Concerned about her daughter's irrational behavior and frail condition, Mother wished to find accommodations as soon as they arrived at Rutland. Axy insisted on stopping at Tuttle's first. She wore the spectacles she had been given in Oswego and the black mourning bonnet to conceal her bad eye.

Not far from Tuttle's was the hotel where Crawford and Chamberlin would be staying. When she completed her business at the book shop, Axy directed Uncle Thomas to drive them there. Mother and Uncle Thomas waited in the carriage while Axy went inside. At the front desk she asked, breathless with the effort, for Mr. John H. Crawford.

"Mr. Crawford is not registered," she was told. But Mr. Philo Chamberlin was.

Axy was too lightheaded to determine if she felt relief or dismay.

"Would you please ask Mr. Chamberlin to deliver a message for me?" she asked.

"And you are....?" the clerk responded.

"I am Miss Sprague. Achsa W. Sprague"

"One moment please, Miss Sprague."

It happened that an envelope had been left there, addressed to her. A pale blue envelope.

Certain she would fall in a faint, Axy clutched at the desk to steady herself. The clerk helped her to a leather settee in the hotel's lobby, where she gripped the unopened envelope for several minutes, oblivious of Mother and Uncle Thomas who were waiting to hear if she had been able to secure two rooms.

John Crawford's handwriting warmed her more than the flush of fever on her brow. Inside the envelope was a poem on his blue stationery:

My Last Night's Dream

'Tis midnight, darkest midnight now,
Deep gloom o'erspreads the land and Sea.
But deeper gloom rests on my brow—
'Tis more than midnight now to me.

Thick clouds like solemn funeral pall
Hang o'er the heavens their midnight scroll,
But darker shadows round me fall.
A pall more black enshrouds my soul.

The pattering drops of summer rain
Are falling from the weeping skies.
But tear-drops, *extacies of pain*—
Flow freer from my streaming eyes.

The howling winds with notes of woe
Now come in waves—like waves depart.
But gales more fearful wildly blow
In waves of anguish through my heart.

The tempest howls, the angry sea
Upheaving piles the shore with waves.
But waves more awful roll o'er me.
A fierce tempest o'er me raves.

Thou'rt "*angry with me*," and hast spoke
These words that thrilled through every vein.
"*Thy life is false.*" Then I awoke
From dream of bliss to hell of pain.

These words of thine have pierced my heart
With javelins, sharp as lightning's gleams;
Their wounds like stings of adders smart,
While darts my blood in firey streams.

But as it flows like driving rain,
Or mountain torrent to the Sea,
I staunch and drink it in again
To feed this sea of agony.

No prayer of mine—no wail of grief
Can reach the Almighty's sacred Throne,
No hand but thine can bring relief,
Thine, dearest Xadie—thine alone.

If thou my inmost heart could know,
Or read its page of history;
If 'twould to thee its feelings show,
This agony were bliss to me.

If aught be false in my life's past
'Tis fault of fancy,—the ideal.
But airy fancy finds at last
In thee my Idol—thee, my Real.

Then grant, Oh! Grant this dreaming prayer,
While on my midnight couch I lie.—
Believe me earnest and sincere.
Believe me Xadie.—lest I die.

"*Xadie.*" The name mystified her. Who was "Xadie?" She read the poem again. And again, noting every clue.

"Lest I die" was underlined.

If one removed the letters "d-i-e" from "Xadie," it spelled "Xa," or Achsa. How typical of her Evil Genius to construct a word puzzle for her amusement.

She knew she was sobbing because she was weak and sick, but why this feeling of fullness overflowing in her heart?

He still bore strong feelings of love. Indeed, even now his feelings for her were true, *earnest and sincere.*

Mother was concerned with her daughter's agitation during the remainder of their trip. Axy's mind was swarming with thoughts, words she must write, actions she must take. Time was running out.

It was not until Uncle Thomas's carriage was approaching the Notch the next evening that my sister realized she had not left a message at the hotel for Mr. Crawford after all.

It was just as well.

What could she have said that she had not already told him?

What could she have told him that he did not already know?

And the following day, I arrived.

I have related what occurred upon my entrance—my shock at the spectre that was my sister, her desperate clutch of my arm, the unsteady stroll to the church, her disturbing confession.

She lay feverish and strangely subdued the next day, and many days thereafter. We had only a few weeks.

The lingering hours spent by my sister's bedside at the Notch were mostly hushed, as she could go outdoors only at twilight and rarely felt strong enough to sit by the window (with curtains drawn due to her bad eye). In moments of her near lucidity, I was able to acquire the account I have described—with the addition of details from others' correspondence and writings she'd copied for safekeeping. On especially "good" days, she was able to sit up and share anecdotes. If her mind was truly agile, we took pleasure in a rare opportunity to converse. She liked to hear the messages that wished her well as I read them aloud once more.

Benjamin Starbuck had written in February, saying that Mr. Crawford had contacted him from Oswego regarding her illness and "some good spirit whispers to my inner consciousness, 'write to her, tell her she is dear to you, and to many others here in Troy…and whose hearts will unite in one prayer, that she may soon be restored to health.'"

Each day when I returned from the general store, Axy turned to ask me if the mail held a pale blue envelope. Sadly, my response was always in the negative.

Her final decline was swift. At times she imagined she was in Oswego and cried out for the sea. Malvina placed her cat Moses on Axy's pillow when she said his loud purr drowned the crashing of the waves.

The usual patriotic music floated up the hill from our rag-tag band on the Fourth of July: "Battle Hymn of the Republic," "Better Days are Coming," and "I'll be a Soldier." The familiar strains of "Beautiful Dreamer" caused a slight smile to cross Axy's haggard face: For the first time she was not agitated by the rejoicing of the crowd, the shots of the controversial canon or explosions of fireworks. *Independence Day*, The Glorious Fourth. How she had raged about "independence" years ago, yearning to be freed from the prison of her infirmity. Now we all knew she would soon achieve her true *independence.*

On Sunday, July 6, I was kneeling by her side, holding her hand, and Oh! the grasp she gave my own I shall never forget. I said, "Axy, you will not leave us now, will you?" A faint "no," was her reply, which were all the words that fell from her lips upon my ear.

She held my hand until her strength was gone, and then as I laid her back upon the bed the beating of her heart could plainly be heard in the room until the spirit had taken its flight. She had dwelt in her mortal body thirty-four years, seven months, and nineteen days.

"Her death seems untimely," Axy's friends lamented afterward, and many found it hard to acquiesce in an event that removed one so young, so active, and so anxious to do good, while the world needed her. This feeling was heightened by the impression that she needlessly overworked herself and did not prudently husband her strength. They claimed she used up life too rapidly, in violation of physiological law.

APOTHEOSIS

"Death is but a kind and welcome servant who unlocks with noiseless hand life's flower-encircled door to show us those we love."

Departure of Miss A. W. Sprague:

Our sister, Miss A. W. Sprague, is no more—no more in the external, sensuous Form—but her blessed spirit, that has just passed beyond the confines of mortality, to expand and grow more wholly in spirit-life, will, we are confident, return to us bearing many blossoms of affection, to guide and direct us in our pilgrimage here; will return with greater power than she possessed when clad with the "flesh of bondage," to reassure us in our beautiful faith, and bid us persevere until the end.

Miss Sprague was a pioneer in teaching the Spiritual Philosophy in her native State, and though meeting the usual opposition from existing religious organizations her influence as a public speaker was remarkable. Always deeply in earnest, elegant and forcible in her style of speaking, equally removed from extravagance on the one hand and tameness on the other, she rose not unfrequently to a chaste and noble eloquence.

She spoke habitually on highest themes, with a scope and vigor of thought and fertility of illustration rarely equaled. In those localities where she was best known, she was prized most, and there her loss will be keenest felt. Hundreds of personal friends in New England, New York, and the West, besides the large congregations she was wont to gather in Boston, Portland, Providence, Philadelphia, Oswego, and in a multitude of other cities and towns in 15 states of the Union, will learn with regret of one whose persuasive words have often called them to a glorious emulation of a true life.

In Vermont she will be sadly missed. Her influence upon that community has been deeper than that of any other mind for a long time. Multitudes who never accepted spiritual intercourse as a fact, were wont to listen to her with unaffected delight. Wherever she went, even in the most sparsely populated districts, she was sure of overflowing houses. It was common to see people at her meetings who had come eight, ten, even fifteen miles to hear "the preaching woman," and thought themselves well paid at that. Indeed, all who ever heard her, loved her. She was eloquent to every feeling soul. She had the elements of a mother's kindness, of a child's innocence, and of a philosopher's logic, blended most happily. No one who had feeling, sympathy, and love, developed, could listen to her without dropping a tear of real Heavenly love, for she always breathed forth the unadulterated affection of the Heavenly world. May God add blessings still to her noble soul, that she may continue to shower them upon humanity.

The Banner of Light
July 26, 1862

I returned to Oakfield and my dear Morris, a week after my sister's funeral. One day, perhaps, my sister's story will be brought to light and my long-sought mission will be complete.

Celia Sprague Steen

⊰ AFTERWORD ⊱

Bury me, friends, where the flowers shall wave
In the early spring, above my grave!
...While the whispers aloft in the leafy tree,
Shall all seem voices that come from me.

From *The Poet and Other Poems*
ACHSA SPRAGUE

ACCORDING TO AN ACCOUNT in the *Banner of Light,* Achsa's "widowed mother, with martyr-patience and calmness, clasped her daughter's dying hands in her own, and only breathed forth, 'Oh, that this cup could have passed me by.'" A friend and fellow medium from nearby Bridgewater, Melvina S. Townsend, officiated at Achsa's funeral, and she was buried in the Plymouth Notch graveyard. The Rev. Mr. Osgood contributed prayers and A. E. Simmons of Woodstock made appropriate remarks. A year later, a blue marble tombstone was placed on Achsa's grave, engraved with these words:

Achsa W. Sprague
Went Home July 6, 1862.
Aged 34 years.
"I Still Live."

On May 2, 1863, *The Banner of Light* published a letter from Melvina Townsend that related the occasion of Achsa's death as it transpired.

Dear Friends of our Angel Sister, Miss A. W. Sprague.

A few words from my pen concerning her and circumstances connected with her and myself may not fail to interest you... an attachment of more than ordinary friendship existed between Dear Angel Achsa and myself. We were always together when we could be, and conversed a great deal upon the subjects connected with our mission. We talked of the cross so much interesting the religious world, and came to the conclusion that *our* cross should be humbly bearing the scorn and criticism of those who could not understand us in our pursuance of truth, right and justice. Nearly eight years had passed since she commenced her angel ministrations when we again met… [and] we made an agreement that whichever of us should go first, should receive the services of the other at the funeral… On Sunday the sixth, Miss Sprague's uncle came for my husband's mother to go and watch with her that night, and I attended her. We had not been in the house an hour, ere the messenger appeared to claim her for the higher home… As she lay in her last moments I saw her angel father and brother standing near her, and three little angel pets floating above her, throwing flowers upon her. It was her request that I should perform the sad office at her funeral. It was also her dear mother's request. And although my own poor heart was almost bursting with grief at her loss from my side… I could not refuse, nor did I wish to, if angels had the power to sustain me through such a trial, which they did, in their own blessed way. And we laid the treasured casket, that had contained such a priceless jewel, beside the parent gone before. 'Tis a dear spot, the grave of Achsa! And my tears will fall upon the flowers when I go there as they do now while I write these lines for your perusal.

M. S. Townsend

Her poems were gathered and published as *The Poet and Other Poems* in 1864 by William White and Company, Boston. Demand for the book was so great that a second edition was printed almost immediately. The copyright is under the name of Achsa's mother, Betsey Sprague. John H. Crawford contributed poems of which her family was previously unaware.

A lengthy biographical introduction to the book was composed by Merritt E. Goddard, who edited the collection. Goddard, then representing the town of Reading in the Vermont legislature, was in theology school when he attended Achsa's first public lecture in South Reading in 1854.

Two-thirds of the poems in *The Poet* comprise a Victorian play that pitches a passionate battle between organized "orthodox" religion and a more transcendent concept posed by the Improvisatrice, Miss Raymond. Many of the lines bear traces of the quarrels and "combat" between Crawford and Achsa. The poem for Elvira Crawford that Achsa left behind at Lakeside View is also included:

"YE HAVE DONE IT UNTO ME"*

When thou hast heard the heart's lone prayer,
Low-uttered in its deep despair,
When sorrow called, and not in vain,
When thou hast sought the couch of pain,
To cheer the sufferer's aching eye,
And speak of hope, if they must die,—
Then angels bent to watch o'er thee,
Saying, "Ye have done it unto me."

When hearts are tempted unto sin—
If thou dost speak, their souls to win
From that dark midnight gulf of pain,
Making them strong and true again;
When wildly by the storms they're driven,
If thou a purpose high hast given,—
Then angels bend and watch o'er thee,
Saying, "Ye have done it unto me."

When thou doest firmly, strongly stand,
With earnest purpose in thy hand,
Though known, or though misunderstood,
Still striving bravely for the good,
Ready the power of truth to claim,
Though others put it unto shame,—
Then angels bend and watch o'er thee,
Saying, "Ye have done it unto me."

When to thy heart and to thy home,
Thy words have bid the wanderer come,
And watched with earnest, heart-felt prayer,
And with a mother's tender care;
When long-enduring, working long,
Through weary months, in purpose strong,—
Then angels bend and watch o'er thee,
Saying, "Ye have done it unto me."

When life's dark shores are left behind,
And Heaven's bright portals thou shalt find,
The angels in their blest estate,
Shall open wide the golden gate;
And friends, and light, and joy, be given,
And all-enduring love in heaven;—
Then God shall bend and watch o'er thee,
Saying, "Ye have done it unto me."

*Dedicated to Mrs. E. R. Crawford

Celia and her husband, John Morrison Steen, continued to live on their Wisconsin farm near Oakfield until her death on May 10, 1867, only a week after her thirty-seventh birthday. Her grave in the nearby Avoca Cemetery is marked simply CELIA, with this line from *Les Miserables*: "Kiss me on the forehead when I am dead and I shall feel it."

Her husband's grave lies adjacent to hers. Morris eventually remarried, but his life came to a sad conclusion on February 12, 1885, at the age of fifty-nine. As reported in the *Fond du Lac Daily Commonwealth*:

MORTALITY'S COIL: It Became Burdensome to John Morrison Steen, and He Shuffled it Off

John M. Steen, a prominent resident of Oakfield, committed suicide last night by drowning himself in the well on his premises. His family knew nothing of it until 6 o'clock this morning, when a letter written by him was found on the table addressed to his nephew, Joseph Steen, relating where his body would be found, and that a grub hook in the granary would be a proper instrument to use in removing it from the well. The horrified members of the family went at once to the residence of the nephew about a quarter of a mile distant, with the letter. Joseph Steen, with another gentleman repaired to the scene of the suicide and removed the body from the well. There was no apparent cause for John M. Steen's voluntary farewell to life. His finances were in a satisfactory condition, and his family relationships were pleasant. His occupation was that of a farmer. He was a member of the Masonic order in Oakfield and in Fond du Lac and was aged about fifty years. The funeral will be held tomorrow, with interment at the Oakfield cemetery.

John H. Crawford saw his fortunes falter soon after Achsa's death. On January 15, 1863, his beloved daughter Jenny, only twenty-two, perished from consumption. Lakeside View, the Gothic Revival cottage the Crawfords were renting at West Lake and Eighth Street, was sold in 1863 and renamed Whitney Cottage. An 1865 census shows him living in the center of Oswego with his wife Elvira, their youngest children, John's elderly sister Sarah, and two servants. That year, the Northern Transportation Company suffered great losses. By then, in addition to their propellers, Crawford and Chamberlin had purchased 43 canal boats and barges and 200 horses to work between Oswego and New York City: The New Oswego Line.

Crawford eventually sold his interest in canal boats, barges, and horses and moved his family to Buffalo, New York. Only a short time later he relocated to Chicago where, for a number of years, he contracted for piers and dredging. Just before the Great Fire of 1871 the Crawford family left Chicago for "pine lands" near Glen Haven, Michigan, where John had purchased land, engaged in the manufacture of lumber and shingles, and managed a large general store. Glen Haven, conveniently located on the Lake Michigan shoreline, supplied 25% of the fuel for the Northern Transportation Company, which by then had a twenty-four-vessel fleet.

According to maritime history, the Northern Transportation line "reached its meridian in 1872." But old-time seafaring men maintained that a "spirit of disaster" hovered over the company, as all of the ships eventually succumbed in a tragic manner. For example, *The Jefferson* was condemned in 1863; in that same year *The Young America* was lost. In 1867 the propeller *Wisconsin* burned at Grenadier Island, near Kingston, Ontario—thirty lives were lost and fifty saved. In 1881, *The Granite State* sank in Lake Michigan near Door County, Wisconsin. Many of the ships were eventually cut down to serve as steam barges in the lumber trade.

It must have been disheartening for him to live so far inland after his deep love for the Great Lakes, but in 1873, due to an unknown reason, Crawford left Michigan for wheat country west of Rochester, Minnesota. There he purchased the Dodge County

Stone Mill at Wasioja, on the south branch of the middle fork of the Zumbro River. The custom and merchant mill, powered by water and steam, had two 40-horsepower turbines and produced six thousand barrels of flour per year. Daughter Lizzy, then Mrs. W. E. Brown, lived nearby in Cheney, Minnesota, which may have influenced the move. A history of the area says he was very active and admired in the community.

On February 6, 1884, John H. Crawford died after only a short illness, described in his obituary as "nervous prostration and general debility." He was seventy years old. The *Detroit Post and Tribune* called Crawford "well known among shipping men on the lakes, having been actively engaged in the propeller and canal business for over 20 years."

Funeral services were held the next day, February 7. Despite heavy snow and drifted roads, a large attendance was noted. He was buried in the Wildwood Cemetery, Wasioja. According to friends, Crawford was a Republican, was "liberal in religious views," and had been married for fifty years. Survivors included Elvira (who would live until 1901), daughters Julia, Lizzie and Molly, and his son, George Lindsey Crawford.

After John H. Crawford left Oswego he continued to correspond with his friend David H. Judson, who owned a dry dock there. A decade before his death, upon moving to Minnesota, Crawford sent Judson a poem in which he reflected on his life:

> . . . I caught a gleam
> Of light from out hope's youthful beam,
> But soon it hid away from me
> Like golden sunset in the sea:
> 'Twas but a dream ~
>
> I launched my bark
> On proud ambition's boisterous sea,
> Whose foaming waves dashed angrily—
> Then all was dark.

John H. Crawford: b. Ontario County, New York, 1813; d. Wasioja, Minnesota, 1884. Ten years before his death he composed a poem that included these stanzas:

> I caught a gleam
> Of light from out hope's youthful beam,
> But soon it hid away from me
> Like golden sunset in the sea...
> Whose foaming waves dashed angrily—
> Then all was dark.

The cold world's frown
Bereft of riches, fame, renown,
Fell on me with its with'ring blast,
Its stony fingers clutched me fast
And held me down.

. . . And will no ray
Of light or hope beyond the tomb
Come to dispel its damp and gloom?
No brighter day

Dispel the night?
Comes there no answer to my prayer
That I may meet my loved one there
In realms of light?

O, love divine!
Let the sweet trust that thou art mine
Sustain and comfort till the last
Of fear and disappointment's past—
Beyond the line.
J. H. C.

—From the *Oswego Palladium*,
reprinted in *Mantorville Express*, February 15, 1884

Until the very end, it seems that John Crawford was thinking of his love for Axy. His hope may have been sustained by her poem, "Hark to the Waves That Roll":

O weary waves, find rest!
In regions of the blest
Must they live sublime.
O soul, be strong! thou'lt meet
The loved in their retreat,
Far beyond all time.

Back in Oswego, the four-story stone structure built in 1828 on the corner of Water and Seneca Streets and used by "Crawford and Co." is still standing today. It is one of the only original buildings on the waterfront.

The Spiritual Harp, a popular Spiritualist hymnal published in 1868, contains at least six hymns co-written by Achsa Sprague and John Crawford. Particularly poignant is "Lock of Hair," attributed singly to Crawford:

> *The sunny spirit passed from sight*
> *The eyes that shed love-beams*
> *Though closed to earth in starry night,*
> *Shone down from land of dreams;*
> *Amid the melting, holy calm,*
> *Removed with tender care,*
> *Suffusing it with tearful balm,*
> *I clipped a lock of hair…*
>
> *Unbroken shall this tie remain,*
> *Though from its owner riven,*
> *Enwoven into ringlet chain*
> *That draws me up to heaven.*

Hymns of Progress (1884), recently reprinted, contains several more examples of the joyous "combat" engaged in by the duo. The hymnal is still used today in Spiritualist churches, and the lines may have been altered to mute their passion and correspond with the principles of the church.

In his letter of February 3, 1859, Crawford told Axy that "some Spirit" had sent him words and music, and he guessed who it was from. He promised to revise the arrangement and write the song for her. The result of their mutual composition appeared as "The Heart's Dream" (see page 430).

LOCK OF HAIR.

1. The sun - ny spir - it passed from sight, The eyes that shed love - beams,

Though closed to earth in star - ry night, Shone down from land of dreams;

A - mid the melt - ing, ho - ly calm, Re - moved with ten - der care,

Suf - fus - ing it with tear - ful balm, I clipped a lock of hair.

"Lock of Hair," p. 151, *The Spiritual Harp: A Collection of Vocal Music for the Choir, Congregation and Social Circle.* Words and composed by J. H. Crawford, "Amid the melting, holy calm / Removed with tender care, / Suffusing it with tearful balm, / I clipped a lock of hair." This is especially poignant, since the hymnal was published after Achsa's death.

Alternate lyrics by A. W. Sprague, "Night Vigils": "Sweet Peace, descend with noiseless wing, / And through the night in sweetness sing / And soothe to quiet rest."

The Heart's Dream

While on my night couch sleeping,
While stars are vigils keeping,
And night winds moan along the sky,
In shadows dim before me,
Or softly bending o'er me,
An angel form seems hovering nigh.
An angel form seems hovering nigh.

In *The Spiritual Harp* the shared effort is attributed only to A. W. Sprague and is sung like this; Crawford's music remains the same:

Mother's Dream

While on my lone couch sleeping,
In dreams sweet vigils keeping,
And night winds moan along the sky;
In shadows dim before me,
Now lowly bending o'er me,
An airy form seems hov'ring nigh,
A form seems hov'ring nigh.

The final verse still echoes the evidence of their eternal love:

Now softly she is going,
One tender look bestowing,
Now vanished o'er the purple sea;
No longer am I only
Sad, desolate, and lonely;
My darling lives and comes to me,
My darling comes to me.

Light	C. M.		61
Life	L. M. D.		86
Live them down			114
Liberty	C. M. D.	A. W. Trask	137
Lock of Hair	C. M. D.	J. H. Crawford	151
Love	8s & 7s, D.	E. T. Blackmer	100
Love on	10s.	Y. A. Leib	49
Make home	8s & 7s, D.		97
Mansions	8s, 6s, 8s, 8s & 6s.		127
Mason	L. M.	Dr. L. Mason	134
Media	S. M.	M. M. B.	243
Morning Light	L. M., 101		45
Mother's Dream	7s & 8s.	J. H. Crawford	51
Morn amid the Mountains			72
My Home in the Spirit-		S. W. T.	179

GRACE NOTES

The papers of Achsa W. Sprague (1827-1862) archived at the Vermont Historical Society (VHS), Barre, Vermont, are used with their permission. The bulk of the papers are from 1852-1861 and deal primarily with that period of Sprague's life devoted to travel and lectures as a Spiritualist trance-medium. *Selections from Achsa W. Sprague's Diary and Journal*, published in the Proceedings of the Vermont Historical Society, September and December 1941, were edited by L. Leonard Twynham. Letters cited here are contained in the VHS archives, arranged by their date of origin.

About the Era: Following the War of 1812, the entire midsection of Vermont became known as the "Burned-Over District" for waves of religious fervor that swept over the area like wildfires and incited devotion to a succession of secular trends. Religious revivals appealed to hundreds of Protestants with one exciting new doctrine after another: Anti-Masonry, Mormonism, Millerism (which became Seventh-Day Adventism), the Shakers, Universalism, Swedenborgianism. These and other fashionable ideologies held special appeal for women, because they encouraged women's emerging leadership and spiritual prowess. As *The Banner of Light*, a Spiritualist newspaper, explained in 1866, "Women in the nineteenth century are physically sick, weak and declining," but if "the functions depending on force and muscle are weak...the *nerves* are intensely sensitive... Hence sickness, rest, passivity, susceptibility, impressionability, mediumship, communication, revelation!"

Seven Years of Grace: Achsa Sprague's experience of convalescence and healing corresponded with the above definition of the nineteenth-century woman. In addition, the transformative function of illness was a popular element in Victorian novels and Spiritualists recognized this as part of the necessary progression toward mediumship. At the age of twenty, Achsa fell ill with what today would be diagnosed as rheumatoid arthritis but then was referred to as a scrofulous disease. At twenty-seven, cheered by angel voices only she could hear, Achsa made a compact with spirit guardians to go forth among strangers as a preacher of a new faith and advocate for social change. S. B. Nichols, a contemporary of Achsa's from Burlington, Vermont, argued, "Was not the seven years of illness which this medium had to pass through a means of purification and of developing the power of spirit over all things, animate and inanimate?" Seven years after her recovery, illness caused her final collapse at the age of thirty-four.

PART ONE (1827-1856)

1. **Achsa** is a biblical name, but several spellings may be found: Achsah, Akhsah, Acsar, Aksar, and Axa. She is someone who refused to give up. Her story may be found in Judges 1.12-15.

5. **Plymouth, Vermont,** was chartered as Saltash on July 6, 1761, when the State of Vermont did not yet exist. Today Plymouth consists of Plymouth Union, a small village, and Plymouth Notch, straight east and up the mountain on Highway 100A. A "notch" is a common term used in New England to describe a small pass that cuts between two hills or mountains. This unincorporated village is almost completely included in the Calvin Coolidge Homestead District, a National Historic Landmark. The 30th president of the United States was born here and in 1923 was sworn into the office of president by his father upon the death of Warren G. Harding. President Coolidge's grave in the Notch Cemetery is only steps away from those of the Sprague family. Coolidge was a distant relative and his father, John Coolidge (1845-1926), would have been Achsa's student when she taught in the local school.

5. **Charles Sprague** (1794-1858), Achsa's father, was the son of Nathan Sprague, who had a tavern in Plymouth. He and Betsey were married in November 1816.

5. **Betsey Moore Sprague** (1798-1869) was the daughter of Ephraim Moore and Elizabeth Sawyer. Betsey's father was the representative from Plymouth to the Vermont General Assembly from 1809-1817 and again in 1822.

6. **Rheumatoid arthritis.** The "scrofulous disease" from which Achsa suffered was probably an inflammatory disease that attacks the joints in symmetrical fashion: If one wrist is affected with swelling, stiffness, and loss of function, the other wrist will be similarly involved. Wrist joints and finger joints are typically affected, as are the joints of the hips, knees, ankles, and feet. The disease can go into remission for long periods of time. Sufferers often experience fear, depression, frustration, and anger.

34. **Petition for equal rights for women.** Some years later Achsa acted on her belief in equal rights for women. Her signature was the first one on a petition for woman suffrage submitted to the Vermont legislature on November 20, 1858, by residents of Plymouth, part of a coordinated effort statewide. The fact that her name is first indicates that she circulated the petition. Betsey Sprague's name was second, followed by Athelia Moore and Thomas Moore, Achsa's aunt and uncle. The petition is in the Vermont State Archives, Manuscript Vermont State Papers, volume 65, p. 217.

35. **Marenda Briggs Randall** (1817-1876) married Nathaniel Randall (1809-1888) in Brockport, New York, on July 28, 1834. Nathaniel was then a homeopathic physician. They were divorced in 1853; Nathaniel married Achsa's sister, Sarah Sprague, in 1854. Marenda served as a vice president of the 1853 Woman's Rights Convention in Cleveland, Ohio, in October of that year, and the subsequent convention in Philadelphia to consider "the Equal Right of Woman to all the advantages of education, literary, scientific, artistic; to full equality in all business avocations, industrial, commercial, professional; briefly, all the rights that belong to her as a citizen." Marenda was also a physician and a devout Grahamite, adhering strictly to the teachings of Sylvester Graham (1794-1851), who advocated a vegetable diet as a cure for intemperance and the use of coarsely ground whole wheat (or graham) flour.

35. **Magnetism.** In her book, *History of Modern American Spiritualism* (1869), Emma Hardinge wrote, "Thousands of persons who are warm advocates of the spiritual philosophy acknowledge that their attention was first attracted to the subject by their interest in magnetism. In all the principal cities of the Union, gentlemen distinguished for their literary abilities, progressive opinions, or prominence in public affairs,

have graduated from the study of magnetism and clairvoyance to become adherents to the cause of Spiritualism, whilst many of the best mediums—especially the trance speakers and magnetic operators—have taken their first degree in Spiritualism, as experimentalists in the phenomena of mesmerism." **Mesmerism** was named for Anton Mesmer (1734-1815), the founder of psychotherapy and today's mental health industry.

44. **Andrew Jackson Davis** was known as "The Poughkeepsie Seer" and is recognized as the father of modern Spiritualism. Born in 1838, he discovered as a young man that he was clairvoyant and claimed he could receive truths from a higher plane of consciousness, read closed books, and diagnose illnesses. Eventually Davis wrote and published more than 30 books on such topics as the seven planes of existence, mental and physical health, astronomy, physics, chemistry, philosophy, education, and government, although he'd had almost no formal schooling.

Modern Spiritualism is a concept that "came about as a reaction against materialism, and the single idea which gave birth to it was that ghosts or spirits were individualized entities subject to law. It is distinguished from ancient spiritualism by its sweeping claim that all spiritual phenomena and the evolution and existence of spirits are by the operation of fixed and ascertainable laws." (From Hudson Tuttle, *Mediumship and its Laws,* 1900).

46. **Gaius Cobb** was the father of Charles M. Cobb, whose diary in the collections of the Woodstock Historical Society documents his life and social observations from 1850-1862. According to Cobb's diary entry of March 14, 1852, General Washington spoke "thro' Horace Wood, and the doings of Miss Randall and Miss Louisa Cady, mediums. Mrs. Marenda B. Randall the 'Grahamite' was author of the book."

47. **John Murray Spear.** Information on Spear is drawn from John B. Buescher, *The Remarkable Life of John Murray Spear: Agitator for the Spirit Land* (University of Notre Dame Press, 2006). He was a gentle eccentric with wild, enthusiastic ideas, many of which he attempted to accomplish and several of which were magnificent flops. He was also a leading proponent of the Spiritualist concept of Free Love. On April

1, 1853, Spear received (via automatic writing) an announcement by a group of twelve spirits of famous people, including Thomas Jefferson, Benjamin Franklin, and Benjamin Rush, informing him they had formed a missionary association in the spirit world and were called the "Association of Beneficents." Spear was to be their agent and communicator on earth. Spear spoke at Woodstock on April 10, 1853; this was Achsa's initial contact with him.

54. **Passing Strange**, meaning extremely bizarre, or stranger than strange. This old New England phrase was spoken by William Shakespeare's *Othello* in Act 1, Scene 3:

> *My story being done,*
> *She gave me for my pains a world of sighs;*
> *She swore, in faith 'twas strange, 'twas passing strange;*
> *'Twas pitiful. 'Twas wondrous pitiful,*
> *She wish'd she had not heard it, yet she wish'd*
> *That heaven had made her such a man*

56. **"Keys Silver and Golden."** This page in Achsa's handwriting was found in the Sprague archives. If not received as automatic writing, this could have been a spoken (and transcribed) message from Andrew Jackson Davis, as it speaks of her as "[a] teacher and a priestess divinely ordained and consecrated," which is similar to a later spirit message he delivered to her.

56. **Delia Pollard**, Achsa's closest friend and distant cousin, was born Clarissa Adelia Pollard on November 1, 1831, the daughter of Abigail Brown Pollard and Moses Pollard of Ludlow, Vermont. Unmarried during Achsa's lifetime, Delia eventually wed Reverend Samuel U. King of Windsor and resided in Putney, Vermont. She was a published poet.

58. **Father Hopper.** Isaac Hopper (1771-1852), a Quaker and member of the Pennsylvania Abolition Society active in the Underground Railroad, was expelled from the Society of Friends for his antislavery activities in the early 1840s. He also worked for prison reform and gave aid to free blacks, the infirm, and the insane. Achsa's eventual attention to those issues may have been partially influenced by her belief in Hopper's role as one of her spiritual Guardians. The message Achsa received by

automatic writing signed "Thy Spirit Friend, I . T. Hopper," is written backwards. **Mirror Writing** is a graphic quirk reported in people who suffer from Geschwind's Syndrome, or Temporal Lobe Epilepsy. Achsa manifested many symptoms of TLE, including hyperreligiosity, hypergraphia, and a neurological state of transcendent consciousness identified as a religious experience. For more information on TLE see Eve LaPlante, *Seized: Temporal Lobe Epilepsy as a Medical, Historical, and Artistic Phenomenon* (Harper Collins, 1993), and V. S. Ramachandran and Sandra Blakeslee, *Phantoms in the Brain* (William Morrow, 1998).

63. **Achsa's initial appearance in South Reading**, July 16, 1854, is accurate as to the date but the details are imagined, utilizing a composite of reactions she eventually experienced and noted in her diary and other writings throughout her career.

69. **Merritt E. Goddard** (1834-1891) was present at Achsa's initial spirit lecture in South Reading on July 16, 1854, when he was a young theological student. Goddard signed only his initials, M.E.G., after his introduction to Sprague's posthumously published work, *The Poet and Other Poems* (Boston: William White & Co., 1864), which he edited at her family's request. He graduated from Dartmouth College and the Harvard Divinity School, with the goal of entering the Unitarian ministry, but poor health prevented the accomplishment of that objective. He represented Reading in the Vermont legislature in 1863-64, and was active in promoting education and libraries. Goddard also wrote the town history of Norwich, Vermont, which was completed after his death and published in 1905.

78. **Warren Chase** of Wisconsin became a follower of Charles Fourier, the French utopian socialist. Several utopian movements found a widespread following in the United States in the early 19th century, and in 1844 Chase founded the Wisconsin Phalanx to implement Fourierism in Wisconsin. Phalanx members established the community of Ceresco in Fond du Lac County on the site of the present-day city of Ripon. Chase lived there until the community was abandoned in 1850. He was a friend and advisor of Achsa Sprague and his memoirs, *Life-Line of the Lone One: Autobiography of*

Warren Chase (Boston: Colby & Rich, Publishers, 1883), has proven advantageous in research for this book.

79. **Nathaniel Tallmadge**, a New York lawyer and politician, was appointed territorial governor of Wisconsin in 1844. He became a highly respected and influential spokesman for Spiritualism and one of its leading figures in the country.

84. **The Charter Oak** was an important symbol of liberty in Connecticut and significant to its history. According to the *Connecticut State Register*, "On October 9, 1662, the General Court of Connecticut formally received the Charter won from King Charles II by the suave diplomacy of Governor John Winthrop, Jr. who had crossed the ocean for the purpose. Twenty-five years later, with the succession of James II to the throne... Sir Edmond Andros. ...[arrived] in Hartford with an armed force to seize the Charter. After hours of debate, with the Charter on the table between the opposing parties, the candle-lit room suddenly went dark. Moments later when the candles were re-lighted, the Charter was gone. Captain Joseph Wadsworth is credited with having removed and secreted the Charter in the majestic oak on the Wyllys estate."

95. **Solitarie.** Achsa may have selected this *nom de plume* as it suggested her isolation in the mountains. It probably also implied one who traveled alone as a solitary figure. In her twenties, Achsa was a *solitarie* as defined by the Oxford English Dictionary, Second Edition, 1989: "keeping apart or aloof from society; avoiding the company of others." Christian hermits or recluses living under a religious vow are described as *solitaries*.

121. **Encounter on the steamboat with a man of mystery**. A detailed entry in Achsa's diary on May 12, 1856, describes this encounter. I have taken the liberty of introducing John H. Crawford as "the person on board" at this time, since their mutual relationship to waves and sea would endure, in many phases, throughout their liaison.

126. **Bell.** Achsa especially used this *nom de plume* with her children's stories that were published in *The World's Paper*.

PART TWO (1856-1859)

128. Thomas Lake Harris (1823-1906) was a former Universalist minister who became a mystic Spiritualist. A mesmerizing speaker, he promoted "Respirationism," the idea that "supernatural breathing" or "divine respiration" came about during sexual intercourse. Harris also believed little fairies lived in women's breasts.

130. Amanda M. Britt Spence of St. Louis gained early fame as a trance lecturer and séance medium. She and her husband "Professor" Spence alienated many faithful Spiritualists when they announced that not all souls survived the death of the body, instead some were simply annihilated. Children, for example, had not yet built up enough substantiality to allow them to persist after they were deceased. Amanda had a loud and commanding voice and often spoke at conventions against "Free Love."

131. Pic-Nic. See the painting by Thomas Cole, "A Pic-Nic Party," 1846.

135. Minister's sore throat. This affliction plagued Achsa throughout her career as a medium. It was perhaps caused and further irritated by the need to project her voice so that it could be heard by crowds numbering in the thousands, eventually numbing her vocal cords.

143. Lucretia Mott, the prominent suffragist and abolitionist, was an acquaintance of Marenda Randall.

143. Sprague relatives in Providence, Rhode Island. With his brother Amasa and cousin Byron Sprague, **William Sprague** (1830-1915) operated the A&W Sprague Manufacturing Company, the largest calico printing textile mill in the world. In 1860, at the age of twenty-nine, he was elected governor of Rhode Island, and from 1863-1875 he served as a Republican U.S. senator.

148. New York Council of Spiritualists with Walt Whitman. Achsa was in New York City, staying at the home of **Dr. Robert Hallock** and his wife, when the New York Conference of Spiritualists met on July 21, 1857. Hallock's book, *The Road to Spiritualism*, would be published by *The Spiritualist Telegraph* in 1858, and in the third lecture he says, "The man who leaves the unstable and dreary marches of poetical tradition, for the solid ground of fact and principle, will never be troubled by the question of theological angels, nor by the *presence* of church devils. In short, the man who sets out to investigate Spiritualism will stumble and fall at every step, or gain with comparative safety and ease, according to the guide he elects at the beginning and the fidelity with which he follows him." This might be construed as a response to the presence of the poet Walt Whitman at the weekly meeting of the New York Conference of Spiritualists on August 1, 1857. The New York *Spiritual Age* reported that the question for discussion that evening was, "What is the difference between being a medium, so-called, and those who are not mediums?" Whitman took the floor and revealed that he had been trying to develop himself as a medium for the past year, without success. Achsa Sprague is not mentioned in the article, but we may easily assume that Dr. Hallock, then residing at 140 East 15th Street in New York, attended this conference, and that his guest, the well-known Achsa Sprague, would have accompanied him. However, the scenario wherein she speaks while entranced and then visits with Whitman are imagined.

159. Funeral of Charles Sprague, January 1858. Controversy over Achsa's behavior at her father's funeral caused prolonged agitation in the area. For years afterward, one Sprague neighbor insisted that Achsa "created a local sensation at the time of her father's death by compelling all the school children to file over to the funeral, at which she stood up and said, 'These are the remains—this is only a shell—he is with God.'" Eliza Ward, *Recollections and Stories of Plymouth, Vermont,* ed. Barbara Chiolino and Barbara Mahon (Plymouth Vermont Publications, 1992), 80.

179. Improvisatrice. The title Achsa gave to Miss Raymond in her play, *The Poet.* She also used this term to refer to herself. The word is Italian, taken from *improvvisatore,* or an improvisator, especially a person who extemporizes verse.

183. Eliza Cook was a British poet (1818-1889) whose songs were especially beloved by John Crawford. These lines from her poem, "Love On," may have held particular relevance for Achsa: *Who would not rather trust and be deceived?*

200. **At Darling's Gap.** Celia Sprague's experiences as a schoolteacher in Wisconsin are taken from her letters to Achsa and diaries of other women who left their homes in Vermont for similar destinations:

Diary of Adelia A. Bartholf of Greenbush, in the archives of the University of Wisconsin-Milwaukee. Bartholf was born on August 17, 1835, in Batavia, Genesee County, New York, and came to Wisconsin to teach around the same time as Celia and in a nearby village.

Pieced from Ellen's Quilt: Ellen Spaulding Reed's Letters and Story, by Linda O. Lipsett. Ellen married and moved to Wisconsin in 1854 from Ludlow, Vermont.

"Pioneer Life in Fond du Lac," by Mrs. S. P. Higbee, Wisconsin Historical Society, (Wisconsin Local History and Biography articles). The Higbees came to Fond du Lac in 1844 from the east, arriving in Milwaukee on the steamer *Missouri*.

Early schools were described in a 1916 history of Greenbush, Wisconsin. "It may be interesting to note the different kinds of punishment in vogue in the earlier days. Sometimes a stick was split and put over the nose of the pupil, or he was forced to bend over a nail in the floor with his finger upon it until the teacher released him." Or he might be instructed to erase the blackboard with his nose.

203. **"Whatever is, is right."** A phrase used by Spiritualists as a premise of their belief. Taken from *An Essay on Man*, by Alexander Pope (1734):

> All nature is but art unknown to thee,
> All chance, direction which thy canst not see;
> All discord, harmony not understood;
> All partial evil, universal good;
> And spite of pride, in erring reason's spite,
> One truth is clear,
> > Whatever is, is right.

206. **Phrenology** was developed in the late 1700s by the German physician Franz Joseph Gall, who became convinced that the shape of one's

skull and its bumps and indentations could be linked to twenty-seven "faculties" that determined a person's specific traits or characteristics.

220. **"Kilmeny"** is the title of a poem by the Scottish poet and shepherd James Hogg (1770-1835) that celebrated Bonnie Kilmeny, a young woman who was spirited away.

239. **Washington City.** Many of Achsa's experiences in Washington were suggested by a similar visit (within a year) by Warren Chase, and documented with much detail in *The Banner of Light*.

240. **The question of Cuba.** Prior to the Civil War, territorial expansion was a popular topic in the United States and many proslavery Southerners wished to expand the territory open to slavery. Cuba was a frequent target, and some people believed that as a great slaveholding republic, the United States could stretch across the Caribbean to Brazil.

243. *Poets and Poetry of Vermont* was edited by Abby M. Hemenway and published in 1858 and 1860.

A. W. SPRAGUE
OF PLYMOUTH

THE INSPIRED

She stands beneath the arching dome
Where thousand burning worlds shine dim,
Her dark hair floating on the breeze,
That softly chants its evening hymn.
Her brow is lifted to the sky,
Her flashing eye burns strangely bright,
As it had caught, from yonder stars
Or some bright heavenly world, its light.
Her lips are parted as to speak,
As if in strange, sweet, glad surprise;
A light breaks over all her face,
Like morning's golden, sunlit skies.

She stands as though her beating soul
Had first caught glimpse of angel eyes,
And chained, enrapt, she lingers there,
Mute, motionless, in glad surprise,
As though her ear first heard the tone
Of seraph voices in the air,
And cheek, and eye, and lip had caught
The glowing smile the angels wear.
As though she stood beneath that sky,
And on that green and grassy sod,
Baptized by angels passing by,
And consecrated until God.

Ah! what a bursting of earth's bands,
And what a glad, triumphant hour—
The human soul asserts its right,
And feels, at last, Immortal Power.
The chords no mortal hand had waked,
Thrill with the symphony of Heaven,
And Godlike powers are born within,
By God and God's own angels given.

Great thoughts and glorious onward sweep
Like torrents that no power can bind,
Sublime in grandeur as they pass
To the great ocean of the Mind.
The mantle of the beautiful
Has fallen o'er her spirit now,
All bathed in light from that bright Home
Where angels and archangels bow.

246. Ships of the Northern Transportation Company in 1858: *Buckeye, Granite State, Northern Michigan, Ogdensburgh, Potomac, Wisconsin, Young America, Bay State, Lady of the Lake, Michigan, Vermont, Prairie State, Jefferson,* and *Cleveland.*

277. **Friends of Progress.** This group professed a Quaker version of Spiritualism that appealed to radical reformers and depended more on scientific reasoning, empirical investigations, and experiments than on séances. The Quakers and early Spiritualists were united in their mutual support of Progressive reforms: abolition of slavery, woman's rights, and temperance. Lucretia Mott was a Progressive Friend who dismissed spirit raps but embraced phrenology.

279. **Aurora Borealis, September 1 and 2, 1859.** An astonishing display of Northern Lights was due to the most massive space storm in recorded history, also known as "the solar storm of 1859," "the 1859 solar superstorm," or the "Carrington Event." At the time, sources other than a solar flare were credited for the show: *Scientific American* said it was caused by debris from active volcanoes, the *San Francisco Herald* theorized it was "nebulous matter" from "planetary spaces," and *Harper's Weekly* blamed it on reflections from distant icebergs.

284. **The Great Blondin** was the most famous tightrope walker in history, born in 1824, who received his name from his blond hair. He believed that a ropewalker was "like a poet, born and not made." When he performed for the final time in 1896, it was estimated that he had crossed Niagara Falls 300 times on his rope.

284. **John Brown** was a fellow member of Ohio's Summit County militia along with John H. Crawford and Philo Chamberlin, all of whom lived near Hudson, Ohio, at the same time (Chamberlin was the mayor of Akron in 1845). John Brown was executed on December 2, 1859, for leading the raid on Harper's Ferry in October of that year. Southerners saw him as a fanatic, embodying all they hated about the North. But Brown was seen differently in the North; Henry David Thoreau called him "an angel of light," and Ralph Waldo Emerson said he would "make the gallows as glorious as the cross."

300. **James H. Blood** would eventually become the second husband of Victoria Woodhull, the flamboyant social reformer who was the first woman to run for president of the United States. She was criticized for her sexual nonconformity and her political ambitions. Woodhull published the first English translation of Karl Marx's *The Communist Manifesto*.

PART THREE (1860-1862)

314. **Achsa's account of her trip from Davenport to Memphis** is documented in a letter from Benjamin Starbuck. The riverboat voyage is based on one made by Warren Chase in January 1859—the same month, same route, but a milder winter.

335. **Achsa's Chicago meeting with John Crawford in 1860** is strongly suggested by correspondence between the two of them, and letters from Mary Richardson in Oswego.

340. **Caleb Wall** operated a Milwaukee hotel, The Bellvue House. In the late 1850s, the behavior of the city's Germans, who filled their beer gardens to overflowing on Sundays, scandalized the Yankees who called for temperance. Wall attempted to conduct his hostelry as a temperance hotel, but it became common knowledge that tipsy boarders easily came and went through the back windows by means of ladders and knotted bedding. Disappointed with his attempts at reform, Wall renounced his temperance effort altogether and installed Milwaukee's most lavishly stocked bar.

344. **The Indian scare.** Similar alarms were sounded throughout Wisconsin during this time in history. The Fond du Lac incident occurred in 1862.

382. **"A Sermon on the Mount."** A lengthy poem written by Achsa just prior to leaving for Oswego in July 1861. It is not included in *The Poet and Other Poems* but was published posthumously in *The Banner of Light*. The last stanza reads:

> A presence passed—but left a flood of glory,
>   A rainbow in my heart, not on the hill.
> And trembling at my strange and wondrous blindness,
>   I bowed in reverence to the Father's will,
> And vowed I'd still have faith in childish dreaming,
>   No matter how they seemed to fade and die,
> Remembering when it seems the darkest, furthest
>   We reach our hands, and somehow touch the sky.

383. Achsa's illness in Oswego is based on her lengthy letter and poem published posthumously in *The Banner of Light*, August 2, 1862.

404. *The Bay State*, one of the Northern Transportation Company's steamships, foundered and sank off Oswego in a gale in November 1862. A nephew of John H. Crawford, Orely Thompson of Vermont, was a cabin passenger. All twenty-two persons on board drowned and the full cargo of merchandise destined for Cleveland and Toledo was destroyed. The wreck was recently discovered: http://www.cnn.com/2015/10/22/us/bay-state-shipwreck-lake-ontario-feat/. *The Jefferson* was condemned in 1863; *the Buckeye* was stranded in 1885 and burned in Georgian Bay. All of the ships of the Northern Transportation fleet eventually perished. Veteran maritime men were heard to comment that a "spirit of disaster" hovered over the Northern Transportation Company. See "Loss of *City of Concord* Recalls Day of Old Northern Transit Line," *Detroit Free Press*, October 15, 1906.

420. Book review, *The Poet and Other Poems*, in *The Continental Monthly*, 6(July-December 1864), published in New York by John F. Trow, 50 Greene Street.

> MISS SPRAGUE was chiefly known to the world as a trance lecturer under what claimed to be spirit influence.... These poems are characterized by great ease of style, flowing rhythm, earnestness in the cause of philanthropy and frequently contain high moral lessons. But it is somewhat strange that the poems of trance writers and speakers, so often marked by exquisite, varied and delicate chimes of ringing rhythm, of brilliant words, of sparkling poetic dust blown from the pages of great writers, and drifting through the world, should so seldom give us those great granite blocks of originality, which must constitute the enduring base for the new era therein announced. Is there nothing new in the world beyond the grave which they deem open to their vision? We ask this in no spirit of censure or cavil, for we have no prejudice against the school of spiritualist literature, save where it militates against the faith in our Redeemer.

422. Celia's death. The inscription on Celia's tombstone in the Avoca Cemetery, Oakfield, Wisconsin, is carved only with her first name and this quote from Victor Hugo's *Les Miserables*: "Kiss me on the forehead when I am dead and I shall feel it." The scene describes the death of Eponine and these are her dying words.

425. David H. Judson was John Crawford's friend in Oswego. The poem "I Caught a Gleam" had been shared with Judson ten years before, in 1874, just after Crawford moved to Minnesota from the pinelands of Michigan, and Judson shared it with the Oswego *Palladium* upon Crawford's death.

428. Hymns jointly composed by Achsa Sprague and John H. Crawford and published in *The Spiritual Harp* (first lines):

> "While on my lone couch sleeping"
>
> "The leaves round thee falling, are speaking"
>
> "Sweet peace, descend with noiseless wing"
>
> "Sweet darling of the mother's heart"
>
> "O take me home, I cannot bear"
>
> "O sail from out the sunrise"

Hymns by J. H. Crawford in *Triumphant Hosannas* (Waco, Texas: Trio Music Co., 1912)

"Glory Over There," first line, "There's a mansion free from sorrow"

"The Master's Orders," first line, "We have been told to tell the story"

⊰ ACKNOWLEDGMENTS ⊱

THIS WORK WAS WRITTEN with the support and permission of the Vermont Historical Society (VHS), Barre, Vermont, which holds the personal papers of Achsa W. Sprague in its archives. I have been as faithful as possible in basing Achsa's story on fact and often retained the very words with which she or Celia Sprague Steen and John H. Crawford expressed themselves. Achsa's lengthy drama, *The Poet*, in which she crafted Miss Raymond, an "improvisatrice," to whom she ascribed her own beliefs, was carefully scrutinized. I also drew heavily from her diaries, journals, children's stories, newspaper columns and articles, essays, letters, poems, unpublished messages, and sundry jottings. A surprising discovery came about when I noticed that, when read chronologically, John Crawford's letters revealed the Free Love nature of their relationship. Her quickly penciled drafts meant for him divulged clandestine and often playful ripostes.

Further details of her public life were found in the words of her contemporaries, such as Warren Chase, Emma Hardinge, and Alonzo Newton, and in Spiritualist publications that alluded to Achsa and her mission.

In September and December 1941, excerpts from Achsa's diary and journal, edited by historian L. Leonard Twinem, were published in the Vermont Historical Society's Proceedings under the pseudonym, Leonard Twynham. He had purchased the box of Sprague papers at Tuttle's Bookshop, Rutland, Vermont, in 1932 and claimed he possessed her entire "literary remains" including "a vast quantity of manuscript material, verses and essays, which await publication," as well as "an autobiographical poem of 162 pages, which she composed in six days, when in such a nervous state that the spinning wheel, latches, and roosters were all muffled for her peace of mind."

The letters were eventually turned over to the Vermont Historical Society by Twinem's brother, Francis P. Twinem, in 1976. The original diary and journal were thought to have been lost until they made an unexpected appearance on eBay in May 2013. Alas, VHS Librarian Paul Carnahan and I were outbid for an astronomical $4,997 by an as-yet-unknown buyer.

Achsa Sprague was introduced to me at the quaint little community of Lily Dale, New York—the center of the modern Spiritualist movement. There a friend loaned me Anne Braude's book, *Radical Spirits: Spiritualism and Women's Rights in Nineteenth-Century America,* and the chapter on Achsa carried a footnote that mentioned her diaries at VHS were, according to Braude, "[A]s far as I can ascertain the only extant personal papers of a nineteenth-century Spiritualist medium."

This seized my imagination and I found myself returning to the annotation again and again. I had earned my MFA in Writing at Vermont College in Montpelier in 1989, and was on the faculty of the MFA in Writing program at Goddard College in Plainfield, Vermont, for several years. As someone intrigued by Spiritualism, a published poet and biographer, and a progressive woman fond of Vermont, I resolved that I was capable of affording Achsa the attention she deserved.

In 2003 I was awarded the Weston A. Cate Fellowship by the Vermont Historical Society to aid in my research. Kevin Graffagnino, then the director of the Vermont Historical Society, expressed his confidence in my pursuit of Achsa's story. In August 2004 I was invited to present a lecture about Achsa, "Green Mountain Mystic," in the same one-room schoolhouse where she taught in Plymouth Notch.

Paul Carnahan introduced me to the Achsa Sprague files in the VHS archives, which contain over a thousand letters received by her. He and Assistant Librarian Marjorie Strong were most generous with their assistance.

The letters as I found them were roughly sorted, but never classified by author. Louise Crowley of my Vermont College MFA program suggested Caroline Mercurio when I asked for a research assistant, and a year of her careful gleaning and copying followed by my transcription provided a wealth of rich, new material—including materials written by Achsa but never before identified as such.

The folks in Plymouth Notch welcomed me and the opportunity to familiarize me with their most intriguing female resident. This picturesque hamlet became the birthplace of Calvin Coolidge, the 30th president of the United States, only ten years after Achsa's death, and as a National Historic Landmark the village remains carefully preserved today. William Jenney, site administrator for the Calvin Coolidge State Historic Site, always offered a warm reception, as did Cyndy Bittinger, then the executive director of the Calvin Coolidge Memorial Foundation.

Eliza Ward, Plymouth historian, drew a floor plan of the original Sprague homestead that proved to be a helpful aid in picturing the arrangement of rooms. Eliza's book, *Recollections and Stories of Plymouth, Vermont* (edited by Barbara Chiolino and Barbara Mahon), became an invaluable resource, and she presented me with a tintype of Achsa as a young girl, which I treasure.

My childhood friend and classmate, Mary Ann Craig, faithfully answered my pleas for genealogical information on the Sprague and Crawford families. I enjoyed working with someone I had known since first grade, and her support meant a lot to me.

The National Association of Spiritualist Churches at Lily Dale granted unlimited access to their library and archives, as did the Morris Pratt Institute in Wauwatosa, Wisconsin.

Mary Ellen Hall, of Jericho, Vermont, shared an early interest in Achsa's life and introduced me to the newspaper file at VHS. Mary Ellen's reproduction of *The Poet*, Achsa's romantic play, is available from Essence of Vermont.

Oswego historian Justin White kindly devoted an entire weekend to showing us around that upstate New York city and pointed out the location where John H. Crawford's "Gibraltar Cottage" stood on the Lake Ontario shore. We had lunch in the same stone building that once served as the office of Crawford's Northern Transportation Company.

Kathy Wendling, Woodstock, Vermont historian, provided me with that city's colorful Spiritualism history and evidenced a keen interest in my project. Reference librarian Dora St. Martin of Somerville, Massachusetts, and Dee Morris searched microfilms and made copies of references to Achsa that I could not obtain elsewhere.

I owe a tremendous debt of gratitude to John Buescher, religious scholar and administrator of an early website devoted to the history of Spiritualism. He retrieved innumerable articles, interviews, and other materials related to Achsa's era that I would never have unearthed or understood without his help. In turn, John introduced me to IAPSOP, the International Association for the Preservation of Rare Spiritualist and Occult Periodicals. This resource is remarkable for its comprehensive collection.

Finally, to Achsa's spirit—which I have sensed all along as she hovered nearby—I offer my heartfelt appreciation. She became my sister, my beloved friend, my continued inspiration. I am honored that she chose me to write the story of her life. And to Celia Sprague Steen, who allowed me to tell this story in her voice, I dedicate the completion of her long-sought mission.

Along the way (or "by the wayside," as Achsa would have it) I relied upon trusted friends and found new allies who have been of immeasurable help. Cynthia Pearson Turich, a dream journalist and scholar, was the friend who loaned me the Braude book during our visit to Lily Dale in 1996.

I owe a debt to Ludmilla Bollow, dear friend and fellow author, whose heartfelt reassurance and blessings I have cherished. My faithful Byliners gang from Milwaukee buoyed me with their support and friendship during the early days.

In Vermont I found Glenda Thistle, whose sweet Farmbrook Motel in Plymouth Notch sadly washed away during a hurricane after our visit; Jim Cooke visited Achsa's grave whenever he was nearby; the Salt Ash Inn, Plymouth, provided cordial hospitality.

Fond du Lac genealogist Sally Albertz led me to Celia's grave in the Avoca Cemetery near Oakfield, Wisconsin, and supplied additional information about the area, the Steen family, and their farms. Here in Spring Green I relied upon Jean Porter at our local library, who utilized her wisdom and contacts to obtain obscure microfilms and other little-known data for my use.

The sustained enrichment of my friends has been remarkable throughout the twenty years of my commitment to this project. I am especially grateful for the love and support of Linda and Ben Bolton, Susan and Nick Jannotta, Eileen and David Roeder, Judy and Joel Marcus, my River Valley Book Club, the Friends of the Spring Green Library, and Sarah Day (my sister from another era, according to a medium during a message service at the nearby Wonewoc Spiritualist Camp).

Raphael Kadushin and Andrea Christofferson of the University of Wisconsin Press have always supported my belief in Achsa's story. Alan Berolzheimer, managing editor at the Vermont Historical Society, never lost faith in our ability to see that Achsa "still lives," and his wisdom and tenacity were appreciated throughout our editing process. Jim Brisson is to be congratulated for his beautiful book design and considerable patience as we processed several complicated style issues.

My children, Laura Rath Beausire and Jay Rath, are both successful writers and understand the unconventional agendas to which writers must succumb. Their persuasion has been unwavering.

If Laura's husband, Robert Beausire, had not accepted a job offer from Rich Products in Buffalo, most likely I would not have discovered Lily Dale in the first place. Thank you, Rob!

Del Lamont, my husband, accompanied me on journeys to Vermont and New York. He drove thousands of miles, helped explore obscure graveyards, and sorted papers while searching the shelves of musty libraries. I could not have completed this project without his love, his reassurance, and his conviction in the significance of Achsa's story.

A chapter of this book appeared in the literary magazine *Hunger Mountain*, as "In My Present Heaven: Achsa Sprague (1827-1862)," 6 (March 2005).

❧ ABOUT THE AUTHOR ❧

Author Sara Rath, standing at Achsa Sprague's gravestone in Plymouth Notch.

Sara Rath is an award-winning author whose poetry, articles, and short stories have appeared in *The Boston Review*, *Poets & Writers*, *The Wisconsin Academy Review*, *The Arkham Collector*, *Green Mountains Review*, and many other publications. A native of Wisconsin, Sara earned her MFA in Writing at Vermont College. She has received numerous honors and awards including fellowships with The MacDowell Foundation, Ucross, Wisconsin Arts Board, and in 2003 the Vermont Historical Society awarded her the Weston A. Cate Fellowship to aid in her research about Achsa W. Sprague. *Seven Years of Grace* is Sara's fifteenth book. She lives with her husband in Spring Green, Wisconsin.